THE BRAVEST AMONG US

K. S. MOORE

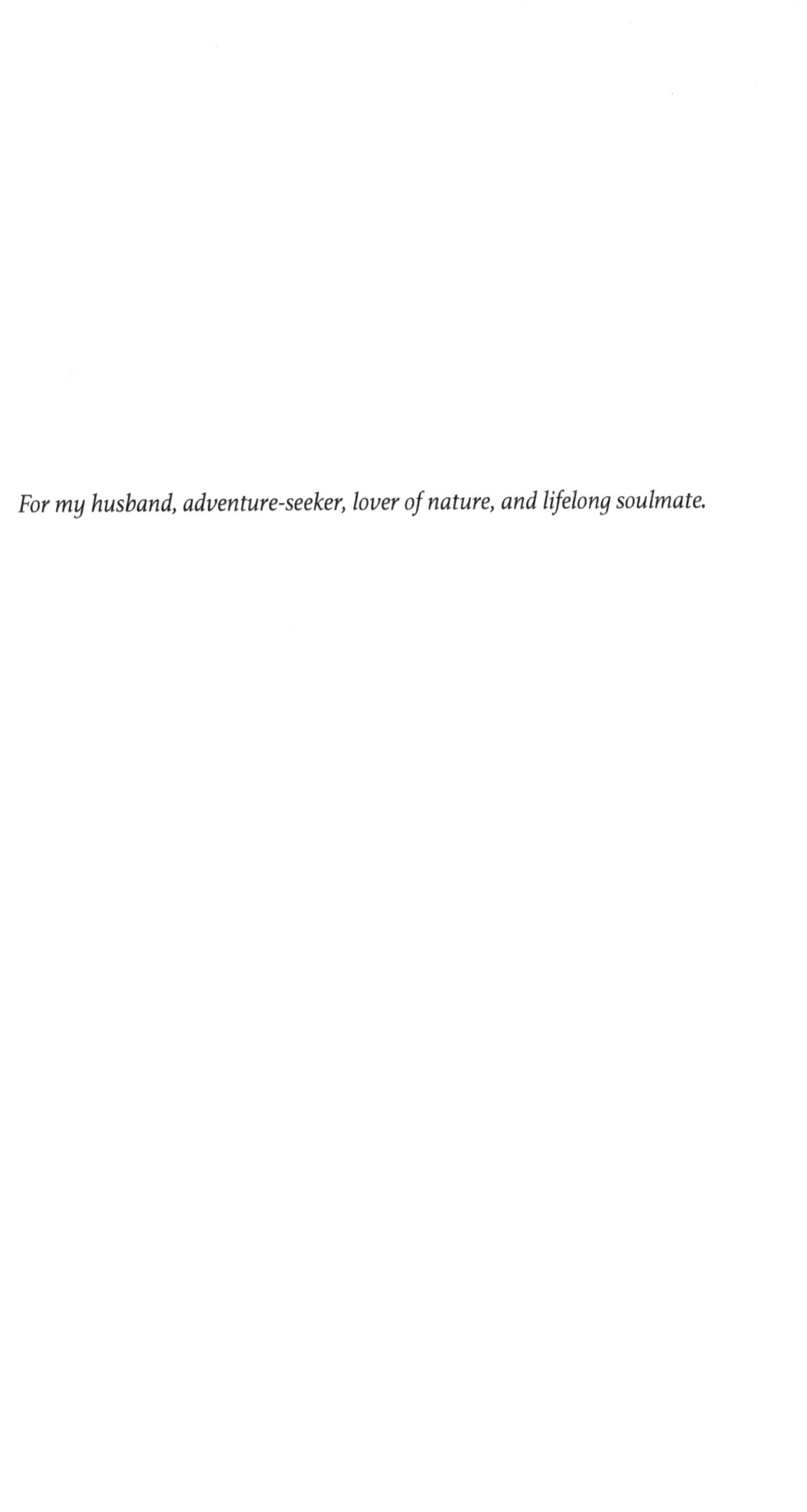

For my husband, adventure-seeker, lover of nature, and lifelong soulmate.

The brokenhearted are the bravest among us. They have dared to love.

— DR. BRENÉ BROWN, RESEARCHER,
PROFESSOR, AUTHOR, AND SPEAKER

Courage is not the absence of fear but rather the assessment that something else is more important than fear.

— THEODORE ROOSEVELT

PROLOGUE

I stare out the windshield at the chain stretched across the empty two-track while the engine ticks, cooling. The headlights blink off, and the darkness seems alive and ominous pressed against the car windows. It's a long trek back to the pond and I know my bum leg is not up to it, but I remind myself that everything worth anything costs something.

I'm certain she's there, probably resting and thinking, maybe crying too, in that way she only does when no one is around. I've seen it before, and the thought of it brings a jagged edge to my heart. At the same time it fills me with hope, because I know, in a way I know few things, that I can help.

The car door closing behind me sounds like a thunderclap in the still, dark night. The scent of rain hangs in the air like sweet relief. I hope I can make it to the shelter of the willow before the skies open up.

As I tuck the old blue toolbox under my arm and start up the grassy lane, I picture myself, a tall shadow figure of a man in the prime of his life, on this fateful journey. The scene plays out in my head as if on a huge movie screen, and I wonder if this is the beginning or the end, if the introductions or the credits are rolling. All of my hard work, sacrifice, blessings, and misfortunes have brought me to this one pivotal moment where my happiness lies in the hands of a broken woman, a woman I cannot imagine life without.

As you read my story, you will discover I am far from perfect. I'm simply a man with my own set of insecurities, selfish motives, and pride. But I hope you will recognize the wholesome intent behind my actions and with a forgiving heart overlook my imperfections.

Rounding a sharp curve in the trail, I see the dark outline of a pickup parked at the barn. The sight is both reassuring and terrifying. My gut tightens. This is it.

Reaching the truck, I pause to catch my breath and sag against the hood. It's cool. She's been here awhile. I gather my resolve, shake the tension from my shoulders, and push on.

I picture her smile and it gives me courage. When I think about all the loss she's endured, all the death, grief, and heartache, it amazes me she can still laugh so easily. She reminds me anything is possible.

As I reach the meadow, a gentle rain begins to fall. At the far edge, beneath the willow, a small shape darkens the horizon. A crouching woman or a wild bush—it's hard to discern from so far away. I trudge on but have to stop several times to rest my leg. I long for my crutches, but I'm tired of feeling damaged, and tonight I cannot show weakness. She'll need me to be the strong one this time.

Some may call this story a romance. Skeptics will call it a tragedy. This night will determine which it will be, but I'm optimistic. I lift up a silent prayer for the strength I know I will need, and I soldier on. I haven't always been a firm believer in God or in the power of prayer. Like many, I've had my doubts. But having lived both with and without faith, I've found my life to be much richer with it, so who am I to question?

They say behind every successful man is a woman. I prefer to think that behind every great man is a remarkable woman of faith. But don't be misled. I do not profess to be a great man. In all likelihood, I'll never be a truly great man, but I'm a far better one than I have ever been, for I have loved another with all my heart. Even if her broken spirit can never return my affections, she has given me the greatest gift in life, for which I am forever grateful.

And to think it all started with a prayer.

Fifty yards away now, I bend to rub the ache in my thigh. When I look up again, a small fire burns beyond the willow's drip line, but the shape is gone. A few steps farther, the soft crack of a snapped twig pierces the stillness of the night. My whole body tenses.

She steps from the edge of the woods, her stance defensive, legs wide, torso turned sideways, fists raised. Despite the moonless night, I can make out a flash of recognition then a languid smile.

"You're here," she says.

1

————

After a week of nonstop meetings, her days packed as tight as seeds in a sunflower, thirty-six year-old Aria Whitmore stood in the security area of the Montreal airport, seething with impatience. Nearby, fellow travelers skimmed through with their Nexus cards, avoiding the long line she'd been standing in for almost an hour.

She should have signed up for the trusted traveler program months ago, but she'd been booked solid, flying back and forth from the States several times a month, working to grow the Canadian division of Hewitt Medical Diagnostics as its North American Key Accounts Manager. When she was busy enough, she didn't have time to dwell on how dire things had become, how her life, once filled with love and family, had turned into a shell of despair.

Aria shuffled forward with the masses, too tired to even think. She glanced at the time on her phone. Lines were such a tedious and unproductive waste of time and energy, and she'd gotten quite good at avoiding them—airports being the one inescapable exception.

"*Bonjour*, hello," the security officer greeted her.

"Bonjour," she replied. They exchanged some pleasantries, and she was on her way. She hadn't needed to take a foreign language in college, but now she was glad she had. Her French was the differentiator that had landed her the North American leadership role. The promotion had come in the nick of time too, as her finances were in ruins.

At her departure gate, Aria maneuvered through the packed seating area to claim an empty space to stand near the windows. All week she'd been sequestered in stuffy offices, restaurants, and a closed-up hotel room. Now she yearned to feel the fresh, cool air on her face.

On the tarmac below, a dozen men in uniform formed into two lines, saluting a flag-draped casket being lowered from the belly of a small plane. Canada's bold red maple leaf on white rippled in the wind. An honor guard. Aria's throat closed on a lump she couldn't swallow. A year ago, she'd been handed a folded-up flag—all she had left of him.

She squeezed her eyes shut. Please, God, please, not here. But what good were prayers now when her husband was already dead?

She'd held the grief at bay all week, but now, riveted by the all-too-familiar ritual playing out below, she faced once again the enormity of her solitude. If only she could stop her heart from beating the awful dirge.

Mourning—the love song you sing to someone who can no longer hear you. Aria knew the tune well. Its opening refrains invaded, unbidden and unwelcome, into every quiet moment.

Refusing to give in to despair, she'd found distraction in staying active and focused. For too long, she'd burned the candle at both ends. Anything to stay busy. It was the only way she knew to prevent the sorrow from overtaking completely.

"Hey," he'd murmur in the dead of night, his voice as soft and tender as his touch trailing across her cheek and down her side.

More than anything, she missed his warmth beside her as she fell asleep, how he always had to be touching her, whether it was a hand on her hip, his leg alongside hers, or his arms wrapped around her like a cocoon.

Even another argument about how his work consumed every weekend would've been welcome. She'd never been a crier, but these days all she wanted to do was crawl into a corner and sob, and too often, that's exactly what she did: in his closet, in the shower, in the endless array of hotel rooms across North America.

Her eyes stung, but she steeled herself. She would not break down, not now, not in front of all these people.

Breathe, just breathe. You've been here before. It's going to be okay.

Feeling trapped in a glass box, with everyone watching as she ran out of air, she surreptitiously scanned the faces around her then exhaled a held breath. No one cared about her pitiful life. How odd to feel so alone in the middle of a crowded terminal. *That's one thing most people don't know about grief—how lonely it is.*

She glanced at her boarding pass—group two. Turning back to the glass, she took out her phone and brought up a picture of her once-perfect family.

How many men does a woman have to lose before God doles out some mercy on her poor, battered soul, before she's deemed worthy of lasting grace? Or was she forever fated to taste only fleeting snippets of happiness? Five years with her father, fifteen with her brother, eleven with Dante, twenty with Adam, almost twenty-one with Jacks—so far.

Oh, God! Please don't take my son.

2

———————

Propped against a post in the crowded boarding area, his backpack at his feet, Eli Van Drie surveyed the other passengers from behind his aviators. He straightened and smiled when he spotted the woman he'd noticed earlier in the security area, the one who'd left him a bit breathless. She passed him and weaved through the crowd to stand near the windows.

Definitely a business traveler, he decided, probably heading home to a waiting husband. As pretty and put together as a cable news anchor, she wore a crisp tan pencil skirt, a navy blazer, and a gentle sadness on her slim shoulders as she stood there, her back to the crowd. A computer bag hung from one shoulder. He tried to picture her in jeans, then decided she probably never wore them. With a trim, athletic build, she had a casual elegance about her that hinted she'd be comfortable dressed up all the time. Not the type of woman he'd ever find in an LA nightclub, wearing a provocative party dress, smiling and laughing, surrounded by friends and admirers. But if he did, would he approach her, and if so, what would he say?

She faced the wall of glass, and he could barely make out her reflection. Were those tears brimming in her eyes? The sight of her standing there, awash in sunshine and sorrow, made his heart stutter in his chest. She tugged at whatever held her honey-brown hair in its smooth ponytail and pulled it loose, setting the long lengths tumbling free. The lighter streaks reflected the sunlight like threads of gold. Such a simple act, but the sensuous effect of it sent a jolt of heat straight to his core.

She'd spoken French to the TSA officer. What if she didn't speak English? In no mood to risk another humiliation, he slumped back against the post and scanned the fellow passengers idling about the boarding area. But he couldn't keep his eyes from returning to the sharply dressed businesswoman.

What's your story, madame? Or is it mademoiselle?

She extended her right hand, palm up, and lowered her head. Praying? Her shoulders slumped beneath some imperceptible burden. Where was all that sadness coming from? And did she really believe God was listening?

He imagined her sliding happily onto a bar stool across from him at the Polo Lounge, where he'd tended bar for almost four years while awaiting his big break. He'd become quite adept at guessing a woman's favorite drink. This lady had a sophisticated air about her that suggested she might enjoy a fine wine—one glass, two tops, never more—and undoubtedly a red: cabernet, merlot, maybe a pinot noir if she was the adventurous sort.

Definitely not a chocolate martini drinker, like his barely twenty-something costar, who'd gotten blitzed at last night's final wrap celebration. He'd invited Makayla Chase to dinner before the party in hopes their on-screen chemistry could turn into something real. But the night had ended with Makayla getting sick and Eli tucking her into bed in her hotel room, little black dress and all. Not exactly how he'd hoped the evening would end.

Thinking back on it now, he realized he wanted more than a meaningless one-nighter with another ambitious young starlet. He longed for the whole package: the heart-stopping, raw, almost feral can't-get-enough-of-you physical need shared by two people consumed by love.

Makayla was smart, funny, and kind, not to mention sexy as hell. Why wasn't that enough? Was it asking too much to enjoy his morning coffee with someone who wasn't ducking out early in last night's party dress?

The French woman would never duck out, he thought, eyeing her reflection in the glass. She'd be the lingering, sleep-until-ten, savor-me-all-day, and when-will-I-see-you-again type. The kind of woman who would pray for his soul.

Or was he just dreaming?

You always miss the shot you don't take, his grandfather used to quote Wayne Gretsky. Of course, it was usually in reference to hockey, but Eli had long since learned that it applied to everything in life, including women.

He slung his backpack across his shoulder and took a step toward the intriguing woman when a call came over the airport's PA for boarding group two. With a wistful longing, he watched her join the line of passengers, then disappear down the jet bridge.

3

On the flight from Montreal to Chicago, Aria prioritized all the follow-up notes that had come out of her meetings that week and made a list of things to do when she returned to the office on Monday. Before she realized it, the plane was landing at O'Hare. After a brief layover in Chicago, she had one more leg to Grand Rapids and then a twenty-minute drive home to Falls Creek.

Within seconds of taking her phone off of airplane mode, it vibrated. "Hey, Glen." She tried not to sound as tired and impatient as she felt. The last thing she needed were more to-dos from her boss.

"Hey. Will you be in the office this afternoon?"

"My flight gets in at 3:00. I wasn't planning on it."

The silence on the other end said he needed something. She waited. "How'd the week go?"

"Good. Great actually." She peered up the aisle. The doors were opening. "Look, I just landed at O'Hare and we're about to deplane. Can I give you a recap on Monday?"

"Fine." His tone was that of a disappointed child, which she was in no mood for.

"Great. Talk then."

She was about to end the call when he interjected, "Wait." A short pause followed. "Any chance you've started on that industry standards presentation?"

Aria rolled her eyes in disbelief. "Glen, I've been in Montreal all week. I've literally been working from breakfast meetings through dinner pitches. No, I haven't even thought about your presentation. But I'll get it to you by the end of next week. Good enough?" Geez, the guy had over a month until the conference. And if he was in such a rush, why didn't he put it together himself? In fact, why'd he schlep if off on her in the first place?

"Fine." Again, short and loaded with unmet expectations.

"Okay, gotta go." She forced a smile into her voice. "Have a great weekend."

"You too."

Aria tucked her phone into her satchel and again glanced up the aisle, now filled with standing passengers, barely moving.

Her boss hadn't always been a total jerk. He used to be tolerable, friendly even, provided direction, escalated issues when asked, and otherwise left her to do her job. But ever since the reorg that had earned her the recent promotion, he'd felt the need to keep her under his thumb with incessant demands to remind her who was in charge.

It was understandable Glen should feel threatened by her. Despite his Ivy League MBA and her lowly BA from community college, he'd gotten his promotion to VP of Sales by default. The role was offered to Aria five years prior, and she'd turned it down. At the time, she wasn't willing to devote so much of her time to travel—the casualties of balancing career and family. She'd been one rung beneath him on the corporate ladder ever since.

She'd had to accept the Key Accounts role a year ago because she needed the money. When it came down to losing her home or being home, it was an easy choice. Even so, the decision weighed on her. It was one thing not to be there for her kids after school.

Leaving her daughter home alone for days at a time was another thing altogether.

Pushing aside the untenable concessions she'd felt compelled to make, Aria vowed to not think about Glen again until Monday morning.

She adjusted the strap of her satchel on her shoulder and craned to see up the aisle. What was taking so long?

Even after exiting the plane, the line moved at a snail's pace, and Aria finally discovered why. Near the front, an elderly woman inched along, clutching the handrail of the jet bridge, while the other passengers cautiously made their way around her in the narrow corridor like peas squeezing through a funnel. Someone should have brought the poor woman a wheelchair.

The two men ahead of Aria split up. The first guy, despite his ungainly size, carefully slipped by. As the taller one followed, his backpack shifted and bumped the old woman, causing her to stumble at the threshold to the terminal.

Aria lunged forward, barely making it in time to keep the lady on her feet, but the woman's bag fell from her arm, its contents scattering. The distraught passenger allowed Aria to help collect her things. Crouched on the floor, Aria glanced up to see the man who had wreaked the havoc amble away down the concourse, totally oblivious.

Fuming, Aria handed the bag to the old woman, who thanked her profusely, switching from English to French and back again as if it were all one language.

"May I walk with you to baggage claim or to your next gate?" Aria asked, concerned.

"Oh, *non, non,* but *merci. Tu es si gentil,* so nice." She explained that her daughter from Minneapolis was meeting her and together they were going to Key West.

"Ah, *c'est bon,*" Aria said. *"Alors, au revoir."*

Once beyond the gate area, Aria dashed through the terminal, determined to catch up with the oblivious jerk. She spotted him up ahead and was gaining on him when he headed for a private lounge. Afraid of losing him, she took off a shoe and hurled it, hitting him right between the shoulder blades.

The man spun around, eyes searching, then bent to pick up the shoe as Aria hobbled to a stop before him.

Tall, well over six feet, she judged, lean and well muscled in jeans, a black T-shirt, and a brown leather jacket, he wore an LA Kings ball cap, dark sunglasses, and a crooked grin. His gaze traveled the length of her, pausing at her bare foot. With a smirk and a head tilt, he offered the shoe.

Aria snatched it, bent to slip it on. "Do you have any idea what happened back there?"

He recoiled at the accusation in her voice then glanced back the direction they'd come from and frowned.

"Are you really that clueless?" She didn't give him time to answer. "You hit an old woman with your backpack! Practically knocked her to the ground." Aria paused, letting it sink in. "And her bag dumped everywhere."

A teenager carrying a skateboard stopped to sneer, "You totally did, man. I saw it," then moved on.

The tall man's jaw dropped and a half-laugh escaped him before he looked back at Aria.

"You know what happens when old people fall?"

He stared at her, speechless.

"*Parlez vous Anglais?*" Perhaps he spoke only French. She could think of no other reason for his continued silence.

His older, shorter, and grossly overfed companion stepped forward. "Excuse me, ma'am. Do you know who you're yelling at here?"

She shot him a piercing glare before turning to gaze at Mr. Clueless again. She recognized him as one of those overblown, self-important, second-rate actors. "I don't care if you're the pope. What you did back there was thoughtless and rude." She stared into the dark lenses covering his eyes, daring him to object.

A slow smile curved his lips. "I had no idea, really. I'm sorry."

His voice was soft and gravelly, a Camel and bourbon baritone, and for the briefest moment Aria forgot her anger. Despite the incredibly seductive smile, his words seemed sincere.

She took a calming breath. "Save it for the woman you almost seriously injured." Aria stepped around him and marched toward her connecting gate.

A few steps away, she turned back. He stood staring at her from behind those dark sunglasses. He grinned, and she gave him a weak smile, then spun around, her face hot. Letting out a defeated breath, she plodded on. He probably thought she was horrible. Oh, well, it was the right thing to do. Besides, she'd never see the guy again anyway.

"Good God," Eli muttered as the angry woman stormed off. Such passion! He'd been so captivated by the fury in those blazing green eyes, he didn't know what to say. That was new.

Returning to their arrival gate, Eli found the old woman sitting alone, rummaging through a reusable bag, white with a green Provigo logo. Her blue-gray hair was carefully arranged in small tight curls.

He slid into the seat beside her and eased his backpack onto the floor at his feet. "Excuse me. I think I may have accidentally bumped into you earlier, and I wanted to apologize."

Her rosy cheeks plumped as she smiled. *"C'est bon."* She patted his hand. "I am well."

"Good." He would have liked to chat with her, reassure her that he really was sorry. But he didn't know any more French than a few greetings and *Où est la toilette?*

Minutes later, as he trudged through the terminal to catch their connecting flight to Los Angeles, his agent prattling on beside him, thoughts of the pretty French woman still swirled in Eli's head. He couldn't believe she'd had the nerve to chase him down.

His agent nudged him and stopped. "What can I get ya?" Max nodded toward a snack shop.

"Nothing, thanks. I'm good."

Max waddled into the shop, no doubt in search of more food. The man ate 24/7. Eli admired his commitment, though. Max Acres had flown all the way to Montreal to coax Eli onto a commercial flight back to LA for a meeting on Monday for his "next big shot."

According to Max, every meeting was Eli's next big shot.

With an oversized nose and a balding pate, the rough-talking Jersey man resembled an elite-level boxing coach, the all-in corner-man in Eli's championship-winning bout. Cleaning him off, wiping him down, talking him up, only to push him right back out for another round. He couldn't have asked for a more dedicated agent. It was only a matter of time before Eli scored a knockout.

This latest film wasn't Eli's first time playing the romantic lead, but it had the potential to launch him to the top of *The Hottest Leading Men in Hollywood* list, maybe even earn him an award.

An Oscar sure would be nice to take home. If he ever went home again.

After twelve years, he finally had the burgeoning career he'd always dreamed of, making at least two movies a year, sometimes three. He'd bought an impressive estate home in Beverly Park, an upscale community popular among actors, directors, producers, and other name-makers in the industry. With several close friends, an abundance of female companionship, and plenty of money to play with, he enjoyed his life. He especially looked forward to premiere night, which he and Makayla would attend together as a couple, even if they weren't still dating.

And yet, something was missing.

While he waited for Max to re-spike his blood sugar, Eli leaned against a post, his backpack at his feet, and searched the sea of travelers for the bilingual businesswoman, hoping for a chance to set things right. He hadn't even gotten her name. The image of the tear on her cheek, along with the tentative smile when they'd parted, played in the back of his mind like an unreachable itch.

When Max rejoined him, a bulging plastic bag dangled from his wrist as he tipped an open can of Pringles Eli's way.

"No, thanks."

Farther down the terminal, Eli spotted the woman handing her boarding pass to a gate attendant. He raced to catch her. "Wait!" He skidded to a stop a few feet away, a throng of travelers between them.

About to step onto the jet bridge, she paused as if considering whether to turn around.

"What's your name?" he called out.

She turned and shot him that adorable shy smile. "Aria."

"Thank you for . . . that." He hitched a thumb over his shoulder.

Max appeared at his side and Eli turned. When he looked back to the gate, Aria had disappeared. He cursed under his breath.

A wild thought occurred to him. He rushed to the counter and checked the board to see where she was headed. Grand Rapids, Michigan. At least it wasn't another foreign place where he couldn't speak the language.

He gave the young blonde manning the counter his most alluring grin and handed her his boarding pass to LA. "Any chance you could exchange my ticket for a seat on this flight?"

She blushed. "I'm sorry, sir, but we're not allowed to change a passenger's destination at the last minute. Besides, your luggage would go to the wrong place."

Eli took off his sunglasses and propped his elbows on the counter. "My agent checked my bag, so technically it's attached to his ticket. And my guess is the front section isn't full. Sure you can't make an exception just this once?"

The attendant's gaze flitted left then right. Eli amped up his smile.

She sniffed. "I suppose. Let me just—"

"This is ridiculous." Max placed a meaty hand on Eli's shoulder. "The interview is scheduled for—"

"Don't worry, Max. I'll make it." Eli smiled as the printer spit out his new boarding pass.

Max groaned and rolled his eyes, accepting that the battle was lost. "You'd better." Tugging the strap of his carry-on, he turned away and disappeared into the crush of passengers.

Eli, the last to board, greeted the pretty flight attendant at the door with his most winning smile. As soon as he was settled in his seat near the front, she was at his side, offering to serve.

He made an outlandish request. Minutes later, she returned and gave him a surreptitious thumbs-up.

He glanced back to see Aria sitting two rows back—next to an empty seat.

4

Aria settled into her new seat with a much needed exhale. She'd been pleasantly surprised when the flight attendant had offered her a free upgrade to business class. The only one in her row, she wouldn't have to make small talk with anyone.

"Something to drink?" the young woman asked.

"I'd love a water, but unfortunately this airline doesn't recycle, so I'll pass. But, thank you." Her refusal almost seemed wrong in light of the free upgrade, but Aria had determined long ago to add the explanation to her response in hopes that fellow passengers might overhear and follow her lead. She loved Michigan, but with at least one landfill within an hour in every direction out of Grand Rapids, she diligently did her part to recycle, reuse, and minimize waste whenever she could.

The attendant moved on and Aria stared out the small oval window, yearning for something she couldn't name. She needed to be alone, to look inward, to grieve. But she knew from experience that once she opened the door on grief, even the tiniest crack, it would barge in like an unwanted guest, and it would be a long time before she could drive it out again.

Aria suppressed an urge to pull the shade down on the sunlight that streamed so happily through the window. Instead, she faced it, along with her reflection. Unbidden, memories of the last sunny day of her marriage flooded in. Two years ago, she'd been planting spring flowers, blissfully ignorant of the tornado of tragedy that would sweep in out of the blue to tilt her world on its axis and blow away the very foundation she'd built her life on. In a blink, she'd gone from enjoying a small hard-earned slice of The American Dream, to being utterly destitute and facing foreclosure. One minute her husband was hunched over a broken sprinkler head, and the next minute he was lying by the side of a road, mortally injured.

Ever since that day, grief was always there, lurking, crouched like a cornered animal. Occasionally its roar diminished to a calm whisper, but it never went away completely. In the most inopportune moments, and without warning, it sprang up again to bring her to her knees.

Determined to focus on something else, Aria searched her mental to-do list and honed in on three pressing events on the horizon: her product launch, Jacks's need for money, and Monroe's high school graduation.

The product launch should be all set. The purchase agreement was signed. The last contingency, delivery and acceptance of the recycling machine she'd developed with the help of her father-in-law, Justus, had been satisfied yesterday when he had delivered, set up, and demonstrated the latest prototype at the EverClean offices. They had only to show up in three weeks to close the deal.

She stared at the seven-figure number, imagining all she could do with it: Pay off the mortgage, cover her kid's college, quit her job or at least stop traveling so much, maybe even finish law school. If only Gibs and Dante could see her now. The long hours they'd spent as kids in their basement workshop settled like a fond memory. How ironic that she would be the one to sell a patent when they were the ones set on becoming engineers.

Pulling the dog-eared pages from her satchel, she reviewed the contract again, searching for any loopholes that could potentially jeopardize the deal. She couldn't afford for it to fall apart. Her house and her kids' futures were riding on it.

Earth Everlasting—she liked the ring of the company name she'd settled on. It was only an LLC, Limited Liability Company, but she'd retain the rights to it. Satisfied all of the *i*'s and *t*'s were dotted and crossed on the deal, she turned her attention to her children.

Two days ago, Jacks had texted her.

Jacks: Did you pay my tuition?

Aria: Not yet. When's it due?

Jacks: A month ago.

Aria: Don't worry about it.

Jacks: I need new pads and a catcher.

Aria: Can't the gear wait until next season?

Jacks: Summer camps start in June.

At that point, she'd called him. He picked up on the first ring. "You can't make do for now?" She couldn't afford any unnecessary expenses.

"My pads are too small."

"Already?" She and Adam had bought him new equipment when he started college.

"They're three years old. You want me to get hurt? And my catcher ripped again. I had to duct tape it, and now it barely folds."

She closed her eyes. Disappointing a child was never easy. "Jacks, I just can't right now."

"You guys said—"

"I know what we said, but that was before."

She and Adam had made a deal with Jacks his freshman year of college: as long as he stayed on the dean's list and the hockey team, they'd pay for school and living expenses so he could focus on his studies. He'd held up his end. He excelled academically, never missed a practice, and started every conference game in the net.

She pinched the bridge of her nose. "I'm doing the best I can." It took everything she had not to let her voice break.

Jacks's only response was an angry grunt.

"You could get a job."

"Seriously?"

"Yes!" The kid was twenty years old, and his last job was at a car wash in high school. Not that he didn't work hard during the school year, but he could've at least gotten an internship during the last summer before his senior year.

She hadn't spoken to her son since that phone call. For two days, guilt had churned in her stomach like curdled milk.

Now, feeling optimistic about the EverClean deal, Aria texted Jacks.

Aria: Go ahead and buy your new hockey gear. Put it on the card.

He responded immediately with an animation of himself in the net, making a save, followed by *TY* and three hearts. She watched the animation a few times, amazed at how tech-savvy he'd become, then "liked" his text.

As the plane taxied to the runway, she put her phone on airplane mode and turned her attention to her daughter's graduation.

If only Adam could be there to see his little girl graduate from high school. He was going to miss so much: moving her into her dorm, helping her pick out her first apartment, walking her down the aisle.

For months after his death, Aria had heard Monroe weeping at night. She went into her room, wrapped her daughter in her arms, and silently prayed for her until she fell asleep. Sometimes when Aria awoke in the morning she found Monroe had crawled into bed with her.

They all missed him. Everything used to be so much easier. She missed how well they did life together, how she'd see the kids off in the morning and he'd be home when they returned in the after-noon. She did the laundry and he grocery shopped. She paid the bills and he took care of the vehicles. She planted flowers and he tended the lawn. Most days they cooked dinner together. As the kids grew older, she managed Monroe's soccer, then tennis, while Adam coordinated Jacks's hockey. They both tried to make it to every game. Two parents in sync.

Grief hit so sharply it took her breath away. Tears threatened. Aria fought them back. Prayers circled in her heart.

The seatbelt signal *dinged,* and within seconds a man slid into the seat beside her. "You!" She cringed at the harsh sound of her voice.

"Hi," said Tall, Dark, and Clueless, shooting her that crooked grin of his. His five o'clock shadow made him look like a rock star— in a scruffy, trying-not-to-stand-out sort of way.

She blinked away her almost-tears. "Are you stalking me?"

"What? No. I wanted to apologize."

"You already did, back in the airport." She shoved the contract back into her satchel.

"Ari, you have to believe me, I had no idea I'd bumped into that woman."

What arrogance! Adam was the only one who called her Ari. This guy didn't even know her.

She peered out the small window as an uncomfortable silence settled between them.

"Can we just start over?" He took off his sunglasses. "Hi, I'm Eli." He extended his hand.

His eyes were the color of a summer sky but it was the lopsided, almost childlike smile that totally disarmed her. "Aria." She accentuated the final *a* as she shook his hand. "You want to make me smile? Think I'll want to let you in?" She quoted lines from a song he'd performed in a movie she'd seen.

Eli laughed. "So you do know who I am!"

Aria softened her tone. "What are you doing here?" Surely this young B-list movie star hadn't switched flights just to follow a bedraggled widow and worn-down mother of two.

"Going to Grand Rapids." He peered out the window as if he could see where they were headed. "Right?"

"Yes. But why?"

"To . . . see a friend, an intriguing woman I just met, actually." His eyes held a mischievous glint.

She almost laughed at the thinly veiled compliment but decided instead to play along. "She must be something."

"Oh, yeah. Full of spunk. Got a fire in her."

"You know all that on such short acquaintance?"

"You betcha," he said with a distinct accent—Minnesota or Wisconsin, Aria guessed. His gaze fell to her lap, where she absently twisted her wedding ring, and he grimaced. "Problem is, I think she's married."

Aria wrung her hands. Part of her wanted to say, *"He died,"* or, *"I'm a widow."* But she hadn't been able to say those words aloud yet, not even to herself, and if she tried now, she'd probably burst into tears.

"Hey, it's all right. I'm still glad I got to meet you and apologize. Do you have kids?"

The awkward moment having passed, she talked enthusiastically about Jacks and Monroe. Her children were the sunlight that got her through her darkest days.

Aria asked him about his time in Montreal, and he described the movie he'd been filming, which was based on a book by one of her favorite authors. Eli asked if she'd read it.

"I've read everything he's written. Wow, can he tell a heartbreaking love story! Did they change the ending for the movie?"

Eli grinned sheepishly. "Not sure. I only read the screenplay."

"Well, was it a happy ending?"

He gave her a sly smile. "You'll have to wait and see the movie to find out."

"No way." She shook her head. "Good stories are supposed to be like a dream you don't want to wake from, and that one had an incredibly sad ending. Real life has enough of those."

"I suppose it does. But hey, I'm glad you chased me down in the airport."

Her face flushed. "Sorry for being so forceful."

"It's okay. I think it's great you have the courage to stand up for others."

I can't believe I did it. That's so not me. She wished it was. "How'd you like Montreal?"

"It was nice, what little I saw of it. Living in a place for months and not speaking the language is tough. I could've used your help getting around."

"How do you know I speak French?"

"I was behind you in security. Plus you asked in French if I spoke English."

That he'd noticed her at all was surprising, but even more so was how it made her feel.

The voice of the pilot broke in to announce the approach to Grand Rapids. "Current weather is eighty-two degrees and sunny."

Eli angled toward her and searched her face. "Your husband's a lucky man."

The warm feeling vanished as quickly as it had come. Yes, Adam was the lucky one; he got to go first. She had to find a way to move on alone.

Alone was the first flavor she had tasted in life, having been abandoned by her father and neglected by her mother. Her brother and mother were gone now. She knew loneliness, and she knew her children, nearly grown, could not save her from it. The reality of it hid in the deep recesses of her heart, reminding her she'd soon have no one.

She stared at the wedding ring. Would she ever feel ready to take it off? She felt empty without Adam. She couldn't feel naked too. A part of her wanted to tell this alluring stranger that she wasn't married. But was she prepared to let someone else in? She closed her eyes and breathed.

"You okay?"

"I'm not married. I was, but he . . . died." The words tumbled out, and hot tears glazed her vision. "Little over a year ago." She tried to sound matter-of-fact, even as images of her comatose husband rose in her mind. Adam had hung on for so long after the accident, she'd been certain he'd pull through, and then—he didn't. So many evenings she'd spent at his bedside, feeling oddly numb as he faded away. Her mouth was suddenly so dry she could hardly swallow.

Something about the way Eli looked at her in that moment told her he knew the pain she tried to mask, as if he sensed how alone she felt and understood it. He placed a hand over hers. "I'm so sorry."

The warmth of his touch undid her. So tender, so gallant, so unexpected. She tore her gaze away. "Thank you."

She'd finally done it. She'd told someone. That was a big step, right? And she'd said it without crying.

She dared a glance at him, and his eyes captured her gaze. "When God closes a door, he always opens a window."

She exhaled, not realizing she'd been holding her breath. Was that in the Bible? She couldn't remember. But she wished it were true. She could use a window.

Beyond him, fields, lakes, and city outskirts rushed by as the plane banked. "Have dinner with me tonight."

She felt as if he could peer right into her soul, see all the grief and sadness lurking there. She pulled her hands away.

"Come on. Say yes." He flashed that charming smile again. It was hard to say no while looking into those incredible eyes.

"Why me, Eli?" He could do so much better.

"I've made you laugh. Like at least ten times. It's time you were happy again, don't you think?" He searched her face. "You never know, lightning could strike." He raised his eyebrows in anticipation, just like Anthony Hopkins in—

The plane hit the tarmac, the impact an exclamation point to his argument.

She stared back at Eli, speechless, as the roar of the reverse engines kicked in. *You never know, lightning could strike*? Of course he'd quote great movie lines. He probably had a whole arsenal of them. "*Meet Joe Black*?"

"One of my faves."

"Mine too."

As the plane taxied toward the terminal, Aria dug out her phone, flipped it off of airplane mode.

"It's just dinner. If you don't have a good time, I won't bother you again. C'mon." He nudged her leg. "Give in to me." He gave her the most endearing half smile—one she felt sure was well practiced—while his eyes twinkled back at her.

"That pretty face probably gets you all kinds of things," she teased.

Eli's smile vanished. "Please don't hold that against me."

A pang of guilt stung her. What right did she have to judge him by his looks?

Aria's phone buzzed with a text from Monroe.

Monroe: Can I go to the movies tonight with Sutton and some friends?

Aria considered. Another lonely evening at home, or dinner with an attractive man who did, she had to admit, make her laugh? "I'd love to."

"Great!" He tapped his phone. "Pick you up at five?"

She hadn't seen her daughter all week. "One sec." She fired off a response to Monroe.

Aria: Just landed. Movies OK. Be home when I get there?

She lifted her gaze to Eli. "How about we meet somewhere. Say seven?"

"Seven it is. But I'd really like to pick you up." He handed her his phone, open to the New Contact page. "Please?"

She eyed his phone.

"Too soon to meet your daughter?"

"It's not that. I barely know you."

"At least your number then."

She entered her number and handed the phone back to him.

He thumbed in a text and seconds later her phone vibrated with a message.

Eli: The best way to find out if you can trust somebody is to trust them. E. Hemingway.

Eli's contact info followed, including a Beverly Hills address.

Any guy that quotes Hemingway can't be all bad. "That's really where you live?"

"Trust me." He handed her his phone again, open to her Contact page, and she entered her address.

When they reached the terminal, he turned to her. "Got any suggestions for where I should stay? I've never been to Grand Rapids before and . . . this was kind of a last-minute thing." He winked.

They discussed hotel options as they made their way through the concourse.

Eli paused to read the overhead signage. "Looks like Ground Transportation's this way." He nodded to the left.

She hesitated, considering whether to offer him a ride.

"I need to rent a car. See, I have this big date tonight."

"Right."

Minutes later, as Aria stood alone at baggage claim amid a cruel sea of reunited loved ones gushing with joy, her phone vibrated with another text from Eli.

Eli: I would be happy to meet you somewhere if you'd prefer, but I get to pick the place, the wine, and pay.

Aria brightened, thought for a moment, then replied.

Aria: Energy and persistence conquer all things. B. Franklin. For all that, you can pick me up.

Eli could have hired a town car, but he decided on a basic rental, figuring Aria would be more at ease with that. The attendant handed him the keys, and he headed toward the parking garage, envisioning the evening ahead. It had to be perfect.

His luggage was on its way to LA, and he had nothing but a few toiletries in his backpack. He rubbed his chin. A shave was definitely in order, a haircut too. Hopefully the hotel had a good concierge.

Tossing his backpack into the backseat of the rented Impala, Eli absently patted his chest pocket where his cigarettes would normally be, then remembered he'd smoked his last one on the balcony outside of Makayla's room last night. Resolving to quit, he slid into the driver's seat and closed the door.

In the sudden silence and new car smell, his heartbeat pounded in his ears, his stomach twisted, and his mouth went dry. For the first time in his adult life, he was nervous about a date.

5

Aria stared at her reflection in the full-length mirror. When had she become such a sad and lonely person? Where was the confident businesswoman? Where was the beloved preschool teacher all the little ones greeted with excitement every Sunday morning?

She forced a smile, then cringed. It looked as fake as it felt. She brushed a bit more powder over the dark circles beneath her eyes, evidence of too many sleepless nights. She longed to feel the fireworks of someone discovering her anew, the old Aria, before she'd become so exhausted, so bereft, so depleted. The little girl who loved to swing, who once believed her toes, if she stretched them far enough, could one day reach the heavens. The teenager who'd vowed to make a difference in the world.

Whatever happened to the vibrant mom who loved to swim and play with her children, to dance and laugh with her husband? *Death happened.* She bent closer to her image in the mirror. *Are you still in there?*

For nearly two years, ever since the accident, Aria had worn her pain like a shroud, allowing it to overshadow everything, darken even the sunniest of days. In all that time, the ache of his absence hadn't faded.

A familiar sting blurred her vision, followed by a feeling she often had of wandering aimlessly inside herself, searching in vain for something forever lost. *What if I never get over him?*

Suddenly weary, she closed her eyes, welcoming the dark, empty void.

When she opened them, the room had brightened. The air seemed light and breezy. Glancing up, she saw Adam over her shoulder in the mirror, his expressive blue eyes staring back at her with a full-faced grin.

"You look pretty, Mom." *Monroe?* Her daughter's soft blue eyes —her father's eyes—appraised her, head to toe. Monroe nodded, grinning—her father's grin. "Really pretty."

Aria blinked, and it took several heartbeats before she could speak. "Thank you, baby." She wasn't at all sure of herself or the plans she'd made for the evening. Afraid of sending the wrong message, a dozen nixed cocktail dresses covered the bed, and she'd finally settled on a simple skirt and sweater. "You sure you're fine with this?"

Monroe wrapped her in a hug from behind. "Yes. It's time. Trust me, Mom, you're ready."

Aria hoped her daughter was right. She certainly didn't feel ready.

"Sutton and I are going swimming," Monroe said, heading for the door.

Aria spun around. "Don't you want to meet him? He'll be here any minute."

"No. You've got this."

A few minutes later, the sound of bare feet pounded the length of the dock, followed by two splashes.

Turning back to the mirror, Aria forced a smile. "You can do this," she insisted. *Ready or not, you have to do this.*

At the sound of a car door, she dashed to the kitchen to check the driveway. Sure enough, Eli was ambling up the sidewalk.

Returning to the bedroom mirror, she took one last look, yearning to see what her daughter had seen. Disappointed, she hurried to answer the doorbell.

A brave smile firmly in place, her heart pounding in her chest, Aria opened the door.

Eli's smile broadened as his gaze swept over her. "You look gorgeous!"

"Thank you," she said, suddenly shy. It had been a long time since a man had given her a compliment like that. Her husband, after eighteen years of marriage, was seldom inclined to appreciate her appearance beyond a quick *You look nice,* and even then, only when she asked.

She backed into the house to allow Eli entry. "Come in."

He walked inside, smelling very expensive, and glanced around. His black pants and perfectly pressed steel-blue shirt accentuated his broad shoulders, narrow hips, and long legs. All cleaned up, he was the gorgeous one. What was he doing here?

Her heart raced. This was a huge mistake. She closed the door and backed against it to face him. "Eli—"

"This place is fantastic!" He gaped wide-eyed at the expanse of windows and French doors, the vaulted ceiling and massive solid-oak staircase.

Seeing her beloved home through the eyes of a stranger, she had to admit, the house was impressive. With its open floorplan done in soft shades of sage, it had an earthly décor that emulated a natural beauty, bringing the outdoors inside. Tall white paper birch trees, long dormant and leafless, rose from large copper pots that framed the doorway to the master suite off the kitchen. Every inch spoke to her and Adam's love of nature.

Eli caught sight of the view at the back of the house. "You live on a lake." His voice rang with awe.

"Haven Lake."

The lake house had been a big step up from the quaint little apartment they'd shared over his parents' barn and a huge improvement from the tiny storeroom over the pool hall in Delray where she'd lived before that—not to mention her mother's decrepit rental on Bowser Street in Detroit where Aria had grown up. How different her life may have been if she hadn't allowed her childhood home to burn to the ground, if Dante hadn't gone to prison for it, if he'd written back just once. At least one of her children would still have a father.

But you'd never have found this wonderful life. A rush of guilt smacked her like a knockout punch from a bouquet of flowers. How could she even think of herself when Dante had given up everything for her? The last time she'd seen him had been through a thick piece of glass at the correctional facility.

"Go, live your life, Lily Fair."

"I'll get you out of here, D. I'll find a way."

How naïve she'd been back then, writing to him for eight years, waiting patiently for something in return. But the mailbox never held anything but bills, junk mail, and the bitter disappointment of her letters, returned to her unread, unopened.

No, she wasn't ready for another relationship. First Dante, then Adam. Every time she shattered, the pieces were sharper, cut deeper, hurt more. She couldn't face losing another man. She wasn't strong enough. Might never be.

She glanced with longing at the kitchen sink, reliving all the times Adam had sneaked up from behind to run his hand, rough and calloused from work, down her side before pulling her in for a kiss.

It's just dinner, she told herself, burying the ghosts of the past along with the guilt of the present.

Eli strolled into the living area, gazed out the windows, and turned. "Is this where you'll sit when I call you later?" He nodded to the back deck with its comfy furniture grouping.

"You're planning to call me?"

"Of course." His voice held a gentle kindness.

His response both surprised and settled her.

Maybe she was ready after all.

SOMEHOW ELI KNEW he was going to want to call Aria later. He sensed tonight was the beginning of something good. Really good.

He couldn't believe how naturally pretty she was with her barely-there makeup. She wore a cream-colored sweater over a frilly, tiny-flowered skirt that revealed shapely legs. Her hair tumbled around her shoulders, and now out of the business suit, she looked soft and totally feminine standing there smiling nervously up at him.

Photographs of her late husband and their happy family were scattered throughout the main living area. Not unexpected. But what did surprise him was that the man's belongings were everywhere. Near the windows, on the floor beside one of the two matching cream swivel rockers, lurked a pair of men's slippers. In the foyer, a man's jacket hung on the hall tree, a pair of men's boots at its base.

Eli felt like an intruder, trespassing where he didn't belong. She'd said he died a year ago. How long did these things take?

She walked to a set of French doors that led to the back deck, opened one side, and beckoned him to follow. "My favorite room."

"Wow, what a view!" The tranquil lakefront yard was incredible. Wildflowers bloomed beneath a stand of pines running along one side of the well-tended lawn. Gardens bursting with flowers and sprinkled with birdhouses anchored the property, while pots overflowing with color edged the waterfront patio. The scent of lilacs and freshly mown grass filled the air. The landscape lush and vibrant green, reminded him of a movie set in Aspen, only this time he didn't have a boom mic inches from his face while he tried to fake feelings for a coked-up starlet. No, this time, it was all real. "You must have a gardener."

"My college-age son takes care of the lawn, a trade for me doing his laundry. But the rest is all me. I always wanted a pretty yard, so I read a few books and *voici*." She smoothed her skirt and leaned a shoulder against the deck post. Her stance said nonchalant, but her timorous smile belied uneasiness.

"It's stunning."

"Thanks. Everyone thinks gardening is so hard, like it's some special gift or something. It's actually pretty easy if you remember one simple rule: plant things where they belong. Everything has a place where it thrives. It's when you don't follow the rule that it gets hard."

Eli's life clock stopped. Standing against the backdrop of her idyllic lakefront house, Aria looked completely at home. Like James Dean belonged in a fast convertible, Aria belonged at the lake. Her eyes mirrored the evergreens, her hair as straight as their trunks, its honey-gold strands reflecting like sunlight on water. Her flowered skirt danced in the soft evening breeze, an extension of the gardens below. It was all so serene he wanted to settle into it, linger, and absorb the essence of it, of her.

Aria waved at two young girls on a water trampoline beyond the end of the dock. She turned to Eli. "My daughter, Monroe, and her friend." The sound of youthful laughter floated up from the girls frolicking out in the lake.

Monroe must be the high school senior she'd talked about on the plane. He'd never dated a woman with kids, but teenage girls adored him. The older son, he didn't feel quite so confident about despite the fact that they shared a passion for hockey. He turned back to Aria. "Mind if we sit for a few minutes?"

"Sure." It came out sounding like *shoor,* and he considered teasing her about her Michigan accent but thought better of it.

He sat on the double chaise lounge and patted the cushion beside him. She joined him, leaving enough space to park a small car.

Eli asked how long she'd lived in the house, and she explained that it had once been a modest ranch-style home that her husband, a builder, had remodeled. Aria seemed comfortable talking about her home, then suddenly she went silent, staring off into space, as if interrupted by a memory she couldn't voice.

He asked about the little hook that hung from the cedar beam above them, and Aria described the circle of mosquito netting she hung from it when she slept outside on warm summer nights.

"You sleep out here?" He pictured her asleep on the chaise, surrounded by translucent netting, moonlight softly illuminating her features, like something from a fairytale.

"I used to. It's amazing falling asleep in the fresh air, surrounded by the sounds of the lake, cicadas, frogs, and an occasional splash when a fish jumps, then waking to the birds at dawn. It's multi-sensual."

"Multi-sensual?" His skin tingled.

"Yeah. In the darkness you hear, breathe, *feel* the world around you." She thumped her chest. "In here."

Eli looked at her, and their gazes lingered. He admired her love of nature.

"Trust me. It's pretty awesome."

"I'll bet it is." Eli faced the lake and let his mind wander. Had Aria and her husband sat together in the evenings like they were doing now?

He tried to imagine what it must be like for Aria to have shared her life with someone for so long, and all of a sudden, he's gone. And then someone new comes crashing in to convince her it's time to move on. His heart ached for her loss.

"Is it weird, my being here?" He hoped the question wouldn't reawaken sad memories.

Several silent moments ticked by. "No. But going on a date isn't something I imagined myself doing." She looked away. "Ever."

He shouldn't have pushed her.

She turned to face him. "But I'm glad you're here."

"Me too."

ELI TOOK Aria to the only upscale restaurant in Falls Creek and was pleasantly surprised. The hotel concierge was right. The River View was an elegant little place and perfect for a first date. When he'd made the reservation, he'd worried that Aria's husband might have brought her here. But he figured it would have been virtually impossible to pick a place nearby they hadn't been to. This was her town, after all, and it was small.

As he held the door open, Aria squared her shoulders and breathed in as if bracing for something.

"Is this ok?" Maybe he should've found someplace further away, more discreet. Again he was having second thoughts about this whole Michigan adventure.

"It's perfect," she said with a questionably sincere smile.

He thought about telling her to relax but she had every reason to be apprehensive. When is it socially acceptable for a widow to be seen in public with another man?

Inside, a millennial in a dark suit, with olive skin, kind eyes, and jet-black hair slicked into a ponytail, stepped forward with menus in hand.

"Sebastian," Aria greeted the maître d' with a happy grin.

"Mrs. Whitmore." The young man's expression brightened. "How are you this evening?"

"I'm doing well, thanks. And how's your father?"

"Very busy at the moment. Chef's out sick so Papa's in the kitchen tonight." With a courteous smile directed at Eli, he motioned for them to follow. "Right this way." He led them to a private corner table on a deck overlooking the river, while Aria, lashes at half-mast, shot furtive glances at the passing tables.

"Tell your father I said hello," she said, slipping into the chair Eli held for her.

"Will do." Sebastian carefully positioned menus and a wine list on the table. "Enjoy your evening." With a slight bow, the young man left them.

Aria nodded toward the retreating figure. "He played hockey with Jacks."

Of course she'd see familiar faces here. But remarkably, so far anyway, she seemed all right with it. Dinner was easy and relaxed and seemed to be exactly what Aria needed. They shared their favorite movies, music, and pastimes. She laughed easily at his stories about growing up on a farm in northern Minnesota, living in Los Angeles, and working in film. He loved the music of her laughter, the way it made her eyes light up. Then he asked about her job and the company she worked for.

"I recently convinced leadership to consolidate our North American operations to provide one cohesive customer experience and they gave me the job of implementing it. So, now I manage Hewitt's entire North American team of forty-some sales reps. Initially, my boss—I report to the VP of Sales—rejected the plan outright: too risky, too much change all at once, Sales would hate it. But I eventually convinced one C-suite executive who, in turn, helped sell it to the others. Sometimes all you need is one shining advocate to help raise you and your idea in everyone's estimation."

"That's a lot of responsibility."

"I suppose it is."

"And how's it going so far?"

"Great. In the past six months we've cut expenses by nearly half to achieve record profits, and we're on pace to double sales for the year. A big part of the plan was to get rid of weekly call sheets and the myriad other tracking reports that had been required for years. All that time previously wasted on paperwork is now spent in front of customers, and our numbers prove the plan's efficacy."

"Impressive." An accomplished and articulate businesswoman, she was modest but comfortable with the power of her own mind. Do you travel often?"

"I do now. I usually limit it to one or two overnights a week, but this last trip was a whole week." She reached for her wine. "What about you? You probably film all over the world."

"Not as much as you'd think. A lot of scenes are shot on sets."

"Did you always want to be an actor?"

"Since high school," he said, thinking back. "I played Danny Zuko in *Grease* my senior year, and I've been hooked ever since. What about you? Did you always want to go into sales?"

"No. I was going to be a public defender, save the world, or at least innocent young men who—" She stopped herself, and her thoughts seemed to go far away for a moment before she came back around with a rueful smile. "—people whose only crime is being poor. I had just started law school when my husband's construction business was hit hard by the recession, so I quit school and joined Hewitt to help pay the bills."

"I could see you as an attorney." He pictured her approaching the bench in a stylish, tailored suit, like Olivia Pope or Ally McBeal.

"Maybe someday I'll finish."

Eli watched her quarter the remaining scallop on her plate and divide the risotto into four equal portions, one for each bite of fish. She had a casual grace about her that he found intensely attractive. He was glad he'd followed his instincts that afternoon at the airport. This dinner was turning into the high point of his week.

"Tell me about your family."

Her eyes went far away, cloaked in sadness. When she looked back at him, she cocked her head as if deciding whether to share something she normally kept close. "My parents are gone." She set her fork and knife across her plate, parallel and pointing toward eleven o'clock, apparently finished with her meal. "Older brother too."

"I'm sorry." As he reached across the table for her hand, he noticed she'd replaced her wedding ring with a small emerald band.

She followed his gaze and gave him a wry smile. He squeezed her hand, wondering if all that death had made her into the resilient, confident woman who sat before him.

"I . . . I used to pretend John Adams was my father."

"Why?"

"He was a good man. He loved God, his family, and his country, in that order. And he was very brave."

"That's your idea of a good man?"

Her gaze wandered as if searching for a better idea. "I suppose so, yeah."

"Do you remember your real father?"

She nodded. "I was five when he left, and . . ." She raised her wine glass, gave it a swirl. "At sixteen, after my mom died, I was placed in foster care in Gross Pointe, an upscale Detroit suburb, and I ran away to find my father. He still lives on the other side of Grand Rapids."

A million more questions circled Eli's brain like a maelstrom. "What's he like?"

"He's a finance manager at a Chevy dealership and plays jazz clubs around town. And he's the exact opposite of John Adams. The man I'd blindly adored as a little girl turned out to be a worthless coward." There was no bitterness in her voice, only resignation, but no wonder she didn't want to talk about her family.

"You don't have a relationship with him then?"

She scoffed. "He has another family now." She took a sip of wine.

"So," he began, searching for a more comfortable topic, "you like to read?"

Her body relaxed. "Love it. When I was five I had a babysitter, Mrs. Wyatt, who held a Bible study in her basement. I couldn't wait to learn to read, so I memorized Scripture verses. Been hooked ever since."

So she *had* been praying in the airport. It saddened Eli to think how his faith had withered over the years. He was still a believer and made no attempt to hide the fact, but he wasn't as active as he used to be. He'd turned his back on God about the time his father had turned his back on him. "Your first book was the Bible?"

She nodded and forced a smile over the rim of her wineglass, but seemed hesitant to go on, as if that part of her life was cloaked in sadness too.

Giving her a moment, Eli panned the nearby tables, made eye contact with an older woman wearing leopard print, heavy makeup, and a coy smile. "What's your favorite book?" he asked, returning his attention to Aria and groping to salvage the conversation.

"*Scarlet Sails* by Alexander Green." She didn't even take time to think about it. "It's a little book translated from Russian."

"What's so special about it?"

Her eyes brightened. "It's the story of a handsome sea captain who makes a young girl's dream come true simply because he can."

"Well, isn't that what we all want, to make someone's dream come true?" The beauty she found in the story's simplicity said a lot about her. He wanted to tell her about his balcony prayer last night in Montreal, how awestruck by a gilded cross rising high atop a church spire, he'd begged for a woman to love. But he didn't want to freak her out. "Or better yet, to be the answer to someone's prayers?"

"Dreams, prayers. I guess the only difference is where your faith lies."

He bent forward, elbows on the table. "And what do you pray for, Aria Whitmore?"

She stared at him, her eyes darkening to a deeper green, like sinking in an ocean. "Lots of things." A frown creased her brow, and she looked away. Obviously that wasn't a safe topic. Maybe she still prayed for her late husband.

"What's your favorite book?" she asked.

"*The Adventures of Huckleberry Finn.*"

She nodded in approval. "Two young men determined to be free."

"Doesn't get more noble than that." Her summation surprised him. Most people would say it's a story of travel and adventure, but she, with her literary intellect, recognized the underlying theme of liberty and the true price of freedom.

The waiter returned, offering dessert. Aria declined. Then, sensing Eli's disappointment, she suggested he pick one and she'd share it with him. He turned his attention to the dessert menu, happy to have extended their time together if only for a few minutes. He decided on apple pie à la mode.

He'd no sooner ordered dessert and the leopard-clad woman

placed a hand on Aria's shoulder. "Aria? As I live and breathe." The woman's voice boomed like a foghorn.

Aria grimaced then turned, fake smile firmly in place. "Denise. Hi. It's been—"

"Ages!" The woman shimmied with excitement. "We've missed you and that handsome hubby of yours at euchre."

"Yeah, well . . . " Aria sat, mouth agape, while an uncomfortable silence settled on the table like an uninvited guest.

"Oh, right. He . . . what a dreadful thing. I'm so sorry." Denise turned to Eli. "Hi, I'm Denise." She leaned over the table, hand extended, her huge breasts straining against the daring neckline.

Was that a onesie she was wearing? Eli stifled a laugh and launched to his feet to meet her halfway, lest her ample bosom spill right out. "Eli—"

"My friend Eli and I were on the same flight home from Montreal this afternoon," Aria hurried to explain. "A business trip."

"Nice to meet you." Eli shook Denise's hand then settled back into his seat, grateful to be the date downplayed to a friend rather than whatever Denise was, or more accurately, wasn't.

"Likewise." Denise said with a sultry lick of her lips. "Do you play euchre?"

"Not in a long time."

"Well, Aria's a ringer. Maybe you two can sub in some time." Denise turned back to Aria and blatantly sized her up. "A business trip, did you say?" A single penciled-on brow raised in judgmental disbelief.

Aria bit her lip, like maybe if she said nothing, the woman would go away.

"Right, well you two have fun," Denise said with a bawdy laugh. "But not too much," she tossed back over her shoulder as she strutted away on matching leopard print stilettos.

Aria blinked and let out a breath. "Sorry about that."

"No worries. Being a friend is a good place to start."

Aria fingered the stem of her wine glass, her eyes unmoving, as if seeing nothing but her own discomfort. The mood at the table had definitely done a one-eighty. If the caption of the pre-Denise scene was *Lonely widow beholds a spark of possibility* it had quickly morphed into *Envious cat squashes hope beneath a well-placed stiletto.*

"Hey, do you want to get out of here?"

Aria visibly relaxed, a definite yes. "What about dessert?"

"We'll get it to go."

He paid the check and dessert in hand, they snuck out the back and down a flight of steps to a long paved sidewalk that ran along the river.

Aria collapsed onto a bench and, elbows on knees, covered her face with her hands, and laughed with obvious relief. While Eli would've loved to join her, the best he could muster was a smile as he pictured the audacious woman in the leopard-print onesie. There was nothing funny about pure meanness.

Eli eased down beside Aria and opened the dessert box, took a bite. Then another. When Aria glanced up, he offered her the other spoon.

"Of all the people," Aria said with a lingering chuckle. She spooned out a hearty chunk of pie while he held the box.

It was clear Aria didn't like the leopard-clad woman but he suspected beneath that humor, hid a certain amount of regret, or shame even.

Two bites in, Aria jumped to her feet and spun to face him. "Let's go for a walk."

Eli took another bite, pretending to consider it when really he was thrilled she didn't ask to be taken home. Most women would— he had to stop making suppositions. He'd already discovered Aria wasn't *most* women.

"This," she motioned to the long sidewalk that extended as far as he could see in both directions, "is the Rails to Trails state park, a converted railroad bed a hundred miles long. It stretches all the way from Grand Rapids to Cadillac and the section through Falls Creek has some of the prettiest scenery along the whole trail."

They say every journey begins with a single step. Eli couldn't wait to accompany Aria on that path.

6

Eli took Aria's hand and they headed north, the path well lit by street lamps. Downtown was mostly a collection of boutiques and civic buildings, not so different from his own hometown. Beyond a park, the lights ended and the path disappeared into dense woods, lit only by the faint moonlight filtering through the treetops.

"Aren't you worried, wandering into the dark with a man you barely know?" Eli asked.

Aria stopped and studied him. "Should I be?"

"No! I mean, not with me. But I hope you don't make a habit of it on first dates," he said, only half teasing.

"I haven't had many dates lately, first or otherwise, but I can take care of myself." She walked on ahead of him, and Eli instantly regretted his comment.

She must have realized he wasn't following because she stopped and turned around. "What?"

"Am I your first date since ...?" he asked gently, closing the distance between them.

Aria tilted her head with a wry smile. "Lucky you." She walked on, stopping at an overlook. Her back to him, she stood on the observation deck and propped her elbows on the railing. Her shoulders rose and fell with a heavy breath.

He had mixed feelings about being her first. On one hand, he was glad no one else was in the picture. On the other hand, she still carried a lot of sadness. There were obviously topics he couldn't breach, things he couldn't say. He had to tread carefully.

After several long moments, she extended a hand palm up, as though reaching for something, like she'd done in the airport. Praying again?

He eased closer and watched the river's lazy run, the stars and half-moon mirrored in its smooth, dark surface.

"I always wanted to go kayaking here," she said softly, "but we— I—never did."

He propped himself against the rail beside her and studied her profile. Her eyes grew distant, and he knew she wasn't looking at the muddy water anymore. Was she seeing a river of regret, memories that should have been made before the hourglass of her marriage ran out? It was hard to witness her pain without pity wringing from his heart, yet something good flickered deep down, set alight with a newfound sensation he hadn't felt in a very long time.

The way the moonlight created a halo around her iris, he imagined he could see right into her soul. A haunting loneliness, a deep-seated yearning for comfort, drew him in. She wasn't beautiful in the usual sense of perfectly shaped features but in a classic, almost ethereal way that reminded him of a child or an angel. She was so much more than simply pretty.

He knew plenty of attractive women, but Aria was different, an intriguing dichotomy. She was delicate—fragile even—and yet she had an inner strength that astounded him. She was elegant but unpretentious, confident but modest, extremely intelligent but with a natural common sense. He especially liked that.

"Can I take your picture?" He reached into his shirt pocket for his phone. She withdrew, and he felt the *no* coming. "Please? The moonlight, the angle—a master couldn't paint a more perfect picture." She gave over with a soft smile. He clicked off a couple of shots, then tucked his phone away, relaxing against the rail. "So why didn't you ever kayak here?"

"I don't know. Never got around to it, I guess." The sadness in her voice was unmistakable. "You always think you have more time, and then . . ." Her voice caught. "You don't." She crossed her arms and rubbed herself.

"Cold?" He wished he had a jacket to offer, but he'd left it in the trunk of the car, worried it probably smelled like smoke.

"A little."

Eli stepped behind her, wrapped his arms around her, and gently pulled her back against the warmth of his chest. "Better?"

She felt stiff in his embrace, but she nodded.

As they stood facing the river, a peaceful silence surrounded them, broken only by the sounds of crickets and bullfrogs. Eventually she relaxed her head against his shoulder and sighed. It was a pleasant sound. He smelled a hint of her perfume—or maybe it was her shampoo—like fresh, ripe strawberries.

Eli bent, his lips to her ear. "It's good, huh?" She felt soft and warm against his chest. He had no idea holding someone could feel so right.

"Very." Her voice, sweet and fluid like honey, trailed away. If only he could banish the sorrow like he had the cold.

A half-moon illuminated the night, and the stars, like millions of tiny pinpricks of light, winked in the blackness. He'd forgotten how different the night sky looked out in the country, how many more stars could be seen away from the city lights, where starlight goes unchallenged. No amount of money could buy a view like this in LA.

"There's something wonderfully serene about moonlight on water," he said, mesmerized by the beauty of the river, the quiet of the deep woods at night, and, God help him, the way this woman felt in his arms.

"I know what you mean."

Aria turned and looked up at him, and he had an overwhelming urge to kiss her. She must have sensed it, because she quickly withdrew.

"Why me, Eli?" She squinted up at him. "LA is chock full of glamorous women, and you could have any of them. What are you doing here, with me?" She tore her gaze away and blinked as if breaking some spell.

"Why not you?" A godly Midwesterner with a brain might be exactly what he needed. He was tired of trying to live up to his current public image. Aria could reconnect him to his own roots and values, help him to be the kind of man he wanted to be.

She stared at the ground. "You're Eli Van—"

"I'm just a guy from Minnesota." Stepping closer, he tipped up her chin, forcing her to look at him. His gaze wandered to her full lips and back to her eyes. His hand threaded through her hair, the long strands dripping through his fingertips like molten gold.

"Aria, you are beautiful, and bold, with a dazzling intellect. I've never met anyone like you." He paused, searching for the right words, while she stared back, doubt clearly etched in the glint of her eyes. "You're genuine, down to earth, comfortable with who you are, not striving to be someone you're not, like the women in LA. Actresses playing a part. I never know who they really are. But you're different." He paused and grinned. "If you wanted to be with me . . ."

She returned his smile, giving him the reassurance he needed to continue.

"I know it would be because of who I really am, not because of my success or my money or how I might help your career. You see the man I am. And maybe the man I could be." Eli brushed a fingertip across her cheek, mesmerized by the smoothness of her skin. "I like that. A lot."

He wondered if he should go on, but he couldn't find the words. And that was okay, because it was too soon to tell her he'd been waiting his whole life to meet someone like her.

He leaned in to kiss her.

She stepped back, searching his face. "Are you playing a part right now, Eli? Telling me everything you think I want to hear? Trying to make me fall for you?"

Her mistrust felt like a gut punch. But the last part of her question gave him a flicker of hope that she was feeling something too.

"No acting here." He took her hand, hoping she could read the sincerity in his face.

She stared back at him, captive in his grip. While his hand held on, his heart let go. She had no idea how amazing she was, which made her all the more enticing.

He took her face between his hands. "Would it be so terrible to let me in, just a little bit?"

She pulled away, her eyes wide with fear. "Oh, Eli, I—I can't."

The sound of his name on her lips almost undid him. The last thing he wanted was to frighten her by moving too fast, but she was intriguing, and smart—probably way too smart for him—and he wanted her.

He swallowed everything he wanted to say to lure her back into his arms. And then what, get her into bed? No, he wanted more than that with her. He wanted everything with her.

"I'm not the man the tabloids write about."

Aria didn't read the tabloids, so she had no idea what Eli's public image might be. But that didn't matter. She'd always been a good judge of character. She'd find out for herself the kind of man he was.

Aria longed to trust him. But did she really want to get involved with an actor? His life had to be so different from hers. He probably had hundreds of women throwing themselves at him—young women, Hollywood's hottest. A man like Eli couldn't possibly be happy with only one woman; eventually he'd get bored with her.

Besides, they literally just met. And she had a past. If he knew what she'd been through, what she'd done . . . Her heart thumped with trepidation.

And yet, a waft of hope fluttered in the periphery, like the scent of fresh-baked cookies—even if you couldn't see them cooling on the kitchen counter, you knew how delicious they'd taste. She longed to hear more of his sweet, uplifting words that made her feel so beautiful, so alive, so—not alone.

Eli eased closer, his gaze intense, until they shared the same breath. When his lips brushed hers, they felt soft and warm, his tongue shy. The wine-soaked kiss was everything she secretly longed for, and yet, everything she feared. When he pulled away, she shivered, and not from the cold.

The intensity in Eli's deep blue eyes made it easy to push aside the guilt and let herself believe.

"We should probably head back." She tried not to let the shakiness she was feeling show in her voice.

He straightened and took her hand, cleared his throat. "I can't tell you how much I don't want this night to end." He looked like he wanted to say more.

She put a fingertip to his lips. "We could go back to my place, sit by the lake, make a fire, have another glass of wine?"

He smiled, relief washing over him. "Sounds perfect. I'm great at starting fires."

"I'll bet you are," she said with a laugh.

7

Seated in Eli's car, Aria glanced at her phone—a missed text from Monroe, asking to have a sleepover at Sutton's. As Eli skirted the hood and slipped behind the wheel, Aria shot back a reply.

Aria: Sure. On my way home. Good night. Love you tons.

When they returned to the house, Eli offered to open a bottle of wine and take it to the lake while Aria changed into warmer clothes. A few minutes later, dressed in yoga pants and an oversized sweatshirt, she descended the deck steps. Eli had the fire going and was rearranging chairs to make room for the double chaise he'd carried down from the upper deck.

"I hope you don't mind. I'll take it back up before I leave." He shot her a sheepish grin as he set it alongside the fire pit and stretched out on it.

"Not at all." She picked up a glass of wine and joined him, pulling her feet up beneath her.

They sat in comfortable silence while the moon hung low over the treetops on the far shore and reflected in a long, tranquil line across the lake. The water, smooth as glass, carried the muted sounds of Friday night revelry from a group of boats parked at the dam. Aria stared into the flames, mesmerized by the flickering glow.

Adam had made the gas-fueled tabletop fire pit shortly after they'd bought the outdoor furniture so sparks from a wood fire wouldn't burn the cushions. He was always so clever, so capable. Now she was sitting here, sharing the serenity of it with someone else. Somehow, it felt all wrong.

"I'll be right back," Eli said, heading toward the house.

Aria closed her eyes and settled in, warmed by the heat and soothed by the sound of the flames dancing from the gas jets, so unlike the wild crackle and pop of a wood fire. So different from the whoosh and hiss of that terrible, long-ago blaze. If she'd only glanced back that night, she would've seen the flames that had consumed her childhood home. But she hadn't. She'd walked away, refusing to look back. If she'd seen the house aflame, she would've felt compelled to call for help, and that wicked man may have lived to go on hurting—

"Hey," Eli called as he crossed the yard, his voice ringing with excitement. "Look what I found." He raised an arm showing Monroe's beat-up guitar, one of her many short-lived interests. Across his shoulder draped the couch blanket from the rec room sofa.

Aria's heart melted like a puddle of wax. He was going to sing. The most vivid thing she remembered from the movie she'd seen him in was his voice. His character had totally drawn her in, and she knew the real man, walking toward her now, would easily do the same, especially after the feelings he'd shared with her back on the trail. Completely unfair.

Aria forced a calm that threatened to elude her. "It won't hold a tune. Has a cracked neck."

"I think it'll make it for one song." He tossed the blanket across the back of the chaise and sat at the end, facing her, positioned the guitar, and plucked at the strings, listening intently as he adjusted the tuning pegs. When his fingers eventually strummed the instrument, the air filled with music, and he smiled as though finding a long-lost friend.

She quickly recognized the tune as the song from his movie she'd quoted on the plane. She could barely breathe. His music warmed her cold, empty heart . *He* warmed her cold, empty heart . Her pulse raced with excitement. But this wasn't right. She wasn't ready to feel this way.

Her hand shot out and wrapped around the neck of the guitar. "You can't sing that to me."

"Why not?" He looked confused. "Let's sing it together," he drawled, slipping into the character from the movie. "You've got a smile that makes me want to sing. C'mon. You know the words."

"I—I can't." She shook her head.

"What is it?" He studied her intently.

"There's only so much a girl can resist," she said with a light-hearted chuckle.

"See, that's where you're wrong." He bent over the guitar, his face inches from hers. "You don't need to resist me." He uncurled her fingers, placed her hand in her lap, and restarted.

He sang the first verse, and he was even better than he'd been in the movie because he was right there in front of her, singing the words to her. For her.

She joined the chorus on cue. Her voice shook at first, but by the time her solo came, she'd calmed herself enough to sing smoothly.

I wanna draw you in
I wanna make you smile
Come on and take my hand
Let's dance for a while

I wanna steal your heart
I wanna be your dream
Come on and take my hand
You'll be my everything

Let me into your heart
Into your life
Let me fill your days
Let me in. Let me in

I wanna give you time
A while to heal your pain
I wanna love you so
You'll wanna let me in

Her heart thumped so loudly she felt certain he could hear it. It was just a song. But the way he looked at her made it so much more than lyrics and chords. His openness made her want to let him in.

ARIA'S VOICE sounded surprisingly soft and breathy—like ripples on water. Awed by the raw beauty of the music they made together, Eli took over the last verse, the one cut from the movie. He wanted to let her know he was going to make her his, if not tonight, then eventually.

I wanna make you mine
I wanna help you see
I wanna be with you
You'll wanna be with me

Let me into your heart
Into your life
Let me fill your days
Let me in. Let me in
Oh, let me in

When the song ended, their eyes lingered and he kissed her,

savoring her softness, the taste of her, the feel of her, the way she smelled. It was mind-blowing.

He pulled away slightly to stare at her kissable lips. *You're gonna wanna let me in, Aria Whitmore.*

Her breath caught. "That was . . . Wow!"

"The kiss?" Her laughter told him she was referring to the song. The tremendous effect it had on her thrilled him.

She created space between them. "Where'd you learn to make music like that?"

"My mom taught me to play piano as a kid, and my grandpa taught me the guitar. I was in a praise band in high school."

"You sang in church?" Her voice rang with surprise.

"Yep. My grandpa was a preacher, and my mom played piano every Sunday, so I pretty much had an in." She seemed more impressed by his music than his celebrity status. He liked the way she looked at him, like she saw more in him than just a good-looking guy, a man worth more than a tawdry one-nighter.

She took a deep breath that quivered on its way out. "I don't stand a chance against you, do I?"

He laughed, then set down the guitar and crawled up beside her. He gently pulled her into his arms, her back against his chest, and hugged her close, inhaling the subtle sweet scent of her hair. He nuzzled her neck, kissed it lightly, then spread kisses across her bare shoulder. Her skin felt like silk beneath his lips.

Her head tilted to one side, granting him better access, welcoming him like a flower reaching for the first gentle rays of dawn.

"What are you doing, Eli?" she said, her voice soft with a glow of happiness.

"Enjoying being with you." He kissed the base of her throat. "Want me to stop?"

After a long minute, she said, "Yes." It came out in a shaky breath.

He knew she didn't mean it, but he accepted it anyway. Nothing more would happen tonight. This was all he needed, for now.

Eli stared into the fire, enjoying the stillness of the cool spring evening. His thoughts drifted to his beloved grandpa, the pastor, the storyteller, the lover of poetry and music. The man Eli had always turned to when he needed advice. Some of his fondest childhood memories were of the endless summer days spent fishing in the streams and ponds around Region, Minnesota. They seldom reeled in many fish, but Eli usually caught a good story or two, great tales of adventure, courage, and woe that taught important life lessons. Grandpa had talked often about following the light, but Eli hadn't expected to find it in a woman's eyes.

He missed those days . . . and the spiritual force in his life that had once been so strong. Most of all he missed the comfortable sense of fulfillment that came from trusting wholly in something bigger than himself.

Eli found himself nodding off. "I should go," he mumbled half-heartedly.

Aria nestled against him and in a sleepy voice, mumbled, "Stay."

He drew her closer and settled in, awash in a contentment he'd never known, and succumbed to sleep.

Eli woke to the sound of birds. The fire had gone out, but he was still warm and cozy with Aria snuggled against him beneath the blanket. He hoped he could lie there a few minutes longer, watching her sleep, feeling her breathe.

The lake shimmered in a pre-dawn pinkish glow. *"There's always hope in a sunrise,"* his Grandpa would say.

He dozed off again and woke when Aria stirred beside him. He kissed the top of her head, breathing in the essence of her.

She nestled deeper into his arms.

"I can't believe we slept out here all night," he murmured against her ear.

She laughed softly. "This doesn't count as sleeping together, you know." She pillowed her hands beneath her cheek.

He pulled her close, basking in her warmth. "You were right about waking to the sounds of the lake and the birds."

She lifted her head. "Hear that soft cooing?"

He listened carefully and heard a throaty *cooh, cooh, cooh* coming from the rooftop.

"Mourning dove," she said. "My favorite."

The haunting sound, like a lost soul, continued for several moments. "Sounds like a nightingale to me."

She playfully pushed against his chest. "Sure it is, Romeo." They laughed together, and she rested her head on his shoulder.

Eli once read that it was the custom of Japanese men to honor their lovers by giving them not jewels but the most exotic birds. Maybe all the homemade birdhouses in the yard were Aria's husband's way of honoring his beloved bride.

As much as Eli longed to linger in the magic of the pending daybreak, he knew he shouldn't. "Suppose I'd better go, huh?"

Reluctantly, they eased from the tangled cocoon. Aria collected the blanket, the guitar, and the leftover wine and glasses, and Eli hefted the chaise over his shoulder. As he followed her up the deck steps, a single thought filled his mind.

He had to see her again. Soon.

8

———————

Eli paused at Aria's front door, aching to take her in his arms, as she stood there in her grand foyer, hesitant and sleepy-eyed.

"Thanks for a lovely evening." The words were rote, but her eyes screamed, *Don't go.* Or was that just a reflection of his own desires?

He stepped closer. She didn't back away. He bent and his lips touched hers, a sensation as soft and gentle as a butterfly's wings.

She sagged against the door. His body pressed against hers while he lingered in the moment, wishing it would never end. "When can I see you again?"

She gently pushed against his chest. "Oh, you'll have forgotten all about me by the time you get to your hotel."

"Not going to happen." He played with a strand of her hair. "Absence makes the heart grow fonder, you know."

She grinned, shook her head. "Out of sight, out of mind."

He was going to miss that smile and quick wit of hers. "I'll call you the minute I get home."

Her gaze fell away and took her smile with it.

"If you want me to." All of a sudden he wasn't so sure.

She looked back at him and slowly shook her head.

"What's wrong?"

"Eli." She swallowed hard. "I . . . I'm not ready for this."

"Ari—"

She tried to pull away, but he held her fast. "I only went out with you because I thought you'd be . . . safe. We'd have a nice evening, then you'd fly to LA and forget all about me."

Was she really pushing him away? He had found something amazing with her, and he was certain she'd felt it too. The song they sang together, the unmistakable passion in her eagerly returned kisses, and she had asked him to stay. He hadn't imagined all of that. He hadn't imagined *any* of it.

Aria rubbed her forehead. "I'm sorry." She stepped away, and his arms fell empty at his sides.

He rubbed his stubbled jaw and slumped against the door. *This can't be how it ends.* "Are you sure?"

She stared at him, an almost smile curving her lips. She nodded. Clearly she was holding on to her grief. But he could also see her trying on these new feelings, slipping into the possibility that she could feel something special again.

He gently cupped her face between his hands. "Ari, it's been—"

"I can't." She pulled free of him and plopped down to the bench.

He sat beside her, took her hand, and laced his fingers through hers. "I can only imagine what you've endured. And I know you're still in pain. But beneath your grief . . . I see something more."

She peered at him with a hint of curiosity. "What do you see?"

"Someone who's strong, fiercely independent, passionate. And lonely."

She speared him with a sideways glance. "Lonely? You can see that?"

He nodded. "I know what it looks like. I see it in the mirror every day."

Her eyes brightened with a tenderness that captured his heart.

She nestled her head against his shoulder, and he pulled her onto his lap. Her arms circled his neck, and he held her like a child. The warmth of her breath, feather soft against his throat, provided a quiet reassurance. Her words were lies meant to push him away, but the way her body spoke to him was unmistakably honest.

He thought about their conversation at the river's edge, the fear in her eyes. She needed time to realize what they'd found together. He wouldn't pressure her.

After several quiet moments, he lifted her chin with a fingertip, and her eyes met his. "I think we both need to get some sleep."

Aria nodded and they stood. The longing on her face was undeniable, like she was drowning in the tears she refused to shed. He hated leaving her so sad. Taking her hand, he brought it to his lips. "Dream about me," he said with a wink.

Aria half-laughed—much easier to walk away from. Funny how a total lack of modesty could be so disarming. Eli kissed her one last time, a soft, slow kiss that bespoke everything she wasn't ready to hear.

After slipping into his car, Eli turned and found her watching from the doorway. Would this be his last glimpse of her?

As he drove away, a voice resounded inside his head, No. This is but a beginning. How lucky he was to have found something that made saying goodbye so hard.

Aria's head sank into her pillow. *Dream about me*, he'd said. She couldn't possibly dream anything more perfect than the last twelve hours. As she lay there on her side, facing the emptiness where Adam had always been, it was no longer her husband she imagined on the pillow beside her.

Her breath caught. Guilt and shame swooped in. She caressed Adam's pillow, squeezed it to her chest, but his image wouldn't come. Reaching for him. Longing for him. Every night flooding her bed with weeping. These had become her nightly rituals—but no more!

It was time she abandoned that pillar of salt beneath her pillow. She bolted upright, the images of Adam shattering, leaving her with a sudden, sharp emptiness.

Finally giving in, she closed her eyes and let herself feel the warmth of Eli's arms around her in the cool dawn-painted morning. The memory of waking up beside him lingered like a warm breeze as she thought about what she'd say to a phone that would never ring.

LATER THAT MORNING, Aria entered the exercise room. Her boxing gloves beckoned from a hook on the wall. Minutes later, she stood hammering away at the speed bag as easily as thrumming her fingers on a desk, finding comfort in the natural rhythm, in the orchestrated coordination, and soon after, the subtle burn in her pectorals.

"Working out again?"

Aria looked up to find Monroe standing in the doorway, wearing the shorts and tank top she often slept in.

"Morning, sunshine." With the back of her forearm, Aria swiped at a bead of sweat dripping from her nose.

"How was your date last night?" Monroe picked up her own gloves and strapped them on.

Aria resumed her rhythm, her fists making small circles in the air: Right-right-strike, left-left-strike. "It was nice."

"Just nice?" Monroe danced in front of the freestanding heavy bag and threw a few punches. "Gonna see him again?"

"Nope." Aria concentrated on the speed bag. "I'm not ready to start dating again."

"But you like him, right?"

Her daughter's movements were awkward, unbalanced. Aria moved to her side. "You need to ground your feet when you punch, move when you're not punching. And don't throw your body into it, just throw the punch."

Monroe grounded her feet, shoulder distance apart, threw a left-left-right, then danced, following her mother's instructions. "You didn't answer me."

"Less power, more breathing."

"Mom." Monroe stood, gloves on hips, facing her.

Aria rolled her aching shoulders. "He was pretty great. But this is where I need to be right now." How could she explain to her little girl how much more important she was than any man. Even Eli van Drie.

Monroe stared at her, apparently at a loss for words. The smile that replaced the blank look said she understood how important this summer would be to her mother. "Let's go shopping."

"How about we spar instead?" Aria removed her gloves and returned them to their place on the wall.

Monroe scoffed and rolled her eyes.

"Come on. You need to be ready."

"For what?" Monroe tugged off her gloves, and tossed them aside.

"Life." Aria knew the helpless feeling of being held against her will. The last thing she wanted was for Monroe's college years to include that nightmare experience. Since their first self-defense classes as kindergarteners, Aria had done her best to ensure both of her children never felt impotent or weak. Jacks now had size, but Monroe was still a petite little thing, and she could easily be overpowered.

"Come on." Aria wrapped her arms around her daughter from behind.

Monroe deftly freed herself, then squared up to face her mother with a triumphant smile.

Aria tried a few more grabs. Monroe, well trained through years of sparring, freed herself each time. Monroe swatted Aria's punches aside like they were cobwebs. For the next half hour, Aria practiced every defensive move she'd ever taught her daughter, and Monroe escaped, blocked, danced, and jabbed, finally breaking out in laughter at her mother's unsuccessful attempts. Aria considered wrestling Monroe to the mat and pinning her, just to demonstrate that she wasn't infallible. Instead, she drew her daughter into a sweaty, breathless hug. "You're ready."

"So are you, Mom," Monroe shot back with a meaningful grin.

9

———————

A flutter of apprehension rose in Aria's chest as she approached her in-laws' farmhouse. Would they know she'd betrayed their son by seeing another man?

She stepped out of the car and took a steadying breath of fresh country air. It smelled of horses and dirt and green—the scents of home.

As she ambled up the cracked sidewalk behind her children, Aria studied the surrounding landscape. It felt familiar, like the way your lips become accustomed to your favorite coffee mug. An array of pastel-hued sheets, hung like oversized dinner mints on the clothesline between the house and the orchard. The barn doors stood wide open, a dozen horses grazing in the main paddock. How could this place remain so unchanged, impervious to the tragedies of life, especially the loss of a son?

The first time she saw Adam he'd been walking up this very sidewalk, home on leave for Christmas. She was sixteen and had been living in the loft above the barn and working at his father's hardware store for a couple of months. Tiny snowflakes swirled in the wind, turning the farm into a sea of white, the whole scene illuminated like a snow globe by the barn's yard light. From the darkened loft window, she watched as he and his parents spilled out of the farm truck and trudged into the house.

In his buzz cut and desert khakis, his military duffle slung atop his shoulder, Adam looked big and strong, a blond version of his burly white-haired father, Justus. From his parents she'd learned he was twenty-one, had joined the Marines right out of high school, and had one more year to serve.

When she walked into the kitchen the next morning, she over-heard him whining to his mom, "You used to bake cinnamon rolls. Now we have banana nut bread? And since when do we eat *turkey* bacon?"

Aria hung her coat on the hook by the door and stepped out of her boots. "Hi. I'm Aria." She slid into the seat across from Adam as Bea set a plate of nut bread and turkey bacon in front of her.

"Adam," he said, obviously perturbed.

She grabbed an apple slice from the saucer in the center of the kitchen table.

He eyed her as she ate. "Little young to be on your own, aren't ya?"

"I'm eighteen," she lied.

"Really?" He cocked a disbelieving brow at her.

"Leave her be." His mother placed a protective hand on the back of Aria's chair. "She's working at the store and helping with the animals and the loft renovations. Least we could do is offer her room and board."

Bea returned to the stove and Adam sat back, crossed his arms, and glared at Aria.

Aria fought the temptation to pull out her fake ID. The less she showed it the better. It had cost her the last of her babysitting money, but she'd needed it to get in to see Dante at the correction facility. And despite him sending her away, the expense wasn't a total loss. She'd landed a good job and a place to stay. If she could make it a year, she could prove herself as an emancipated minor, then she'd hire a lawyer and get Dante out of there.

She hated lying to the Whitmores though—they were such nice people.

Over the next few days, she caught Adam watching her often, even smiling more than once. He never said it, but she got the feeling he liked her being there, helping his parents. The farm and the store were a lot of work, and his parents were as old as Texas.

When Bea and Justus gave her ice skates for Christmas, Adam taught her how to skate on the pond beyond the barn. She'd felt safe with his strong arms holding her up. Like she'd once felt with Dante.

If only she could shake that snow globe again. *Oh, sweet if-only.*

"Mom?" Jacks called from the front stoop. "You coming?"

Bea and Justus stood behind Jacks in the open doorway.

Aria followed her kids into the house, where hugs were exchanged all around.

"You look good," Justus said, holding Aria's gaze a trifle longer than usual before enfolding her in his massive arms. The flutter was back, squeezing her diaphragm like a fist. *He knows.*

She clung to him, basking in the familiar scent of his work clothes: earth, sunshine, horses, and home. Justus, ruddy with fuzzy ears, was a gentle giant of a man who could read people in a single glance. That first day in the hardware store, the scent of pine and a single needle clinging to her hair told him that she was homeless and had slept beneath a tree the night before. He saw things unspoken that lingered in a person's gaze: loneliness, anger, disappointment. What did he read in her simple *Hello*?

Aria had no intention of telling her in-laws about Eli. But Justus would see it.

"Looks like you got the corn in," Aria said, turning to gaze out the front picture window.

"Almost. Plan to finish the south field tomorrow."

"Perfect timing." Aria stepped out of her shoes and nudged them beneath the little bench beside the door. "I think it's supposed to rain on Tuesday, then warm up a bit."

"God willing," Justus replied with a grin, hitching his thumbs into the pockets of his jeans.

Tied to the rhythms of nature, Justus never wasted hope on the weather. His trust in the earth and in providence was resilient, passed down through generations, like the land of his forefathers, life giving and a solid foundation on which to raise a crop—or a family. Adam had been like his father: from the earth, strong, with unshakable integrity. From deep roots sprout strong trees.

But Adam was gone, returned to the earth, dust to dust. Is that why she clung to her father-in-law with such tenacity? His strength, like Adam's, held her up. His love, like Adam's, never failed.

Justus turned to Jacks. "How's about a game of chess whilst we wait on dinner?" With that, the two men headed for the living room.

"Smells wonderful," Aria said, following Bea into the small country kitchen. The scent of fresh-baked bread and bubbling cheese filled the air. The old round breakfast table where she'd first met Adam still anchored the cozy U-shaped space.

"Just meatloaf and potatoes," Bea said. "Hope you don't mind."

In contrast to her towering husband, Bea stood all of five feet nothing in her cowboy boots. Wearing a perpetual smile on her heart-shaped face, Bea was an accomplished horsewoman and an amazing cook who took great pride in caring for her family. To Bea it was nothing. To those around her it was everything.

"Aw, Grandma, you make the best meatloaf." Monroe picked up the stack of dishes from the counter. With a backward glance of sheer adoration directed at Bea, she disappeared into the dining room to set the table.

Later, seated around the dinner table, hand in hand while Justus said the blessing, Aria offered up her own silent prayer of thanks for their Sunday dinners, glad they'd survived despite Jacks going off to college, the kids' sports schedules, and Adam's—well, she was grateful for the only real family she had left.

Bea dumped a heaping spoonful of scalloped potatoes onto

Aria's plate. "For having spent a week on the road, you look well rested."

Aria's cheeks warmed with the unexpected memory of waking up Saturday morning, having slept through the night for the first time since Adam's accident two years ago. Like a newborn, she was still getting used to her new cruel world, crying for the warmth and comfort she'd been mercilessly yanked from, for needs she had no idea how to articulate. "I finally had a good night's sleep."

And there it was, Justus's knowing smile, exuding understanding and empathy. *It's okay to move on,* it said. *It's time.*

Aria slumped with renewed guilt. If he only knew that she'd found her elusive slumber in the arms of another man . . . As parents, they'd hold on to their grief for a lifetime. But was she expected to do the same?

10

Tuesday morning, in full-on work mode despite another sleepless night, Aria wrapped up her weekly sales meeting and followed her team out of the conference room, her laptop tucked under one arm.

"Caleb." Aria stopped her latest new-hire outside the door. "Got a sec?"

"Sure." Caleb, a quick-witted squirrel of a kid with bushy brown hair, rosy cheeks, and a ready smile, stepped aside to join her while the others dispersed.

"Great job landing Saint Mary's." Aria wasn't the least surprised the young man had acquired his first sale within a month of coming on board. Well spoken, confident, and personable, he'd crushed the interview.

"Thanks. I thought it went well." Caleb stood a little taller.

Aria's phone vibrated, but she ignored it. "You missed your recognition at the start of the meeting. Be on time next week. It's important."

Aria did not abide her team being late. She liked her reps prepared and punctual. In fact, she insisted on twenty-five minutes in lieu of half-hour meetings, fifty minutes versus a full hour, allowing time for participants to get from one place to the next with a few minutes to regroup and prepare. The practice was quickly being adopted throughout Hewitt's two-thousand-plus home office staff.

"I will." He nodded curtly, sufficiently chastised.

"Welcome to the team," Aria said with a smile, softening her tone.

"Thanks."

As Caleb scurried away, Aria's phone vibrated again. She glanced at it.

Hewitt Reception: You have a visitor.

Normally he mentioned who it was, at least a company name. Aria wasn't expecting anyone. She stepped to the railing to peer down into the lobby. Seeing Eli, she raced down the steps.

Aria strode toward the front desk, her heels *click-clicking* across the tile. In tan slacks, with his sunglasses tucked into the neck of a black sport shirt and holding a ball cap in his hands, Eli looked ready for the golf course.

"What are you doing here?" She laughed from the sheer joy of seeing him again.

He gave her hand a quick squeeze as his gaze swept her outfit. In a navy pencil skirt and white blouse and with her hair pulled back in a clip, she felt like a librarian, but from the light in Eli's eyes it was a look he liked. "I was hoping I could take you to lunch."

And just like that all thoughts of sales figures flew right out of her head. Part of her wasn't prepared to feel like this. But a much stronger part relished the memory of his warmth as he'd held her in the early morning. "That would be great. Noon work for you?"

"Perfect. See you then."

He walked away with a casual ease that she found incredibly attractive. His stride was confident, sturdy, strong. At the door, he turned, shot her a knowing grin, and winked.

With a conscious effort to suppress her giddiness, Aria waved, then hurried back up the steps for her next meeting.

Cadence May, one of her best sales reps and a good friend,

stood waiting at the top of the open stairway. "Was that Eli Van Drie?" She nodded toward the front door.

Aria didn't want her coworkers to know she was seeing someone, but she didn't want to lie either, especially not to Cadence, who'd helped her through so much lately. Aria checked the time on her phone. An explanation would have to wait. "Looks like him, doesn't he?"

"A lot." Cadence fell in step beside her. "Lucky girl."

She did feel lucky. Lucky that he wasn't giving up on her, at least not yet. "Let's do lunch tomorrow."

"I'm on the road the rest of the week. Next Monday?"

"Sounds good. I'll put it on my calendar."

"Hey, I saw your dad play last night at GR Noir. He was really good."

Aria stopped walking and turned to give her friend an exasperated stare.

"What? You're going to run into him eventually."

"I know, and I've planned for it. I'll say hello. If he starts a conversation, I'll be cordial but aloof. If he doesn't, I'll just walk away and go on with my happy, fatherless life." She had Bea and Justus and they were all the parents she needed.

"If you say so."

As her friend walked away, it came back to Aria, the thing she loved most about Cadence. It wasn't that she was a top performer on her sales team. It was the girl's honesty, directness, and the way she accepted Aria for who she was, never judged.

Minutes later, alone in the empty conference room, Aria took a seat and scrolled through her email while she waited for the others to show up. Despite her best efforts, thoughts of her father crept in, as they always did whenever Cadence brought him up. She almost wished she'd never shared that part of her childhood with her friend.

She closed her eyes in the white-noise-filled room, and took a deep, centering breath. Despite her best efforts, her mind carried her back to that frigid February afternoon when, at sixteen, she'd walked into the Chevy dealership where her father worked—eleven years after he'd walked out on his family.

"Can I help you?" he'd asked from behind a desk in the small glass-walled office. *James Farrow, Finance Manager*, announced a shiny brass nameplate on the desk.

"You don't recognize me?"

"Should I?" He studied her for a fleeting few seconds, then motioned for her to take a seat. "I'll be right with you."

She slid into the chair opposite him. His hair was more salt than pepper now, but other than that, he looked exactly as she remembered—dark and handsome, like a fairytale prince.

She licked her dry lips. "I'm . . ." *wondering why you left us.*

The din of heavy footsteps echoed in the showroom. High heels skittered down a hallway. Power tools buzzed in the service bay. Somewhere a door opened and closed.

Her father stamped some papers on his desk, scribbled a few notes, then shuffled them into a folder, which he tossed into the shallow wooden box at the corner of his workspace. He glanced up, and when their eyes met it was as though the ruins of all the broken promises melted away.

She imagined herself settling onto his lap, and him pulling a storybook from his desk, opening it to a dog-eared page, and reading from where he'd left off. In reality, all he did was blink a few times and then fold his hands on the desk in front of him. "Now, what can I do for you?"

Her lip trembled.

He peered at her, and his eyes widened in recognition. He bounded from his seat, closed the door behind her, then returned to his desk, practically falling back into his chair.

"Lily?" He breathed heavily as he eased back. The chair creaked with his weight.

Aria nodded excitedly, thrilled at having found him. But she didn't know what to say. He looked . . . angry. Where was the man she remembered from her childhood? The man who'd spoken to her in loving, gentle tones of heartfelt trivialities, those silly things little girls needed to hear from their fathers.

"I should've known you'd be the one to track me down. You always were the most needy."

Needy? *I was five!* She pushed the words past her lips, "Everyone else is gone."

"What do you mean?"

"They're dead. Mom, Gibs."

"I'm sorry." They were the right words, but his expression remained indifferent.

"I went by your house the other day. Your daughters are sweet. Are they my sisters?"

He clenched the arms of his chair and leaned forward. "You went to my house?"

The breath went out of her lungs. "I wanted to see you."

His knuckles turned white as his gaze panned the showroom behind her. "Why?"

Why? "Because you're my father." *Aren't you happy to see me?*

His hands raked through his hair like his head might explode. "No, Lily. I'm not your father."

"What?" A tear trickled down her cheek. She swiped it away, determined not to cry.

He edged closer and spoke slowly. "I am not your father."

"I don't understand."

"What's not to understand?" His somber voice turned to an angry growl.

She bit her lip to stop it from trembling. "How do you—"

"Your mother told me you're not my kid! There."

Realization hit like a slap in the face, and suddenly it all made sense. Her selfish, angry, vindictive mother. "She screamed it at you, didn't she? During a fight, I bet. Well, newsflash! She lied. To hurt you. She would do that, and you know it." She found it impossible to fathom the vicious wounds parents inflicted on their defenseless children, and her mother was the worst of all. "And you believed her because it made it easy for you to walk out like none of us mattered."

"What do you want from me?" He glowered at her.

"I want—*you to love me*—my father."

"Are you in trouble? Do you need money?" He reached for his back pocket.

"No. I just want you to be my father."

"I have a new life now. A wife and two daughters."

But I was your daughter first.

"They don't know about you. And I don't want them to. Ever. You hear me?"

I hear you.

"You need to go." He stood and opened the door, then backed up, waiting for her to leave. "And don't come around my house again."

She swallowed all the angry words she wanted to hurl at him and stood. "Don't worry. I won't." She walked past him.

"And Lily?"

She stopped and turned to face him, hoping against hope he was changing his mind, that he'd remembered how much he'd adored his Lily-bear and sweep her up into his arms, cover her with kisses and—.

"Take care of yourself." He sounded like her mother, sending her on her way with nothing more than some trite parental admonishments.

"Promise me, Lily, you'll never let a man mistreat you."

"I won't, Mom."

"And promise me you'll stay in school and live a better life."

"I will."

The weight of yet another rejection, like a boulder on her back, almost brought her to her knees. Instead, she swallowed her disappointment, almost choked on it. "I will. *Dad.*"

Her hand cradled her belly. She'd vowed then and there to give her child a better life. And to never use the name Lily again.

~

WHEN ARIA CAME DOWN to the lobby at noon, Eli was waiting for her. As she slid into the passenger side, she eyed a picnic basket in the backseat. While Eli slipped behind the wheel, she peered at the dark and threatening sky, then at the weather app on her phone. "It's supposed to rain."

He grinned. "There's a pavilion in the park." With an arm across the seat behind her and a backward glance, he eased the rented Impala from the parking spot in the guest lot.

She doubted they'd stay dry if the storm was as bad as predicted. But she was willing to go anywhere with this man.

"Were you surprised to see me this morning?" He pulled into the flow of traffic.

"Definitely." She thought she'd never see him again, let alone at her office. "Please tell me you didn't fly all the way back here just to take me to lunch."

He shot her a raised brow and a wide grin.

She shook her head. "You're crazy."

"Think so?" He winked at her.

Behind them, Hewitt's three-story office building got smaller and smaller as Aria fidgeted with an undercurrent of excitement and danger. This last-minute venture out into what was bound to be a raging thunderstorm felt like playing hooky, something she'd never done, at least not for the sheer fun of it.

He nudged her knee. "Hey, I had a great meeting with a new director yesterday."

Aria faced him. "For another role?"

"Yep, a good one."

"Did you get it?"

"I won't know for a couple of weeks. My agent, Max, says I'm up against at least one other big name."

He turned into a small neighborhood park she hadn't known existed. As raindrops began to patter the windshield, he pulled up in front of a pavilion.

"We could eat in the car," she suggested. He had no idea what a little rain would do to her naturally wavy hair.

"It'll be fine. Come on." He jumped out, grabbed the picnic basket from the backseat, and made a dash for the shelter.

She joined him as quickly as she could in her heels. He spread a red-checkered cloth over the wooden table and set a carafe of white daisies in the middle.

"I have an antipasto salad and a ham-and-cheese stromboli." He pulled out a Romano's Deli bag from the picnic basket. How did he know what she ordered there at least once a week?

"I showed the owner your picture," he said, answering her unspoken question as he pulled the items from the bag. "So, what's it gonna be today, *Signora Whit-amore*?" he asked in a rough Italian accent, mimicking Mr. Romano to perfection.

"Oh, that's good." Aria laughed as he set both meals before her. She chose the salad.

Eli reached back into the basket and pulled out two lidded cups, sliding one her way. He upended the Romano's bag. "Hmm, no straws. Sorry."

"He knows I never use straws. Bad for the environment." She said a short, silent prayer before uncovering the salad. "I can't believe you bought an expensive last-minute plane ticket just to take me to lunch."

"Why not?"

"Seems like a waste of time and money."

"Not to me." He unwrapped the sandwich. "In fact, I think it might be the most worthwhile thing I've done all week."

"Really?" She didn't believe for a second that this picnic lunch was more important to him than the meeting with the director. "What if I'd had lunch plans?"

"Then I would've invited you to dinner." He took a bite of the thick sandwich loaded with Italian meats, onions, and green peppers. After wiping a drip of marinara from his chin, he turned serious. "Ari, I haven't been able to stop thinking about you. I was starting to think I might've imagined the time we spent together. I had to come back to see if you were really all I remembered."

Aria wanted to laugh, but his sincerity was unmistakable. "So," she said, drizzling vinaigrette over half of her salad, "am I all you remembered?"

"More." He set down his sandwich and took her hand. "We found something special last weekend. It'd be a shame if we didn't see where it could go. Don't you agree?"

Aria poked at her salad with her plastic fork. Her mind drifted to that frigid December morning when she'd walked into Bea's kitchen and met her son, Adam, home on leave from the military. He had treated her like a child at first. But as he learned about her situation from his parents, he became empathetic, showing her the same warmth and concern that had made her fall in love with Bea and Justus.

Adam returned to duty a few days later, but he called home often after that, always asking to speak to her. She thought he was simply a good guy with a heart of pity for a young girl left alone in the world. But over the next two years they built a lasting friendship through all of those phone calls and occasional visits.

One night, when she was particularly sad and missing him, not knowing where things were headed, she commented to Adam over the phone how great it would be if there were a book they could read to learn how long-distance relationships were supposed to work. Adam had told her, "If there were such a book, I know it would end with the words 'ever after.'"

Tears stung to her eyes as she stared at the man sitting across the picnic table, holding her hand and inviting her into another long-distance relationship. Common sense told her to listen to the voice of reason instead of the pleas of her lonely widowed heart. "We live so far apart. Three time zones."

"But only a four-hour flight," he said without hesitation.

Aria stared at him, her tangled thoughts churning with indecision.

"We'll take it as slow as you want." His thumb caressed the back of her hand. "Tell me you haven't been thinking about me too."

Her heart softened. "I enjoyed last weekend very much."

"And?"

And your hand is so warm. "And I do like you."

He straightened with a satisfied smile. "Yeah? What do you like most about me?"

She laughed. "Come on, what's not to like? You're a movie star."

He shook his head, causing unruly dark waves to fall into his eyes. He brushed them back. "I happen to know that doesn't impress you at all."

He had her there. "Fine." She studied him. "You're really hot." It was no secret; she was incredibly attracted to him. What woman wouldn't be?

He lowered his voice. "If that's all it was, we would've had sex already."

Aria recoiled. Did he really think she would have slept with him on a first date just because he was good looking?

"Okay, maybe not." An uncharacteristic self-doubt clouded his features. "But it's more than just a physical attraction. Isn't it?"

She nodded, warmed by his insecurity. "Eli, you've touched my heart deeply. You made me laugh, and it felt good to laugh again. I liked your stories. Your song. Your gentle ways."

His expression softened.

Oh, that boyish smile. He had to be closer to her son's age than her own. "But you're so young," she blurted out.

"What?" His brows shot up in disbelief. "I'm thirty-one."

"Yeah, right." She didn't believe him for a minute.

"Well, I will be. In April."

"I'm thirty-six."

"Five years apart is nothing." He stroked his jaw and looked out at the rain falling in torrents around them. "I didn't expect my age to be the showstopper here."

It wasn't so much his age as it was hers. "Don't you want a family one day?"

"Yes. But we can figure that out when we get there."

Silence settled between them like the heavy clouds that had stolen the day's sunshine.

"You should be with someone younger, someone who can—"

"I want to be with you." He drew nearer to recapture her gaze. "Ari, don't you want to be happy again?"

What a cruel thing to say. Of course she did. More than anything, she wanted her husband back. She wanted her life back. Most days she struggled to just go on. She couldn't start over again.

Rain poured from the edges of the pavilion like tears from heaven. A blanket of sadness smothered her. She swallowed the emptiness and squared her shoulders, resolving not to cry in front of him.

"I was pretty happy before . . ." She glanced away, searching for words to explain how hard it was to face her life now. The nightly prayers that she wouldn't wake up in the middle of the night in a puddle of tears, seized by an indescribable panic, and every morning, begging for the strength to just make it through one more day without totally losing it.

She poked at her salad and tried to smile through the tears pooling on her lower lids. She sniffled and, giving up, lifted her gaze to his. "The tears still come sometimes, and there's nothing I can do about it." She swiped them away with the back of her hand. "You must think I'm so weak."

"I don't think you're weak. I think you've been strong for way too long."

No one should have to be this strong.

He threaded his fingers through hers and she felt it all the way to her heart. "It's time for you to let yourself be happy again."

He knew she was broken, but he wanted to be with her anyway.

He took both of her hands. "You ever stop to think maybe the best hasn't happened yet?"

Of course he could be cavalier about a leap like this. Indifferent to fate, he'd obviously never fallen.

A crack of lightning streaked across the sky, and they both jumped. Eli grinned. "Lightning."

You never know, lightning could strike. A small laugh fell out of her.

Eli bounded from his seat, jumped to the top of the next table like Peter Pan, and with three more leaps he was standing on the table behind her. She shifted around to face him. The rain coming off the roof formed a splashing backdrop while the sky beyond flashed, illuminating his silhouette. "Where's your next business trip? I'll meet you there."

Stepping onto the bench, one foot still on the tabletop, he lowered his head and breathed deeply. When he looked up again, the tenderness in his eyes spoke volumes. "Ari," he said, his voice soft and deep, "open the window, just a crack. You never know what might blow in on the breeze." He held out his hand as though inviting her to fly away with him to Neverland.

Could Eli be the strong guiding hand she'd been reaching for in her prayers? Not to replace the one she prayed to but someone who could physically walk this path of life at her side.

His outstretched hand didn't shake or falter. All she had to do was take it.

The rain fell in steady torrents behind him. Lightning splintered the sky, followed by a rolling thunderclap, the whole storm a cacophony amid her silent torment.

As her eyes lingered on his face, solemn and serene, something flickered inside her chest. It was hope—but for what, she didn't know. Aria stood, blinking back tears, and placed her hand in his.

He pulled her up to stand with him on top of the picnic table, crushing her against his chest.

"Are you sure about this?"

Eli tenderly laid a hand along her cheek. "I flew two thousand miles to ask you out again. I'm sure."

She leaned into his touch, taking strength and comfort from it.

He grinned. "Does this mean I won't have to beg for a third date?"

Aria laughed.

"God, I love that sound."

God, she loved this feeling.

ENCHANTED by the woman in his arms, Eli stared, as a jolt of excitement coursed through him, like every nerve ending in his body was firing at once. Even his toes tingled. Was it her nearness or the storm raging around them?

Rain pounded the roof of the pavilion, waterfalling to the pavement and joining the roar of wind bending trees, the clang of chains on nearby swings, and the shimmy of metal fencing. He breathed deeply, the cool, moist air filling his lungs.

As a kid he'd hated storms. They'd frightened him. But now, with Aria in his arms, he felt invincible, crazy drunk with the intoxication of her, an electrifying high like nothing he'd ever imagined. Every flash burned like lightning in his veins.

He kissed her, and it was alive with passion. He finally withdrew, but only long enough to inhale. Foreheads touching, lips parted, he shared her breath. It was warm and sweet and life-giving.

And the feeling . . . it wasn't just the storm.

11

———————

Eli stood on hesitant legs in the white-columned and chandeliered lobby at the Fairmont Palliser, his heart pounding every time the elevator doors opened. This evening could be his last date with Aria or one of many more to come. He'd never had to convince a woman to go out with him, so this niggling doubt felt foreign to him.

He knew with certainty that she liked him. She'd said as much. Plus, at lunch last week she'd gazed at him like he was her saving grace, her lifeline from a pit of despair. But he also knew that she teetered on a precarious emotional cliff and could easily call it quits at night's end.

He hoped Jubilations lived up to all the hype. On the list of Calgary's top ten to-dos, it boasted an abundance of five-star ratings. The hotel's concierge and doorman confirmed it was a guaranteed good time, which perfectly fit his goal for the evening: keep Aria smiling. All-out laughter would be a bonus.

Matt would call him crazy for chasing after a woman like this. Thoughts of Matt Desmond led to images of his wife, Heather, her long blonde hair splayed on the pillow next to Eli's and that feeling of a floor dropping out from under him. "You were wonderful, Eli," she'd said in parting that morning. Maybe he *was* the guy the tabloids wrote about.

Ding. The elevator doors slid open, quickening Eli's pulse again. When an elderly couple emerged, Eli slumped back against the column.

His grandfather told him often that everything worth having was worth working for. Grandpa himself waited three long years for his grandmother to realize he was the one for her. But what if Aria never gave herself another chance at love?

She arrived at exactly seven o'clock. Sporting a sleek black cocktail dress with her long hair pulled high into a silky ponytail, she conveyed an understated elegance that said she had it all together. A fluttering tickled Eli's center as she crossed the expansive lobby to join him, her smile as sexy and demure as her attire.

He kissed her on the cheek, lingering to steal a breath of her. "Perfect."

"Perfect for what?" She raised an eyebrow, still in the dark about where they were headed.

"For everything." He offered his arm and led her out the revolving door.

Beneath the portico, the doorman stepped forward. "Good evening, Mr. Van Drie, ma'am." He hurried down the steps to open the rear door of a waiting black town car.

"Does your company always put you up in such fancy digs?" Eli asked as they settled inside the car's plush interior.

"I have a pretty generous expense account, but my local sales rep recommended the Palliser. It's close to The Bow tower, which is where two of my meetings were this afternoon. I don't need to rent a car or take a cab since I can walk everywhere."

He glanced at her black pumps. "Hence the sensible shoes."

"You prefer stilettos?"

"Heels are hot," he admitted.

"They're also impractical." She shouldered him playfully. "Next time I'll wear heels for you."

Next time? That was a good sign. "How was your day?"

"Full of meetings. Started at eight with my local rep and one of his customers, then over lunch we met with a new client at the hotel. This afternoon I called on two different GPOs—Group Purchasing Organizations—potential new accounts." She glanced out the window, craning to peer up at the high-rises. "Did you have a good flight?"

"It was fine. I love coming to Canada. Fewer people know me. And those who do have the good sense not to hound me."

She chuckled. "Tough life."

"Hey, fame isn't always a jar of cookies."

"What do you do when you're not filming?"

"Pretty much anything I want. Like fly off to an exotic locale to meet a beautiful woman."

She side-eyed him. "You do this often?"

"Never. But I may start. This is fun." He leaned to the center to look out the windshield. With its concentration of soaring office buildings, diverse population, and massive bridges, downtown Calgary resembled Manhattan.

Aria shook her head. "Seriously, what does your everyday life look like?"

"Well, I read scripts, try to line up my next role. Max has a few he wants me to read . . . if the audition with the director I met with on Monday doesn't pan out."

"What else?"

"In a few weeks I'll start promoting my latest film. Penelope, my publicist, has a bunch of interviews and photo ops lined up. And I think Max is trying to squeeze in a Pixar voice-over."

The town car pulled to a stop at their destination. Aria gazed up at the marquee while the driver got out. "A dinner theater?"

"A comedy dinner theater." He escorted her into the cavernous three-level room, lined with rectangular tables angled perpendicular to the stage like spokes on a wheel. The hostess seated them at a four-top close to the stage.

While they browsed the limited menu, Eli asked, "Montreal, Calgary, are most of your trips to Canada?"

"Lately, yes. Before my promotion, I only covered the Midwest, so most of my meetings were day trips. Now I've got all of North America, so I've been meeting and working primarily with our Canadian team the last few months."

"How does your daughter feel about that?"

A sudden melancholy settled over her and she blinked it away. "She says she's okay with it. She often asks her brother to come stay with her or she'll invite a friend to sleep over. I feel horrible, though, leaving her home alone."

"I get that. But I'm glad I get to see you."

She smiled coyly. "You meeting me here does make the trip a little more bearable."

Their waiter arrived dressed as a stress-test dummy and introduced himself as Mayhem. Pad in hand, ready to take their order, an invisible force from behind caused his knees to buckle, sending the pad and pen airborne, and he crumpled to the floor like a deflated long-arm balloon. He quickly righted himself, retrieved the pad and pen, and with a chuckle, asked what they'd like to eat.

Eli and Aria's laughter subsided and they made their meal choices.

After jotting down their order, Mayhem went to the next table, where he did a similar but different routine.

All of the waitstaff was in costume: a mime, a scarecrow, an angel, a dog, and a beaver, proudly sporting a Calgary Flames hockey jersey. While Aria watched them—smiling, giggling, and sometimes laughing out loud at their silly antics, Eli thrilled to see her enjoying herself so much.

"Maybe you could visit me in LA sometime?" Eli hadn't meant to express his secret longing, but it was out before he could think it through.

She turned to him, her face glowing. "I'll be in San Diego for a three-day conference in mid-June. I'll have meetings during the day, but my evenings will be free."

A whole month before he'd see her again? No way!

Mayhem arrived, set their drinks on the table, then backed

away with a low bow. He stumbled, sending the tray and two balls flying into the air. He caught himself in time to juggle the tray and the balls. Aria's face lit up with astonishment. He collected the objects, everyone nearby clapped, and with a quick bow, Mayhem moved on.

Eli was about to ask Aria what she was doing the upcoming weekend when she said, "Monroe has a tennis match this Friday."

"I love tennis."

Aria drew a perfectly manicured hand back and forth beneath her chin. "Monroe's going away to college this fall. I want to spend as much time with her as I can before she leaves."

"We could spend Saturday together, the three of us."

She shifted in her seat. "Let me think about it."

Maybe it was too soon for him to meet her kids. Though he ached to know everything about her—and even get to know her children—he couldn't push.

Shortly after their meals were served, the lights dimmed and the real show began. The parody, *Ferris Bueller's School of Rock*, was all-out hilarious. Eli couldn't remember when he'd laughed so hard, and seeing Aria's tears of laughter made his heart soar.

As they enjoyed chocolate eclairs following the performance, Aria gave him a tentative smile. "How about a day at the lake on Saturday? We can show you how to wake surf."

Eli nearly dropped his dessert fork. "That sounds fun."

The pirate waiter, having cleared a nearby table, brandished a used fork like a sword and challenged Eli to a duel. Aria giggled as they mimicked a few fencing moves. The server snapped a quick bow and scurried away.

As Eli walked out of the theater, Aria on his arm, his insides shimmied like a breeze through window blinds. The evening could not have gone better. He not only had another date, but she'd invited him to meet her daughter. And while he had zero experience dating a single mother, let alone a widow, it didn't take an expert to realize that extending that invitation had been no small deal for Aria.

12

—————

Aria trudged up the stairs leading to her son's second-story apartment, lugging four canvas bags of groceries. She probably should have called first, like she usually did. But she wanted to tell Jacks about Eli before their next date, and her son often put off her visits. His car in the parking lot assured her he was home.

When Jacks opened the door, she detected a slight grimace. Yep. Definitely should've called first.

With a nervous backward glance, he invited her in. The source of his reluctance became apparent as she stepped inside. A knee-high mound of pizza boxes cluttered one corner, and pop cans and empty dishes covered every flat surface in the room. Half-turned socks, shorts, and T-shirts draped the furniture and littered the carpet. The smell was a trifecta of locker room, stale pizza, and something yeasty. Aria stifled a gag and a reprimand.

Well-trained on the polite expectations of his gender, Jacks took the grocery bags from her with a smile that said he appreciated her peace offering. Aside from the mess, Adam would have been proud. The thought made her eyes sting. She pushed it away and returned to the car for the rest of the groceries and a gulp of fresh air.

Jacks had chosen Davenport University, a small school south of Grand Rapids, mainly for its Division 1 hockey team but also for its entrepreneurial business program. Like his father, he wanted to run his own company one day. Only a half hour from home, the college was far enough to be "away" yet close enough to return home often, which he did—especially in the summer months to enjoy the lake. Aria was determined to keep their promise to pay for school and living expenses despite her financial straits, even if it meant selling the boat. But the filthy apartment made her question whether Jacks fully appreciated the sacrifice.

She took her time, hoping Jacks would at least clear a path to the kitchen. When she returned with the last two bags, Jacks met her at the door and held it open. "Any more?"

"This is it."

He took the bags from her, and she followed him inside.

He had grown since Adam's accident. His lanky teenage frame had stretched to over six feet. At almost twenty-one, he'd filled out with broad shoulders and real muscles. His face held a maturity she hadn't noticed before. At the funeral, the pain he'd worn had made him seem so much younger, and in the weeks that followed, when he lashed out in childish anger, Aria struggled with how to comfort him. Growing up wasn't always the painless process it was supposed to be.

The young man before her now was no longer the vulnerable fatherless boy, inconsolable and angered by the unfairness of his father's death. Jacks moved and talked and walked like a grown man, comfortable in his own skin and in his small apartment, messy as it was.

As Aria handed Jacks the food for the fridge, she held back a suggestion to throw out the takeout-turned-petri-dishes. The last thing she wanted was for him to get defensive. She'd come to ask something important.

"So," she began, hesitant to broach the subject, "have you talked to your sister lately?" Maybe Monroe had already shared the news.

"Not really." Like his father, Jacks was a man of few words.

"Well, I met someone, and—"

"Yeah, she told me."

Aria regrouped. "I'd like you to meet him. He's coming—"

"No way."

"Saturday." Aria emptied the last of the grocery bags and handed Jacks a carton of OJ.

Jacks cocked his head as he set the juice on the counter. "Don't you think it's a bit soon?"

"Do you think so?"

"Dad's only been gone a year." Jacks grabbed a glass from the sink and raised it to the light.

"It's been two years since the accident." Aria tucked the dry goods into the cupboards while Jacks wiped the glass clean on his T-shirt. He offered it to her, but she shook her head.

Aria folded the grocery bags into a neat pile, trying not to feel defeated, while her son poured himself some juice.

When he looked up, she saw love and compassion in his rain-colored eyes, so like his real father's. Without warning, she was back on the playground in Delray, swinging, toes stretched to the sky while Dante pushed from behind. *"Higher, D, higher!"* she'd squeal until the chains went slack and they both became breathless for a heartbeat. *"I'm going to marry you when you grow up,"* Dante teased, and she always shot back at least three reasons she would never marry him: he was too old, too skinny, and a handsome sea captain was going to come whisk her away.

"An actor, Mom? Really?" Jacks sneered.

"He makes me laugh." Thinking of Eli, something bubbled up inside her. "Actually, he makes me feel a lot of things I haven't felt in a long time."

"Ew!" Jacks set his empty glass on the counter and put the juice carton in the fridge.

TMI, as Monroe used to say. Her son wasn't any more ready for this than she was. "It's fine. You don't have to—"

"I'll come." He swung the fridge door closed.

Aria hugged him. "Thank you."

Sliding into the driver's seat, Aria felt she'd accomplished something significant. If Jacks could get over Adam's death and accept someone new in his mother's life, maybe she could too.

13

———————

Standing at the kitchen sink, Aria stared in disbelief at the For Sale sign rising from her front lawn like a conqueror's flag. She had two more weeks to return her mortgage to good standing. Aria snatched up her phone and called the listing agent. After five rings it went to voice mail, so she left a polite but urgent message asking for an immediate call back.

She jammed her phone into her hip pocket and glanced at the clock. She didn't have time to take care of her flowers *and* yank that sign out.

Aria hurried down the deck steps and grabbed the weed bucket and clippers from the garden bench. Deadheading the potted flowers on the lakeside patio, her hands trembled.

As much as she tried to convince herself today would be like any other friends-are-coming day at the lake, something foreboding lurked beneath all of her careful preparations. Eli Van Drie was coming, and she couldn't uninvite him any more than she could unpick the lilacs she'd arranged in an antique pitcher for the dinner table last evening.

She wasn't ready for the day ahead. For two years, she'd been adrift with no one at the helm. Did she dare let someone she barely knew take the rudder?

Determined to push aside her apprehension, she raised her face to bask in the warmth of the sun. A spattering of puffy white clouds danced across the brilliant blue sky. She loved these crazy late-spring days that acted like summer.

Maybe Eli could help her sail beyond the sea of grief to a place where healing and happiness skimmed the surface unhindered. He'd already lured her off her sad little beach. That was a start.

When she looked back to the lake, a blue heron glided gracefully across the smooth water and alighted on the sandy bottom of the cove. Despite the serenity of the moment, Aria's stomach felt as twisted as a pretzel.

For some reason, today felt significant. On their first date, she'd found safety in considering it a one-time thing. In Calgary, they'd both been on unfamiliar ground, two strangers getting to know a new city and each other. This time she'd invited him into her world, into her home, into her real life.

Her kids needed to see she was going to be all right—especially Monroe, who always seemed to worry about her. She was moving on, finding joy in life again, setting a good example for her children. It's what parents were supposed to do. But she still felt all tied up in knots.

She tossed her cutters into the weed bucket and pulled out the hose. Her phone vibrated– the listing agent calling back. As she moved from pot to pot, thoroughly soaking each one, she introduced herself and, with a calm professionalism that belied her emotions, convinced him to come over immediately to remove the sign. From years of working in sales, she'd learned how to direct a conversation, how to make people listen, and how to lead them to a desired outcome.

Satisfied, she tucked her phone back into her pocket and turned toward the house. Eli stood in the side yard. Dressed in shorts, T-shirt, ball cap, and sunglasses, he spread his arms wide in a silent "Ta-da!" Then he bowed low, as if humbly accepting applause for a magnificent performance.

Aria gave in to girlish laughter. The anxiety and the unwanted sign both forgotten, she remembered why she'd cast off in this tempest-tossed sailboat. Eli Van Drie made her laugh.

"HEY, THERE," Eli called, striding forward. He tossed his beach bag onto a chair and planted a quick kiss on Aria's cheek. "Don't you look all fresh-faced and beautiful."

Her wavy hair was twisted into an adorable side ponytail. A tiny-flowered bikini peeked from beneath her loosely woven white top, and small gold earrings winked in the sun. She definitely seemed to be in her element. The carefree way she moved as he'd watched from the side yard—perhaps for a little too long—made him wish he had her all to himself for the day.

But today was about meeting her family. He had to win over her kids. Like food was the way to a man's heart, children were the way to a mother's heart. The seventeen-year-old daughter would be easy. It was the older son he worried about. Would the boy be any more ready than his mother to have a new guy in the picture?

"Would you like something to eat? Or coffee?" Aria moved to the edge of the patio, turned off the water, and coiled up the hose.

"Coffee would be great." He picked up his bag and followed her up the deck steps. "What's with the For Sale sign?"

"It's a mistake. I just called the Realtor to come get it." The terseness in her voice spoke volumes.

He didn't know her well enough to push for details, so he let it go.

Aria offered a cruise of the lake while they waited for her daughter to wake up.

Minutes later, coffee in hand, Eli followed her down to the water. Alongside the dock, near shore, was a rack holding two paddleboards. Closer to the end of the dock, the boat, maybe a nineteen-footer, sat on a lift, nestled beneath a canopy. Malibu Wakesetter in bold cream-colored letters ran down the classy black and caramel hull. Aria flipped open a black box about the size of a cooler that sat on the dock beside the boat.

Eli inspected the wake surfer's mechanicals at the rear of the boat. "Looks high tech."

"It is." Aria moved to his side. "That's the power wedge." She pointed to a thick silver plate the size of a skateboard that extended down, parallel to the water's surface. "It essentially acts like a hydrofoil, creating drag at the back of the boat." With a Birkenstock-clad foot, she motioned to one of two vertical plates hinged at each back corner. "These surf gates control the curl of the wave so you can surf left or right."

She returned to the open black box and pressed a button that lowered the boat into the water with the high-pitched squeal of a hydraulic motor.

"The wedge though is what makes the waves?"

"Partly." She kicked off her sandals, leaving them beside the box, handed him her coffee, and stepped onboard, then turned back to take both mugs from him. "We also fill six hundred-gallon water bags to create ballast. Then we can dial in some seriously sweet waves."

"Can't wait to try it out." He followed her lead, stepping out of his sandals and onto the the seat cushion as she'd done. He took his mug from her and slipped it into a cup holder. "What can I do?" He eyed the large metal frame that lay across the boat. Obviously, it needed to go somewhere.

Aria set her mug on the dash. "Just have a seat for now. I'll have you help me with the tower in a sec." Using a fob hanging on the key ring, she lowered the boat the rest of the way into the water, then turned the key. The engine roared to life. With well-practiced ease, she backed the boat out of the lift. Then she stood and raised the tower. "Hold it here, if you don't mind."

She stepped aside as he took her place, then moved to the rear to click a latch on each side. The tower securely in place, he was about to take a seat when a glint of light on the opposite shore caught his eye. He lowered his sunglasses to peer across the lake. A manned tripod sat atop the grassy knoll. It was all Eli could do not to swear out loud.

In and around LA, paparazzi were everywhere. But here? Pictures in a tawdry gossip rag, accompanied by some made-up story, could ruin everything.

"That's the dam," Aria explained, following his gaze. "It runs along the main road that borders the neighborhood. The only public shoreline."

Either Aria hadn't noticed the cameraman or she had no idea what it meant. Eli had no intention of telling her, at least not yet. He didn't want her to realize this was part of his life . . . and would be part of hers too if she was with him.

At least with the media relegated to the one sideline of the earthen dam, they'd have limited access. He tore his gaze away, resolved not to let it ruin the day.

As they continued around the lake, the boat gliding along the shoreline, Eli began to relax. He stretched his arms across the back of the seat cushions, fully appreciating the warm sun, the fresh air, and the hot coffee.

But throughout the tour, he kept one eye on the dam.

When they returned to the house, thankfully, the tripod across the lake was gone. Back inside, a younger, blond version of Aria stood at the kitchen counter amid the loud whir of a small blender.

"Morning, sweetie," Aria called over the noise as she set their coffee mugs in the sink. "This is Eli."

The girl shut off the machine and turned. "Monroe," she said, extending a hand. Despite the fact she was still in her pajamas, the girl met him with a confidence that mirrored her mother's. Gangly and coltish with smiley blue eyes, long blond hair and her mother's perfect bow-shaped mouth, they were like two shades of the same theme.

"Nice to meet you. You and your mom are going to show me how to wake-surf, eh?"

"That's the plan," Monroe said with an excited smile. She twisted the lid off of the blender cup, rinsed it in the sink, and turned to Aria. "Sutton's coming, okay?"

"Of course." Aria peered out the kitchen window with a satisfied smile while Monroe, smoothie in hand, headed toward the hallway.

Eli followed Aria's gaze. No surprise, the FOR SALE sign was gone. Aria was a woman who knew how to get things done.

Minutes later, towels, boards, and life jackets stowed and water bags filled, Aria turned the boat toward the far end of the lake, opposite the dam, and Eli felt a rush of relief. The tripod was back, so the farther away from the dam and the photographer, the better.

The girls went first while Eli enjoyed watching Aria at the helm, taking control. Her skin, smooth and tan, glistened with sunlight, while wisps of long hair escaped, twisting in the wind and taking his heart with it. She seemed so at ease with her world. He wished he could pull out his phone and snag a picture.

Monroe drove when it was Aria's turn to surf. With an impressive sense of balance Aria tossed the rope within seconds of getting upright and free-surfed with a delicate grace that the younger girls lacked.

When it was his turn, Eli donned a life jacket and jumped into the water. A die-hard surfer, he hoped wake surfing was like the real thing. He sure didn't want to embarrass himself.

While Sutton collected the rope, Monroe, perched on the swim platform at the back of the boat, handed him the board and instructed him how to position his feet on it, knees bent to chest. Sutton tossed him the rope and Monroe showed him how to hold it vertically between his knees.

"Remember," Aria called from the captain's seat, "let the boat do the work to pull you out of the water."

It took a couple of tries, but Aria and the girls were patient and encouraging, and once he'd gotten the hang of popping up, he couldn't believe how easy it was. Like surfing the Pacific except that the wave was predictable and perpetual, sculpted by the finely engineered boat. It didn't take long before he felt comfortable enough to toss the rope aside. The girls shouted with excitement as Sutton pulled it in.

After a couple of turns around the deep end of the lake, Eli did a three-sixty, surprising them all. The girls hooted and clapped. He finally fell trying to see how much air he could get jumping the wake.

Aria circled the boat around to pick him up. "You said you'd never done this before! Yeah, right."

"It's like surfing the ocean." He started to hand up the board, but the girls insisted he do the three-sixty again so they could capture it on video. After extracting a promise they wouldn't share it on social media, he agreed.

On the way back, Eli finally got that shot he'd wanted of Aria driving the boat.

As they approached the dock, Eli scoured the dam and the nearby lakeshore but the camera was nowhere to be seen.

They enjoyed lunch al fresco on the covered deck, a chicken and tortellini salad paired with a French loaf and ice-cold home-made lemonade, a perfect light meal for the hot day. Monroe and Sutton surprised him with how much they knew about his career and pop culture in general and despite being obviously in awe of his stardom, they were well spoken, polite, and their seventeen-year-old perspectives made for entertaining conversation.

When Aria returned inside for more lemonade, Monroe leaned over to him, her eyes on the door, and spoke in a hushed tone, "I'm glad you're here."

"Me too," Eli said.

A few minutes later, a friend of Monroe's came by on a jet ski and Monroe and Sutton hurried away to join her.

So far, so good. The daughter approved.

As Aria tucked the leftovers into the fridge, a tall, muscular young man with caramel-colored skin and a head of unruly dark curls walked in the front door, accompanied by a stocky guy of a similar age with a buzz cut and a ready smile.

"Hey, Mom," the tall one said, tossing a large laundry bag into the mudroom on his way to the kitchen.

"Hey, buddy." Aria hugged him, then turned to his friend. "Hi, Nate. Good to see you."

"How ya doin', Mrs. Dub?" the stocky kid asked. Eli stifled a laugh at the young man's economy of syllables for Aria's last name.

"I'm good, Nate. Thanks." She turned to Eli and gestured to the tall young man. "This is my son, Jackson." She looked at him. "Jacks, this is Eli." She seemed to hold her breath in anticipation.

The boy gave Eli a hot-potato handshake, then hastily stepped back. Aria shot her son an expectant glance and Jacks introduced his friend, Nate, whose handshake was much warmer.

Aria retrieved the salad from the fridge. "You guys hungry?"

"No," Jacks answered, apparently speaking for both of them.

"Thanks, though," Nate added.

Aria eyed the salad bowl. "It's—"

Jacks cut her off with a scowl, then strolled toward the French doors. Nate gave Aria an apologetic smile and followed Jacks.

Facing the lake, Jacks barked, "Monroe's got the jet ski?"

"With Sutton and Hannah." Aria swung the fridge closed, having stowed the salad.

"Mind if we take the boat out?" Jacks glanced back to his mother, Eli quickly forgotten.

"Not at all. I think we saved you some gas," Aria said, with a grin directed at Eli.

With a curt, "Come on," Jacks and his friends disappeared out the back door.

"Don't forget towels," Aria called after them, "and sunscreen."

A few minutes later, Eli and Aria where halfway down the back steps when Jacks, standing on the patio beneath the deck, exclaimed, "Seriously?"

"What?" Aria asked, hurrying down the last few steps.

"My life jacket's wet," Jacks sputtered, holding it out in front of him with an accusing glare at his mother and totally ignoring Eli who now stood beside her.

"Of course it is," Aria said calmly. "We used it."

"Sorry, Jacks. My fault." A die-hard surfer, Eli understood the personal nature of a lifejacket and how uncomfortable it was to put on a wet one.

Jacks stomped across the yard and hurled the life jacket into the boat with an audible grunt, his friend trailing behind. Aria's shoulders rose and fell with a silent sigh.

"I'm sorry," Eli said, placing a hand on her shoulder.

Aria whirled to face him, her face a mixture of disappointment and anger. "No, I'm sorry. He's, well, I don't think he's ready either."

Either? Maybe this meet-the-children day was a bit premature. "Let's take the paddleboards out," Eli suggested.

Aria studied the lake as Jacks and Nate joined the cacophony of other ski-surf boats, pontoons, and personal watercraft. "It'll be tough with all these waves. But we can try."

As Aria predicted, the waves dumped them several times, which sent them both into fits of laughter. When Eli caught sight of the tripod back on the opposite shore, he nearly gulped a lungful of water.

Maybe the camera wasn't trained on him.

Who was he kidding? No one else would set up a camera on a tripod and hang out there for hours.

He considered telling Aria, but she wouldn't appreciate being spied on any more than he did. So he kept his sunglasses on and did his best to maintain enough distance from her so as to not allow any photo opportunities of the two of them together.

They gave up on paddleboarding and while Eli returned the boards to their rack, Aria pulled a couple of floats from beneath the deck steps.

His back to the dam and the infernal camera, Eli eased onto a float, settled back, and paddled out with his arms. "These are great." Made from wine corks encased in mesh fabric and kept in place by stitched rows, the float conformed around his torso like a Sleep Number bed. "Did you make these?"

"I did." Aria paddled out to join him. "Inflatables don't last very long around here."

He ran his hands along the wide rows of corks keeping him afloat. "Big wine drinker, are you?"

Aria laughed. "My friends collect them for me."

"You should sell these."

"Think so?"

"Absolutely. They're ingenious. And eco-friendly. You could make a fortune."

"Maybe."

He closed his eyes, soaked in the warmth of the sun on his face, and floated as if he didn't have a care in the world. If it weren't for that blasted camera, this would've been a perfect day.

Aria floated up alongside him. "Are you staying downtown again?"

"Nope. I rented a condo at the end of the lake." He'd discovered the unit the afternoon he'd taken Aria to lunch. It wasn't the high-end accommodations he'd grown accustomed to, but it came fully furnished and was nice enough. "A full month's rent is about the same price as two nights downtown." Of course, the cost was insignificant. He'd rented it to be closer to her.

She raised her sunglasses and squinted at him like sighting down the barrel of a gun. "Think you'll be around that long?"

"Hoping." Eli pulled her float closer. "It's an open-ended lease, so I could stay even longer." He didn't mention that the owner only rented by the month.

"Good." She replaced her sunglasses and relaxed back on her float. Intermittent birdsong competed with the distant hum of boat engines and the gentle lapping of waves against the rocky seawall.

Good.

He couldn't take his eyes off of her. Watching Aria afloat on the lake, all smiles and grace, felt like watching a movie teaser. *This is what your life could be like, Van Drie, if you play your cards right.* Everything he'd ever wanted was on the table, right there in front of him. He hoped he had a winning hand.

"Something to drink?" She asked, her eyes still closed to the sun.

"Sure, but let me get it."

"There's another pitcher of lemonade in the fridge on the walkout level, but help yourself to a beer or wine cooler if you'd rather. I'll take a water."

Inside, near the small kitchenette, a door stood ajar. Peeking inside, he found a well-furnished exercise room: treadmill, elliptical, weight bench, mats, a speed bag, and a heavy bag. Trophies and medals lined one wall: hockey, tennis, boxing, downhill skiing.

"That's quite a workout room," he said, wading into the shallows to hand her a bottle of water. "I can guess who plays hockey and tennis. But who's the boxer and the skier?"

Aria sat up, took a sip of water. "My husband raced downhill. I kick box."

He pictured Aria boxing: all muscular, sweaty, and angry, a veritable Lara Croft Tomb Raider. No wonder she was in such great shape. "Kind of a rough sport, isn't it?"

"I haven't competed in a long time. The kids' activities have kept me pretty busy the last few years."

Eli returned to his float and paddled out to join Aria.

The girls returned on the jet skis and Aria rose to help Monroe stow theirs back on the lift while Sutton landed hers next door and the new girl beached hers. Monroe introduced her friend, Hannah, to Eli then the girls swam out to the water trampoline.

Within minutes Jacks and Nate returned in the boat. As expertly as Aria had done, Jacks eased it gently beneath the canopy, shut it off, and raised the lift enough to keep the boat in place while Nate disembarked. From the boat, Jacks collected towels, life jackets, and boards, handing everything over the side to Nate. They laid out the life jackets on the patio to dry, hung their towels on the hooks along the deck steps, then set up a volleyball net on the lawn.

Eli loved volleyball, especially on the beaches around LA. He glanced at the dam. The tripod was gone. Yes!

As if reading his mind, Aria nudged him. "Want to play?"

Eli almost launched off of his float. "You betcha. I mean, if you don't think they'd mind."

Aria grinned. "You betcha—is that a Minnesota thing?"

"Hey, you guys want to play?" Nate called from the yard, the volleyball spinning on the tip of his finger.

"You betcha!" Aria answered with a smile directed at Eli.

If Eli had any chance of winning over Jacks, this was the time.

Nate jogged to the dock and called to the girls out on the tramp but they declined.

Resisting every competitive bone in his body, Eli allowed Aria's son to smash across the net more than once when he could have easily blocked. He also let slide the kid's numerous net-touches, illegal even in backyard volleyball. But as the game went on, Eli matched Jacks's aggressive play, smash for smash, block for block, mindful to toss out a "Nice one!" when Jacks or the others made an exceptionally good play.

It did little good. Jacks ignored the recognition, only intensified his game, and didn't smile or speak except to Nate. When the boys won, Jacks sealed it with an abrupt bone-crusher handshake. Overall, the game was a double-edged loss for Eli. He was no closer to winning over Aria's son than when the kid had walked in the door.

Eli and Aria cooled off in the lake, then settled into the lounge chairs on the patio in the shade of a cottonwood while the boys took turns in the outdoor shower.

Eli wondered how Aria's husband had fit into days like this. Did he surf with the kids, play backyard volleyball, relax on the floats with his wife? Or did he work most weekends, leaving his family to manage on their own? They were all adept at driving the boat, easing it in and out of the lift, pulling it alongside the dock, getting equipment ready and putting things away. All of that didn't happen over the course of only a year or two. He had a feeling they'd been flying solo for a long time.

"Thanks for having me, Mrs. Dub," Nate called down from the deck railing.

Aria sat up and turned toward the house. "Of course, Nate. Any time."

Jacks bounded down the steps and trotted across the lawn to the patio. Bending down, he kissed his mother's cheek. "I'm taking off."

Aria propped her sunglasses atop her head and squinted up at him. "I thought you might join us for dinner. I've got steaks."

Jacks glanced at Eli with derision. "Sorry. I made other plans."

She nodded, momentarily crestfallen, then stood and hugged her son. "I'm glad you came. Love you." Her face radiated pure joy.

Jacks stepped back and eyed his mom with a flash of surprise. "Love you too." With a lingering grin, he turned to Eli, hand extended.

Eli stood to shake the boy's hand. Finally, a normal handshake. "Great to meet you, Jacks."

"Same here." The boy gave his arm a quick squeeze, almost a reluctant thank-you, as if Eli alone had put the happiness back in his mother's face.

"Hey, before you go . . . I brought you something. It's in the kitchen, by the chalkboard."

"The Kings hat?" Jacks said. "That's for me?"

"Your mom told me you were a big fan."

"Their goalie had the best save percentage in the whole league last year." Jacks turned and raced across the yard.

"You didn't have to do that." Aria's gaze followed Jacks as he bounded up the steps.

"I know."

Within seconds, Jacks reappeared at the railing, holding the hat. "Thanks, man." His smile was laden with guilt, as he stared at the hat's bill and the Jonathan Quick autograph there.

"My pleasure."

Jacks settled the hat on his head, gave Eli a thumbs-up, then disappeared into the house.

Eli turned to Aria. "He's a great kid." Not many college-age guys kissed their mom goodbye, without being asked, and in front of a friend even. Eli envied this close-knit family.

"Yeah, he is."

While Aria threw together a salad, Monroe set the table, her friends filled glasses with ice water, and Eli manned the grill. When the steaks were done to perfection, they took their seats at the deck table. The cameraman loomed again on the other side of the lake, so Eli chose a seat with its back to the water, despite Aria's insistence that he switch spots with her so he'd have a better view. "I like how the sun lights up your skin," he reasoned.

During dinner, Hannah and Sutton dominated the conversation with questions about his "glamorous" life.

"What's it like going to all those glitzy parties?"

"How does it feel to walk the red carpet?"

"How many times have you been on a magazine cover?"

"What's Matt Desmond really like?"

He ignored the question about Matt, the last person he wanted to think about after what happened with Matt's wife, but Eli did his best to answer the girls' other questions, expounding on what he most liked about his life in LA: the near-perfect weather, the laid-back pace when he wasn't filming, the lazy afternoons spent poolside, at the beach, or driving up the coast.

Monroe and her friends were easily impressed, but Aria sat quietly, as though sizing him up. It seemed like everything that elevated his standing in the girls' eyes lowered him a notch on Aria's yardstick.

When the young ladies finally paused their inquisition, Eli turned to Monroe. "You're all graduating this year, right? Tell me about your college plans."

"I'm hoping to get into premed," Monroe said.

"Me too," Sutton said.

"Do you know Timothée Chalumet?" Hannah broke in.

So much for turning the conversation around.

Aria stood and took Monroe's empty plate and stacked it atop hers, clearly signifying dinner was over.

Monroe jumped up and took the plates from her mother. "I've got this. We'll clean up." She shot Eli an apologetic smile, as if she'd suddenly realized she and her friends had been more interested in who he knew than who he was.

The girls cleared the table with the efficiency of a Michelin star restaurant and disappeared inside, leaving Aria and Eli to relax, enjoy their wine, and watch the sunset. Seeing no sign of the tripod, Eli moved to the chair beside Aria that Monroe had vacated, facing the lake.

"I think the girls are pretty smitten with you," Aria said.

He shot her a lopsided grin. "I know the feeling."

Aria blushed—or maybe the color in her cheeks was merely a remnant of the day in the sun. She turned to the lake and swirled her wine thoughtfully, then finished it.

Eli topped off their glasses, reclined in his chair, and laced his hands behind his head, content and yet aching for more. He yearned for this laid-back life, the love of a family, and the incredibly brave, resilient, and accomplished woman at the center of it all. Her comfortable home, the serenity of the lake, the reverence of the sunsets, each one a welcome splendor to bid goodnight, a perfect close to a beautiful life with a wonderful wife.

"What a great day!" he said.

"I'm glad you came." Aria's gaze drifted from the lake to the yard and the trampled patches of lawn where they'd played volleyball. Her smile widened.

As they quietly sipped their wine, a pair of hawks whistled across the treetops. There were a million questions Eli wanted to ask about her husband, about her life before his death, but today was for making new memories, with him. "So, what are you doing tomorrow?"

"Church. Want to join me?"

Though thrilled at the prospect of seeing her again, he certainly didn't want to make a scene in her church. He'd managed to get by almost unrecognized at dinner last week, at her office, and hopefully today. He didn't want to push his luck.

"I'd better not. Maybe we could go kayaking after?"

An awkward silence. Was kayaking a memory she'd reserved for her husband?

"We're going to Sutton's now," Monroe shouted from the kitchen.

Aria turned toward the door. "Hey, we'll start a fire later, so we can make s'mores if you want."

"Sounds great! We'll be back." The sound of the front door closing carried through the house.

Aria turned to Eli. "Do you like to hike?"

That was a more appealing option. Most kayaks sat only one person, and he wanted to get close to her. The night on the chaise effervesced in his thoughts like fine champagne. "Sounds great. I'll bring lunch."

"Meet here around noon?"

"Perfect." All of his anxiety evaporated.

She smiled, satisfied, and he was again struck by her natural beauty. Still with no makeup, her cheeks and the bridge of her nose wore a healthy pink glow, despite the sunscreen she'd reapplied throughout the day. It made her bottle-green eyes even brighter.

"Maybe next time you could come visit me," he ventured.

She ran a finger along the rim of her glass.

"We could go shopping on Rodeo Drive. And I could show you where my star is going to be on the Walk of Fame."

Her jaw dropped. "You're getting a star?"

"Well, we don't have a date yet, but my publicist promised it within two to three years, five tops."

She swirled her wine and stared into it. "You really are from a different world."

His heart sank. The last of the sun's rays danced off the water like tiny diamonds. Twilight came slowly to Haven Lake. "But I really like your world."

She gave him a rueful smile. "You're just passing through."

"I'd like to stay."

"For how long?"

"As long as you'll have me."

She returned her gaze to the lake, a profound sadness in her eyes. "Being with you is like holding my breath on the lake bottom. Cool and serene, but I know it can't last."

He cocked his head. "Why so cynical?"

She shook her head without even looking at him.

"Come on, Ari." He draped his arm across the back of her chair. "Give me a chance. I might surprise you."

She took a breath almost as deep as the lake. "Eli, my grief is not going to go away overnight."

"Neither am I."

That brought a smile to her lips, but it was short-lived.

He tried another tack. "Bring Monroe. Jacks too. You'll have your own rooms. Have you ever been to LA?"

"Just for business." She glanced around uneasily. Too much, too soon. She was going to turn him down.

"Ari." He bent forward to recapture her gaze, but she kept staring at the water. With a fingertip he tenderly turned her face to him and placed a light kiss on her lips.

She pulled back, but only inches. "Eli—" He could see the conflict in her eyes. She wanted to say no, but her face warmed with a smile that was all *yes*.

His lips found her ear. "Tell me what you're thinking." He could smell his own breath against her hair, red wine mingling happily with traces of sunshine, coconut, and lake water still clinging to her skin.

When he pulled back, she was breathing heavily.

"Eli," she began again, "I like you very much." She spoke carefully, as if the words were razor sharp. "Please don't play with me." The plea came out feather soft, but the sheer anguish of it hit him like a cannon blast.

"I'm not. I never would."

She studied him for a long moment, as though gauging his sincerity and considering whether to trust it. "I'll ask the kids and let you know."

"Fair enough." It took great willpower to keep his grin from wrapping clear around his head.

Somehow he knew she'd come, with or without her children. Eli could hardly contain himself at the thought of another weekend together. He scanned the opposite shore for the tripod. Not seeing it, he kissed her like he'd yearned to do all day—freely, deeply, and completely. He ran his hands through her hair, then rested them at the back of her neck while she returned his kiss with all the passion she'd had at the river's edge, like a woman longing to be kissed, a woman used to being kissed regularly. When her husband was alive.

He pressed his forehead to hers, savoring the moment, but wondering, as the day bled into night, if her passion actually belonged to him at all.

LATER THAT EVENING, after s'mores over the fire and Monroe's friends had wandered home, Aria walked Eli to his car where they parted with a chaste goodnight kiss and plans to meet again tomorrow at noon. Aria tidied the kitchen then peeked into her daughter's room. Monroe sat propped against the headboard, swiping away at her phone. With a light rap on the door, Aria entered and Monroe scooted over, making room for her mother to sit on the bed facing her.

"He seems really great," Monroe said, setting her phone aside. "You're going to see him again, aren't ya? Is he around tomorrow? Cause I could definitely hang here."

"We're going to hike The Willows tomorrow after church. But I'll be back in time for dinner with Grandma and Grandpa."

Monroe nodded then grinned. "That sounds chill. He'll like that."

"He invited the three of us to LA."

"Me and Jacks too? He's just being nice."

"Would you like to go?"

Monroe's brows knit together. "When? I have state finals next weekend, and the week after is graduation, the senior overnight. I don't want to miss all of that."

Aria wouldn't miss her daughter's state tourney or her graduation for anything in the world. "I was thinking the weekend after graduation."

"But there're so many open houses that weekend. I can stay with—"

"Monroe." Aria crossed her arms, the familiar guilt settling in. "It's one thing to leave you alone for work, but—"

"Pleeeease?"

"Jacks won't even consider it if you're not going."

"Unless Eli can score playoff tickets."

"The Kings aren't in the finals."

Monroe's face fell. "Oh."

"You really don't want to go?"

"I do but . . ." Monroe let out a frustrated sigh. "I want to stay here more. But you should definitely go. You like him, right?"

"He's ok." Aria's smile betrayed how she really felt.

"Yeah, I thoughts so," her daughter said knowingly.

14

Arriving early, Aria walked through the doors of Falls Creek Community Church, a renovated paper mill that her husband, a deacon, had helped bring to fruition. Thankfully, this morning she'd beat even the greeters, which meant she could forego the forced smile.

On her way to the children's area, her sandals echoed on the concrete floor, reverberating off the high ceiling of the broad open space. The industrial garage-style doors of the sanctuary were up. Inside, a *strum*, a *plink*, and a *boom-boom-boom* filled the space as the worship band warmed up. The pastor, an agile forty-something who still ran marathons, stood amid the chairs off to the side, chatting amiably with a young couple. The twelve-foot-tall rough-hewn cross Adam had handcrafted still anchored the stage and seemed to glow beneath the track lighting.

Entering the preschool room, Aria smoothed her skirt, donned her badge, and busied herself organizing the morning's lesson. She laid out the craft supplies, slipped the CD for the song they'd sing along to into the player, and waited for her team of helpers to show up. It wasn't much, but leading the preschool ministry helped her feel plugged in, and when she'd volunteered, it was all she could take on at the time.

Monroe and Sutton used to help with the little ones, but a few years ago they'd started attending the youth ministry on Wednesday evenings.

There was a time when Aria loved attending church every Sunday, their kids excitedly running off to their respective rooms. But after Adam died, it was too hard to walk in without him, to sit by herself in the sanctuary, surrounded by benevolent but pitying looks from people who used to greet them with genuine smiles.

These days Aria found more comfort in the preschool room, where the littles didn't know anything about grief or ask uncomfortable questions like "How are you, really?"

She missed attending the service—singing along to the music, drawing strength from the message and pastoral prayers. But now she found her strength and solace in the Book itself, especially the Psalms, Job, and Jeremiah. They reminded her that she wasn't alone, not truly, not ever. No matter her despair.

On the way to her car afterward, her phone vibrated with a text from Jacks.

Jacks: Gonna shoot today with Nate so I'm coming by to get some guns, k?

Always happy to hear from her son, Aria replied with a thumbs up then added,

Aria: What did you think of Eli?

Jacks: He didn't seem like the guy I checked out online.

Aria: He told me not to believe anything I read about him.

Jacks: Yeah, if I were him, I'd tell women that too.

Ugh! Aria slid into her car, blinked hard, then stared at her phone, tempted to do her own online search. When it went dark, she slipped it into its cubby in the console. Everything she'd seen so far told her Eli was a good guy: compassionate, affectionate, patient and kind. The hat for Jacks was a thoughtful touch. No, he deserved a bias-free chance. Didn't he?

Arriving home, Aria changed into jeans and a light cotton shirt.

When she entered the kitchen, Eli stood at the island, closing the lid on his picnic basket. The delicious scent of strawberries permeated the air.

"Hey!" Aria couldn't hide her surprise. She hadn't heard him pull in the drive.

He planted a kiss on her cheek. "Jacks let me in."

"That boy. Might've been nice if he let me know. I could've come out half-dressed."

Eli raised a brow as if to say that wouldn't have been all bad.

Jacks emerged from the lower level, carrying a rifle case and a box of shells.

"Hey, buddy."

"I can't find the Glock."

Aria stiffened. Having decided to give Jacks the keys to his father's gun safe was one thing—it only contained shotguns and rifles—but allowing him access to a handgun was another thing altogether. "Why do you need it?"

Jacks rolled his eyes. "I'm going elk hunting with Grandpa this fall. I want to take it for bear." He tucked the box of shells into a side pocket of his shorts. "Please tell me you didn't get rid of it."

"I still have it. But I'd like you to hold off using it until Grandpa or I can go with you."

Jacks opened his mouth as if to argue, but Aria cut him short with a stern look.

Eli nodded to the case. "Can I see what you've got there?"

"Sure." Jacks glared at his mother then moved to the kitchen island. He set the case on it, popped the latches, and opened the lid.

Eli peered at the gun. "Whoa, a 300 Weatherby?"

"Yeah."

"May I?"

Jacks nodded and stood a little taller.

Eli lifted the gun from its case, angled the barrel toward the floor, opened the chamber to ensure it was empty, then sighted the gun toward the lake, his eye to the high-power scope. "Nice."

The two of them huddled together, talking guns, scopes, and

ammo, like Adam had done with his son hundreds of times before. It was all so déjà vu Aria's heart swelled with the memory, and happiness squeezed in. The realization brought a fresh twist of guilt.

Aria caught Monroe watching from the hallway and went to her. "Is it wrong that this makes me happy?" she asked quietly.

Monroe shook her head. "No. Mom, you deserve happiness, wherever you find it."

Jacks packed up the gun and headed for the door.

Aria straightened. "Be sure to bring that right back—"

"—to clean it and lock it up. I know," Jacks snapped. "Love you." He one-arm hugged her. When he stepped back, he glanced at Eli, and guilt crept into his eyes. Was he feeling the same shame she had of allowing someone else into that hallowed space that had once belonged to his father?

The door closed behind Jacks, and Aria turned to hug her daughter. "Be good while we're gone."

"Always." Monroe grinned.

Aria turned to Eli. "Ready?"

"You betcha." Eli grabbed the picnic basket.

Aria led the way to the garage. "We should take the truck. There's not much of a road where we're going."

As she backed out, Eli eyed Adam's dog tags swinging from the rearview mirror. Aria hadn't driven the truck in months, and she'd forgotten how many memories it still held.

"Jacks has access to your gun safe?" Eli asked as she pulled out of the neighborhood.

Aria bristled. "He's almost twenty-one, and he's been shooting since he could read." She didn't intend to sound defensive, but he had no right to question her. It was hard enough making all the parenting decisions alone.

His silence clearly said he didn't agree. Or maybe he was doing the math. People often hesitated—she called it the judging moment—when they realized she'd been sixteen when Jacks was born. It always disappointed her how ready people were to lower her a notch on their social strata.

"Why do you even have a gun like that?"

"Why not?"

He turned in his seat to face her. "You live in a nice neighborhood in a small town. What are you afraid of?"

"I am not afraid." *If there's one thing I will never be again, it's afraid.* "I'm a woman living alone with a teenage daughter. I have to protect myself and my family."

The silence between them crouched with uncertainty. When she glanced over, he looked as if he wanted to say something more but didn't dare risk it.

Aria pulled into a narrow drive and got out to unlock the chain that crossed the lane. She returned to the truck, drove through, then went back to replace the chain.

When she hopped into the driver's seat again, Eli looked her way. "You think someone's going to follow us in?"

"Just habit, I guess." She usually brought the Glock too. Okay, maybe she was afraid. Not of the woods or the isolation of the property. Nature had never done her any harm. Only people.

About a mile in on the winding, tree-canopied two-track, she pulled to a stop in front of the barn. "We call this The Willows." Her gaze spanned the dense woods to the east, the grassy lane that continued north past the barn, and the sprawling meadow beyond, all painted golden by the sun.

Memories flashed before her like pages in a scrapbook: the lazy afternoons spent meandering through these woods with her family, Adam and Jacks fishing from the pond's edge while she and Monroe gathered wildflowers in the meadow.

"Is this all yours?"

The images of her happy young family scattered like autumn leaves, leaving her with a sudden, sharp emptiness. "From the fence east." She pointed to the split-rail fence that ran north from the barn, then stepped out of the truck.

The clear-blue sky and a cool breeze welcomed her, as gentle as a first kiss. "This is where I come to refresh when work gets crazy or after I get back from a long trip. I love the quiet. And I can actually breathe here." She closed her eyes and inhaled deeply, absorbing the peace she so often sought, the calm settling over her like a cool mist.

"It's . . . lovely."

Aria turned and saw Eli watching her from the other side of the truck. His eyes seemed to drink her in, giving the distinct impression he wasn't referring to the landscape.

She wanted to explain how her connection to the land grounded her, how even when life was one big hot mess, the land remained solid, resilient, and virtually unchanged save for its ever-reliable stroll from one season to the next. But she didn't understand it herself, this inexplicable draw. So she simply pulled the blanket from the backseat and slung it over her shoulder.

Eli grabbed the picnic basket and took her hand as they headed toward the meadow. A small cabin at the east end of the field dredged up bittersweet memories of overnights spent camping with the kids. Two swings still hung from the huge maple, one slightly askew, both empty now save for the echoes of her children's playful giggles dancing on the wind. In the precious, fleeting moments of her children's youth, Adam's absence felt like lake weeds pulling her under, drowning her in the sorrow of the forever lost. She shuddered.

Chasing away the melancholy, she headed toward a stand of willows on the far edge of the meadow. Beyond the trees the earth sloped away to a small pond bordered by cattails and wild iris, her favorite spot to rest and recharge whenever she came alone.

They deposited the blanket and picnic basket in the shade of the largest willow, then Aria led Eli toward the woods beyond. The trail head was obvious, but farther in it became a challenge to make out the path. Every spring, Adam would clear the trail, but it hadn't been done since—

Well, the hike would be a little harder this year, like everything else.

The woods were cool and damp. Sunlight filtered through the treetops to dance on the forest floor. Ferns and apple blossoms had begun to unfurl their new fronds, carpeting the way. The scent of wet, decaying leaves compressed by winter snows and the fresh green growth lent a musky earthiness made more intense by the rising warmth of the day.

At a familiar bird sound, Aria stopped abruptly and crouched, pulling Eli down beside her. She pointed to the top of a dead birch as a large brown-and-white bird lit on the edge and disappeared within. "A barred owl," she explained. "Did you see it?"

Eli nodded excitedly.

They stayed there, watching, until the owl came out and flew away.

Aria rose. "Listen." Baby owls chirped hungrily in the nest. She remembered the day Adam had shown it to her. "They roost here every year."

"Wow." Eli stared up at the tree, his eyes bright with wonder.

Did he actually share her love of nature, or was he faking it to impress her? He was an actor; pretending was part of his job. But she had no reason not to trust him, especially about something as trivial as an owl's nest.

They continued on until they reached the creek with its old wooden bridge. A rickety barnwood sign read Pooh Sticks Bridge. She stopped at the center of it. "When Jacks and Monroe were little, we'd come here and play a game called Pooh Sticks." She picked up a twig and dropped it into the water on the upstream side of the bridge. Then she hurried to the opposite side and pointed to her twig floating downstream. "Simple, I know. But for a toddler, it's great fun."

How silly she'd been as a young mother. And oh, how she missed those days.

"When they got older we started a new game, and it became an annual tradition. On Midsummer's Eve, we'd come out here at dusk, each of us holding a little cedar boat with a candle on it. We'd light the candle and place the boat in the water while we made a wish out loud. If the candle stayed lit for as far as we could see, the wish would come true." She smiled, feeling as if she'd given up something special and private. "It's an old English tradition I read about."

He cocked his head and squinted. "Out loud? You know—"

"Yeah, yeah. If you tell a wish, it won't come true. Well, I think that rule is stupid. How many more wishes might come true if they were known?" She recalled some of the wishes her kids had made over the years, many of which she and Adam had brought to life.

She also remembered the day Dante, her brother's best friend, turned fourteen. As he blew out a single candle and the family sang, Gibson insisted he say his wish aloud. Dante hesitated, looked at Gibson, then whispered with a childlike breath of hope, "I wish our friendship would last forever."

Aria hadn't made a wish in a long time. She chose to focus instead on the goodness that came from family rituals. "You can never have too many wishes, right?"

"Right." He took her hand, brought it to his lips, and kissed it. The gallantry of the simple gesture soothed something inside her.

Still holding her hand, he led her deeper into the woods, weaving through the thick brush as though determined to reach some specific destination.

A crashing sound came from the brush behind them. Aria whirled as a mass of tawny brown fur bore down on them then gasped as Eli pulled her out of the way of the charging animal.

A gangly white-speckled fawn raced past, not two feet away, and disappeared into the dense undergrowth.

Crushed against Eli's chest, Aria erupted in laughter. "You were protecting me from a rampaging fawn!"

"Hey, you were scared too." He broke into all-out laughter along with her.

Aria pulled free. "I don't need saving, you know." She wasn't sure where the words came from or if they'd come from her at all. Was it weakness he saw in her? She wasn't weak. She'd never be weak again.

"That's good. Because I don't need to be a hero."

Aria didn't believe him. Every man needed to be a hero. "I'm glad we understand each other."

He reached for her, but she escaped his grasp and took off running.

Eli chased her, finally catching her where the path gave way to the edge of the meadow. They tumbled together into the soft grass. Eli rolled to one side, pinning her half beneath him. For his size, he moved with a gentle grace. "Are you making fun of me?" His voice held a hint of indignation. Real or mock, she couldn't tell.

"Maybe a little." She giggled. "I'm sorry. It was just so sweet that you—" She exploded into a gale of hilarity and laughed so hard she had trouble catching her breath—like when you laugh so much you can't stop, not because something's so funny but because it just feels good, because you need it, because it's been too long.

Eli's laughter started deep in his chest and ended infectiously in hers. When their frivolity gradually settled, the tenderness in his eyes made her heart ache with longing.

He brushed a lock of hair from her forehead, then traced a fingertip along her jaw to her chin and across her lips, which opened at his touch. His gaze was intense, as if he were memorizing every line on her face.

"Ari, I . . ."

Was he about to tell her something she wasn't ready to hear?

"I'm glad you can still laugh."

Relieved, she relaxed into his arms. "Me too."

They lay there in silence, sharing the poignant moment. His eyes caressed her face, every inch of it. A man should have words to go with a look like that. It was like he could see all of her shattered pieces and was trying to figure out how to put her back together. And she didn't care. She liked the way he looked at her. So what if she was broken. Wasn't everyone?

A butterfly landed on his shoulder.

"Don't move," she mouthed.

Eli tried to peer at his shoulder by only moving his eyes. "Jiminy Cricket?"

Did he think he needed a conscience? "A Spicebush Swallowtail. A butterfly."

"Whew!"

Aria stifled a giggle.

The butterfly flew away, and he bent to kiss her. His lips were feather soft on hers. He kissed her so deeply, so completely, she didn't care that she was flat on her back in a wide-open field of grass that could be full of ticks. All she could think about was this man who made her feel things she thought she'd never feel again.

When he finally pulled away, his eyes were alight with rapturous surprise, like he'd found something—or someone—long lost and cherished. She knew that look. Adam had looked at her that way once, when she'd fallen against him while learning to ice skate. A mere flash of wondrous recognition.

Eli rolled onto his back with a happy sigh. Aria lay beside him, propped on an elbow, basking in the afterglow. Hands beneath his head, eyes closed, he had a casual ease about him. He stretched, apparently unaware of the effect he had on her, a lonely widow. His long, self-assured frame seemed to say, *This is who I am: a golden boy, deservedly content in my place at the top of the heap. I didn't ask for any of it—my looks, my size, my strength—but still, it's mine. I know who I am, I'm aware of my place in the world, and I'm comfortable with both.*

Aria raised her gaze to the meadow, where lush field grasses swayed in the spring breeze and birds, bees, and butterflies flitted about. She paused to savor the moment because after so much uncertainty, so much death, joy-filled moments like this were fleeting and precious. She'd learned firsthand how one minute you could be rolling along on a happy-path and then *wham!* It's gone, all of it. Just gone. And you're left reeling, wondering what happened, what you did wrong, *Why me?*

Days like this were to be cherished, because when life turned ugly, memories of the good times were sometimes the only things that got you through another day. She looked back at Eli, utterly relaxed lying in the grass, and imagined bending down to kiss him. But would he construe it as an invitation for something more—something she wasn't ready to give?

He opened one eye to peek at her, and the idea vanished. "Hungry?" she asked.

"Starving." In one swift movement, he pulled her to him again. His mouth pressed to hers, while his caress slid down her side.

She grasped his wandering hand and twined her fingers through his, her other palm pressed against his chest. "Eli . . ."

He withdrew. "Oh, right. Lunch." He licked his lips as though the taste of her lingered there. Then he jumped to his feet and turned to help her up. "Let's eat."

Aria wasn't sure what Eli saw in her, but she knew it was something strong and good, maybe even beautiful. Giddy with this discovery, she suppressed the urge to skip as they crossed the meadow to the pond.

Aria parted the willow branches, weaving each side back like opening drapes, providing an unobstructed view of the water. The faint smell of mud mixed with the scents of grass, trees, and wildflowers enveloped her in sheer perfection. She breathed deeply, taking in the serenity of her favorite place in the world.

Eli handed her a chicken croissant sandwich. She knelt on the blanket beneath the tree, and he laid out fresh strawberries and cheese cubes on a cutting board, then opened a bottle of merlot. A meadowlark perched on a nearby pine and sang his mating song. "Choose me, choose me," it seemed to call over and over in a voice like the sound of a violin.

Eli pulled two stemless wine glasses from the basket, and she held them while he poured. A gentle breeze set the long branches rustling with the marshy scent of the pond. Kingbirds flittered around in pairs while the distant call of pheasants floated on the wind, the sounds of the wild Aria found so incredibly refreshing.

"Tell me about your childhood," he said, recorking the bottle.

Aria stiffened, his innocuous request yanking her from calm to dread. It's sad how people always try to measure others based on how they grew up. She'd spent years suppressing the painful memories of her past. The horror of her youth was the last thing she wanted to talk about. "I'd rather not."

His brows shot up.

"I'm worried that you'll be disappointed when you learn some of the not-so-great things about me." She couldn't bear to let him see the wounds of her childhood. Maybe he'd decide she was too broken after all.

He squinted, studying her. "Who are you, Aria Whitmore?"

How could she admit to him that her life was one big lie? Pretending for years to be an upstanding wife, successful business woman, and devoted mother, simply emulating her mother-in-law, neighbors, women from church, and the mothers of her children's friends. All she'd ever wanted was to be one of them. Normal, good, unbroken. No, she never even let Adam see that part of her.

"I'm the woman God and my past have made me. Let's leave it at that for now." She shot him a hopeful smile.

"For now."

Aria sipped her wine. "How about you tell me more about your family?"

He stretched out on his side and propped on an elbow to face her. "My mom's an incredibly talented pianist and music teacher. With her Italian roots, she's sort of Sophia Loren meets Mary Poppins—dark-skinned, with auburn hair, a voice like an angel, and a joyful heart. My dad's more the Grumpy Old Men sort, stocky and gruff. He'll pull out a chair for you at the dinner table and then ignore you the whole meal." He laughed, but she had the feeling he was making light of it only to cover some deep-seated concern.

"You said you had a brother and sister."

"Oh, yes." He popped the remainder of his sandwich into his mouth, then washed it down with a sip of wine. "My sister, Anna, is twenty-six and a kindergarten teacher. It's her life mission to try to embarrass me in front of women. Her husband, Cameron, is a good guy. Their daughter, Chloe, is three or four, a little sprite of a thing.

My brother, Nick, is a year younger than me." A dark scowl chased away Eli's smile. "Nick's a hard worker like our father, but where my dad's a storm cloud, Nick's a sunny day. His wife's name is Joy, which suits her. They have two kids, Olivia and Asher."

A brother, just like her. If only he had lived. She didn't remember ever meeting any of her grandparents, aunts or uncles— she'd been only five when her father left—and when she'd entered the foster care system at sixteen, after her mother's death, the agency hadn't found any relatives either. She blinked back the familiar longings.

She loved how he'd brought each one of his family members to life with his animated portrayals, building pictures in her mind so she almost believed she'd recognize them when they eventually met. Despite a niggling uneasiness about his dad, she looked forward to meeting these people who had helped mold the confident and carefree man so eager to share himself with her.

While puffy clouds glided overhead, Aria's thoughts turned to her mother and the endless paper-cut disappointments that defined her childhood. With two kids, Mona Farrow had nothing left when it came to her youngest. Like in the wild, when resources are slim, the smallest suffers most. Aria couldn't remember a single time her mother had held her, kissed her, or told her she loved her. Water under the bridge now—but it had almost drowned her as a little girl.

"I can't wait till you're all grown and out of the house," she'd rail at her and Gibs when their play grew noisy. Aria often wondered if her mother was bitter because her husband had stopped loving her, or did her husband stop loving her because she was bitter?

On her good days, her mother was merely indifferent, as if providing a roof over their heads and food on the table was all the parenting she was capable of.

They rarely went hungry, but a single parent too proud to live on the dole meant they were always short on comforts and long on hardships, content with little but forever wishing for more. They often subsisted on boxed mac-and-cheese and hotdogs for weeks on end. Bill collectors, disconnection notices, missed school events —it was the kind of poverty they couldn't get out of once it sucked them in, the kind of childhood Aria vowed her children would never experience.

Thoughts of her mother always crushed her, so she pushed them back down where they belonged. "My in-laws live on the other side of those woods." She pointed beyond the pond. "This property was their wedding gift to us."

Eli popped a strawberry into his mouth and stretched out, propped on an elbow. "They probably hoped to keep you close."

"No doubt." She remembered how happy Bea and Justice had been the day they presented them with the deed. Even if she had to sell her house to pay the bills, she could never sell this property.

Aria reclined beside Eli, arms wish-boned beneath her head. She closed her eyes and inhaled deeply, soaking in the scents and sounds. "Willows are my favorite tree. They're so romantic and grand . . . and mournful." She stopped thinking about it because it made her sad. She'd learned long ago it was best to avoid focusing on things that brought her down.

Eli shifted, and she opened an eye to find him watching her as if he were figuring out a difficult math problem.

He looked so deeply into her eyes, she thought she might fall in. *If only.* When he bent to kiss her, his hand brushed the curve of her hip. Lulled by the breeze rustling the leaves and the intoxicating taste of strawberries, wine, and passion, Aria lost herself in his kiss.

He pulled back, and his gaze caressed her face. Did he have any idea how his size looming over her made her feel so small and warm and safe? "I know we said we'd take it slow, but I want to . . . be with you." His voice was hoarse and little more than a breath. The low, steady moan of the breeze in the trees was louder. "I want to make love to you, Ari. Now. Here."

She couldn't breathe. With one touch, he'd awakened something in her she hadn't felt for a long time. His hunger frightened her. Her own hunger frightened her more. "I barely know you."

He placed her palm on his heart. "You can learn me."

The beating in his chest was so strong she could feel it. "Eli, I—"

"I want to be like the air you breathe," he said, his voice soft and gravelly. "If only for a moment. That unnoticed, that easy, that necessary."

He touched her cheek with a gentleness that made her heart race, bringing warmth to her hands and face. His fingertip trailed down to her chin and he tipped her face to his. She could almost see his thoughts swirling and brewing, as if he would spill over any second. "If I'm not careful, I could really fall for you, Ari."

The raw emotion in his eyes made her heart hurt. She couldn't speak. She couldn't do anything except . . . give in, pull his head close, and brush her lips against his, drinking in his breath.

He kissed her, starting with her lips, then moving to her chin, neck, collarbone. His fingertips lingered at the V of her shirt, then unfastened the top button.

Aria shut her eyes and the world fell away, the rustle of the leaves above, the birds whirring in the meadow, the scent of the pond.

When no more buttons remained, he opened her shirt. His fingers traced the lacy edges of her bra, then trailed across her stomach, stirring her hunger, robbing her of her breath. More kisses followed, light as a thought. At the edge of her jeans, his fingertip fluttered along her skin.

Lost in the feelings he had awakened in her, she trembled and gasped, then responded with a kiss wild with reckless abandon.

"I want you, Ari," he said, his voice husky with passion.

His touch, familiar and warm, elicited sensations so long foreign to her, she ached in places she'd forgotten existed. "Oh, how I've missed you," she moaned.

He pulled back and cupped her face roughly in his hands. "Ari, look at me."

She didn't want to open her eyes, didn't want to see the face that belonged to the voice, the voice that didn't match the touch.

"Ari!"

Her eyes snapped open and she gazed into a face clouded with unbearable disappointment. Eli's face. It hadn't been Adam touching her, making her feel things that only belonged to her husband.

Struck with the horror of what she'd done, she tried to push Eli away, but he pinned her within his arms.

"Ari, what do you mean, you've missed me?"

Her mind raced for an explanation, but she quickly gave up the chase. It was clear from the devastation on Eli's face that he'd already guessed the answer to his question. She'd never felt so ashamed. Oh, why did she have to keep thinking about Adam? He was gone and never coming back. Why couldn't she let go?

Aria rolled away and buried her face in her arms. Eli reached for her, and she pushed his hand away. Sometimes it hurt more to be comforted than to be alone. And right now, she needed to be alone.

"Ari." His voice was soft, soothing, talking her down from her emotional precipice. He swallowed her in his arms. "You weren't ready. It's okay."

"No, it's not." She choked on her words. "It'll never be okay."

"You need more time. That's all."

She didn't know what to say. *I'm sorry* fell so far short.

He held her for several minutes. Then he eased her onto her back and tenderly re-buttoned her shirt.

She raised her eyes to him. "I can't give you what you need. Not right now."

"I want more than your body, Aria Whitmore. I want all of you, your whole heart and soul. I've waited my whole life for you. I can wait a little longer."

Despite his reassurances and the warmth of his touch, she shivered as if a cloud were passing over her.

His eyes traveled from her eyes to her lips. "God, you're beautiful." He breathed deeply, as though struggling for some elusive inner calm.

He made her feel beautiful, and it was a feeling, she realized now, that she'd missed. "I," she began, breathless. "I need a minute."

He stood and his gaze roamed the landscape. "Yeah, me too," he said and walked away.

Aria sat up, propped against the tree. In the silence that followed, her mind flooded with regret. The way Eli had touched her was gentle and adoring, like Adam had always been. She shuddered to think what might have happened if he'd begun to—

I can't do this. She hung her head in her hands.

She wasn't sure how much time had passed when Eli slid down to sit beside her.

"Hey." Eli shouldered her.

She forced herself to meet his gaze and saw nothing but love. "Oh, Eli, why do you have to be so wonderful?"

He smiled at the compliment, that adorable half-grin. "Guess that's the way heroes are," he said matter-of-factly. "Wonderful, by definition."

She laughed. "I thought you didn't need to be a hero."

He took her hand, twining his fingers with hers. "Maybe for you I do."

His tender touch reminded her of the warmth of his breath on her skin, his soft, wet kisses, and the feel of his hands gliding over her quivering skin. "You were so gentle."

"Like Adam used to be?"

She stiffened. "I wasn't going to say that."

"But you were thinking it."

How could he see into her thoughts so clearly? She squeezed her eyes tight, wanting to close off his view, shut out the things she didn't want him to see, things she didn't want to think about.

He cupped her face. "Look at me."

She opened her eyes. The doubt in his gaze was a heavy burden on her frail resolve.

"I need to ask you something. And be honest."

Dread settled over her like a wool blanket on a sweltering day. But she nodded ever so slightly.

"When I first kissed you at the river in Falls Creek . . ." He licked his lips nervously. "Were you thinking about him?"

She couldn't turn away. He was holding her face. All she could do was blink. Honesty stinks sometimes.

His hands dropped, and he exhaled like it was his last breath of life.

"I wasn't. Not at first." She swallowed, remembering the perfection of the moment. "I was only thinking about how good it felt to be held and kissed like that. I was thinking how much I'd missed it. And then I thought of Adam."

He slumped back against the tree, staring at his empty hands. "I know I'll never measure up to your husband."

"You don't need to."

He took her hand, and the light returned to his baby blues. "You're not ready to take the next step, and that's fine. I just want to be with you."

A gentle breeze rustled the leaves. She felt an overwhelming urge to rest her head on his shoulder and eventually, she did. A comfortable silence filled the space between them.

Eli stood and helped her up, holding on to her hands. "Take all the time you need." His eyes gleamed with hope in the tree-speckled sunlight, his crooked grin so boyish and innocent. "I'm not going anywhere."

"Good," she said. "Neither am I."

"When you're ready, I want it to be right here, in this magical place."

Something inside of Aria warmed as she imagined giving herself to him in this very spot. When the time was right. If that time ever came.

"Don't make me wait too long, though," he said with a chuckle. "It might be tough when there's snow on the ground, eh?"

"Eh?" she echoed with a nervous laugh, wondering if that Canadian habit of speech had immigrated across the border to become part of his Minnesota upbringing.

As they trekked back to the barn, Eli held her hand, and she had an inexplicable feeling that something good and promising had crept back into her life. He made her feel like a child, trusting and innocent of the ravages of love.

When she started school at five years old, Gibson and Dante, both nine at the time, held her hand everywhere they went, often swinging her between them. As they got older, Gibson held her hand—until she turned fifteen, and he was no longer there. Then Dante stepped in.

Adam was never one for holding hands, but he touched her in other, more intimate ways: a hand on her hip, an arm across her shoulder, a pat on the knee.

She never imagined it could feel this good to hold someone's hand again.

15

Well after midnight in Michigan, Eli sat on the back deck of his lakeside rental reliving the events of the day as fireflies flickered on the lawn below. An ache started deep in his core as he conjured up an image of Aria's pulse racing at her throat, the quiver of her stomach, her lips soft and warm—

In his shirt pocket, his phone buzzed with a text.

Aria: You awake?

Eli: Very. It's only 9:30 in LA. Smiley-face emoji. How was dinner with the family?

Aria: Nice, as always.

A row of dots danced on the screen as she typed.

Aria: I know you have an early flight, but do you want to come over?

He hesitated but only for a moment.

Eli: Be right there.

Aria: I'm at the lake. Come on around.

He gave her last text a thumbs up, brushed his teeth, then ran his hands through his hair and pulled the condo door closed behind him.

At Aria's minutes later, he parked in the driveway and scanned the street in both directions for unwanted media. Only an empty boat trailer sat parked at the curb halfway down the block. Still watchful, he walked around the house and peered from the shadows of the side yard to the lakefront patio where Aria sat in a chair illuminated by moonlight, her knees pulled up, her arms wrapped around them. No fire burned tonight in the center of the outdoor seating arrangement. Was she thinking of him or of the ghost he couldn't push from her thoughts?

He panned the opposite shore. No tri-pod silhouette loomed on the dam, at least that he could make out. He studied the neighbor's deck to the west, the only one with a view of Aria's backyard. Empty. Quiet.

Aria's shoulders rose and fell with a big breath and she rested her head on her knees.

Eli crossed the lawn and she perked up. "Hey," he said, giving her a quick kiss on the cheek, then slipping into the chair beside her. "You all right?"

"Couldn't sleep."

"Me neither." The night settled between them, as still as a held breath. He ached to draw her into his arms but struggled against the memory of what happened beneath the willow.

She glanced up at him, making eye contact for a split second before looking down again. The sadness in her eyes made his chest ache.

"Can I hold you?"

She nodded, stood. He held his arms out, and she settled on his lap.

He pulled her against him and reclined back in the chair. She felt warm and soft and relaxed in his arms. Moonlight painted the lake water silver while the cool tranquility of the evening settled like a summer rain.

"It's always harder at night," she said.

Despite the looming sadness, Aria was the strongest woman he'd ever met. It was the first thing he'd noticed about her when she chased him down in the airport. He admired the way she held herself, her determination and confidence. But it was nice to see this side of her too, the vulnerable side, the side that might need a shoulder to lean on. He kissed her hair, lingering in its softness.

They sat in silence, neither apparently willing to bring up what they both must be thinking. How was this going to work if she couldn't move on?

"So many stars," Aria said.

He glanced skyward. "You're pretty easy to please."

"Would you rather I be more demanding, high maintenance, needy?" A smile colored her voice.

"Demanding, no. High maintenance, definitely not. Needy? A little might be nice."

"Oh, Eli, I do need you." She pulled back to look at him. "More than you know."

"You do?" He stared into her big doleful eyes, a starlit evergreen forest.

"Yes." She rested her head on his shoulder and nestled against him.

A pontoon puttered by beyond the end of the dock, and a dog barked in the distance. Aria clambered from his lap and smiled down at him, then plucked something from the air.

Fireflies had settled on the yard like the Milky Way, and Aria strolled among them, arms outstretched, scattering the "stars" and filling him with awe at how effortlessly she'd captured his heart.

She then collected several more. "I've never seen so many," she said, her voice whisper soft as if afraid the sound of it might frighten them away.

She twirled to face him. "Come dance with me," she said, extending a hand.

He pulled himself from the comfy patio chair and with a quick glance at the neighbor's deck and the dam across the lake, he ambled toward her. "There's no music."

She closed the distance between them and opened her hands, releasing the fireflies to flicker up between them. As the little bursts of light scattered, a huge grin settled on his lips. How could he possibly stay angry when he was so helplessly in love?

He tipped Aria's face up to meet his gaze. "Your ability to take so much pleasure from something as simple as a few bugs is one of the things I love about you."

She pulled her phone from her back pocket and with a few taps, a soft ballad started playing. She adjusted the volume and slipped it into his shirt pocket. "Music." She gave him a satisfied smile and wrapped her arms around his neck.

Blissful contentment washed over Eli as he circled his arms around her waist, and they swayed as one to the soft melody. Her body was warm and supple, and she smelled like strawberries and vanilla ice cream. She was broken. He knew that. And he loved that about her too. What else could he do but help her heal?

When the song ended, he stepped back. "Did you decide yet about coming to LA?"

Aria gave him a questioning look. "Are you sure you still want me to come?"

He frowned. "Do you think I'd change my mind because of what happened this afternoon?"

She shrugged.

Another man might wonder if she was worth all the trouble. But not him. Because he knew exactly where his heart was. "Ari." He held her hands, took a deep breath, and stared into her eyes. "I'm not going to lie and say it didn't hurt. It cut right to the quick, in fact. But I understand. You spent years with your husband, and it's going to take time to get used to having someone else in your life."

Her eyes twinkled with hope and maybe something more.

"I want that someone to be me."

She released a long breath.

"This afternoon . . . I lost myself in kissing you, touching you, being close to you. I wanted to show you how I feel." He brushed a fingertip across her lips. "I'm sorry if I went too far."

She rested her head against his chest, and a pulsing hunger shot straight through his core.

"I have no idea how long it might take," she said.

"No problem. We'll have all weekend." Aria looked up and he winked.

She playfully punched his arm. "Gee, thanks. You're such a patient guy."

"I can be," he said. "For you." He pressed his lips against her ear. "Please say yes."

A long exhale came from her mouth, like a boxer before entering the ring. "Yes."

He swung her around, then set her back on her feet. "You won't regret it, I promise." His mind raced through the myriad things they could do, places he would show her.

"But Monroe has a tennis match next weekend—state finals. Can we make it the weekend after?"

"You betcha." More time to plan. It had to be perfect.

"And it'll just be me."

"Oh?" He hoped with a single word to hide his lack of disappointment.

"Monroe has a lot going on the next few weeks, with graduation and open houses. You know how it goes."

"You bet." She would be all his for a whole weekend. His heart raced. But he resisted the urge to kiss her. Because kissing only led to wanting more. And he needed to wait until he felt certain that she thought of no one else but him.

Eli's thoughts drifted back to the night of their first date, falling asleep on the chaise in front of the fire with her wrapped in his arms and waking up in the cool morning air, her warmth beside him. He'd never felt such contentment, as if the whole world had stopped to entrance him in its simple beauty, draw him into another realm, one he'd never known before, something sweet and powerful and complete. With a deep-seated ache, he yearned to feel that way again.

Eli looked skyward, admiring the blanket of stars. A bright

white light streaked across the heavens in a long arc, the longest shooting star he'd ever seen. "Did you see that?"

"I did!" Aria's excitement matched his own.

He gave her a gentle squeeze. "Tell me what you wished."

"That I could fall asleep with you tonight. What did *you* wish for?"

"Same thing." She grinned up at him. "Is Monroe—"

"Asleep." She took his hand and led him up the deck steps to the chaise. "Is this ok?"

"Perfect." He lowered the backrest, sat, and waited while she disappeared inside the house.

Minutes later, she returned with a pillow and two thick quilts, which she draped over him.

Lying on his side, he opened a corner of the bedding, and she slipped in beside him, sharing the pillow. He wrapped her in his arms under the covers.

A soft murmur welled up from deep inside her. "I'm sorry for being such a sad person. I just don't want to forget him."

"You won't. And that's okay."

"Thank you." She kissed his hand and tucked it beneath her chin. "Good night, Eli."

"Good night, baby."

Eli lay awake for a long time. The night was too perfect to waste on sleep. The moonlight, the cool fresh air, the warmth of the woman nestled in his arms, the smell of the lake, the smell of her— another memory to add to his rapidly growing stack of moments to remember.

He didn't care that she'd been thinking of her late husband moments before. Or that she wasn't ready to be intimate with him. So what if she was simultaneously a wonderment and a torture? He'd take whatever she could give him and wait patiently for the rest.

Eli eventually dozed off. When he woke just before dawn to the cacophony of birdsong, he helped Aria carry the bedding into the house and kissed her goodnight—or good morning, more accurately.

In the sudden silence of his rental car, he lingered, basking in an afterglow he couldn't explain. He'd never felt so content, so needed, so hopeful. Now he understood the way Grandpa always talked about Grandma. *This is what it's like to truly love someone.*

16

Less than six hours after waking up with Aria, Eli entered the main concourse at LAX to absolute mayhem. A surge of media and crying, screaming—some even swooning— teenage girls rushed straight through a hastily built crowd fence. There were so many of them, the half-dozen airport security guards couldn't deter them. EMTs followed in their wake.

Blinded by flash after flash, surrounded and outnumbered, all Eli could do was jostle among them as hands groped, tugging at his jacket, his hair, his backpack, whatever they could get their greedy little fingers on. His hat was snatched from his head, but he spun around just in time to yank it back, then tucked it under his back- pack, which he cradled like a football.

He pushed his way through the crowd as gracefully as he could manage, shaking a few hands and mumbling, "Thanks," and, "You're beautiful," as he tried to extricate himself from the fray.

A large man in a black suit appeared at his side and cleared a path with the skill of someone who'd done it a hundred times before. Never in his life—even at recent premieres—had he garnered so much attention. A part of him wanted to be thrilled about what it meant to his career, but a stronger part was genuinely afraid for his personal safety. If not for the brute ahead of him, he wasn't sure what he'd have done.

Finally bursting through the exterior doors, Eli was ushered into a black limousine waiting curbside. His publicist and his agent sat inside, both grinning like Cheshire Cats as the car door shut behind him.

"Hey, buddy!" Max set aside a bag of Cheez-Its to shake Eli's hand.

Eli ignored the proffered hand, which Max he hadn't even bothered to wipe on his pants. "What's going on, P?"

Penelope lipped her red lips, a lioness relishing her kill. "Stardom is a manufactured commodity."

"You arranged all that? And didn't tell me?"

The thug who had ushered Eli through the airport slid into the driver's seat.

"Eli, meet James Anderson, your new bodyguard. Anders, Eli."

"Nice to meet you, Mr. Van Drie." Anders reached over the seat for a handshake.

Eli shook the man's hand then turned to glare at Penelope. "We talked about this."

"I know, I know. And you said I could hire you a bodyguard when I got you to the top. Based on what I just saw, I've done it!"

"I said we'd talk about it." Eli stretched forward to pat Anders's shoulder. "No offense. It's not that I don't appreciate what you did for me back there. I just don't require your services."

"Consider me a driver, then. My job is to take you places . . . and get you out of places. You won't even know I'm around until you need me."

Eli's jaw clenched so tight his teeth hurt. He glared at Penelope. With her fire-red hair and purple-and-black pantsuit, she resembled a bruise.

"Give him thirty days. If it doesn't work out, we'll revisit."

"It's for the best, man." Max stuffed another handful of crackers into his mouth.

Eli couldn't fight them both. He was paying good money for

their experience and career guidance. He ought to trust them. With a groan, he stared out the window as the car pulled onto the freeway.

Max nudged him with a stack of folders. "Got you five new scripts to consider."

Penelope settled into her seat with a satisfied smile. "Told ya. You're hot right now."

Yeah. So hot he was about to torch whatever spark he might have started with Aria.

17

———————

At the sound of a tap on her office door, Aria swapped the phone to her other ear, spun in her chair, and motioned for Cadence to enter.

The young woman stepped inside, eased the door closed, and sagged against it, arms behind her back. An ominous look darkened her normally bubbly countenance.

Aria held up a finger and spoke into the phone, as calmly as she could manage. "We can push it to the thirty-first, Sam, but that's it."

"Listen, we need—" Benson began.

"No, you listen. The contract—"

"We can amend—"

"No. We cannot. We *will* not." Aria shot Cadence an apologetic smile. "I'll have my attorney call you, and we'll go from there."

Aria ended the call, and it took all of her willpower to not slam the desk phone into the cradle. They absolutely could not delay again. Not when she was days away from losing her home. She turned to Cadence. "EverClean wants to push back the closing."

"Again?"

"Yes, can you believe it?" Aria took a big breath and reached for her cell phone. "I just need to make a quick call and I'll be ready."

She called her attorney, and of course got his voice mail—because she only ever got his voice mail. So she left a brief message detailing EverClean's request, her express desire to hold firm to the agreed upon close date, and provided Benson's number, even though he already had it. As an afterthought, she also provided David Harris's number, EverClean's CFO and Benson's boss. Then she fired off a quick text to Benjamin Thrasher, her advisor from the Small Business Development Center.

Aria: EverClean is pushing to delay again. Left a message for Hainey to call Benson.

She didn't know what else to do except hope that the contract law attorney Benjamin recommended would prove worth his outrageous retainer.

Aria set her phone aside and pulled her purse from the desk drawer. "You wouldn't believe this guy, Benson, their R&D director. The most arrogant, overbearing . . ." She glanced up to where Cadence still stood, back against the door, hands tucked behind her, looking almost as frazzled as Aria felt.

"Cadie?"

Cadence bit her lip. "This is the last thing you need right now, but—"

"Oh, please tell me you're not quitting." She'd never find someone to replace her.

"No, God no. I love my job."

Aria stood. "Whatever it is, let's talk about it over lunch. I'm starving."

"Actually . . ." Cadence stared at the floor, as if searching for words. "We should probably talk here."

Aria slumped back into her seat. "What's up, Cadie?"

Cadence slid into the chair opposite Aria's desk. "I picked this up on the way in this morning." She pushed a copy of *The Hollywood Scoop* across the desk. The tabloid cover featured a photo of Eli and Aria in the boat. The headline read, "Van Drie's Latest Conquest: Mysterious Midwest Sweetheart."

Aria's mouth went dry. Eli wasn't some B-list actor. He was

front-page material, for crying out loud. She should've known, seeing as he had an agent and a publicist. *How famous was this guy?*

Cadence flipped to the center. The two-page spread featured a photo of the two of them cuddled together on the chaise by the fire.

Aria closed her eyes, feeling nauseous. *Breathe. Deal. You can handle this.*

"Why didn't you tell me?" Cadence's voice broke with disappointment.

Aria steeled herself. "I was going to. At lunch today."

"It doesn't really look like you." Cadence gazed at the cheesy newspaper. "I recognized your boat."

Aria shook her head. "I should've known this would be part of the deal."

"It shouldn't have to be," Cadence said, sounding protective. She opened her mouth again but said nothing. She probably wanted to ask more questions. *Where did you meet him? What's he like? Are you two really a thing?* Were they?

"Mind if I take a rain check on lunch today?" Aria didn't know what, if anything, she could do about this latest debacle but on the heels of the EverClean hiccup, she'd certainly lost her appetite.

"No problem." Cadence moved to the door.

"Thanks for showing it to me." Aria didn't know what else to say.

Cadence paused with her hand on the doorknob.

"Cadie?" Aria prompted.

Cadence turned, leaned against the door. "He's out with a different woman every weekend. And did you know he did a stint in rehab?"

Aria's cheeks grew hot. "No. But he told me not to believe anything I read about him."

"Right. Well . . ." Cadence looked skeptical.

"This is a bad idea, isn't it?" Aria trusted her friend's judgement almost as much as her own.

Cadence bit her lip like she often did when she was mulling something over. "Maybe not. You're smart. I know you'll be careful."

"Thanks, Cadie. We'll talk soon, and I'll tell you all about him."

"Sure. And don't worry. I'll keep it to myself." Cadence closed the door behind her.

Aria wasn't sure what bothered her more, the disappointment in her friend's eyes, being the mystery girl on national display, or Eli's reputation. Not to mention, the closing on her product launch being at risk.

It struck her that there was little more she could do about the closing, so she sat back and, resisting the urge to Google Eli, she studied the angles of the photos. Most had been taken from across the lake. The one of them lying together on the chaise was from land, though—up high, like from a deck. And there were leaves in the corner—Bradford Pear leaves.

"Oh, no." Sutton's mom, Kate, must have taken that picture. *How could she betray our friendship like this?*

At least the photo didn't show their faces.

Aria fumbled for her cell phone and called Eli. "Did you know our pictures are in a tabloid?"

He gave a low growl. "I was afraid of that. But don't make too much of it. I'm a public figure. Media attention comes with the territory."

"How can you be so calm about this?"

"Hey, we weren't doing anything wrong."

His nonchalance set her mind racing. "You knew, didn't you? You saw photographers on the dam that day."

"It was only one guy—"

"And you didn't tell me?"

"Ari—"

"There's a photo of us on the chaise, which had to have been taken from my neighbor's deck. Either Sutton's mom let the photographer take it or she took it herself and sold it to the paper!" She wasn't sure which was worse. Aria knew Kate had a subscription to *People* magazine. Occasionally it landed in her mailbox by mistake. It wasn't very far-fetched to assume she read *The Hollywood Scoop* too. But would she take a picture and sell it to them?

"Or . . . the photographer might have snuck onto the deck while your neighbor was sleeping," Eli suggested. "We were out there all night. Remember?" She could almost hear the smile in his voice.

"If it wasn't Kate taking the pictures, how did the newspaper know to come back the following weekend?" She wasn't sure whether she was more angry at Kate for betraying her or Eli for not warning her.

"Don't let it get to you. Nobody reads that trash."

Aria winced. "One of my sales reps saw it."

"Is that bad?"

Bad enough.

"Besides, my publicist says there's no such thing as bad publicity."

"What a genius to come up with that profound scrap of wisdom!"

"I pay my publicist an obscene amount of money for that kind of stuff. Since hiring Penelope Fenquist, I've gotten one film offer after another, top billing too. I know my public image is . . . distasteful, but it's working for me. And I hope you know by now, that's not the real me."

Aria stared at the pictures and read a few of the captions beneath the photos—all benign, but still.

"Look, don't blow it out of proportion. It's really not a big deal."

"Not to you, maybe, but I have a past, Eli. I'm not the—what did they call me?" She flipped to the front and read the headline aloud, "'Mysterious Midwest Sweetheart.' There are a lot of things you don't know about me, things that could hurt your career."

"Maybe you'll share them with me sometime," he snapped.

Aria recoiled at the accusation in his voice and stifled a retort. "I should get back to work."

Eli let out a long breath. "Call you later?"

"Sure." Aria ended the call, resisting the urge to hurl her phone against the wall, and returned to her computer screen full of emails.

ELI PACED the length of his back patio, phone in hand. Finally, Penelope picked up. "Eli! Darling—"

"Have you seen it?"

"Seen what, dear?"

"*The Hollywood Scoop.* 'Mysterious Midwest Sweetheart.'"

"Ooh," she cooed. "Catchy headline. Congrat—"

"That's going too far, even for you." He felt his cheeks grow hot.

"I didn't even know, honestly. But I like it."

He didn't believe her for a New York second. She not only knew, she'd likely orchestrated the whole spread, right down to the tawdry headline. "My personal life is private. Period. If you can't respect that—"

"Darling." Her voice held the condescending tone of one speaking to a child on the verge of a meltdown. "Did you or did you not hire me to make you a star?"

He held the phone away from his ear and breathed deeply, reining in his temper. "Yes, but—"

"You're close, Eli. And it's those very glimpses into your personal life that are going to take you to the top."

He stifled a curse. "Aria is off limits."

"Who?"

Her feigned cluelessness infuriated him even more. "Listen carefully, P. I don't want to ruin this relationship with her. Not for stardom, not for anything."

"Well, then." She paused and he could almost see her folding her hands on her cluttered desk in that smoke-filled skanky office she kept in West Hollywood. "Guess Anders stays."

"I don't need a bodyguard," he snapped. "I just need you to stay out of my business."

She cleared her throat. "It's my business to make sure you're seen, often, everywhere, and especially with attractive women. Is she pretty?"

Eli pictured Aria the morning he'd arrived at her place for their day on the lake. "Of course she is."

"If you really care about her, you'll keep the bodyguard."

Let it go with the damn bodyguard already. "Get me to the top first, and then we'll talk about it."

"Oh, I'll get you there, darling. Remember, stardom is a manufactured commodity. You'll see."

~

MID-AFTERNOON ARIA's phone buzzed with a call from her neighbor.

"Hey, Janie," she answered. "How are you?"

"Oh, good. We're fine, yes, just fine, but," a short pause, "I, well, are you at home?"

"No, I'm at work. Why?"

"Well, dear, the street in front of your house is lined with news vans. People with cameras are all over your front lawn. Pounding on your door. It's really quite a circus." Her voice raced with a mixture of excitement and panic.

Aria bristled at the thought of paparazzi invading her home. For Janie's sake, she forced a calm response. "Oh, well, I hope they're not bothering you. Don't worry, I'll take care of it."

"What do you think they want? Is something wrong?"

"No, no. I'll explain when I get home. I'm sorry. And Janie, *please* don't talk to them."

"Oh, no. Absolutely not."

"I'm glad you called. Thank you."

"Of course, dear. Let us know if there's anything we can do."

Aria ended the call and shot off a text to Monroe.

Aria: News vans are at our house. Don't pull in the driveway. Go straight to the Polenskis and ask Mr. P. to walk you through the yards to the back door. Once you're inside, close all the blinds. Under no circumstances are you to answer the door or speak to any of those people. Understood?

Aria waited for a response that didn't come, then glanced at the clock. The final bell hadn't yet rung and cell phones weren't allowed in the classrooms.

Aria: I'll be home as soon as I can.

After sending a quick email to her team, with a copy to her boss, Aria packed up her laptop and headed for home. On the way, she called a friend who was a county sheriff. By the time she arrived, the street was cleared.

As Aria tucked Monroe into bed that night, her daughter confessed that she and her friend had spied on Aria and Eli the night she returned from Montreal. "We didn't mean to. We were coming home from Hannah's, and we heard music. We only watched for a couple of minutes."

Aria admired her daughter's honesty. And it was sweet that Monroe felt bad about intruding on them. But a seventeen-year-old shouldn't have to deal with paparazzi. As funny and charming as Eli was, Aria knew there'd be a downside to dating an actor. And this was likely just the flower on the long-rooted dandelion called fame.

Aria brushed a blonde lock from her daughter's brow. "How would you like to stay with Rachel for a couple of days?"

"On school nights? Cool!"

"I'll call her mom." Aria planted a kiss on her daughter's cheek. "Love you."

"Love you more."

Aria's heart softened. Monroe hadn't responded that way in years. She turned off the light before her daughter could see her eyes go misty.

When Eli called, he must have read something in her face because he immediately asked what was wrong, as if he'd totally forgotten about the tabloid. She sat on her bed, leaned against the headrest, and told him about the news vans and reporters. "Monroe had to go to a neighbor's and sneak through the backyards to get into the house." Aria pressed her lips together, reluctant to voice the full extent of her frustration.

"I'm sorry. Really. But it's gonna be okay." He seemed tense, like he could sense her balancing on the precipice of breaking it off with him. "It's a momentary infatuation—"

"It is not okay. They know where I live."

"Trust me. They probably won't even come back and if they do, they won't stay long."

Her silence filled the air between them like the two thousand miles that separated them physically, and he must have taken it as acceptance, because he rushed on with excitement in his voice. "I had a fantastic photo shoot and interview this afternoon. With *Us Weekly*. It was supposed to be about me and Makayla—"

"Makayla?"

"My costar. It's good publicity to let the public think we're an item before the movie releases. The issue will hit the stands in July, the first of many summer promos Penelope has scheduled leading up to the premiere in September."

A million questions circled in her mind. "Why are you telling me this?"

"Because when you read it, I want you to know that I was thinking of you the whole time."

Right, whatever that means. "Eli, it's late—"

"Oh, sure. I'll give you a call tomorrow."

Aria scowled as she hung up.

Soon Eli's face would be on newsstands—cover story, no doubt —touting his relationship with another woman. She added another tick to the cons side of her virtual *Dating Eli* sheet.

The next day at work, on the heels of a voice mail from her attorney assuring Aria that the closing at EverClean would proceed as scheduled, a bouquet of pink and white tulips was delivered to her office. She sank into her chair and read the note. *"Sorry you had to deal with the press. But there's an upside to my job you haven't even seen yet. Love, Eli."*

She didn't even stop to consider what the upside might be. He'd signed it *love*. Her chest tightened—with excitement or panic, she wasn't sure which.

18

A trickle of paparazzi reappeared over the next few days, but Aria ignored them, and by the following week, they'd dissipated altogether like fog in the wind, leaving behind tire tracks on the lawn, a broken sprinkler head, and an eerie sense of foreboding, as if they still crouched in the bushes, ready to pounce again at any moment.

Early Tuesday morning, after picking up Justus from his home, Aria met Benjamin Thrasher at the commuter lot northeast of Grand Rapids for the ninety-minute drive to the EverClean Tech Center in Grand Haven. Somehow she always felt taller, stronger, and braver when she drove Adam's truck, and she needed to be all of those things today. Plus, with the memories it held, she felt as if a small part of him was with her. Which was right, because he was the reason she started the recycling-machine project in the first place.

She'd felt so alone after her husband's death, in the strange emptiness of the house when Monroe was gone—the long days, the even longer nights, and her whole barren life. Throwing herself into the project was how she'd coped.

But now, as Benjamin hefted himself up into the backseat, Aria wondered if her company car might have been more appropriate. She'd met the elderly, gray-haired man through the Small Business Development Center. A retired auto industry executive, he'd been her mentor and had helped her through each step of the process: filing patents, obtaining financing, negotiating the purchase agreement. She could not have done it without his encouragement, direction, and advice. He'd also recommended her two attorneys, one who specialized in patent law, the other representing her contracts and financial interests.

They arrived twenty minutes early, signed in at the front desk, and were escorted to a boardroom with a massive polished mahogany table at its center. A spread of coffee, water, and breakfast pastries covered a counter at the rear of the room. The prototype of the recycling machine was set up and plugged in at one end of the long table. Too nervous for coffee, Aria helped herself to a bottle of water and joined her colleagues near the machine.

A few minutes later, the attorneys arrived, followed by Sam Benson and several other people sporting EverClean employee badges. Benson, the R&D Acquisitions Lead, had been Aria's main contact on the deal since their meeting at the International Consumer Electronics Show in Las Vegas last January.

After introductions and the customary but loathsome small talk, Benson suggested a demonstration of the prototype.

He tossed a copy of the tabloid on the table in front of her. "How about shredding this?"

Aria leveled a searing gaze at Benson and silently counted to ten.

Benson's entourage snickered.

As composed as she could manage, Aria stood, placed her palms on the table, and stared Benson down. "Mr. Benson," she said in a calm, even tone, "we had six offers come out of the Vegas show, and yours was not the highest."

Silence filled the boardroom as Benson boldly returned her stare, a slight smile spreading across his face.

"Aria Whitmore!" David Harris breezed through the door, his

cheerful greeting breaking the tension. EverClean's Director of R&D, and Benson's boss, exuded a charm and energy rarely found in the business world. He greeted Aria with a warm two-handed shake and welcomed her and her associates to their offices. He apologized for his tardiness, then requested a moment alone with his colleagues.

Aria and her team filed out. In the hallway, Benjamin asked Aria about the newspaper, and she reluctantly explained her recent association with Eli Van Drie.

"You handled yourself well in there," he said. "But don't lose focus. This is a big day. Remember why we're here."

Aria nodded and forced a smile.

Benjamin drew closer and lowered his voice. "But between you and me . . . I'm glad you're finally getting out there."

Aria felt her cheeks warm. "Excuse me. I'll be right back."

Alone in the ladies' room, Aria peered at her reflection in the mirror and tried to convince herself that the woman who looked back at her was smart, educated, well-dressed, and strong. "You can do this." For an instant she considered giving in to the inner voice that told her she wasn't good enough. But she couldn't. She wouldn't. Not today. Her home, her kids' education, everything she and Adam had planned for was riding on this meeting. And she'd worked so hard to get here. She would see it through, whatever it took.

She smoothed her jacket and donned a happy-and-confident smile that she almost believed.

As Aria rejoined the group in the hall outside the boardroom, Benson disappeared around a corner. Her colleagues offered no explanation and Harris opened the door and beckoned them to rejoin the meeting. Inside the board room, a capable looking young woman stood near the head of the table. The tabloid was nowhere to be seen.

"This is Lauren Atkins," Harris said. "She will be running the meeting today."

Aria shook her hand. The young woman's eager smile said

clearly she was quite thrilled to be called in to clean up her colleague's mess.

When everyone was seated, Harris rubbed his hands together and said, "Let's close a deal, shall we?"

The rest of the day went without a hitch. Lauren Atkins proved herself not only competent and knowledgeable but extremely adept at negotiating the discussion points step by step.

After a catered lunch, the attorneys broke out to another room to cover the finer points of the contract while Ms. Atkins led Aria and her father-in-law on a tour of their production facility. Despite his lack of real-world manufacturing experience, Justus provided the EverClean operations team with an abundance of detailed guidance for setting up their production line.

By the time they wrapped up at the end of the day, Aria was a very wealthy woman. And despite his inevitable objections, Justus was also going to be rich too when she transferred half of the funds into his account.

As Aria and her team were preparing to take their leave, Harris invited Aria and Justus to a press conference on Friday morning.

"Thanks," Aria said, shaking his hand. "But I think I've had more than enough of the press lately."

Harris laughed. "I understand. And I wish you the best, in everything you do."

After Aria dropped off Benjamin, Justus called his wife, barely containing his excitement as he parlayed the events of the day. His voice held unmistakable pride whenever he mentioned Aria's name.

She wished she felt the same enthusiasm for herself. The struggle to make this multimillion-dollar venture a reality was finally over. She was rich—truly rich. No more foreclosure hanging over her head. She could cover her children's college costs, pay off the mortgage and the past-due bills, and invest the rest. If she played her cards right, she'd never have to work another day in her life.

But she couldn't help wishing Adam were there to share in her success. If she'd done this while he was alive, they would've had an easier life. He wouldn't have had to work all those weekends. They could've spent more time together, and more time with Jacks and Monroe, enjoying life together as a family.

She'd run the idea by him years ago, but he'd said there wasn't a market for a recycling machine when the manufactured goods were so cheap to buy. If only she'd have trusted her instincts back then.

Her brother, Gibson, and his best friend, Dante, would've totally been on board. They were both so good at tinkering, figuring things out, fixing whatever they could get their hands on. They'd spent hours playing Whacky Inventor in the basement of their old house on Bowser Street, disassembling toys and small appliances found in alleys, and putting them back together to make something altogether new.

When she was six, Gibs and Dante dismantled her Tinker Bell music box—a gift from her father the year before he walked out on them. She'd almost cried when she saw the inner workings on a plywood table in the basement, splayed open like a gutted animal. But she trusted Gibson. He would never destroy anything so precious to her.

When Dante turned the simple brass cylinder, its bumps passing beneath the metal comb, the "You Can Fly" tune rang forth, clear and true. Aria had giggled, bounced on her toes, and begged him to do it again and again.

Gibs put the music box back together, smoothed the thin cardboard bottom, and glued the paper back into place. With a satisfied smile, he handed it to her. But when she opened it again, Tinker Bell fell into the box like a marionette cut from its strings. She slammed the lid shut and thrust it back at her brother.

Dante snatched it and reattached Tinker Bell with a length of pink telephone wire and needle-nose pliers.

She'd had complete trust that Gibs and Dante could fix her toy. But then, she'd also believed her father would come back one day. She didn't know which was worse: a father like Dante's who hadn't stuck around long enough to even meet him, or one like hers who said he loved her and then changed his mind.

Both boys should've gone to engineering school. If they had, Gibs wouldn't have been at her lame fifteenth birthday party and Dante wouldn't have been forced to make that stupid promise.

"Aria?"

Aria felt herself yanked back into the present. Justus was peering at her, waiting for an answer to a question she hadn't heard.

"Yes?"

"Does this deal mean you won't be selling the house after all?"

"Who said I was selling the house?"

"Mrs. Kratz said she saw a sign in your yard." Running the local hardware store, Justus got more than his fair share of town gossip.

She looked away. "The house was in foreclosure."

"Oh, Aria-girl."

She liked it when he called her that. It always preceded a *How can I help?* conversation. With a heart as pure as the gaze of God, he was one of the few people who recognized she wasn't always as strong as she tried to appear. And for some reason it was okay, because he only ever wanted to help, to let her know he was there for her and always would be.

"But today's sale will fix all that." Aria patted his knee.

"You should've told me. We could've helped."

The last thing Aria would ever do was bankrupt her in-laws. She'd forever be grateful that they took her in as a teenage runaway, but she was a grown woman now, capable of standing on her own two feet.

"We'll always be your family, Aria. You know that, right?"

She nodded, not trusting her voice. God, she loved that man.

"And don't think for a minute Bea and I will be taking any of these proceeds."

Aria held her peace. It wasn't worth arguing about. She'd be giving them a healthy share despite his refusal. They could give it away for all she cared.

When Eli called that evening, he commented on the smile in her eyes. "Good day?"

"Great day." She eased onto the chaise, a huge sense of relief washing over her. "But I'm beat, and I probably look as tired as I feel. Do we always have to video chat?"

"I like to pretend I'm with you. I miss you."

An unexpected warmth crept over her as she settled back in the chaise and raised her knees to steady the phone. Eli appeared to be outdoors too with a mass of greenery and a pink flowering vine in the distant background.

His smile gleamed as bright as the white T-shirt he wore. "Tell me about your day. Something obviously went well."

Well was such an understatement, she wanted to laugh. "I can't talk about it until Friday when the press release comes out, and since I have Monroe's tennis tourney this weekend, I'd much rather wait and tell you about it when I see you next. Do you mind?"

"Sounds very high tech."

Aria couldn't suppress a wide grin. "It is."

"I wish you were coming this weekend. My mom and sister will be here."

"Oh? Do they visit often?"

"Every year after school gets out. I could use your help entertaining them. After three or four days of endless shopping and garden tours, I'm toast."

"You're assuming I love to shop."

"You don't?"

Aria shook her head. "Sorry."

"You're one surprise after another."

Aria dropped her phone, picked it up, and repositioned it atop her knee, careful to keep a grip on it this time. "Whoops! Sorry about that. The garden tours sound fun though."

"Maybe next year."

Aria fell silent at the sheer hope in Eli's long-term outlook.

Eli propped his phone on the table and leaned back in his chair. "I told my mom about you."

"You did?" Aria picked at a thread of her ripped-knee jeans.

"Of course."

Of course? Did he tell his mother about all of the girls he dated —even his girl "friends"—or was this a first? She didn't want to know.

He glanced away as if regrouping. "What were you doing when I called?

"Reading."

"Reading what?"

"A Ben Franklin biography."

Eli chuckled. "Big fan of the rebels, are you?"

"He was a pretty amazing man. Not a very good husband or father but an incredible statesman, a literary genius, and a successful inventor."

"Hmm, rotund and balding but smart and successful. Your kind of guy?"

Aria chuckled. "The type of intellect I'd like to measure up to. How about you? Who do you admire?"

Eli's gaze went far away before returning with a wry smile. "My grandfather taught me everything I know: how to fish, hunt, fell a tree, farm, tend animals. What it meant to be a man." His voice caught. They were obviously close. "He died eight years ago. I haven't been home since."

Aria sat up a little straighter. "What happened?"

He rubbed the stubble along his jawline. "I don't know where to begin. I have a lot of scars."

"Tell me. I want to know the real Eli Van Drie, scars and all." She gave him an encouraging smile.

He let out a heavy breath and stared off into the distance. "My brother and I grew up playing hockey. The invincible Van Drie brothers, people called us. State champs three years in a row. Nick had a real chance of going pro. Then the summer before my senior year, we crashed my car into a tree. I walked away without a scratch. Nicky was medevacked out by chopper. Crushed his leg and his

NHL dreams all in one fell swoop." He leaned forward, elbows on knees. "My father blamed me."

"You were driving?"

He closed his eyes and breathed in and out. Once. Twice. "Didn't matter. I was older. I should've known better."

Aria wasn't sure that answered her question.

"After the accident, my dad never came to watch me play. Nicky was his favorite anyway. He'd probably been coming to watch *him* all those years." Eli shifted in his chair. "Senior year I signed up for theater because it was an easy elective. And I loved it. Performing on stage was a high like nothing I'd ever felt. I could pretend to be someone else. Someone who hadn't ruined his brother's life." He let out a small, bitter laugh. "Of course, that's all it was. Pretending. It didn't change anything. Dad still didn't come to any of my performances."

"Oh, Eli."

"When I announced I was turning down a hockey scholarship for U of M to pursue an acting career in LA, my father practically disowned me."

He shook his head as though to dislodge the memories, the hurt, the terrible accident that had changed the trajectory of two lives and rent the fabric of a family.

When he didn't say anything else, Aria said softly, "So, what happened eight years ago?"

Eli dialed back in. "My grandpa's funeral. When my brother wanted to have it out with me over 'family responsibilities' it hit a nerve. I only threw one punch before we were pulled apart, but it blackened his eye pretty good. My dad told me to leave and not come back until I remembered who I was. And that's the last time I was home." He finally met her eyes. "I wasn't going to go back until I'd earned an Oscar."

Aria squeezed her eyes shut. An Oscar?

"I don't have one," he said. "Not yet." He shot her a grin. "But I have you."

She gave him a little smile in response, then gazed out over the lake. Was she simply a trophy for him to present to his father? A paltry replacement for an Academy Award? And was he really so naïve to think that a little gold statue or a girlfriend would have any effect on his broken family relationships?

On the upside, if and when she did finally meet his family, she probably couldn't make things worse.

On Friday, Aria tried to catch a few minutes with her boss to fill him in on the sale of her recycling machine. Glen Corbett was as attuned to the goings-on in the business world as he was to the health app on his smart watch. He'd see the news as soon as it hit the internet.

Shortly before lunch, she found him in his office with the VP of marketing. After apologizing for interrupting, she gave them a quick summary of her recycling machine, the company she'd started, and the closing at EverClean.

She wasn't quite finished when Glen interrupted in his all-too-frequent outdoor voice, as if speaking louder lent more importance to what he had to say. "So, is this a prelude to a resignation letter hitting my inbox?"

Aria suppressed a smile. "Not yet."

In the doorway, she turned back. "By the way, check out Earth-Everlasting.com if you're interested."

A niggling of conscience followed her back to her desk. She fell into her chair, let out a huge breath, threw back her head, and spun around. With the consolidation of their North American operations, not to mention the likelihood of landing both of the Calgary-based GPO accounts she'd met with, she'd accomplished more in the last twelve months than Glen Corbett had in his twenty-odd years with the company.

Aria straightened the Platinum Club award on the credenza. Even if her boss never recognized her accomplishments, at least the company did. If and when she did decide to quit, she'd be departing on a high note, and that was way more than insecure, overbearing Glen Corbett could even begin to crush.

Aria turned to her computer and checked her bank account

online for about the tenth time since Tuesday. The proceeds from the closing were still there. She rested against her seatback and stared at the screen. The deposit—all nine figures of it—took up a lot of space on the account details page, and just below, the debit for the mortgage payoff, shined like an Olympic gold medal. She blinked several times.

Now what?

Aria plugged in her headphones, found her favorite playlist, ignored all thoughts of work, and allowed herself to daydream. A list immediately began forming in her mind. At the top, was more time with her kids. Only three months remained of summer break. Then Monroe and Jacks both would be in college. The thought brought a familiar ache to her heart. She considered marching back to Glen's office and giving her notice, but resolved to take at least the weekend to think it through.

ESL– Monroe, part of the district's Spanish immersion program since kindergarten, had always wanted the two of them to volunteer together to teach English as a Second Language to Spanish families. But Aria had always said later, when she wasn't so busy, when things settled down at work, when she had more time. As a working mother, she'd learned that there is never *enough* time. There are only priorities. This summer, she could make teaching ESL with Monroe a priority.

Law school had long been a dream. Dante was out of prison, but there were thousands more like him who still needed help. Being a public defender wouldn't be easy. It was notoriously a stressful job with heavy caseloads and a lack of resources. But it could be a meaningful and satisfying new career, fighting for social justice one poor person at a time. But what if she could make more of a difference doing something else, something bigger, like Franklin, Adams, or Lincoln big? She'd definitely need to give that idea more thought, but she had time. Soon, she'd have plenty of time.

Her computer screen flashed; the bank's website logged her off due to inactivity. To the left of her monitor sat the vase of tulips from Eli, fading fast but still somehow beautiful.

Aria had no idea what kind of future, if any, she might have with Eli. Would she be relegated to following him around from one movie set to the next like some groupie, trying to eke out a sense of purpose with the sliver of life that would be hers? That sounded loathsome. And lonely.

Eli said he wanted a family, and she was already feeling the heartache of missing hers. Was it too late to want all of that again? She used to be someone's wife, someone's mother. And she'd been happy. But was Eli even the right man to have another child with? She liked him, sure, maybe even more than liked, but they'd only been dating a few weeks. She barely knew him.

But she was working on that. She couldn't wait to see Eli's face next weekend when she told him about the closing on her recycling machine.

Aria's heart raced as she thought about having an entire weekend alone with him. He'd said she could trust him. But did she trust herself?

19

———————

After an oddly cool video chat with Aria, during which Eli got the distinct impression she did not struggle with their temporary separation nearly as much as he did, Eli tried to focus on a script in the double-chaise lounger that had been delivered earlier that day. The comfortable and capacious chair anchored the new al fresco seating area beneath the magnolia tree in the center of his garden. A chandelier hung from a branch, making the setting almost as enchanting as the firefly-strewn backyard of Aria's lake house. She was going to love it!

That he wasn't invited to Monroe's tennis tournament still irked him a little. He'd offered to meet them there, but Aria had insisted on no distractions. Monroe needed to focus. A mother protecting her child—he got that. But he would've loved to have been there to help cheer the girl on, to have seen Aria's face as she watched her daughter win first place in a state meet, and to have replaced the husband-memory at her side. *One man's loss is another man's dream.* How long until Aria allowed him into that hallowed place in her life?

His phone chirped with a text from Makayla.

Makayla: Hey, E! Let's par-tay! Party-hat emoji. I'm with Matt

and Heather. Leigh's here too with some guy. Join us. We'll make it a six-some.

Three double-heart emojis followed.

If he'd learned anything from his time with his recent costar, it was that the number of emojis Makayla used was in direct proportion to her alcohol consumption. Despite the indication she was well past tipsy and flirting with all-out wasted, he considered the invitation. He needed to talk to her. He didn't know what he might have with Aria, but he knew he couldn't be with anyone else while he figured it out. And that required a one-on-one conversation, with both of them stone cold sober, and definitely not in the company of Matt and Heather.

Eli: Can't tonight. Meet me for lunch tomorrow?

Makayla: Come on out, E. Have some fun. All work and no play . . . Five scary-face emojis.

He remembered their last attempt at fun.

Eli: Another time, Mak.

Makayla: Sad-face emoji. Lunch then. Pick me up at noon tomorrow.

Eli: Meet me. Polo Lounge at noon. See you then.

She "liked" his response, then replied with two martini glasses cheering.

The next afternoon, he'd been waiting on the red brick Polo patio for twenty minutes when Makayla finally swept in, looking like she owned the place. With its spectacular array of palm trees and flowers, the restaurant was one of Los Angeles's premier outdoor lunch settings, well known as an epicenter for power dining and deal making, and always filled with familiar faces. Makayla's carefully chosen outfit of white capris and cropped jacket over a hot-pink top—the exact shade of the towering bougainvillea behind her—matched the patio's décor to a T.

She greeted him with a peck on the cheek, and before he could even pull a chair out for her, she slipped gracefully into the one at his elbow.

Eli relaxed back into his seat. "You're late."

"I was hoping you'd call," she said coolly.

He tossed the menu aside. "Thanks for coming."

In a blink her demeanor transformed from ice maiden to winsome coquette. "A lunch date with my handsome costar? How could I refuse?"

She tucked her oversized white-framed sunglasses into a stylish white clutch, which she set on the table, and turned to him with her most alluring starlet smile. "I'm sorry about our last night in Montreal. I'd love for a chance to make it up to you."

He sipped his iced tea. "Well, that's what I wanted to talk to you about."

She straightened and smiled expectantly.

A waiter appeared between them. "Excuse me. Can I offer the lady a beverage?"

Makayla kept her eyes fixed on Eli. "Champagne, please. No, wait. A Bloody Mary. Yes, that will do perfectly."

Eli nodded to the waiter, who quietly retreated.

Makayla glanced coyly around the room as if sizing up her audience, then eased closer to Eli. "We left some unfinished business in Quebec." She blinked her incredibly long eyelashes. "Didn't we?"

His mood withered, along with his estimation of this picture-perfect young actress he'd almost slept with. He had more to offer a woman than a one-night stand, didn't he? Why didn't Makayla want more from him? Why didn't she want more for herself? What a shame that a woman with so many assets could value herself so little.

"That's not what I need right now."

"Are you sure, E? The last love scene we shot . . . I could feel how much you needed me."

Makayla was right. He did have needs. But when an image of Aria danced before him, he knew whatever Makayla was offering wouldn't satisfy. He had no idea what might become of his relationship with Aria, but it would be more than that.

Given his long history of avoiding entanglements, this sudden change of heart felt foreign to him. He was probably setting himself up for disappointment because Aria came with complications, a sadness in her eyes that came out of nowhere. But he wanted her, all of her. He wanted everything with her.

"See, that's the thing," he said, eyeing Makayla, "I have needs and right now I think what I need is completely different than what you're looking for."

She lifted her chin and gave her long, black curls a toss. "I can do casual."

"I can't." Not anymore.

Makayla scoffed. "So you think your 'Midwest Sweetheart' is the real deal?"

"Maybe."

She teared up, as if what they'd shared on set was real. "Okay, then," she said bravely.

"Mak, I'm sorry." Eli placed a hand over hers, playing along with her melodrama. He didn't want to hurt her feelings if she really did think their on-screen chemistry meant something more than what it was—acting.

She withdrew her hand to dab at the corners of her eyes with her napkin.

Her cocktail arrived and they ordered lunch. When the waiter left, Makayla took a long sip, then drew an olive from the skewer, making a show of it as she eyed Eli and pressed it to her full hot-pink lips. "My mom and her new husband are throwing a party Sunday night. Want to come?"

"Penelope has a can't-miss event for me on Sunday night."

"At Michael Lang's house in Malibu?"

He stared at her. "Yes."

"He's my new stepfather."

Eli rubbed his forehead. "Your mom married a producer? Nice *in* for you."

"For you too. Seems he's got this epic historical romance, the next *Titanic,* and they're looking for the male lead." She drew a gherkin from the skewer and rubbed it across her lips, then gently sucked the tip of it, making a delicate slurping sound.

He tried to remember the last time he had sex, then forced himself to look away. *You don't want her, not really.*

"I told him it had to be you."

"You insisted on me?"

"Well, yeah. Before you dumped me." She tossed the pickle into her mouth with a crunch.

Eli rubbed a tightness from the back of his neck. "I owe you one."

"That's what I was thinking too."

Eli let out a sigh. "What do you want from me, Makayla?"

One elbow on the table, the other on the arm of her chair, she edged closer and eyed him seductively. "What every woman wants."

Braless beneath her gaping pink tank, a full third of each creamy white breast screamed for his attention. His pulse raced and his face grew hot.

He pulled away and rubbed his palms down his thighs. He'd never had to sleep his way to the top and he wasn't about to start now. "Is that what it's going to take to keep your friendship?"

Her hungry gaze raked over him.

"Mak—"

With a childish huff, she settled back in her chair. "No."

He glanced around the restaurant and smiled at a couple of elderly ladies who'd obviously been entranced by their little tête-à-tête. Turning back to Makayla, he considered what came next. "We're going to have a lot of promos over the summer with the premier in September. It's not going to be weird for you, is it?"

"Don't worry. I'm a big girl." She straightened and forced a smile, but he could see the hurt she tried to mask. She was a good actress, but not that good.

20

———————

Between her new accounts and her growing team of sales reps, her own company's first product launch, and all the last-minute planning for Monroe's graduation party, Aria ran at chipmunk speed, constantly adding tasks to her to-do list only to scratch them off minutes later. All the frantic activity at least gave the appearance of her life being normal.

By the time Aria landed at LAX on Friday, her apprehension about the weekend ahead threatened to overwhelm her. How she wished Jacks and Monroe had joined her. She always felt like she had a sense of purpose with them along.

As she descended the escalator in the terminal at LAX, she spotted a guy holding a placard with her name on it. Built like the Terminator with the dress and demeanor of a man named Jeeves, Anders introduced himself, took her carry-on luggage, then led her to a black Escalade with tinted windows. Eli had offered to meet her in person, but wanting to avoid the inevitable media attention, she'd agreed it would be best to send his driver into the airport instead.

Aria hadn't even buckled her seatbelt before Eli cupped her

face in his hands. "God, I've missed you." He kissed her like they were long-parted lovers. So much for taking it slow.

As the car pulled away from the curb, Aria retrieved the *Wall Street Journal* from her satchel, folded to the article about her product launch. So excited to tell Eli her news, she could barely hold a thought in her head.

Ignoring the newspaper, he gazed deep into her eyes. "I'm so glad you're here. I have a great weekend planned. Any chance you can stay until Monday? There's a party Sunday night, and I'd love for you to go with me."

But she still had a job. She'd given her two-week notice to her boss on Monday morning, but he didn't tell her she could go ahead and leave, like they sometimes did with other positions. If they needed her to stay the full two weeks, she would. She wasn't one to burn a bridge.

Eli described all the plans he'd made for the weekend, and his energy and excitement were so infectious, Aria quickly decided to save her news for later. Before she knew it, they were pulling into a gated driveway. The car stopped in front of a vast Italianate villa surrounded by a carefully curated lawn and towering palms. A stone pathway ambled in a graceful arc to the front door. Its authentic Old World style boasted a subtle magnificence. "This is your home?"

"You betcha!" Eli jumped out and skirted the hood to open her door while Anders retrieved her luggage from the back.

Aria returned the newspaper to her satchel, took Eli's hand, and stepped out of the car. A motorcycle sat in the drive, gleaming black and chrome and sinister in the California sunshine. Her insides clenched. "Is someone else here?"

He followed her gaze. "The bike? That's mine. I thought we could go for a ride later."

Her heart sank, and her whole body almost followed. Adam's smiling face swam before her, morphing into the emaciated visage she'd visited for almost a year: pale, graying flesh hanging gaunt on angular cheekbones, his head wrapped in layer upon layer of white gauze, flat and misshapen on one side following the craniotomy. She pushed down the panic, hoping Eli wouldn't notice.

Anders preceded them inside with the luggage while Eli took Aria's arm and led her toward the front door. A few shaky steps later, he stopped and studied her face, his excitement withering to concern. "What's wrong?"

"Nothing." She forced a smile—a lame attempt.

He placed an arm around her shoulder. "Please tell me."

Aria nodded toward the motorcycle without looking directly at it. "Adam—"

"Oh," he said quietly. "A motorcycle accident?"

She nodded.

"Oh, Ari." Eli wrapped his arms tightly around her. "I'm so sorry."

Three little words, those overused platitudes people say when someone dies. So trite, so rote, so insufficient. Honestly, she was sick of hearing them.

Aria pulled out of Eli's embrace and marched through the open front door. She paused on the threshold. One step down, an expanse of travertine blurred before her eyes.

Images flashed before her, like some macabre carousel she couldn't jump off of: Adam, life-lined by tubes and machines, wasting away day by day, month by month. A tiny hospital consult room, a box of tissues on the small round table. The doctor's prognosis: *Little hope*. Bea's silent tears. Justus's words: *Whatever you decide*.

Unable to breathe, she stumbled forward and grasped the railing of a sweeping staircase that curved up along the wall to a balcony and beamed ceilings. An even larger house to be left alone in.

She could turn around right now. Take the next flight home. Run away like the coward she was. There's a point where everyone breaks.

"Baby, I didn't—"

His voice behind her was like a shotgun blast. She whirled at the sound. "Eli, I'm sorry, but *that*?" Her voice broke as she pointed to the driveway. "That's a deal-breaker. I can't go down this road again."

He took her hands into his. "Hey, don't worry. I'll get rid of it."

Her heart thundered in her chest. "Really?"

His somber blue eyes held sympathy, understanding, and a willingness to do whatever it took to ease her terror. "Absolutely."

It can't be this easy. He was simply placating her. He'll keep it hidden until she's sucked in so far, and then, like Adam . . . Trembling all over, her body went limp. She would've fallen if Eli hadn't pulled her against his chest.

Breathe. Just breathe. You've been here before. You know what to do.

Eli's arms tightened around her, his breath warm against her ear. "It's gone. I promise." He pulled back and held up two fingers. "Scout's honor."

She exhaled, smiled, and held up three fingers. "It's three fingers."

He raised a palm to the ceiling. "Okay, so I was never a boy scout."

She wanted to laugh but couldn't—not yet. She sat on the bottom step and took a deep centering breath.

"How do you feel about Jeeps?"

His boyish expression brought forth a tiny chuckle.

"I'm sorry I overreacted."

He sat beside her on the step and faced her. "Don't be. I should have asked how it happened a long time ago. I just didn't want to be the one who made you think about it." He smiled ruefully.

She finally let slip a real smile.

He took her hands, suddenly earnest. "What was he like?"

She cringed. She didn't want to talk about Adam any more than she wanted to think about his accident. Yet a deep longing compelled her to share something special with this man who honestly cared about her.

"Adam was a good man and a good husband." She stared at Eli's hands, large, soft, and warm, their hold on hers, gentle and relaxed. "I always felt like the best version of myself when I was with him."

Eli's silence was deafening and she rushed to fill the space between them. Maybe if she got it all out now, she—they—could get past it.

"We had a great marriage. Our strengths and weaknesses dovetailed instead of clashed. When he struggled, I'd say, 'It's okay, babe. I've got this.' And he did the same for me. Doing life together made each of us better than we could have ever been alone. Like one plus one in binary makes ten."

"So that's love according to Aria Whitmore?" His easy smile made her feel warm all over.

She eyed him. "You betcha."

He laughed at her borrowing his turn of phrase—and her poor attempt at imitating his Minnesota accent. "But what was he like?"

She swallowed the lump in her throat. "He was a devoted father, a loving husband, thoughtful, sensitive, easygoing. Always put his family first. Well, almost always." She choked, blindsided by the one thing he'd done that hadn't put them first. Getting that blasted motorcycle.

"Adam was homespun and humble, close to his parents, proud of his roots. He knelt to pray and stood up for his neighbor. He was a Marine when we met, always bought American, did his civic duty, served as a deacon in the church. And he could build or fix anything. He loved adventure and the outdoors." She paused and took a deep breath, determined not to cry. "He loved the kids and me very much." She studied the room, certain that if she so much as glanced at Eli, she would totally fall apart.

"When did you know you were in love with him?"

"When he moved back home to help with the hardware store after his dad's heart attack. He gave up his dreams to help his parents when they needed him. He was an adventure guide. I didn't realize until two years later that he stuck around for me."

Suddenly, she didn't want to think about Adam anymore. He was loyal. He had loved her. But in the end, it wasn't enough. She took a breath and faced Eli's tender gaze. "Your turn. Tell me about your girlfriends."

His gaze boldly raked over her, as if forming comparisons, and his eyes lit with a burning hunger. She immediately regretted asking about them.

"My last real girlfriend I met in seventh grade. Her name was Natalie and we dated all through high school. But after graduation, I set out for Hollywood and she left for college, and that was the end of Nat-Eli."

"Nat-Eli—Cute."

"At the time, I thought I was in love with her, but she wanted no part of my acting dream. Last I heard, she was married and had a couple of kids. She found her dream with someone else."

"You haven't had a girlfriend since high school?"

"I've been pretty focused on my career."

"Come on."

He shrugged. "There are a few women in LA that I see occasionally, but nothing serious."

Aria raised a brow.

"Taylor, Kirsten, Makayla." His gaze caressed her face. "All very pretty, talented, accomplished. But none can hold a candle to you."

She didn't believe him for a minute.

"And they're just friends, really. Who happen to be female." He smiled that boyish half-grin and pulled her up into his arms. "I don't know what you've got that those other women don't, but . . . whew, it's powerful."

Was he always this charming, or was this a well-played scene he'd honed to perfection? She wanted to trust his words, his eyes, the way his heart beat for her beneath her palm.

"So am I your girlfriend?"

"If you want to be."

"I do."

"I'm falling in love with you, Aria Whitmore." He rested his forehead against hers—she loved the way he did that. A handful of heartbeats later he pulled back to catch her gaze. "I know you're not able to say it back to me. Not yet. But I think you feel something too."

A fragrant breeze wafted in from outdoors, birds tittered, and her pulse pounded in her ears. He was right—she couldn't say it. But she could show him. She wrapped her arms around his neck and pulled him down for a long, slow kiss.

When they parted, his smile left no doubt that he'd heard what her heart had wanted to say.

"Come with me." He took her hand and led her to the front room, a spacious living area done in deep reds, rich cherry woods, and creamy whites, with ample seating centered around a Monet-inspired tapestry rug. Anchored by an oversized rough-hewn table, the tasteful and eclectic mix of fine furnishings and well-worn rustic pieces blended exquisitely, while a grand piano dominated the far corner. He sat on the bench and opened the keyboard. "I was going to save this for later, but…" He patted the seat beside him and she joined him on the bench.

His long fingers danced over the ivories as he brought to life a song about starting over, moving on after a tragedy, resilience borne in faith. The lyrics of the song, which could only have been titled, "Tell Your Heart to Beat Again," spoke to her on a deeply personal level, emotional and raw, filling her heart the way Eli's rich baritone filled the cavernous room.

When Eli finished, he stared straight ahead, hands in his lap. Stillness owned the house. Was he afraid to look at her, expecting to see her crying? She wasn't. And she silently vowed to never cry in front of him again. Not over Adam at least. She'd get past her grief eventually, and she would be strong in the interim.

"That's a lot of black keys," she said.

He glanced at her and grinned.

"Did you write that song for me?"

"I wish. It's by Adam Gokeye."

She nestled against his shoulder and squeezed his hand. "I am trying, you know."

He rested his head against hers. "I know."

Several long, quiet moments ticked by as they drank in the serenity of the silent room. He caressed her hand, and she was awed by how soft and gentle and incredibly gifted his hands were, how tender and thrilling they'd felt as they'd trailed across her stomach beneath the willow.

He pulled back to look at her, his eyes shining with the light of love, life, and hope. She imagined kissing him, falling into his arms, getting carried up that grand staircase to his bedroom.

His hands returned to the keyboard, and as he began to play again, she blinked away the dangerous yearnings. The uplifting lyrics of Elton John's "Your Song" brought joy to her heart.

"I love how you make me smile even when I don't think I can," she said when the song ended. "I love that you're so understanding. I love that you want to be with me when I can't even—"

"Of course I do." He kissed her forehead, then jumped to his feet as if he'd forgotten something. Spinning to the center of the room, he held out his arms. His eyes roamed upward, shining with excitement. "Welcome to LA."

Aria stood and did a quick three-sixty, taking it all in. A stone fireplace she hadn't noticed earlier flanked the sitting area and anchored the room where they stood. Beamed ceilings, intricate wrought-iron railings, and antique built-ins made the stone-and-mortar interior reminiscent of a Tuscan villa. "It's gorgeous."

Eli pulled her toward the back of the house, where a huge expanse of arched windows and doors framed a stone patio with a fireplace at one end, a sprawling garden beyond, and a swimming pool off to one side. Past the bougainvillea-draped fence, distant mountains thrust from the horizon, washed gold by the early evening sunshine. The Gold Rush wasn't the only reason California was called The Golden State. Awed by the beauty rolled out before her like a red carpet, Aria stood captivated, lost in the splendor of Eli's private Eden.

Strong arms encircled her waist as he pulled her back against his chest. "In Beverly Hills you have two choices: a view of the valley with the ocean in the background or a view of the foothills and the San Gabriel Mountains. I prefer the mountains."

"Good choice." She whirled to gaze up at him.

He grinned. "Want a tour of the rest of the place?"

"There's more?" she teased.

Holding her hand, he led her up the broad staircase. "I bought it a few months before I left for Montreal, so I still have some empty spaces to furnish."

He opened the door to the first room on the right. Done in restful shades of cream and sage, like her own home, it smelled vaguely of fresh paint and new fabrics. A window seat ran the length of one wall and overlooked the back gardens.

Over a long dresser hung a landscape print that seemed oddly familiar. She moved closer. The Willows! Her jaw dropped as she stood transfixed by the scene, the branches pulled aside framing the view of the pond, a small corner of her red plaid picnic blanket visible in the foreground—a moment in time, captured for all eternity. He must have taken it when he'd walked away after she'd mistaken him for Adam.

She turned to see Eli's satisfied grin.

"Do you like it?" he asked like an insecure child aiming to please, unsure of his place in her world.

"Are you kidding? I love it." She squeezed his hand.

A vase of fresh baby pink roses and white daisies sat on the dresser. She bent to breathe in their subtle fragrance.

Her neighbor had given her a bouquet of daisies and sunflowers at their impromptu dinner party last week. Aria had never felt more alone than when she'd stood in that kitchen full of laughing happy couples, staring at the lovely sympathy bouquet. *"Why do awful things happen to good people?"* Sandy had asked.

Aria had said the first thing that popped into her mind. *"Maybe so someone like you would have a reason to give me flowers."*

Was it really that simple? Was tragedy merely a catalyst to get good people to extend compassion and kindness to others?

Aria turned back to Eli. "They're lovely. Thank you."

An almost scowl flashed across his face, but she couldn't help the sadness that seeped through the cracks of happiness he'd planted with his carefully chosen gifts.

He pulled her forward and opened the door to the adjoining room with a wink. "In case you need me in the night." .

The next room was cream and gray, with French doors that led to a balcony. Aria walked a few steps to look out over the well-tended gardens below, lush and bursting with color and life, glowing golden in the fading light. Stone paths wound in and out of sight, beckoning. On the patio below, a long teak table was set at one end with plates, linens, and wine glasses. A small candle sat in the center of the two place settings, ready to cast a romantic glow when daylight faded to dusk. Her insides danced. "You must have a gardener."

"I do. But I like to work out there too I am a farmer's son, after all."

Their eyes met and sheer happiness lit across his, as if her reaction to his elegant house and gardens was precisely what he'd aimed for.

On the way out, she paused in front of a long dresser, an array of framed photographs on one end. She picked up what appeared to be a family photo, a younger Eli at its center. "Your family?"

He nodded with a sentimental longing that seemed to suggest he might miss them more than he let on.

She had nothing like this from her childhood, only a single well-worn photo of herself, and Gibs. It was the only photograph she'd taken with her when she'd moved out at fifteen, the only one to survive the fire that had totally destroyed her childhood home. Despite that single treasured image, she had only a fading memory of her brother. Like a face under ice, he sank further with each passing year.

"You live in this great big house all alone," she said as they returned to the stairs. "You need a dog."

"Hardly. When I'm off filming, I can be gone for months. What would I do with a dog?"

"Good point. Is that also why you don't have a girlfriend?" When he didn't answer right away, she wondered if she'd been too direct.

"The reason I don't have a girlfriend is because I haven't found the right one." Halfway down the steps, he stopped and took her hands. "Until now."

He stared at her as if searching for a mirror of his sentiment in her eyes. Then he kissed her, backing her against the wall and leaving her breathless. When he pulled away, his lips curved into a small, satisfied smile. She couldn't help showing him exactly what he'd been hoping to see.

At the foot of the stairs they met a sturdy, middle-aged woman with a welcoming smile and hair as black as night heading toward the door with a handbag on her arm. Eli introduced Mrs. Rodriguez, his housekeeper.

"*Buenas tardes,*" Aria said.

"Ah! *Buenas tardes, señora.*" Mrs. Rodriguez beamed at Aria. She turned to Eli. "Good evening, Mr. Van Drie."

"Have a great weekend, Mrs. Rodriguez. Thanks for coming today."

"But of course." She gave Aria a huge smile. "*Mucho gusto.*"

"*Igualmente,*" Aria said. "*Adios.*"

When the door closed behind the housekeeper, Eli turned to Aria with a look of astonishment. "You speak Spanish too?"

She shrugged. "A little." She hadn't spoken it in years, not since high school. She rubbed the scar beneath her chin, refusing to let the memory ruin this perfect start to what was bound to be a weekend to remember.

21

———————

S tanding at the foot of the sweeping staircase in the foyer of his magnificent new home, with a captivating woman who spoke three languages, Eli felt suddenly small. Maybe he should have listened to his father and gotten a college education before pursuing his acting career. But if he had, he certainly wouldn't be here, standing in this spot, with Aria.

"You hungry?" Eli turned toward the kitchen and held out a hand to Aria.

"Starving." Aria glanced at her phone. "It's ten o'clock in Michigan."

"I had Mrs. Rodriguez make us dinner before she left." With a spring in his step, he led Aria to the kitchen and opened the fridge. "Chicken kabobs sound good?"

"Perfect." She gazed out the window above the sink to the patio and gardens beyond. "Does your whole house face the gardens?"

"Only the rooms I spend a lot of time in." He pulled out the plastic-wrapped platter and set it on the counter beside a bottle of merlot, then added two salads. He set a pair of long-handled tongs on the platter and slipped a wine opener into his back pocket.

They took everything out to the back patio, where the table his housekeeper had set awaited.

Eli pulled out a chair for Aria, then fired up the gas grill.

Returning to the table, he opened the wine, handed Aria a glass, and slid into the chair beside her. "A toast," he announced, capturing her gaze. "To new beginnings, getting swept away, and dancing like a dervish."

She chuckled as glass met glass with a soft *tink*. "How many times did you have to watch *Meet Joe Black* to remember that line?"

"Three." Actually it had been four, but three in the past few weeks. What else was he supposed to do with nothing but free time on his hands and thoughts of her filling his head?

She shook her head and laughed. "I'm going to grab a glass of water. Want one?"

He shot her a grin. "Shoor."

"You betcha, eh?"

While she disappeared into the house, he put the kabobs on the grill.

The moment the back door closed, Aria's phone vibrated on the table where she'd left it. Eli glanced at the Caller ID. Will. Eli swore under his breath.

When she returned, Eli nodded toward her phone. "You missed a call."

She set down the water glasses and picked up her phone. After a quick glance at Eli, her gaze flittered away.

Eli raised a brow.

She slipped into her seat. "I was going to tell you. It's no big deal, really."

Eli felt his whole body tense.

"My neighbors invited me over for cocktails last week and, as it often happens, drinks turned into dinner and . . . Well, apparently it was a setup. I didn't even realize it until afterward, when my friend Sandy asked me what I thought of him." She thrummed her fingers on the table.

Eli eyed her phone. "You added him to your contacts?"

"Sandy sent me his number. I added his name so I could choose not to answer if he called."

Eli swirled the wine in his glass. "What was he like?"

"Smart. He's an anesthesiologist. Sandy's husband's a surgeon. They work together."

"So he puts people to sleep for a living. Sounds like an exciting guy."

Aria did a little head tilt—cute. "He was nice."

"Did he ask you out?"

"No." She laughed lightly. "He did offer to walk me home, though. I pointed to my deck and said, 'Thanks but my door is right there.'"

Eli relaxed a bit.

"Even if he had asked me out, I would have said no." She gave him a reassuring smile. "My heart's already heading in a different direction."

With a relieved chuckle, Eli returned to the grill. "Good to hear." He couldn't ask for a better segue. "And just so you know, I'm not seeing anyone else either." Turning the kabobs, he added, "Although I did have lunch with Makayla earlier this week."

"Oh?"

He turned to gauge her reaction. No woeful despair, not even surprise, just a relaxed smile as her gaze swept over the gardens. Of course she'd be confident. She knew where she stood because he'd practically laid his heart at her feet.

"Nothing happened between us."

"I know."

He closed the lid of the grill and returned to the table. "You do?"

"Of course. You're a good guy."

She'd either been married for far too long or was naturally the trusting sort. "Do you really think so?"

She smiled as she studied him. "I wouldn't be here if I didn't."

He could be a good guy. For her, he could be whatever she needed him to be.

She jumped up. "And because you're such a good guy, you deserve an impressive *girlfriend*."

He smiled at her emphasis on girlfriend. "I do?"

"I have something to show you. Be right back!" She disappeared into the house.

He checked on the kabobs. His confession of lunch with Makayla had gone so much easier than he'd anticipated. He'd had a whole speech planned, and not a word was needed.

Aria burst from the house, clutching her satchel. She slipped into her chair, propped the bag against the leg of it, and pulled out a newspaper. Not a tabloid, thank goodness. He returned to the table.

Thrusting the paper into his hands, she pointed to a picture of a machine about the size of a large microwave.

He read the first paragraph of the news article beneath it, then glanced up. "This is the product launch you were working on?"

She nodded, barely containing her excitement, like a kid on Christmas morning contemplating which gift to unwrap first.

He searched the article but found no mention of the company she'd told him she worked for. "I thought that was for Hewitt."

"They had nothing to do with this. I got this deal on my own."

He shot her a puzzled look, then returned to the article. She'd apparently sold a patent for a recycling machine to EverClean, helping to cement its position as one of the largest US manufacturers of household appliances. Toward the end, the article called it a "multi-million-dollar deal." His mouth fell open as awestruck morphed into gobsmacked.

"Your big meeting was about a . . . a recycling machine?"

She beamed with a mixture of pride and humility. "We closed the deal last Tuesday."

"You sold a recycling machine." He wasn't tracking. He thought she worked for a company that made medical devices.

"Yes! And not just any recycling machine. This one turns junk mail into fresh household paper products: napkins, bath tissue, paper towels, printer paper. Did you know paper towels and toilet paper alone kill ninety-four thousand trees a day?"

Eli was speechless.

"I started working on this a couple of years ago—after the accident, you know, to keep myself busy. I've always been obsessed with recycling, minimizing waste, and all that. After Adam died, I lost my passion for it. But Justus used my plans and built our first prototype."

Of course. Her father-in-law, hardware store owner . . . and apparently, mechanical genius.

"Once we had a working machine, he made me file for the patents. We presented it at the International Consumer Electronics Show in Vegas last January, and the media described it as 'phenomenal.' We received several offers. EverClean's wasn't the highest, but it was the only American company."

He knew she was bright. Those wine cork rafts she'd made were ingenious. But a patented inventor? Incredible. "You own your own company?"

"Yeah, but I sold all of its assets: designs, patents, marketing plans, and the prototype to EverClean."

Eli scratched his temple. This new side of her was something he never could've imagined, not in a million years.

She tapped a fingertip on the table, as if patiently waiting for him to grasp it all before doling out more. "Want to see the website?"

He scooted closer while she opened her laptop and launched the site.

After rotating the computer to face him, she clicked on the image. It enlarged into a pop-up box, and the 3D rendering of the machine slowly rotated.

She teetered on the edge of her seat as if she might catapult right out of it at any second. "When my kids were little, we loved doing all kinds of crafts. When we got into paper-making, I realized that paper could be broken down into cellulous fibers and then mixed with water and reconnected to make new paper. And I started to wonder if maybe the whole process could be done at home on a larger scale. So I started experimenting. Once I had the process down, Justus built the machine that brought it to fruition."

His mind was reeling. "How do you build machines, start your own company, and run a website with a full-time job?"

"Justus is an electrical engineer. He built the machine. Jacks helped me create the website. As for starting my own company, I read some books and contacted the Small Business Development Center in Grand Rapids." A sadness seemed to settle in her eyes, but she quickly blinked it away.

Even in the midst of her grief, Aria had focused on doing something positive with her life.

Eli looked at the screen again. "Earth Everlasting, huh?"

"Do you like it?"

"It suits you."

"I thought so."

"Wow. And I thought you were pretty remarkable already."

"I don't know about that." She shrugged. "Like Einstein said, 'It's not that I'm so smart, it's just that I stay with the problem longer than most.'"

She had no idea how brilliant she was. Which made her even more special.

"I want one," he said. "How much do they cost?"

"I'm sure the first models will be expensive." She closed her laptop. "Any new technology initially has a high unit cost. But I'll get you one of the first ones off the line. No charge. I made a few high-ranking friends there."

Eli pulled the kabobs off the grill, set one on each of their plates, and positioned the platter on the table between them. Then he took her hand in his. "Ari, you could have any guy you wanted. Why are you here with me?"

"You invited me," she answered, incredulous, as if it were that simple.

"I'm sure I wasn't the first man to ask you out after your husband died." He tipped his head, waiting for a real answer.

"I like you, Eli, very much. You know that, right?"

He nodded, but he needed more. He was in love with her, and she'd given him little in the way of reciprocation. Beyond the way she kissed him and the look in her eyes, he had no idea how she felt.

She caressed each of his fingertips. They were clean and callus free, obviously not the hands of a man who did physical labor for a living, probably not at all like her husband's, a builder.

"You make me laugh." She held his gaze. "I like the way you look at me. The way I feel when I'm with you. And when you sing to me." She threaded her fingers through his.

He kissed her. She tasted of red wine and warmth and promise.

When they parted, Aria tucked away her computer and the newspaper and described her meeting with her boss and the VP and how good it felt to share her success with them.

"So what's next?" Eli asked. "You could quit your job if you wanted to, right?"

Like popped champagne, she looked about to bubble over. "I gave my two-week notice last Monday."

Just when he thought the night couldn't get any better. "So there's nothing stopping you from moving here."

Her excitement vanished. "Eli, my kids and my home are in Michigan. I'm not going to up and move across the country. Besides, if you get that new role, you could be off to who knows where."

"Italy."

She raised a brow.

"The new film I spoke to the director about—it'll be shot in Italy. Do you speak Italian?"

"No."

They were both quiet.

Aria broke the silence. "You have that condo in Falls Creek for the month, right? You could come back next weekend." She bit her lip as if she'd said something she hadn't intended to say, then raced on. "Monroe's graduation open house is next Saturday. And the rest of the weekend, I'd be all yours."

Eli grinned, her invitation a potent cocktail of relief and anticipation. "Sounds great."

As the sun went down, Eli lit the candle, and they took their time eating the meal and finishing the wine. He couldn't remember ever being so relaxed with a woman. He wasn't planning his next move. Wasn't wondering how the night would end. In fact, he wasn't thinking about sex at all. All he cared about was getting to know this astonishing woman.

"Want to watch a movie?" he asked.

"I'd rather stay here."

"I have a pretty extensive collection. What are some of your favorites?" He hoped she'd name at least one that he was in.

After naming a few popular films, she admitted she'd never seen *Brotherhood,* his first box-office hit. They carried in the dishes and then settled in together on the sofa in his media room.

Twenty minutes later she fell asleep on his shoulder. He didn't take it personally—it was three hours later in Michigan. He muted the movie and listened to her soft, steady breathing. He still couldn't believe she was actually here. Attractive and incredibly smart, she made the other women he'd dated seem like paper dolls, flat cardboard beneath a pretty façade.

Aria wasn't impressed by his fame either. In fact, she saw it as more of a negative. And she certainly didn't need his money, especially now. His looks and charm only took him so far with women like Aria, the intellectual sort.

Had she chosen him just because he was a "good guy?" What if he wasn't as good as she thought?

"Ari." He brushed aside a stray lock of her hair. She didn't stir. "I'm gonna win you over, you know. You're going to fall in love with me."

Reluctantly, he woke her, walked her upstairs, and kissed her good night at her bedroom.

~

ELI WOKE with a start and stared into the darkness. What had wakened him?

Aria's muted voice filtered through the closed door. His listened a moment. Was she on the phone? The name that had shown on her caller ID flashed again to his mind.

No, she wasn't talking. She was crying out.

He rushed to the adjoining door and opened it a crack, only to find her sleeping peacefully. Had he imagined it?

She rolled over. "Please," she whimpered, so softly he could barely hear the word, "Please, Adam, let me go."

Eli eased closer and knelt beside the bed. He longed to comfort her, and for a brief instant he considered curling up beside her to chase away her nightmares. But if she woke up and thought he was Adam again—he couldn't take that.

He watched her a while longer. When her muscles relaxed and her breathing steadied, he quietly retreated to his own cold bed.

22

On Saturday morning, Eli woke to find Aria already enjoying breakfast on the back patio. "Morning, beautiful." He kissed her cheek and slid into the seat beside her. Despite crying out in the night, she seemed well rested, barefaced and radiant in the soft morning light.

"This is amazing." She spread her arms to indicate the bowl of strawberries and the plate of bakery croissants in front of her. By the smell wafting from her mug, she'd also found the decaf hazelnut beans and the caramel-flavored creamer. Monroe had been only too happy to list a few of her mother's favorite things while Aria wake surfed the other weekend. And just like last night's dinner, Mrs. Rodriguez had nailed it.

"Glad you're enjoying it." He helped himself to a cup of coffee, took a sip, and eyed her over the rim. "Do you know you talk in your sleep?"

Her serenity evaporated like a puddle in sunshine. "What did I say?"

He kicked himself for making her uncomfortable. "Couldn't make it out."

She squinted at him. "For a talented actor, you're a horrible liar."

"You admit I'm a talented actor?" He winked and placed a croissant and some berries on his plate.

Eli's phone rang, the familiar train whistle—loud and long, like the woman on the other end. "That's my publicist. Excuse me." He snatched it up from the table and wandered into the yard with his coffee.

Penelope's voice was clipped and harried like she was rushing out the door. "The LA Boys & Girls Club invited you to host a fundraiser. I turned it down."

"What? Why?"

"Charity events are for people who can't get good publicity any other way, and you're above that."

"What if I want to do it?"

"Why on earth would you?"

"You know I hang out there a lot. Those kids mean the world to me, and there's no substitute for face-to-face communication."

"Gotta do better than that."

Eli gazed out over the gardens, lush and green and peaceful. Like his life, fresh with renewed growth and purpose. "I met someone and—"

Penelope swore.

"It's time to change my public image. I don't want to be Hollywood's proverbial bad boy anymore. I want people to see the real me." The man worthy of a woman like Aria Whitmore.

"Are you seriously ready to derail your career, throw away all of our hard work, just to impress your shiny little Midwest Sweetheart?" Penelope huffed. "Eli, darling, we're nearly there."

He spoke through gritted teeth. "Her name is Aria." Knowing anger would get him nowhere, he took a calming breath. "Look, I'm rolling with the new bodyguard. You owe me this one."

"Sorry, but—"

"Make it happen, P." He pressed End so hard his phone almost flew from his grip.

As Eli slipped back into his seat on the patio, his lingering disdain from the phone conversation vanished with Aria's inquisitive smile. "The LA Boys Club invited me to host a fundraiser. Penelope hates me doing charity events, always turns them down."

"Right. Wouldn't want to tarnish that Hollywood hellion thing you got going."

"I told her to book it anyway."

Aria's smile shone with pride . . . and something more. Admiration maybe? "Surfing this morning, right?"

He glanced at the time on his phone. "You betcha! If we go now, we'll catch some great waves. And we'll still have time to come back, change, grab a quick bite, and then go shopping."

"Or we could hang at the beach all day, or go hiking?"

"Penelope made dinner reservations for us at Catch tonight, and we're going hiking tomorrow." His publicist had also made certain the press would be at the renowned celebrity hot spot, but he kept that detail to himself.

"I brought a dress—"

"I'd love to buy you a new dress or two . . . or five." He raised a brow, questioning. Maybe in a new dress, she'd feel better about being photographed with him. He loved the limelight—the more media attention, the better. It meant he was getting closer to *making it*. He wanted Aria to love it too.

"Thank you, but I can buy my own clothes."

"There's also a party in Malibu Sunday night."

"I fly home Sunday."

Eli sat back in his chair and eyed her. How was he going to convince her to stay? He wanted her at that party with him.

"But we can still go shopping if you want. I'll be ready in five." She drained the last of her coffee and dashed inside.

Within minutes, Eli had his boards loaded into the jeep and, top down, they headed for the beach.

Aria was a quick learner, popping up and enjoying a nice long ride on her second attempt. A couple of rides later, she tumbled in the surf, scaring Eli half to death and scraping her hip on the bottom, despite the rash guard he'd given her to wear. She claimed she was fine and was adamant about heading back out, but Eli examined the scrape and reminded her the Pacific Ocean wasn't Haven Lake. "You don't go in the ocean when you're bleeding."

They returned to the house around noon, enjoyed a quick lunch, then slipped into the SUV for an afternoon of shopping.

Thanks to his sister, and his good friend Leigh Campbell, Eli knew precisely where to go. He had more fun than he could've imagined stretched out in a butter-soft white leather armchair in a private shopping lounge, sipping champagne while Aria paraded before him in her rather austere selections.

They narrowed the choices down to two dresses they both liked and he talked her into getting both. "Just in case," he said with a wink, hopeful she would change her mind about staying for the party Sunday night.

After the dress shopping, he pulled her into Tiffany's and despite her numerous objections, he convinced her to let him buy her an emerald necklace. Standing behind her while she lifted her hair, he fastened the pendant around her neck, peered over her shoulder at her reflection in the mirror and smiled. The emerald matched her eyes perfectly. "What do you think?"

Aria touched the dark-green jewel hanging delicately at her throat. "It's too much."

"It's not enough."

She eyed him in the mirror, her face beaming. "Thank you." She spun around and kissed him.

They strolled along the Walk of Fame and he showed her where his star was going to be just beyond the legendary Chinese Theater. Despite his sunglasses, several people recognized him, and Anders discreetly stepped in to clear a path for him to join Aria at the curb, where his black Escalade stood waiting. Eli had never been so gracefully extricated from a crowd of fans.

On the ride home, his phone vibrated with a text from his buddy Matt. Eventually, he was going to have to face Matt and his wife, but not today. He silenced it, tucked the phone back into his shirt pocket, and turned his attention back to Aria, who was fingering the necklace at her throat.

He was glad she'd let him buy it for her. Aria was by far the most self-sufficient woman he'd ever met. Though intrigued by Aria's autonomy as well as her beauty and intellect, he wasn't sure if all that independence was a good thing or not. Would she still need him once she got past her grief?

He'd have to find a way to make sure of it.

23

––––––––––

While Aria finished getting ready for dinner at Catch, Eli stood at the piano, plinking the keys, his center thrumming with anticipation for the evening ahead. On the drive to the restaurant, he'd tell her what to expect with the media attention. She'd undoubtedly want to avoid it, but hopefully he could talk her into seizing the moment with him. If she insisted, they could slip in the back door.

At the sound of heels clicking on tile, he glanced up. She entered the room looking like she'd walked right out of a dream.

The necklace he'd given her perfectly complemented the dress she'd bought—a simple forest-green tunic with a sheer trim peeking from beneath the short hem. Paired with a wide leather belt draped low over her hips and strappy honey-brown heels, the look was part Robin Hood, part fair maiden, and totally goddess.

"Wow," was all he could manage.

It wasn't the dress or the necklace that left him speechless. It was the sparkle in her eyes and the expectant way she peered at him, a gaze that instantly brought to mind whispers in the dark.

"Thank you." She set a small beaded handbag on the hall table and crossed the room to him. "You look pretty fantastic yourself."

Propped against the piano, he pulled her in by the belt to stand between his legs.

She winced. "The scrape," she said, repositioning the belt.

"Sorry." He moved his hands to her waist and brought her closer. She seemed stiff in his arms, tense. "Are you nervous?"

"Should I be?"

"Not at all." Might as well broach the subject of the media now. "Anders will drop us off right in front of the restaurant. There will be cameras, of course. But it's a short walk to the door."

Her brows shot up. "Cameras?"

He gave a slight shrug. "Hollywood rule number one: cameras are everywhere. Plus, it's one of the hottest restaurants in town. And it's Saturday night."

She straightened as though bracing for a challenge. "I was looking forward to a quiet dinner."

"It will be, as soon as we're inside. Just smile and flash those emerald eyes. The press won't know what hit 'em."

"And I'll be tomorrow's headlines. Again."

"That's not so bad, is it?"

She looked away. When her gaze returned, the sparkle was back. "No. I can deal with it."

"Great." He pressed his forehead against hers, wrapped his hands in her hair, and inhaled the scent of her, breathless and hungry at the same time. "How is it you always smell so delicious?"

"I was starving, so I raided your fridge." Her mouth curved into a smile. "You know, strawberries make little hearts when you cut them in half."

"You don't say." He kissed her long and deep. She tasted as good as she smelled.

Anders entered and cleared his throat. "Excuse me, sir. There's a gentleman at the gate, a Mr. Desmond. Says he's a friend of yours."

Matt! Eli checked his phone and read the text he'd ignored earlier.

Eli groaned. He hadn't seen Heather, Matt's wife, since waking up beside her months ago. His plans for a nice evening out with Aria were about to be blown sky high. "Let them in."

While Anders used the app on his phone to open the gate, Eli led Aria outside.

Stepping out of his Beamer, Matt appeared much thinner than Eli remembered. His sport coat hung loosely on his wiry frame, and his chin seemed even sharper.

"Hey, man, good to see you." Eli stretched out his hand.

Matt pulled him in for a man hug. "You got my text, right?"

"Not till a minute ago. We were just leaving. Penelope got us a rooftop table at Catch." Matt would know what that meant, the orchestration involved so Eli could be seen in public with Aria.

Heather emerged from the passenger seat, wearing a dress that matched the small red triangle tucked into Matt's breast pocket. "But we brought sushi."

In public, there was never any doubt those two were a couple. Behind the lights was another matter altogether. Matt's acceptance —even encouragement—of his wife's promiscuity was beyond Eli's comprehension.

"Aria, this is Matt Desmond and his wife, Heather."

Aria shook their hands. "Nice to meet you."

Simon and Leigh emerged from the back seat.

"Simon McGill, set designer extraordinaire," Eli continued. "And Leigh Campbell, from—"

"*Brotherhood*." Aria brightened as she shook Leigh's hand. "I just loved your character in that movie."

"Aw, you are so sweet!"

"Eli, it's been far too long." Heather air-kissed one cheek, then the other. A former model, she was smarter than most people gave her credit for, including herself, and she always dressed to impress. Tonight was no exception. In a curve-fitting Versace dress with a plunging neckline and tiny black buttons running like ants down the sleeves, her blonde hair pulled into a sleek ponytail, she could've been strutting the red carpet instead of standing in Eli's driveway.

"Howdy, Eli," Leigh chirped in her Alabama accent as she wrapped him in a hug. Leigh Campbell was petite and cute, a doe-eyed beauty with a tiny upturned nose. In blue jeans and a black top, with thick, dark curls tumbling loosely around the shoulders of a black leather jacket, Leigh dressed to blend in rather than get noticed.

"Welcome back, mate," Simon said with a friendly handshake, his voice as hearty as his ginger hair, ruddy cheeks, and glib sense of humor. Wearing a signature avant-garde tee with "Phenomenally Red" emblazoned across the chest stuffed into fashionably ragged blue jeans, a black leather vest, and shiny black ankle boots, every detail screamed artist. "How was the great white north?"

"Cold." *In more ways than one.* "It's good to be back." By the time Eli returned to Aria's side, Matt had convinced her that dinner at home with friends would be much more fun than going out to some overcrowded restaurant, and they were already heading inside.

While Eli was disappointed with the change of plans, he shouldn't have been surprised. Aria preferred simple pleasures, and she seemed enamored of his friends. Of course, this also got her out of having to face the media.

As Matt helped Eli with drinks in the game room, Simon opened the double doors to the terrace, and Aria led Leigh and Heather to the kitchen for plates and napkins.

The girls' voices floated in from the kitchen as they opened up to one another like poppies to sunlight. Aria complimented Leigh's dessert. Heather and Leigh admired Aria's necklace.

"Thank you. Eli bought it for me today. Does he do that often?"

"Buy women jewelry? Never," said Heather.

Matt nudged him. "She seems great." He sounded perturbed.

"She is."

Now Heather and Aria were talking about their kids.

Matt slapped the bar. "Any chance I could get a drink?"

He didn't intend to ignore Matt, but Eli really wanted to listen to

Aria's conversation. He poured a glass of bourbon, neat, pushed it across to Matt, then perused the wine options.

When Eli pulled out a bottle of Napa Valley merlot, Matt raised his glass. "Am I drinking alone here?"

"I'm having wine."

Matt rolled his eyes. "You're in love with her."

Eli ignored Matt's derisive tone and gave him a wry smile. "One look at her and my whole world spun on every axis."

"Does she feel the same?"

Eli winced, the stab of pain still as fresh as the afternoon she'd mistaken him for her husband.

"Nevermind." Matt laughed and slapped a palm on the bar. "You're wearin' it on your sleeve, bro," Matt said with a guffaw.

"I should've known better than to tell you anything." Eli turned to grab the wine glasses.

"I'm sorry. But you have to admit, it's ironic. Ever since I've known you, women have been throwing themselves at your feet, and now you fall in love with one you actually have to work for? You've never had to fight for a girl in your life." He took a sip of his bourbon then stared longingly at the contents of the glass. "Do you think that's why you're in love with her?"

"No." Though, if he was honest with himself, Eli had considered that.

"Careful, dude," Matt said. "Falling so hard that fast always leaves scars."

Eli hadn't felt anything for so long—since Natalie—he was ready to feel something, anything, scars be damned. "Oh, and I quit smoking, so if you need a cigarette, please go to the side yard." Eli set three wine glasses on the bar and started mixing a martini for Heather.

Matt stared slack-jawed. "What has that girl done to you?"

"My decisions have nothing to do with Aria. I'm just tired of booze and cigarettes."

"Right," Matt said, his voice dripping sarcasm.

"Believe what you want." Eli couldn't care less. He'd wanted to quit for a long time. Being with Aria made it easy.

"And you're already buying her jewelry?"

He set the martini in front of Matt and spread his hands on the bar. "So?"

Matt raised his brows. "Don't get me wrong. It's about time you started spending some of your money. But come on. You and I both can spot those kind of women."

"She's not like that."

Eli pulled a beer from the fridge for Simon. He tucked a wine opener into his back pocket and the bottle of wine under his arm. He picked up the wine glasses in one hand and the beer in the other. "Grab that," he said, nodding toward the martini.

As they crossed the patio, Aria's voice was easier to make out through the kitchen doors. "Don't get me wrong. Being independent is good. But time goes by so fast, you know? I miss the cuddles, the story times, the way my kids used to need me."

Eli's gut warmed, like an internal smile. Maybe Aria did want more children.

Heather agreed, probably just being polite. Her kids were toddlers. She couldn't miss things she was still smack dab in the middle of.

"I suppose I should be excited as they set their feet on the path my husband and I have led them to. They're making it their own, in ways I never imagined. But I just miss them, so much." Aria broke off when she noticed Eli in the doorway. She smiled at him, and her nostalgia vanished.

Dinner was a casual affair with his friends seated around the patio table, Matt on his left and Aria on his right. With her favorite music app station softly streaming from the outdoor speakers, Aria closed her eyes and bowed her head to say her little silent prayer. Matt eyed her with a smirk. Eli kicked him under the table, hoping his friend wouldn't make a big deal of it.

His friends all seemed to be drawn to Aria, and she came alive with them, thoroughly immersed in the relaxed camaraderie.

When Matt asked her what she did for a living, she described her job at Hewitt but didn't mention her recent success with the recycling machine.

As darkness descended, the conversation turned to Eli and the boys club downtown where he played basketball and mentored inner-city kids. Aria's eyes gleamed with interest as he described the club's program, the boys he hung out with there, and the reason he was so adamant earlier about accepting the invitation to their fundraiser.

Matt raised his glass in mock salute. "To Eli, a great champion of impoverished youth."

"Hear, hear," Simon lauded with sincerity, and the rest followed suit, raising their glasses to Eli.

A mild political disagreement arose between Simon and Matt, centered on the role of government in funding social programs. Simon, an outspoken conservative, admired Eli's work and thought the boys club was a worthwhile cause, but he felt strongly about overspending on costly programs that had driven California into bankruptcy and would soon, in his mind, break the federal government as well, potentially even threaten the democratic ideals on which the country was founded.

Matt, a die-hard liberal, argued there were millions of Americans living in poverty, starving and homeless, and it was everyone's moral obligation to help the needy . . . and taxes were the perfect means to do so.

Aria remained silent throughout the debate. While Eli wondered what her views were, he accepted that she might not feel comfortable sharing them with his friends.

"Where does the funding for the boys club come from?" Simon asked Eli.

"Private donations mainly. Some from churches, but mostly from people in the movie business."

"See, mate?" Simon turned to Matt. "If you give people half a chance, they'll help the downtrodden voluntarily. Like Eli's doing."

"I support a lot of great causes too," Leigh chimed in. "But I agree, we have way too many wasteful programs. They might feed the hungry for a while, but people are depending on handouts as a way of life. And the problems are only getting worse, especially in cities like LA."

Matt looked at Aria. "You're awfully quiet, Michigan. What do you think?"

Aria glanced furtively around the table. "Personally . . . I think if you make poverty easy, there will be more of it."

A moment of silence hung in the air.

"I like that," Eli said, impressed.

"It's a Ben Franklin quote." Aria set down her chopsticks. "Like Leigh, I'm all about the betterment of the underprivileged. But it's not the job of government to dole out tax dollars so freely."

"Aye, the crux of conservatism," Simon added.

Aria nodded. "For too long, our social programs, especially welfare, have encouraged single women to have children out of wedlock and—"

"That's not true." Matt shook his head emphatically.

"The more children they have, the bigger the handout. And if they get married, the benefits decrease. So it perpetuates single-parent homes, leaving more children being raised without a father. And honestly, I resent having my tax dollars support immoral social programs. I don't want my hard-earned money funding someone else's bad behavior."

Matt huffed. "But it's the role of government to protect and care for its citizens."

"Protect, yes. Care for, no. That's not government. That's charity."

"What about the people who really need help?"

"There will always be a segment of society that can't function by themselves. And I'm all about helping the helpless. The clueless—not so much."

"Coo-ee!" Simon slapped the table. "Couldn'a said it better myself!"

Matt held up a hand. "What if some of the people who receive assistance get back on their feet and become a contributing part of society again? I mean, miracles can happen, right?"

Aria looked at him thoughtfully, a deep sadness settling over her. "Rarely. I believe most people want to work, to be self-sufficient. But when poverty is all around you, when it's all you know and all you've ever known, the way out is either invisible or illegal."

She sounded like she knew what she was talking about.

Aria shot Eli a tentative smile then turned back to the others. "Eli is inspiring those boys at the club to say no to gangs and drugs, to stay in school and make something of themselves. He's showing them what a good life looks like. It's no longer invisible. Those are the miracles the poor need. And only people can make them happen, not government."

Eli hadn't thought about making miracles out on the basketball courts. But now that he'd heard her say it, he realized it was exactly the reason he spent so much time there. He wanted to make a difference. "You should come with me sometime."

Aria took a deep breath.

Like a wolf sighting wounded prey, Matt picked up on her uncertainty. "I'm sure that's the last thing she wants to do, Eli. She's probably afraid of poor people."

Aria glared at Matt. "I'm not afraid of the poor. Only the ignorant."

Silence settled on the table as Matt tossed back the last of his bourbon.

Aria used her chopsticks to flick roe off a piece of sushi on her plate. "Let me guess. You had a privileged childhood: big house, private school, vacation home?"

"Minibike and a beach house," Matt admitted.

"Usually the people who grew up with plenty think everyone should share in the burden of caring for the poor, while the people who grew up in poverty and worked hard to get out of it think everyone else can and should do the same." Aria picked up her wine glass and smiled at Matt over the rim as she took a sip.

"So which are you, a *have* or a *have-not*?"

Aria set down her glass. "Oh, I was definitely a have-not. I grew up in poverty, knew it well. My family lived in a small house in one of the worst parts of Detroit with no furnace for an entire winter. I shared a twin bed with my brother, and at night we piled on all the blankets we owned and snuggled together to stay warm. At sixteen, I was sleeping in a storage room over a pool hall, and by God's grace and Pell Grants, here I am tonight, in this magnificent home, with you fine people."

Matt shot Eli a side-eye, as though this new tidbit of information confirmed his earlier suspicions about *those kind of women.*

"How could a house in Michigan not have a furnace?" Simon asked.

"Someone stole it." Aria swallowed hard.

No wonder she'd become so independent and courageous. And she didn't like talking about her childhood. Eli felt proud of her for overcoming so much. And her recent success. If his friends only knew.

"Wait." Matt narrowed his gaze at Aria. "You took government assistance?"

"Grants for higher education are a hand *up*, not a hand*out*," Aria threw back.

Simon raised his glass. "To opportunity!"

Everyone joined in the toast, and the tension slunk from the table like an unwanted dinner guest.

"Aria has a spectacular lakefront home in Michigan," Eli said, hoping to dispel his friend's concerns about her.

"Oh?" Matt sneered at Aria. "You must have married well."

Eli wanted to smack him but settled for another swift kick under the table.

Aria stared at Matt, her lips set in a thin line.

"You're very polished and smart for not being a silver-spoon kid." Matt grinned, as though his feeble attempt at flattery would soften the blow of his sexist comment. He nabbed the last piece of sushi from the platter in the center of the table and stuffed it into his mouth.

Aria stood. "Who wants dessert?"

"I'll get the plates," Eli offered.

"I'm sure we can find them," Leigh said, standing with Aria.

The two women disappeared into the house, and Eli reeled on Matt. "What is your problem, man?"

Matt's gaze focused on the doorway. "She's hiding something."

"Her husband died recently. If she's hiding anything, it's her grief."

Matt rolled his eyes and relaxed back in his seat. "Right."

"Don't mess this up for me, eh?"

"Yeah, be nice." Heather swatted her husband's arm, then turned to Eli. "I think she's great."

"I like her too," Simon added.

Aria and Leigh returned with the bananas Foster. While Leigh prepared to put on her flaming show, adding a generous drizzle of dark rum to each ramekin, Aria returned to her seat.

"So, God's grace," Matt said, eyeing Aria, "let your husband die."

"Matt!" Leigh slapped the table so hard the spoons clattered.

Eli bounded to his feet. "That's enough!"

Heather hid her face behind her hand. Simon picked at the label of his beer bottle.

"Yes, well—" Aria rested her chin on her knuckles and faced Matt, not looking a bit ruffled—"To everything a purpose."

No one spoke as they all stared at her.

Aria reached for Eli's hand. "It's okay."

Eli returned to his seat with a warning glare directed at his friend.

Aria panned the table then scrunched up her nose. "Everyone's got a sad story," she said matter-of factly. "I prefer not to dwell on my own."

"Don't curse the darkness. Light your own little candle, right?" Leigh set the dessert dishes aflame, startling everyone.

When the flames died away, Leigh topped each dish with a scoop of ice cream and Aria passed them out. As she handed one to

Matt, she tipped it slightly at the last minute, so his thumb jabbed into the ice cream. "Oops! Sorry," she said with a giggle.

Eli laughed so hard tears came to his eyes.

SO MUCH FOR a quiet evening at home. Aria steeled herself for round two as she carried a beer and a bourbon to the media room for Simon and Matt. Second-guessing her decision to forego dinner at Catch for the political debate with Eli's friend Matt, Aria could only surmise that she was right where she was supposed to be. Maybe Matt needed to hear her story as much as she needed Eli to hear it. Because sometimes a person doesn't understand the other side of things until it's articulated clearly and passionately. She hoped she'd given her views justice. It was the most she'd shared about her past so far. And yet Eli still looked at her like she was his own personal angel.

Leigh was adorable, as bright and sweet as her sunny disposition. She liked Simon too, friendly and outspoken but not combative, like Matt had been. Heather was nice but painfully passive. And there was something off about the way Eli seemed to pull into himself around Matt and Heather, a friction, like magnets being forced together at opposing ends.

The night was young, with plenty of time to win Matt over. Aria found a smile and entered the room. Matt was in mid-sentence.

"... couldn't stand another minute of Saint Brainiac's music. Eli can't possibly—" Matt stopped short when Simon nodded toward the entry where Aria stood.

With Simon's touch of the remote, the blare of the hockey game on the big-screen TV filled the silence.

Simon's cheeks flushed scarlet as he accepted the beer from her. "Thanks."

Aria forced a smile as she crossed the room to Matt. Eli had asked her to put on her personal playlist during dinner. He liked her selection of songs, mostly Christian rock with some country and popular new artists mixed in. She couldn't care less if Matt liked it. "Did you know Eli was in a praise band in high school?"

A sardonic grin streaked across Matt's features like a skid mark. "Is that what he told you?"

Aria didn't bother to hide her annoyance. She'd had more than enough of Matt Desmond and his blatant condescension for one night. Mustering restraint, she held out the bourbon. As Matt took it, she snatched his phone from his shirt pocket and backed away.

"Let's see what Cali-boy listens to." She hit Play on his music app and recognized the song instantly, having deleted it from her son's music cache years ago. "Oh, yeah. I'm down with this," she said, borrowing her kids' vernacular. "Let's kick to some cop-killing, f-bombs, and girlfriend beating, 'cause that's *sooo* dope."

Matt's gaze darted behind her. Aria whirled to see Eli standing in the doorway. Heather stood beside him, mouth agape.

Aria tossed Matt's phone on the couch and headed for the door.

Eli stopped her as she passed. "Hey."

"It's all good. But I'm gonna—*tag out for a few minutes*—check in with Monroe. I'll be back." She forced a reassuring smile, but inside she wanted to scream. So what if Matt didn't like her politics or her music! *Who cares?* Maybe Eli? Apparently Matt was a good friend, although Aria couldn't imagine why.

But after Eli's lame silence at dinner, Aria had a niggling feeling, if came down to her or Matt, she'd be the one knocked out.

24

———————

The cool night air felt like blessed relief as Aria wandered the gardens in Eli's backyard, determined to shove all thoughts of his smarmy friend Matt to a dark corner of her mind.

Missing Monroe, she tapped and swiped her phone, searching for some assurance her daughter was safe and having a good time at her open houses. Ignoring the notification of another missed call from her boss—the second-to-last person she wanted to think about—she found a picture her daughter had posted on Instagram, a cute shot of a half dozen kids on a pontoon, Monroe in the center. Smiling, Aria tapped the heart icon.

Her boss had called three times since she left the office on Friday. What was so Important it couldn't wait until Monday?

She fired off a text.

Aria: What's up?

Within seconds her phone vibrated.

Glen: Call me.

Aria: It's the weekend.

Glen: I know. I need a favor.

She tapped her foot while the cursor blinked. The San Diego conference was next week, and Glen was scheduled to present. This had to be about that.

She prompted him with a question mark.

Glen: I can't make it to the conf next week. You'll need to present.

The man was astoundingly predictable in his unconscionable irresponsibility.

Aria: Can't. Already canceled my registration.

Glen: I un-canceled it. Tried to catch you before you left yesterday.

Aria seethed. It didn't make sense to fly home for a day and then come right back for the conference on Tuesday. But if she didn't, she wouldn't be there for Monroe when she got home Sunday night. She should say no. She was sick and tired of being where the buck stopped.

Aria: It'll cost you.

Glen: Name it.

Aria grinned, relishing the upper hand. More than anything she wanted to be done—with the job, with the travel, with him and his incessant, inconsiderate, infernal demands.

An idea struck her and she typed before she could reason herself out of it.

Aria: Promote Cadence to replace me.

Her friend would be perfect for the job, would enjoy the travel, and she'd hit the ground running. Aria wouldn't have to interview candidates or train someone new. It would be a win-win-win.

Glen: Done.

Aria felt giddy with freedom.

Aria: Great. Thanks.

Glen: Whatever.

What a childish way to end a conversation. At least she'd be done in a week, and the presentation was no big deal. She'd practically written it for him anyway.

She gazed around the moonlit yard. The cool night air, fragrant with jasmine, radiated calm. Her tension vanished like stars with the dawn.

She wandered to the magnolia, perched on the edge of the chaise, and fired off a text to Cadence.

Aria: You up?

Cadence: I am now.

Aria slipped off her strappy heels, put her feet up, and pressed Call.

"Wassup, girlfriend?" Cadence answered sleepily.

Aria got right to the point. "I gave Glen my resignation last week."

"You sold your recycling machine!"

"I did. And tonight Glen called, needing a huge favor, and I managed to take advantage of the situation. My condition for helping him was that he promote you to replace me. He agreed."

"He didn't!"

"What? You don't want it?"

"I don't *not* want it. But yours are some seriously huge high heels to fill."

"Aw, Cadie, you'll be great."

"Thank you. For always encouraging me, always thinking of me."

"Of course. What are friends for?"

"When do I start?"

"Friday's my last day." Aria couldn't mask the pure glee in her voice. "But don't worry. I'll be back in the office on Wednesday and we'll have three days to go over everything. I just wanted to let you know because, well, you know Glen. He may not wait until Monday."

Cadence's phone dinged and she giggled. "He just texted me to call him in the morning."

So predictable. "Congratulations, Cadence."

"Thanks, Aria. Now, get off the phone and go be with your guy. And I want to hear all about your weekend when you get back."

Aria ended the call, bounced up from the chaise, and did a little happy dance in the moonlight like a madwoman.

When she'd finished, she retrieved her heels, and with the straps dangling from her fingers, she turned toward the house. Her insides slumped. Illuminated behind the wide glass doors, Eli and his friends sat in front of the television, watching the hockey game. They looked like a beer commercial: incredibly attractive people all laughing and cajoling. She longed to be part of a close-knit circle like that—sans Matt, of course.

Not ready to reenter the fray, Aria eyed the empty game room, its soft light beckoning like a safe haven, its arched doors open wide.

As Aria entered, the muted sounds of the hockey game floated in. She dropped her shoes on the floor at the end of the bar, poured herself a glass of wine and admired the room. Beyond the long oak-and-brass bar, which took up most of one wall, a full-size pool table dominated the room. Two pinball machines and an OutRun 2 arcade game loomed silent and dark from the wall opposite the bar, like a carnival after hours, entertainment at the flick of a switch. Drawn to the pool table, Aria brushed her fingertips across the crimson baize top, then rapped it with a knuckle. Slate, not wood, of course—high-end like everything in Eli's lovely home.

Memories of learning the game all those years ago seemed as vivid as yesterday. The gangly silver-eyed boy who'd taught her to play. The little room above the pool hall where she'd lived for almost a year. She closed her eyes and could almost hear the clack of the balls drifting up through the floorboards to lull her to sleep as she lay on the twin mattress where she'd first—

Her eyes flashed open. No, she couldn't go there. She could never go back there.

She racked the balls, selected a stick from the stand against the wall, and chalked up. After a strong break, she chose her next shot, feeling a somber reverie as the ball glided whisper soft into its intended pocket.

She made an easy bank shot. Someone once told her she had a

head for angles. She wasn't sure about that, but she could picture the shots. And if you can picture something, you can make it happen. Someone once told her that too.

She lined up a two-cushion draw shot. The trick would be leaving the cue ball in place for the next shot. She made the bank, and the cue ball curved back to the center as footsteps echoed from the hall.

Matt came through the doorway. "Nice shot." He stood too close, empty glass in hand.

"Thanks." She moved away, eyeing the table from the opposite end.

"Let's play." He selected a stick from the wall.

Sure. Underestimate me. This'll be fun. She hadn't played in years, but once upon a time, she'd been pretty good. And he'd be fun to beat. But this wasn't how she wanted to spend her evening. In fact, she had no intention of staying in the same room with Matt Desmond any longer than necessary.

"No, thanks." Aria set her stick on the table. "I'm not in the mood for another jousting match."

He snickered like a mustache-twirling villain. "Is that what we did at dinner?"

"Pretty much." She retrieved her phone from the edge of the table and eyed her shoes at the end of the bar behind Matt. Deciding to leave them, she headed for the door.

"Eli's really got a thing for you."

She turned back to him. "I kind of have a thing for him too."

Matt sauntered behind the bar and splashed a generous dose of bourbon into his glass. "A lot of women do."

She thought of several responses to that, none of which deserved to be spoken. "Are you happy for him? For us?"

"Of course." Fresh drink in hand, he skirted the bar and propped himself against the front of it on his elbows. His stance said relaxed and nonchalant, but from the tripwire-tight set of his jaw, there was a caveat coming. "But you know, he's been with both of the other women here tonight."

Aria did her best to remain impassive. He was goading her, like some ADD adolescent prodding for a jolt of excitement.

He swirled his drink and returned her stare, his gaze boldly raking over her body as though her dress were invisible. "And if you're into that sort of thing, I'm sure my wife would agree." He sauntered forward, daring in his eyes, and ran a fingertip down her bare arm.

Aria made a concerted effort not to shudder. "Don't touch me."

He grabbed her arm, his grip rough, and sneered. "Come on, it'll be fun."

"You're hurting me. Eli would never—"

He pulled her close, his breath reeking of bourbon. "Oh, he would. He has. You think you're the first? You're just another one of his street projects, one more lowlife he thinks he can save to make himself feel better about his self-indulgent lifestyle."

A shiver of revulsion ran down Aria's spine. She threw up her arm, breaking free. Her phone flew out of her hand, smacked her forehead, and made a loud *crack* as it hit the floor. She faced Matt in a ready stance, left foot forward, elbows tucked tight to her chest, fists covering her face.

A gasp came from the doorway.

Before Aria could even glance sideways, Matt grabbed for her. She blocked first one arm, then the other, then slammed him in the nose with the heel of her palm. His hands flew to his face as he stumbled backward.

"Matt!" Leigh's voice.

Matt gaped at his blood-soaked hands. His face crimson with rage, he lunged for Aria like an angry bull.

Aria front kicked him square in the chest, sending him crashing into the bar, where he slumped to the floor amid a jumble of overturned stools. Blood oozed from his nose and dripped from his chin, spreading like an inky stain on his fancy white dress shirt.

Heart racing, body shaking all over, Aria stared incredulous at the unconscious form crumpled like a rag doll across the room. A gentle touch on her shoulder made her flinch.

"You all right?" Leigh's voice was soft, comforting.

Aria nodded, barely breathing.

Eli rushed in, his gaze darting between Aria, Leigh, and Matt. "What the—?" He dashed to Aria and gripped her shoulders while his gaze raked the length of her. "You're shaking. Are you—"

"I'm fine." Aria said, stepping out of his grasp.

"He totally deserved it," Leigh said, surprisingly calm.

Eli rushed to the bar, tossed aside chairs, knelt beside Matt, and turned back to Aria, "He was coming in here to apologize."

"Well, I think he forgot that part," Aria snapped back.

Eli recoiled, as if shocked she would respond in the same angry tone he'd used.

Aria lowered her voice. "He's a weasel, Eli, and believe me, that man is not your friend."

Eli's jaw dropped.

She wanted him to comfort her, to make sure *she* was all right. Instead, he turned to Simon, who now knelt beside Matt, holding a bar towel to his bloody face. Matt's head lolled on his shoulders as he slowly came to.

"He'll be all right," Simon said. "I'll get the poor bugger home."

Heather appeared in the doorway. When she saw Matt, she hurried to her husband's side, then stared accusingly up at Aria.

"I'm sorry. I didn't mean to . . . but he . . ." Aria didn't know what else to say, to Eli, to Matt's wife. But it didn't matter because no one was listening. And aside from Leigh, who still stood at her side, no one cared. She wanted to scream *He attacked me. What was I supposed to do?*

Aria snatched up her phone from the floor and bolted for the open door. Between the game room and the kitchen, she felt so light-headed she had to rest against the wall to catch a breath. A sharp pain throbbed above her left eye, where the phone had hit her. She pressed a fingertip to her brow and winced.

In the kitchen, she wrapped some ice cubes in a towel and held it in place. Then she trudged up the grand stairway to her room, where she slammed the door, dropped her cracked phone on the nightstand and plopped down on the bed.

It took several deep breaths before she stopped shaking. Anxious to see the damage to her brow, she moved to the dressing table, lowered the makeshift ice pack, and studied her reflection. No broken skin, only a puffy redness—and a scowling woman.

She'd felt so good earlier, so confident and pretty. And the way Eli's face lit up when she walked into the front room confirmed it. How could she have messed things up so badly when all she wanted was to make a good impression with his friends?

No! She did nothing wrong. It wasn't her fault. Just like what happened with Cueball wasn't . . .

A soft knock on the door interrupted Aria's pity party, followed by Leigh's friendly "Hey."

"Come in."

"Oh, my God!" Leigh peered at Aria's temple. "Did he hit you?"

"I'm all right." Aria leaned an elbow on the dressing table and replaced the ice pack.

Leigh stood behind her and gazed at Aria's reflection. "It's not your fault, honey. Matt treats all women that way. It's like he has to feel superior or something."

"Why would Eli be friends with a guy like that?"

Leigh shrugged. "He's got connections. I've landed at least three roles because of him or people he's introduced me to. When Matt got the role of Heavy in *Brotherhood*, he insisted on Eli being his costar."

Aria tried to manage a smile. "He didn't even ask—"

"I told Eli what happened. He'll see it too when he watches the video later." She placed a reassuring hand on Aria's shoulder. "Anyway, Eli asked me to check on you while he and Simon get Matt into the car."

Aria studied Leigh's reflection in the mirror. "Thank you, Leigh. You're a good friend."

She smiled. "Thanks, hon. So are you." Leigh sat on the edge of the bed.

Aria turned to face her. "Do you ever feel like being pretty is more of a liability than a benefit? Like you have to constantly prove to everyone you have a brain?"

"Yeah, sometimes. People think just because you're pretty, life's a Sunday stroll." Leigh stood. "I should get out of here. I'm sure Eli'll be up soon to check on you."

Aria joined her. "I'm sorry I ruined the evening."

"Are you kidding? You're my hero."

Aria wanted to laugh but the best she could manage was a small smile.

"I'm glad you're okay," Leigh said, closing the door behind her.

Aria turned back to the mirror. The night had been a disaster, as bad as or worse than when she'd mistaken Eli for Adam. How could she have let things get so out of hand? Hopefully Matt wasn't seriously injured. She shouldn't have lost her temper. But his vile words, the reek of his bourbon-soaked breath in her face, the way he'd pulled at her . . . reminded her too much of Cueball. She pushed the nightmare away.

Returning from the bathroom, she found Eli standing beside the bed. Before either of them could say a word, her phone vibrated on the nightstand. Their heads turned in unison.

"Go ahead," Eli said, nodding toward the phone.

Aria picked it up, relieved it still worked. There were three notifications: another missed call from her boss and texts from Jacks and Justus. Not ready to deal with Eli, she checked her son's message and smiled at the wake surfing video he'd sent. The text from Justus was simple:

Justus: Not keeping the money.

Stubborn old coot.

She took a deep breath and faced Eli. He sat on the bed, bent forward, elbows on knees, his shoulders heavy. "I'm so sorry. I'm sorry I let my friends intrude on our evening. I'm sorry Matt was such a jerk. Most of all, I'm sorry I got angry with you. I've never seen him get physical like that."

She returned the phone to the nightstand. "How is he?"

"He'll have a shiner, probably two. You may have broken his nose."

"I didn't mean to hurt him." She eased onto the bed beside him and noticed her shoes neatly propped on the carpet beside the dressing table.

"I know."

An uncomfortable silence filled the space between them.

"Disappointed you didn't get to rescue me?"

He made a half-hearted attempt at a lopsided grin. "The hero always gets the girl."

"You've already got the girl."

He pressed his forehead to hers, and she winced. He withdrew, brushed her hair aside, and eyed the bump on her brow with a scowl. "Did he hurt you?"

"Actually, I did that to myself." Aria rubbed her bicep, where Matt had grabbed her. It was already turning an ugly purple-green.

Eli moved her hand aside and inspected her arm, then caressed it with his fingertips. "Leigh says you're an inspiration."

"Did you two ever date?"

"No. We're just friends. We were in the same movie once. We've gone to a few parties together, when neither of us feels like finding a date. But I've never *been* with her, if that's what you're asking."

She nodded, relieved, then glanced in the mirror and cringed. Her eye had grown redder and puffier.

He followed her gaze. "Makes you look tough. And goes well with your beach scrape."

"Just the look I was going for."

He shot her a sympathetic smile.

She lowered her gaze. "You know, I'm not as tough as you might think I am."

With a finger beneath her chin, he lifted her face to him. Admiration twinkled in his smile. "You may not be tough, but you are strong." He stroked his knuckles along her cheek. "To get through everything you've experienced and still be able to smile and laugh? That takes incredible strength." He drew her into his arms.

She pressed her cheek against his heart. He fit her perfectly.

And she liked the way he saw her.

25

S leep eluded Eli, his mind flooding with thoughts of Aria as he lay in bed, painfully conscious of her presence in the adjoining room. Images of the sad young widow swirled into the laughing beauty, fragile and grieving one minute, strong and bold the next.

Eli grabbed his phone and swiped through the photos he'd taken of her, each one a frozen moment in time, a captured emotion as varied and unpredictable as the woman herself. One second he pictured her laughing in the sunshine on the beach, the next quivering like a frightened child. The warrior he'd come to know definitely wasn't invincible.

Giving up on even trying to rest, Eli stole to the door between their rooms, eased it open, and peered through the crack. Kneeling beside the bed, her back to him, Aria rested her head on clasped hands.

He shouldn't intrude, but he couldn't tear himself away.

Finally, she raised her head toward the dim moonlight streaming in through the windows. In the dressing table mirror, he caught a tear slide down her cheek, reminding him of the first time he saw her in the airport. Now he knew the reason for her sorrow. A fist tightened around his heart. He longed to go to her, hold her, comfort her. But he didn't have the power to take away her pain.

Reluctantly, he slipped back to his room.

Some time later, he was awakened by a sound that caused him to bolt upright. Aria's muffled whimpers carried to his ears like the cries of a wild animal caught in a trap—desperate, mournful, resigned.

He threw off the covers and rushed to her room.

Lying on her side, her back to him, she hugged the pillow to her chest as though it were a life preserver. She wore the shirt he'd had on earlier. "No . . . no . . ."

He sat on the edge of the bed and placed a hand on her shoulder. "Ari," he murmured.

"Don't go . . . Please." She sobbed with a ragged breath.

He stroked her hair, pushing aside the tousled mass covering her face. "Shh. It's okay."

Her breathing calmed. He sat there for several minutes, his heart in his throat. *It's always harder at night*, she'd said.

He was about to return to his bed when she sniffled, took a deep breath, then rolled over to face him as if it took her last ounce of strength. Extricating her legs from the jumble of bedding, she struggled to a sitting position, her back against the tufted headboard. She pulled a hand towel from the tangle of sheets and wiped her face with it.

She lowered her head, as though shamed by her tears. "Please go."

He held her hand.

Another sob wracked her thin frame.

A woman's tears had never particularly affected Eli. His little sister had turned them on and off to suit her needs, knowing their mother would come running every time. He'd assumed all women used tears that way. So he'd learned not to trust them. But Aria's grief hit him hard.

He didn't know what to say. She seemed so lost, so broken. He enveloped her in his arms. "I'm here, baby. Tell me what you need."

"I'm sorry." She sniffed, her face pressed against his chest. "I just miss him so much." Her warm tears cooled on his bare skin while her words seared his heart.

Eli wished he had the perfect response to comfort her. Any of the characters he'd played in his movies would know exactly what to say in this moment. But no line from a script would suffice now.

"I don't want to feel like this anymore." She choked back a sob. "I'm tired of being so weak. I want to stop waking up in the night with this huge hole inside me, this emptiness, like someone's ripped out every vital organ. Sometimes I wish—" Her hands flew to her mouth, as though trying to shove the words back inside.

"What?"

She cradled her knees and hung her head on her arms, clearly trying not to weep but failing. "Sometimes I just want to go to heaven."

To be with her husband. Instead of here with him.

"Oh, Ari." He took a deep breath. This was about Ari and her needs, not his. His grandpa would know what to say, and suddenly it came to him. "Don't despair. You're never alone, even in your darkest hour."

She raised her eyes to him. "I want to be with you, Eli. Very much. But . . ." She forced a smile. "This is way more than you bargained for, I know. I'll understand if you—"

"Shh." He pulled her against his chest and stroked the back of her head.

After several quiet moments, Eli pulled back and cupped her face. "Ari, I'm not going anywhere. I'm in love with you. And I know you want to be with me. That's enough for now."

A glimmer of hope shone in her red-rimmed eyes as she bunched up the hand towel in her fist. "I don't deserve to be loved like this."

"Yes, you do." He took the towel from her, found an unused corner, and gently dabbed her cheeks. He shuddered to think how many times she'd cried like this.

She eyed the towel in his hand and smiled weakly. "I didn't want to ruin your shirt."

He tossed the towel aside, and with his thumbs he gently wiped away the last of the wetness. "That first night when we fell asleep together by the fire, you slept like a baby. You didn't cry out in the night, you didn't wake at all. And on your deck you slept right through too. Let me hold you tonight."

She studied him, wary but obviously considering it.

"I promise to be a perfect gentleman." He thought about their picnic beneath the willow, when she'd mistaken him for her husband. The last thing either of them needed was a repeat performance of that debacle.

Gazing at the mess she'd made of her bed, he stood and offered his hand. "My room?"

She placed her hand in his, and he led her through the adjoining door. She took off his shirt and draped it over the back of the chair. In a tank top and girl boxers, she looked like a teenager, all long legs and skinny arms.

She climbed into bed beside him, and he spooned her. Within minutes, her breathing slowed, the soft, steady rhythm of unencumbered sleep. He nuzzled into the softness of her hair and its familiar strawberry fragrance.

He'd never felt so needed.

26

Eli woke to find Aria lying beside him, her head nestled on the pillow next to his, her face bathed in a soft golden glow from the pale morning light. He watched her sleep, marveled by how peaceful she looked, as if the tears, like rain, had washed away her grief, at least for a while. He considered waking her with a soft kiss and a gentle caress, but that might lead to—well, something more. He couldn't stop himself from imagining what it would be like to touch every soft, warm, fragrant part of her, make love to her. How exquisite it would be, skin to skin.

Aria stirred, and her hand brushed his face.

Her eyes flew open. "Oh!" She yanked her hand back. "Sorry."

"It's okay." He led her hand back to his cheek.

She blinked her sleepy eyes and smiled.

"Ari," he choked out, his voice sounding like an animal growl to his own ears. "I—I want you."

She pulled back. Her eyes darkened with fear or desire, he couldn't tell which. "Eli—"

He covered her mouth with his. His hand trailed over her breasts and down her side. His kisses followed, hot and hungry.

She moaned softly, exciting him even more.

He gazed down at her. "You're gonna love me soon, Ari. Me and only me." He said it with confidence borne of hope.

She snuggled her head on his shoulder with a satisfied murmur. He held her for a few more lingering minutes while he willed his body to calm down.

With a fingertip, she traced shapes on his shoulder, as if writing a message for him to decipher. He tried to focus on the shapes, not the way her touch sent shivers through his core.

"You hungry?" he asked, barely breathing.

"Sure."

"Shoor."

She laughed. God, he loved that sound. "Don't move. I'll be right back." He jumped up, stepped into his pants, and fled from the room.

When he returned a few minutes later, she was lying on his side of the bed, her head on his pillow, eyes closed, hugging it to her.

Eli cleared his throat. Her eyes fluttered open, and she scooted over so he could set the breakfast tray on the bed between them. While he poured them each a cup on the nightstand, adding cream to hers, she pushed herself up to lean against the upholstered headboard. Gingerly, he eased in beside her and handed her a cup.

"I like that shirt," she said, smiling over the rim of her mug.

"It looked better on you." The way she sat there, cross-legged, a picture of youthful innocence and yet an implausible contradiction to the grown woman and experienced lover he envisioned her to be. He couldn't help but imagine how tangled up he'd be if she slept in sexy lingerie.

Eli sipped his coffee. "Hey, I want to apologize for last night. I never should have let my friends intrude like that."

"It's okay. I'm glad I got to meet them—most of them anyway. And it was fun until—well, until it wasn't." She set her mug on the nightstand and plucked a strawberry from the tray.

He pushed all thoughts of Matt away, choosing to concentrate instead on tonight's party at the home of Michael Lang. He had to go. Penelope had called it "career critical." According to his publicist, who kept an ear to the ground for the latest industry rumors, what Makayla had told him about Lang was true. He was looking for a male lead for a new epic romance.

Eli turned to face Aria. "Is there any way I can talk you into staying one more night?"

She paused, a strawberry to her lips. "I have a conference next week in San Diego. I'd canceled it—but my boss called last night and said he needs me to present for him because, for some reason, now all of a sudden he can't make it."

"Which means . . ."

"I can stay another two days. If you don't mind."

He threw back his head with a laugh. "Of course not. This is perfect. It means you can go to that party with me tonight."

Aria popped the strawberry into her mouth. "I'd rather do a quiet dinner out."

"Penelope says I have to go."

"Of course she does."

"It'll be fun. And we can have that quiet dinner out tomorrow night, in San Diego. I'll drive you. Well, Anders will drive us."

Aria tore off a bite of croissant. "All right."

"Great!" If they were standing he'd have snatched her up and swung her around, but they weren't. They were in bed . . . together . . . so he settled for a chaste kiss. "Hey, can I come watch you speak? I'd love to see you do"—He shrugged—"whatever it is you do."

She shot him a sideways glance. "I can probably get you in. Do you have a tech geek disguise?"

"I can get one." He set down his cup. "So . . . tell me what started the thing with Matt in the media room last night."

She took a sip of her coffee, then relayed Matt's comment about her music. Eli laughed at Matt's use of *Saint Brainiac* to describe her.

"What happened in the game room?"

She scrunched her nose "Matt said some pretty awful things about you."

His gut screamed, *don't ask,* but he had to know. "Like what?"

She shook her head. "Nothing worth repeating."

"Please tell me."

She screwed her eyes shut. "He said you've been with Leigh and Heather," she blurted out. "Then he asked if I was into that sort of thing." She eyed him furtively, as though asking, *Are you?*

He tensed, dread sinking in. "What sort of thing?"

"Group sex."

He caught his breath. He could only remember fragments of that last night with Matt and Heather before he left for Montreal. But he did recall waking up beside Heather the next morning.

He wanted to be honest with Aria, but this could ruin everything.

"I have gone out with Leigh," he said, buying time while he figured out a way to spin the Heather fiasco. "But she's just a good friend. We've never been together. Never even kissed—except on set."

Silence filled the space between them. He blinked hard, mustering courage. "But I did sleep with Heather."

"Before she married Matt?" Hope and trust shone in Aria's gaze and he was about to crush them both.

Eli held her hand, stared at it, caressed it. "It was a crazy night. I don't even remember most of it. Kirsten and I met up with Matt and Heather at a club, then we all went to a party in Brentwood. The next day . . ." He swallowed the lump in his throat. "Matt told me we did some ecstasy at the party. All I remember is waking up beside Heather the next morning."

He dared to glance up. Aria's deflated expression, like a pinpricked balloon, made his chest hurt.

"Ari, I don't do drugs. Never have—that I remember—and never will. And I don't drink more than I can handle. Ask anyone who knows me. I don't know what happened that night, but there's a huge part of it I don't remember."

She pulled her hand away. The look in her eyes was poisonous. "How can you not remember?"

He shook his head. "I don't know. Believe me, I was shocked

when I woke up to find Heather, of all people, in my bed. I don't fool around with married people."

Aria wrapped her arms around her middle as if she were physically ill. Her face went pale, and she jumped up and raced to the bathroom.

"Ari!" Eli bolted after her but stopped short at the door slamming behind her.

Eli returned to pick up the tumbled breakfast tray, fell back onto the bed, and stared at the ceiling.

The sound of the shower filtered through the closed door.

Scattered images of the Brentwood party flashed before him like some amateur-spliced outtake: music too loud, colors too bright, margins too crisp, then the whole room vacillating like heat waves. He'd definitely been high.

After what seemed like an eternity, he bounded from the bed and rapped on the door. "Hey, you okay?"

No response.

His heart raced. He knocked again. Nothing. He tried the door —locked.

"Ari!" He banged on the door. "Open up."

ARIA STOOD IN THE SHOWER, still in the clothes she'd slept in, palms braced against the glass tile while she choked back sobs beneath the cascade of water.

LA was a horrible place. She pictured Eli on some midwestern farm, the way his parents had raised him. The man she'd spent the day with on the lake and at The Willows was a good guy, wholesome. The man in this stylish Hollywood Hills home was someone she didn't know. Didn't want to know.

So this was what fame and money did to people. Made them forget consequences, ignore the morals that shaped their childhood. How could she have been so wrong about him?

Regret brought her to her knees. Crouched in the corner, she wished the water splashing over her could cleanse the hurt, wash away the disappointment, and dull the dismay. Instead, reality crept in—Eli banging on the door, calling her name . . . and crushing her fragile grasp on hope.

ELI COULD BARELY BREATHE. He envisioned her falling apart in there, because of him and his disgusting revelation. Unable to take it any longer, he kicked open the bathroom door.

Aria sat curled in a ball on the floor of the shower, wearing the tank and shorts she'd slept in. He shut off the water, grabbed a towel, and knelt to drape it around her shoulders.

"No!" She pushed him away, turned her back to him, and huddled into the corner.

"Ari, baby." He choked on the words. "I can explain."

She shrugged him off. "Leave me alone."

He placed a hand on her shoulder.

She shrank away.

Reluctantly, he rose to his feet and stared down at her. He had no idea what to do, what else he could say. He couldn't leave her like this, but she obviously needed time to calm down. He had no choice but to retreat, easing the splintered door closed behind him.

He wandered aimlessly through the house, trying to figure out how to explain away that awful night when he didn't even know what happened himself. He paced the foyer, stared up the empty stairway, then paced some more.

Finally, unable to take the waiting any longer, he headed for the stairs.

She stood at the top, luggage in hand.

"Ari, no." He bounded up the steps two at a time. He reached her halfway up, took her suitcase, and set it aside. "Please don't leave like this."

She refused to look at him. "I have to go." She reached for her bag.

He clutched her shoulders and eased her down to sit beside him on the step. "Ari, please. Give me a chance. Give us a chance." He looked into her downcast face, willing her to look at him.

"This isn't the life I want." Her voice was solid, determined, strong.

He gently lifted her chin, forcing her eyes to meet his. Pain was written all over her face. Her heart was shattered. He'd smashed it to pieces with his brutally honest hammer of drugs and adultery.

But he had to convince her to stay. He'd waited his whole life to meet someone like her. He couldn't let her slip away, not like this. "I love you," he said, his voice breaking.

She shook her head with conviction, but her eyes still held a whisper of hope.

"I can be the man you need. I won't disappoint you. I promise."

He reached for her, but she shoved his hand away and glared at him. Tears hung on her lower lids. "I wanted to love you, Eli." She gave him a weak smile. "The man I met on the plane, the boy from Minnesota . . . I'll admit he captured my heart. These last few weeks have been amazing. But the man who lives here—I don't know him at all. And I don't want to." Her gaze dropped, and she squared her shoulders. "I can't be with someone who does drugs and sleeps around." She glared up at him with a painful resolve. "I won't."

"Baby, I'm the same man you met on the plane."

"No, Eli, you're not." She stood and picked up her suitcase.

The doorbell intruded like a barking dog. Anders was off today. The gate should have been locked.

"Wait here. Please, Ari."

As Eli reached the tile, the door opened and Matt poked his head inside, his nose red and swollen from the night before, his eyes circled purple and blue.

"How'd you get in here?" Eli rushed forward to slam the door on him, but Matt shoved a foot in the threshold.

"I came to apologize."

"Not a good time, man."

Matt shoved past him and into the front hall. Quickly taking in the scene, he dashed to the bottom of the steps. "Aria, don't leave because of me."

Eli stormed after him and spun him by the shoulder. "Get out! You've done enough damage already."

Matt shot Eli a weak grin. "I was an idiot last night. Afraid of losing my wingman." He looked up at Aria. "I'm sorry for acting the way I did. Those horrible things I said ... they were all lies."

Matt turned to Eli. "Nothing happened with you and Heather. She told me you passed out as soon as she got you home. And you didn't do ecstasy with us—at least not willingly. You said no." He backpedaled, as if fearing Eli's reaction to what else he had to say. "So I slipped it into your beer."

"You son of a—" Eli slammed a fist into Matt's jaw. Matt sprawled against the railing. In two long strides, Eli hovered over him, intent on picking him up and giving him more. A lot more.

"Dude, give me a break!" Matt scrambled backward like a crab. "I'm trying to do the right thing here." With the back of his hand he swiped at the blood oozing from his lip.

"And I told you to get out!" Eli lifted him by the shirtfront and shoved him toward the entry.

Matt stumbled, picked himself up, and snarled from the opening, "You're gonna regret this Van Drie!"

Eli slammed the door and banged his head against it. He shook all over, searching for his center. Adrenaline pulsed at his temples.

Two slow claps sounded behind him. He whirled to see Aria, standing on the steps.

"Bra-vo." Her look of stoic resignation was soul-crushing.

"You think that was a show for your benefit?" He nearly choked on the words.

A long moment unraveled between them. He had no idea what to say to those accusing eyes. A dozen curse words raced through his mind. He'd just lost a good friend, and now, even though the truth was out, Aria still didn't believe it.

Something inside him hardened. "You can go. Or stay. I don't care anymore."

He stormed out the back, seeking refuge from that condemning glare that made him feel so small, worthless, dejected.

Pacing the patio, he struggled to grasp Matt's betrayal. Of all the reasons he'd imagined for his blackout that night, the last thing he would have believed was Matt doping his drink and lying to him about things that didn't happen.

The front door slammed. The sound of tires on the driveway sent Eli racing back through the house. He shoved aside the drapes to peer out the front window as a gray SUV disappeared through the gate.

Feeling as though his core had been scooped out, leaving only a barren shell, he turned to face his empty foyer.

Only it wasn't empty. Aria sat on the bottom step.

He blinked and let out a slight moan. "You're here."

She closed the distance between them, her gaze soft and wary. She pressed herself against him, encircling him in her arms. "I'm so sorry," she whispered against his chest.

"Don't be." He took a step back and kissed her eyelids, still moist from her tears. "You didn't know. I didn't even know."

He cupped her face and let his forehead rest against hers as the last splinters of panic and anger eased from his body,

27

———

While Aria napped upstairs, Eli sat poolside, finalizing his plans for Monday. He'd had to pull more strings than Geppetto, but the surprise would absolutely blow her away. He leaned back in his lounge chair and pictured her as he'd left her, tucked beneath the covers, her chest rising and falling with the slow, steady rhythm of sleep, her face peaceful, even smiling slightly. Considering the events of the night before and the emotional scene that morning, it was no wonder she was exhausted.

He'd done the right thing In telling her about Heather. He knew that now. It had almost gone sideways, but they'd gotten through it. Considering their short time together, they'd already been through a lot. But she was worth it. He'd known that from the start.

As he swam laps in the pool, he thought about the anguish she had shared with him upon her arrival. It was the most she'd talked about her husband's death so far. His emotions twisted so wildly he could hardly count reps.

He jumped out of the pool, dried off, and returned to his computer at the patio table. It only took a couple of clicks to find a news article about the motorcycle accident. It happened almost a year before Adam's death . . . and he died a year to the day before Eli first saw Aria at the airport terminal in Montreal. No wonder she'd looked about to cry.

He found Adam's name on several other websites as well: advertisements for his construction company, accolades for his successes, a picture of him and Aria in his pickup pulling a parade float. Eli read them all—along with Adam's obituary.

He looked further and came across a condolences page where Adam's friends and family had left unbelievably heart wrenching farewells. When he read, "God bless you, Aria, for never giving up on our beloved son," he'd had enough and returned to the page of search hits.

He found a Care Pages blog site hosted by the hospital where Adam was treated. Aria had used it to update their family and friends about Adam's prognosis and recovery. For the next hour Eli meticulously combed through each of her posts.

They were painful to read, each one carefully worded to focus on the potential for recovery. She did her best to remain positive even when the diagnosis was discouraging. Adam had sustained a serious head injury, was in a persistent coma, and given poor odds of ever coming out of it. She thanked everyone for their thoughts and well-wishes, meals and support, and continued prayers.

Her misery bled through even while her eloquent words revealed her deep love for him and her steadfast hope that he would recover in time. If tearstains could be seen on a website, these pages would have been soaked.

After a few months, Adam was moved to a nursing home, but Aria remained confident, her faith in God and the power of prayer unwavering. Eli's heart ached for her as he read post after post, each one conveying the same unfaltering belief that Adam would eventually recover.

About eleven months after the accident, she wrote that Adam had opened his eyes and smiled at her. Extreme joy and unbounded hope overflowed her words.

The next post was the last, almost three weeks after his death.

. . .

To our dearest friends and family,

As you know by now, Adam has gone to be with his Lord and Savior.

I want to thank each of you for your endless prayers, kind words, hugs, and generosity over the past year. Knowing so many shared in our suffering, and were praying for the same thing we prayed for, softened the ache of our grief and gave us hope in our weakness. In the waiting, in the searching, in the hurting, your strength and steadfast encouragement sustained us.

And now, in our loss, your prayers and gifts continue, blessings in the brokenness. We are comforted in knowing we do not walk alone.

God bless you for standing by us, for reaching out, for your kindness, and most of all, for the light you've shined into our darkest hour.

Love,

Aria, Jackson, and Monroe

"Oh, God," Eli moaned. As if the wound of Adam's accident wasn't bad enough, she'd endured having him rent from her life like a Band-Aid, one hair at a time.

He stared at Adam's photo on the screen for a long time. He was a good-looking guy, clean cut, with kind blue eyes. His hair was so blond it was almost white, which made him appear much older than Eli had imagined him to be.

He must have been a good man to engender that kind of unwavering love and commitment. He wished he had known him.

Eli closed his laptop and cradled his head in his hands. Was he a man deserving of that level of relentless devotion? He could be. He'd give Aria new memories, like a blanket so warm that those cold, dark days of loss and grief couldn't penetrate.

He wandered up to check on her and found her still asleep, her face peaceful, content. He perched on the wingback chair opposite the bed and watched her as his mind pored over all he had read. How did she make it through even a single day with that kind of heartache?

He showered, then grabbed the folder of scripts his agent had given him and returned to the chair in Aria's room to read, determined to take his mind off the overwhelming melancholy that had enveloped him.

None of the scripts were for the role he had recently auditioned for, but they were all excellent, with action-packed story lines and endearing leads. But he had a hard time focusing on any of them.

He wanted the "big one" Max and Penelope were so excited about. Max had said his chances were good he'd get the part, and Max wasn't one to build false hope. They would find out next week. Eli had never worked with the director before, but he was hugely successful. And if it was indeed Michael Lang's project, it was bound to be a megahit.

Italy! If only he could talk Aria into coming with him. He almost laughed aloud, imagining how wonderful that would be. She didn't speak Italian, but maybe they could learn together.

He looked over at Aria. She was watching him with a drowsy smile.

"Hey, you." He set aside the script and moved to the edge of the bed. "Sleep well?"

"Hmm." She stretched like a kitten. "What time is it?"

Eli tapped her phone on the nightstand. "A little after three."

Aria bolted upright. "I slept all day? My flight!"

"You said you were staying, right?"

"Oh, yeah." Aria plopped back onto the pillow and breathed a heavy sigh. "Wow, guess I was tired."

"I'll say." Her eyes were cool and soft, like the shallows of a lake on a sunny day, and he imagined himself blissfully drowning in them.

She took his hand, placed it alongside her cheek, and smiled up at him. The urge to lie down beside her was hard to resist.

"Feel up to going to that party tonight?" He straightened,

holding on to her hand. "I hear Michael Lang's Malibu mansion is amazing. And we can spend the night at a friend's beach house nearby so we don't have to drive home late."

She groaned softly. "You really want to go?"

He stretched out beside her and pulled her into his arms. "What I really want," he murmured, planting small wet kisses along her collarbone, "is to stay right here the rest of the night." *And make wild, passionate love to you until the sun comes up*, he wanted to add. Instead, he found her lips and kissed her softly, taking care not to overwhelm her—or worse, lose himself completely. He pulled back to see her response. She swallowed hard, as though she'd heard his thoughts. "Tell me what you want."

She inhaled, and her exhale shook on its way out. Good. He wasn't the only one finding it hard to breathe.

He rested his forehead against hers.

"I-I can't."

He leaned on an elbow to gaze at her. "Can't go to the party? Or can't be with me?"

She closed her eyes. "Do you like living here?"

He should have seen the question coming. Hollywood could be such a decadent place, full of temptations and so many bored people with virtually unlimited money to spend on whatever vices enticed them. He'd lived here long enough to see it firsthand. Not everyone succumbed, of course, but many did to varying degrees.

"I don't know," he said, being as honest as he could. "There's a lot I like about living here. It's fun: parties every weekend, interesting people to meet, near-perfect weather, surfing, hiking, beach volleyball. And now that I'm finally getting some decent roles, the money is great."

She eyed him, doubt clearly brewing in the glint of her gaze.

"I'll admit, sometimes I long for something simpler. I've been chasing this dream for twelve years, but now that I'm on the precipice of success, it's not all I thought it would be. It's lonely."

"Lonely, yes," she said as though remembering their first goodbye.

"I can tell you one thing, though. If I had to choose between this lifestyle and true love, I'd definitely choose true love."

Her lips formed a slight but short-lived smile. "Really? You'd give up all this for the woman you love?"

"Absolutely," he declared without hesitation, "'Cause life isn't worth living without love. All the fame and money in the world mean nothing without someone to share it with." His phone vibrated. "That's probably Leigh, wanting to know if we're going." He handed her the phone. "You decide."

Aria read Leigh's text, eyed Eli, then thumbed a response and handed his phone back with an impish grin.

Eli: You betcha. See you there, eh?

He laughed. "Very funny." He kissed her forehead. "I promise you won't be disappointed."

Leigh replied immediately.

Leigh: Fantastic! Tell Aria I'll be there in ten. Taking her to do H&M.

Eli showed it to Aria. "Hair and makeup. She probably has an appointment for the two of you."

Aria narrowed her eyes.

He raised his palms. "Hey, this is all you. You're the *inspiration*."

28

True to her word, Leigh pulled up ten minutes later in a red Porsche 911 Cabriolet, top down. On the way to what Leigh proclaimed was one of the best salons in LA, Aria asked her to share everything she needed to know about the party that night.

"First," Leigh started, her voice bursting with excitement as she turned out of Eli's driveway. "Producers fund the films, and they're the final decision makers on who they want to play major roles. Their parties are not to be missed. Being invited is a golden opportunity. Did Eli tell you he was invited by Michael Lang personally?" One glimpse at Aria and Leigh raced on. "Which means he's likely being considered for an upcoming role. Plus, producer parties are always top-shelf. They go all out to attract top talent."

Aria didn't recognize the name, Michael Lang, but then again, she knew about as many movie producers as she knew NFL quarterbacks, which was maybe two.

As if guessing Aria's thoughts, Leigh continued. "Lang's a big shot." She rattled off several of his movie titles, none of which Aria had seen. "Well trust me. Tonight's a big deal for Eli. Me too, actually." She thrummed the steering wheel with nervous excitement. "If you wouldn't have been able to go tonight, I was going to be his date. I hope that's okay. We're just friends though, you know that, right?"

"Yeah, Eli said the same thing. And of course, it would have been fine." It occurred to Aria that now Leigh might not have a date. "Would you like to come with us?"

"Oh, no. Thanks, though. I have a date. But you're sweet to think of me." Stopped at a light, Leigh eyed the plum-colored bruise on Aria's upper arm. "I have the perfect arm bangle to cover that up if you want to borrow it."

Aria rubbed the spot and winced. It was still tender. "I'd like that. Thank you."

"We'll stop by my place on the way back. You were great last night, by the way. The way you handled Matt. How do you do that?"

Aria stared straight ahead, remembering the way Matt had made her feel like she was back in high school, a subjugated part of the not-cool crowd. "Do what, knock him out? I didn't mean—"

"No. How'd you stay so composed and confident when someone you hardly knew was bent on making you feel small?"

"I suppose experience has taught me that guys like Matt, while they can sometimes be dangerous, they're usually not worth the bother. The only thing that bothers me is how he might influence Eli."

"Influence Eli? About you?" Leigh's voice rose in disbelief.

"Yeah." Aria wasn't so naïve that she could easily brush off the potential hold Matt had over Eli. There must be something there, something more than an occasional referral. Heather came to mind.

"Eli's crazy about you. And nothing Matt, or anyone else for that matter, could do or say would make a lick of difference about that. Eli's his own man. Matt might try to push him around, but Eli's beyond needing Matt."

"To further his career, you mean?"

"Exactly. Matt used to be at the top, used to recommend us for supporting roles in his films. But Eli's getting top billing on his own now. And maybe that's why Matt was in such a tiff last night. Seeing his protégé, with you, and no longer needing him. He hasn't done a film in almost a year, not since . . ." She broke off and bit her lip. "Anyway, after last night, I doubt Eli ever wants to see him again. Or work with him. And Eli can call his own shots now. He certainly doesn't need to put up with the likes of Matt."

Aria liked the sound of that. "Is that what's called 'Making It' in this business?"

Leigh laughed, a lovely musical sound. "Yes ma'am."

Aria thought about their earlier conversation about living in LA. "Do you think he'd ever give it up?"

Leigh grew serious. "Would you ask him to?"

"He said he wanted a family someday."

"People in film have families all the time."

"But their marriages—"

"Don't last?" Leigh glanced at Aria. "Eli's would. He's a good man, and he's good at prioritizing. Do you know his grandpa was a pastor? Ask him to tell you about his grandparents some time." She nodded with a smile. "Yeah, I could see Eli having it all."

Eli's words sang to her. *If I had to choose between this lifestyle and true love, I'd definitely choose true love.*

Leigh whipped the car into a parking spot at the salon and shut off the engine, then turned in her seat to face Aria. "Honey, Eli and I have been friends for a long time, and I can tell he adores you. I've never seen him," she paused as if searching for the right word, "shine quite like he does around you. My advice?"

Aria nodded expectantly.

"Let him revel in his spot at the top for a while. He'll know when it's time to take a break."

Aria nodded, relieved. Eli couldn't have asked for a better friend than Leigh Campbell. "Thanks. I hope we can be good friends too."

"Absolutely!" Leigh reached across the console to hug Aria.

Leigh put the top up on the car, and they walked into the salon.

Aria's anticipation turned to dread when she met her stylist, a barely twenty-something reed-thin guy with a flat top, long white diamonds like exclamation points cut into the sides, and sporting a nose stud and tattooed wrists. He greeted Aria with an enthusiastic, "Well, hello doll!" then led her to a chair and ran his hands through her hair as he spoke to her reflection in the oversized mirror.

Aria glanced at the time on her phone, wondering if she'd have time for a redo at Eli's before they had to leave, then decided to trust her new friend, Leigh.

"Tell me about the dress," FlatTop said, pursing his lips.

"Cream colored, one shoulder, tea length, asymmetrical hemline. Simple but elegant."

He tapped a finger to his cheek three times. "Side ponytail," he said, gathering her hair and pulling it forward, "with cascading curls, in the Greek-Roman goddess style, to flow down the bare shoulder."

"Sounds perfect."

The girl who came next to do her makeup raved about her eyes and played them up, adding quite a bit more *drama* than Aria was comfortable with but Aria didn't object. It was an evening party, after all, and this was Hollywood.

When they were finished and Aria and Leigh met again at the front counter, they twirled for each other, oohed and aahed, and laughed and hugged. Aria felt good. She hoped Eli liked it and she silently prayed the night would turn out better than the one before.

29

Eager to see the results of Aria's salon visit, Eli knocked on her bedroom door. When he heard no answer, he eased open the door and peeked inside. Aria sat at the dressing table, staring absently at her reflection in the mirror, her expression distant, unreadable. It definitely wasn't the gaze of a woman appreciating how lovely she was.

The simple cream-colored dress she'd bought the day before accentuated every curve of her thin frame. Her shoulders rose and fell with a heavy breath and she closed her eyes as if drawing strength from a bottomless well of endurance. On her lap, her hand lay palm up. Praying again. Well, he supposed, everyone has their own source of strength. His grandpa would have adored her.

He moved to stand behind her and caught her gaze in the mirror. She glanced up, and her melancholy vanished like dew at sunrise.

He brushed his fingertips beneath the curls tumbling over one bare shoulder. "Stunning."

She placed a hand over his while her eyes caressed the length of him in the glass. "And you're as handsome as a movie star."

He had on what he usually wore to these parties: a tailored

black suit with a steel-blue dress shirt. Penelope made him buy a dozen shirts in that color, claiming it would "amp your sex appeal tenfold" because it matched the color of his eyes.

He traced a finger along the silky-smooth skin of Aria's collarbone to her neck. Her pulse raced beneath his touch. Suddenly all he wanted to do was hold her until she forgot what it was like to feel alone. For an instant he imagined himself telling her he didn't want to go to the party after all, pulling her into his chest for a deep, lingering kiss, and leading her—

She swiveled on the bench, as though sensing his thoughts. "Ready?"

Something unmistakably sad lay almost hidden beneath the forced smile. He wanted to ask what was bothering her, but maybe it was better to ignore it, like she was obviously trying to do. Pretend everything was fine and maybe it would be.

As he pulled her up into his arms, she seemed taller than usual. He glanced down and smiled. "Nice heels."

She giggled. Genuine laughter. It was exactly what he needed to hear.

Minutes later, settled in the backseat of the SUV, luggage stowed in the back, Eli handed Anders the invitation. "Let's take the scenic route, Sunset to PCH."

"Yes, sir."

Eli settled back and took Aria's hand. "Excited?"

"A little nervous, to be honest. I know how much this night means to you, to your career."

"You do?"

"Leigh told me. The producer's probably considering you for an upcoming film, right?"

"Yeah. But hey, relax. It's going to be fun. And I promise, I won't leave your side."

"You should've told me."

"I didn't want you to feel pressured."

Aria smiled—that forced smile again—and gazed out the window. "Is there always this much traffic?"

"Only from dawn to dawn."

No response, not even a glance.

"You're going to love the beach house."

She recoiled with a gasp as a motorcycle zipped by between the lanes, mere inches from her window.

Silence filled the backseat, settling like a dense fog between them.

"Are your girlfriends going to be there?" she asked, still staring out the window.

"My female friends, you mean?"

"Sure."

"Shoor," he repeated, drawing it out. It was enough to garner a smile, a real one this time. "Maybe. But don't worry about it. I'm all yours tonight."

"Tonight," she echoed.

He eased closer and faced her so she had no choice but to look at him. "Tonight and every other night you'll give me."

He waited. Like a game of chess, it was her move. After too many heartbeats of eye gazing, she smiled and kissed him, a kiss that said clearly she'd pushed through the doubt. Forget the powerful host, the intimidating guests, and the female friends. She wanted to be with him.

He couldn't wait to show her one of the best parts of his world. Fame had its rewards, and tonight's party was sure to be spectacular. She'd see it wasn't all bothersome paparazzi and lost privacy.

Or so he hoped.

ARIA RELAXED BACK in the seat, closed her eyes, and breathed while her insides tightened into a knot. She hated parties. Ever since she turned fifteen. For years she'd suppressed the anxiety they always elicited. But the more she tried not to think about this one, the more the memory persisted, like grabbing onto a hot tailpipe, feeling it burn but unable to let go.

On her fifteenth birthday, she stood on the avocado-green-painted front porch of the rundown house on Bowser Street in Delray, dressed in a pale-yellow sundress despite it being mid-October. It was the only dress she had. A handful of girlfriends from school came for the celebration. Gibson and Dante were the only boys. Amy Grant's "Helping Hand" streamed from inside the house.

One minute she was blindfolded, swinging wildly at a brightly striped donkey piñata while everyone around her laughed hysterically as she struck thin air. The next minute shots rang out. Someone—Gibson, she discovered later—threw her to the floor. Bodies scattered. Girls screamed. Tires screeched.

Aria was crushed beneath the weight of her brother.

Finally Gibson was pulled off of her.

"Mrs. Farrow!" a girl called.

Aria rose to her knees and yanked off the blindfold. Dante sat on the porch a few feet away from her. Beside him lay Gibson, still and silent, blood spread across his white T-shirt. Dante pulled him onto his lap and pressed a hand to the hole in his chest.

"Gibs!" Dante pushed harder on Gibson's chest, with both hands now.

Gibson's eyes fluttered open, filled with horror. Then he turned to where she knelt at his side, and a peace seemed to settle over him. He raised a hand to her cheek and smiled. With his other hand, he grabbed a fistful of Dante's shirt, staining it red. "Watch out for her." Blood trickled from the corner of his mouth. "Promise."

Dante nodded, breathless. "You know I will."

Gibson smiled, satisfied, and his eyes, wide open, stared into nothingness as his hand fell lax and lifeless from her face. Aria clutched it. The acrid, coppery smell of blood filled the air.

Helpless, Aria stared in disbelief as the life flowed out of her brother. Her mother appeared beside her, tugged at her, but Aria couldn't let go of Gibson's hand.

Minutes later, EMTs arrived. Still she refused to release her grip. There was so much noise, so much commotion, everyone pulling at her, trying to get to Gibson.

Dante finally pried her fingers loose so the EMTs could take her brother. Then he held her head to his chest, but she still saw the sheet drawn over Gibson's face. She may have screamed, she didn't remember.

An unnatural silence settled on the small porch. The music had stopped. The ambulance pulled away quietly—even the flashing lights shut off halfway down the block. Another life cut short in the hood. And beyond the grief-stricken few left behind on the bullet-riddled porch, no one cared.

Aria shivered and pulled herself back to the present.

You can do this. Forget the pathetic poverty-stricken girl she'd been; forget *that* party in particular. Be the woman Eli fell in love with in Falls Creek—strong, smart, witty.

As she always did before an important customer wine-and-dine or a presentation before a convention-size audience of doctors, scientists, and other professionals all much smarter than she, Aria talked herself down from the ledge of unworthiness, donning instead a well-focused air of confidence. It was never easy. Sometimes it felt like squeezing into a suit two sizes too small. Occasionally she faltered, like at the EverClean office, but most of the time it worked. If you hear something often enough, you begin to believe it, even if it is your own voice. Positive thoughts and self-deception were her superpowers.

Eli loves me. I'm everything he's ever wanted. I look stunning. Tell, believe, repeat.

Over the din of her desperate self-talk, Eli's voice echoed in her mind. *Life isn't worth living without love.* She wanted to love and be loved—needed it like air—but she'd never survive another loss like Adam. She could live the rest of her life alone—lots of people did.

But did she want to?

Somehow, she was going to have to get past her fear. She sighed, weary of the battle.

You can do this. She thought about the kiss beside the river, waking up in Eli's arms at the lake, the afternoon at The Willows, and dancing in the cool Michigan moonlight.

Eli did love her. She really was everything he'd ever wanted. And she did look stunning. He'd told her he was willing to wait for her. *Tell, believe, repeat.*

The SUV stopped at a wrought-iron gate where Anders showed Eli's invitation to a security guard in a black suit. They continued on a winding drive that ended in a circular piazza, a massive fountain at its center. Aria's heart raced as she gazed out the window, searching for the mansion hidden among the lighted palms.

As Anders skirted the car, Eli gave her hand a reassuring squeeze. "Relax, okay? He's just a guy with a nice house."

"And a production company."

Eli grinned. "Just be yourself. You'll win everyone over."

Eli loves me. Just be myself. I'll win everyone over. Tell, believe, repeat.

30

———

Aria took Eli's arm as they followed a meandering flagstone path through lush gardens and towering palms set alight with hundreds of tiny white lights. Her first glimpse of the sprawling estate revealed sun-washed adobe arches, ironwork balconies, and a red tile roof, like something plucked out of the Spanish countryside.

Another black-suit-clad guard stood at the ornate wooden door. He checked the invitation, then bid them welcome and directed them down a long marble-floored hallway. Sounds of music, laughter, and conversation grew louder as they made their way through the stately home. With a hand at the small of her back, Eli ushered Aria into a large ballroom overflowing with guests, chatting in small groups on the polished wood floor.

Arched windows and doors stretched from floor to ceiling and spanned most of two walls. A small band played at one end, and beyond the arches more people danced and mingled on the veranda. A salty breeze wafted in.

Between the sunset over the Pacific, three massive crystal chandeliers, and the endless strands of lights on the veranda, the whole scene seemed to pulse with light and life.

"I've never seen so much sparkle."

Eli pressed his lips against her ear. "Don't tell me you've never noticed what happens when you walk into a room."

Aria laughed and shouldered him. "You must lie awake at night thinking up these things to say."

"Oh, I lie awake at night, but that's not what I'm thinking about."

Aria scanned the elegant guests, many of them actors she had seen in movies, on television, or in magazines. They were all so perfect as they laughed in their tight little circles with their gleaming white smiles, flawless skin, and sculpted bodies. Suddenly Aria felt like she was back at Grosse Pointe High in her secondhand clothes, the chunk of dusty inner-city coal amid the polished diamonds of well-to-do suburbia.

Eli gave her a reassuring smile. "It's a room full of people having a good time, and they're just like you and me."

She straightened, determined to exude confidence.

"Something to drink?" He nodded toward one of several bars.

"Van Drie!" A woman's voice boomed from the crowd before them.

Eli threw his arms wide. "Latisha!"

The sea of guests parted as a large Black woman in an immaculate cream-colored suit teetered forward on shiny black heels so tall and thin it was a miracle they didn't snap. Her long hair was pulled back in an animal-print headband that seemed to accentuate her smooth complexion, high cheekbones, and full deep-cherry lips.

Eli snatched her up in a bear hug. "Drop-dead gorgeous, as always." He set her from him and kissed her cheek. "This is Aria Whitmore. Aria, this is—"

"Oh, I know who she is," Aria said, a little breathless. "Latisha Lafevre, it's such a pleasure to meet you."

"The pleasure is all mine, truly," Latisha said, extending a hand. The light hit Latisha's midnight skin, like obsidian in flesh, shimmering with perfection like some Nubian princess.

Aria shook the woman's hand. "*Like No Tomorrow* is one of my all-time faves."

"Well, thank you." Latisha grinned and glanced sideways at Eli. "I like her already."

"Honestly." Aria went on to quote her favorite parts. "'I only have time for real reality.' Oh, and the best line: 'Girl, look at you. Next time you don't be so scared.' Words to live by."

Latisha's brows shot up.

Eli stared, speechless.

Aria's hand flew to her mouth. She'd been gushing like a crazed fan. "Wow, I'm so sorry."

"It's a'right, baby. I love hearing how great I am." Latisha put an arm around Aria's shoulders and erupted in a full-bellied laugh. Eli and Aria joined in.

As the laughter faded, Eli nodded toward the bar across the room. "Hey, we're heading to get a drink. Join us."

"You go on. She'll be fine right here with me." Latisha raised an almost empty martini glass. "But I will take another of these apple-tinis, thank you very much."

Eli arched an eyebrow at Aria.

"It's okay," Aria said.

Eli nodded. "Wine?"

"Please."

He hesitated briefly, then disappeared into the throng.

"What do you do, Aria?" Latisha asked. "You in the business?"

"Oh, no." Aria shook her head. "I'm in biomedical technology at a company headquartered in Michigan. Well, until next week."

"Mm-hmm. And what happens in a week? You losing your job?" Latisha's gaze didn't wander. She looked Aria in the eye when she spoke, as though she actually cared what Aria had to say.

"No, I'm . . . retiring." It felt odd to say aloud, but what else should she call it?

Latisha craned her neck back. "Aw, come on, now. Honey, you are not old enough to retire."

"Well, I recently launched a new product—one I designed—

and it was a much bigger success than I ever imagined." It was hard to say, even harder to believe. "So, I don't need that job anymore." She cringed. She'd tried for modesty, but the way it came out didn't sound humble at all.

"A new product?" Latisha's voice raised an octave. "You mean like an invention?"

"Exactly."

"How exciting. Tell me about it. I love new things."

Latisha seemed genuinely interested, so Aria went on to describe her recycling machine, a little embarrassed as she wrapped up, thinking she probably sounded like a veritable tech geek.

"Well, ain't that ellissim'?" Latisha fist-bumped her, obviously impressed.

"I never thought it would actually sell." Aria remembered her father-in-law's constant words of encouragement. *Have faith, Aria-girl. Ask and you'll receive.* She'd followed his advice; she'd asked often.

"You designed it and built it yourself?"

"It's my idea, my design, but my father-in-law helped me build it."

"Father-in-law? You're married?" Latisha's eyes finally broke off from Aria's and searched the room—for Eli, no doubt.

"I was. He died." It was getting easier to say, sadly. At least when she didn't overthink it.

"I'm sorry." Those two words again—so overused, so trivial, so inadequate.

"Thank you." Before the melancholy could ruin their lovely conversation, Aria rushed on, nodding toward Eli, who stood near the bar having what appeared to be an intimate conversation with a petite black-haired beauty. "Who's that with Eli?"

Facing them, Eli caught Aria's glance, and his expression brightened. He raised a glass of wine to her. *I'm coming,* it said. The woman took it from him and raised it to her pouty red lips. Eli glared at her with a look of consternation, glanced to

Aria, rolled his eyes dramatically, then turned back to the bartender.

"Makayla Chase," Latisha said with a hint of disgust.

So that's Makayla. "She's beautiful." Aria tried not to stare but with her black hair and ruby lips, and sporting a figure-hugging sky-blue dress, Eli's costar looked like a bona fide Disney princess.

"Beautiful disaster. She's a spoiled rotten little wench . . . and Michael Lang's new stepdaughter." Latisha waved her hand in their direction. "They're supposed to be seen together. Good press for the movie and all. But don't you go believing everything you read online about Eli."

Aria eyed Latisha, feeling as though she'd missed something.

"Seriously? You haven't Googled your boyfriend?"

"I like to make my own decisions about people."

Latisha gave her an approving smile. "Smart. Well, Eli's a good guy, one of the best."

"That's what I'm finding out."

Aria's gaze drifted to Eli. Makayla's hand rested on his lapel. His eyes were laser focused on the little black-haired beauty as though he was about to ravish her. Or kill her. A few feet away, a woman with a full mane of red hair stood with her phone poised, taking their picture. Poured into a skintight violet evening gown, the woman reminded Aria of an overinflated Jessica Rabbit.

Latisha followed Aria's gaze and wrinkled her nose. "That's Eli's publicist, Penelope Fenwick. Now, that woman's a walking tire screech."

Stunned by the woman's brutal honesty, Aria laughed. No wonder Latisha and Eli were friends.

"So what's next for you?"

The question startled Aria. She hadn't thought much beyond saving her home. She'd been living one day at a time for so long, it was impossible to look that far ahead. "I don't know," she finally said.

"Maybe it's time to give back," Latisha suggested with a hint of challenge.

"Maybe. What would you do?"

"I'm doing it, baby!" Latisha said with a raucous laugh. "I mentor inner-city kids. You've heard of Big Brothers and Big Sisters?"

"Oh, sure."

"I have two little sisters." Latisha whipped out her phone to show Aria their pictures, swelling with pride as though the two little cuties were her own children.

"Aw, they're adorable."

"Yeah, they're something else a'right. I feel like I'm making a real difference in their lives." Latisha tucked her phone back into her evening bag. "Did you know that when pandas have twins they only care for one and leave the other one to die? A lot of these kids are like that extra cub—abandoned, neglected, expected to survive on their own. All's it takes is someone to come along and teach them how to live, someone who shows up every week regardless, with no preconditions. So many kids live in poverty, right here in our own country. On their own, they don't stand a chance. Or at least they can't see it."

"I know, right?" Aria admired Latisha's passion and like-minded spirit. "The American Dream is so far out of their reach, they don't even know it exists. How do you convince a child to trade mud pies for sand castles when they've never even seen a beach?"

"Well, there you go. There's your cause."

"Solving poverty?" Aria asked, incredulous.

"Perpetuating the American Dream."

"Oh, I don't think I can—"

"Girl, if you wait until you think you can, you'll never do anything."

An idea sparked in Aria's mind, setting alight years of lost hopes and noble aspirations. In what seemed like another life, Aria had wanted to be a public defender, to ensure everyone, especially poor kids, got a fair shake, equal justice for all. That was before Adam had seduced her with his promises of a safe and wonderful life as wife and mother. She'd cast aside her lofty ambitions to focus on her family. But now, soon to be on her own again, she was at a crossroad. Maybe it was time to dust off that dream. "You ever read Daniel Keyes's *Flowers for Algernon*?"

Latisha's blank look said she hadn't.

"He posed an interesting question that's always stuck with me: 'How many great problems have gone unsolved because men didn't have enough faith in themselves to let go for the whole mind to work at it?' Not that I'm a genius or anything, but I have faith in myself. Sometimes I think it's all I have."

"I have a feeling you're smarter than the average bear."

Aria laughed. How could she not love a woman who transitioned so easily from espousing social philosophy to quoting Yogi Bear? Latisha was right—she should set her mind to solving something big, something beyond her own sorry troubles. She'd recently read Ben Franklin's autobiography. Now, there was a man of ideas and action.

Aria eased closer to be heard but not overheard. She described Franklin's ideas about the social integration of Blacks, especially remarkable because his writings on the subject were almost a hundred years before the emancipation. Even in his time, Franklin knew slavery wouldn't last. He wrote a fairly detailed plan, which included the formation of four committees, each with a focus area for assimilating Blacks into white society. "Maybe his ideas could be broadly applied to people stuck in poverty."

"Now, that's what I'm talking about," Latisha said. "Use the foundation he laid out to build something that'll work in our current culture. 'Great thoughts speak to the thoughtful mind, but great actions speak to all mankind.'"

"Theodore Roosevelt!" God, she loved this woman.

"You know it, baby."

Aria had once been among the poverty-stricken. But . . . "You think the poor would listen to anything I have to say, a privileged white woman?"

"You think poor people only listen to poor leaders?" Latisha twirled the raspberry garnish in her near-empty cocktail and popped it into her mouth.

Aria mulled over the idea. "I think, at best, a certain amount of resonance is lost when the leader and the led don't share common ground. They'd see me like you do—nothing more than another white woman in a fancy dress."

"So don't wear a fancy dress." Latisha laughed. "Seriously, though, we may live in the world as it is, but we can still work to create a better world. And don't underestimate yourself. One person can make a difference, even if it's only planting a seed. It's gotta start somewhere. Why not with you?"

Aria smiled, encouraged by Latisha's challenge. She wanted to believe she could be one of those people to plant seeds of change to make the world a better place. "I like gardening."

Latisha tipped her glass to her, a silent *You go, girl.*

Eli emerged from the crowd, and his gaze found Aria. An intimate smile shone in his eyes as he made his way toward them. "Hey." He handed them each a drink.

Aria glanced beyond Eli to where Makayla stood alone in the crowd, eyes brimming with tears.

"Thank you," Latisha said, accepting the fresh martini. "I like this girl, Eli. A lot."

His eyes darted between the two women, and his crooked grin emerged. "Me too."

"Hey, girl, you got your phone with you? I want to give you my number." Latisha held out her hand.

Aria hid her astonishment, drew her phone from her purse, and exchanged it for Latisha's drink.

"You call me when you start working on those ideas of yours," Latisha said, her head down, typing. "I mean it. I might have some influence in that community, and I would be happy to give you my . . . unique perspective." She giggled.

"Thank you. I will."

Latisha returned Aria's phone and turned to Eli, "This girl's a real treasure."

Eli laughed and raised his brows at Aria.

"I don't know how you tolerate them other two." Latisha added, waving a hand toward the bar where Makayla and Penelope were huddled over, no doubt reviewing the pics they'd taken.

"Aw, Penelope's not bad in small doses," Eli said with a chuckle. "Like cough syrup. Tough to swallow but makes you better."

"If you say so." Latisha rolled her eyes, then turned to Aria. "It was a pleasure to meet you, Aria, truly. And Eli, great seeing you again. Y'all have fun tonight."

"The pleasure was all mine." Aria replied calmly, resisting the urge to hug the woman.

Latisha wandered off, and Eli turned to Aria. "We haven't been here twenty minutes and Latisha Lafevre gave you her number?"

Aria shrugged. She had no explanation. Anyway, Aria was feeling much better about the evening . . . and about her future.

Eli moved closer, his expression somewhere between enchantment and utter fascination. "The first time I saw you in the Montreal airport I imagined what you'd look like in a setting like this." His breath was a warm waft against her ear, his voice deep and throaty, incredibly seductive. "And what I'd say if I got the chance to meet you."

He stared at her all starry-eyed, the way Adam used to do before he'd lead her—

Aria swallowed the lump in the back of her throat and refocused. "What would you say?"

He raised her hand to his lips, brushing her knuckles across his bottom lip. "Be with me."

It was so innocent, so spontaneous and forthright, like a child saying, *I want it*. She almost laughed, but the sincerity in his gaze was heartbreak serious. "I am with you."

He cocked his head, as if to say, *You know what I mean*. She had to look away. She couldn't be with him that way.

"C'mon. There's someone I want you to meet." He took her hand and led her away.

Penelope appeared in their path, and Eli introduced Aria to his publicist.

"Well, aren't you country fresh." Penelope shook Aria's hand with limp fingers as if she were contagious.

"Pleasure to meet you." Aria donned her professionalism like a well-tailored jacket. "I've heard so much about you from Eli."

"Oh, I'm sure." Penelope smiled as though Aria had just validated the woman's spot at the center of Eli's universe. "Ah, this is perfect." She backed up, her cell phone poised. Aria started to object, but Penelope cut her off. "It's my job, darling."

Eli pulled Aria to his side, leaving her no choice but to don a smile while Penelope captured the moment.

Another one for the tabloids but at least she was poised this time. *And Eli loves me. I'm everything he's ever wanted. I look stunning.* Tell, believe, repeat.

31

As Penelope scurried off, Aria took Eli's offered arm and allowed him to lead her to the far end of the ballroom, where Bret Carlisle and Olivia Dubois stood chatting and laughing at the center of a large group of guests. Each of them megastars in their own right, Bret and Olivia seemed happily married, at least according to the media. Aria had seen them in a few films together. Unlike Eli, their public images were near-saintly: they adopted impoverished kids, built orphanages in third-world countries, and hosted huge fundraisers.

Were they the friends Eli wanted her to meet? Her stomach twisted into a knot. *Relax. They're just people.*

"You're the most beautiful woman here tonight," Eli said, as if sensing she felt out of place, uncomfortable, ordinary. Comparison, the curse of self-esteem.

Even if he hadn't said a word, the adoring look in Eli's eyes would have been enough to reassure her. Maybe with all the pressure of late, her coal was on the way to becoming a diamond after all. "Thank you."

He nodded toward Bret and Olivia. "We could be mega stars like them someday."

Aria scoffed. "I'm no movie star."

"You're a much better actress than any I've ever worked with. You pretend to be happy, but I've seen you cry when you think no one is watching."

Everyone has to play-act sometimes. For her, it was a matter of survival. "Not interested, thanks." If Eli was looking for a costar, he'd have to find a woman willing to subject herself to the scrutiny of stardom, and that certainly wasn't her.

Bret and Olivia broke free from the group and joined Eli, who made introductions.

Determined not to carry on as she'd done with Latisha, Aria greeted them politely, as if she were simply networking at a medical conference.

The two celebrities chatted with Eli like old college roommates. Bret wasn't as tall as Aria had expected, a couple of inches shorter than Eli. But with those puppy-dog brown eyes, chiseled jaw, and broad shoulders, he was every bit the stereotypical leading man. Olivia, with her full lips, regal cheekbones, and a body like Venus di Milo, was undeniably glamorous. Eli fit right in.

Aria felt like a mallard among swans.

"Thanks for the use of your beach house tonight," Eli said. Aria echoed her own gratitude, hiding her awe that these were the "friends" Eli had mentioned.

Bret waved them off. "I only wish we could stay too."

"And be proper hosts," Olivia added.

"But I'm expected on set early tomorrow. You know how that goes." Bret raised a bottle of Perrier in salute.

Bret asked Eli about the movie he'd recently wrapped up and what he had planned next. Eli began with a brief recap of his Montreal project, cited the Pixar voice-over, and a promo-filled summer, but he didn't mention the director he'd recently read for or the scripts he'd been given. Apparently only the work under contract was deemed worthy of sharing with these friends. When he finished, he asked the same questions of each of them. Their conversation reminded Aria of her own interactions with customers, friendly but impersonal, businesslike.

Bret pointed out Michael Lang, their host, across the room, where he stood talking with Penelope. Catching Eli's gaze, Penelope waved him over.

"Duty calls," Eli said with a chuckle.

Tall and thin, dressed in all black, Lang had long, angular limbs, small round eyes, and jet-black hair, graying at the temples and slicked back. He looked part Hollywood mogul, part mantis.

But Aria did not even try to hide her delight at seeing Leigh Campbell on his arm.

Leigh beamed with excitement when she noticed them approaching. "Hey, there!" As she hugged Aria, she whispered, "I told you that arm band would look perfect with your gown."

Penelope introduced Lang to Eli, bubbling with praise over the media's insatiable appetite of late for her client.

"It's a pleasure to meet you, Mr. Lang." Eli wrapped an arm around Aria's waist. "This is my girlfriend, Aria Whitmore."

As the producer greeted Aria with a limp handshake, he repeated her name as though trying to place it. "Ah, yes!" He raised a long finger. "You were in the *Wall Street Journal* last week."

Aria shot Eli a nervous glance, and he nodded his encouragement. "I was."

"A recycling machine, if I recall correctly. Sold for a pretty penny. Congratulations."

"Thank you."

Lang gazed at Eli. "Where in the world did you meet *this* lovely young entrepreneur?"

"O'Hare airport. We were on the same flight from Montreal." Eli shot Aria a crooked grin. "She chased me down, nailed me with her shoe, then yelled at me in French. Twenty minutes later, I'd swapped my flight to LA for one to Michigan so I could get to know this fascinating woman."

Lang and Leigh both laughed. Aria joined in, resisting the urge to fill in details and explain her side of the story.

Lang rubbed his palms together. "Ah, *vous parlez Francais?*"

"*Oui, un peau.*"

Penelope cleared her throat, apparently not used to the prolonged lack of attention.

"*Comment allez-vous ce soir?*" Lang asked, ignoring Penelope.

"*Tres bien, merci. Et vous?*"

"*Tres bien, aussi, merci.*"

"Charming and beautiful." Lang slapped Eli on the shoulder. "Hang on to this one."

"You betcha." Eli placed an arm affectionately around Aria's shoulder.

Penelope gave Eli a quick peck on the cheek, told Lang, "We'll talk later," then excused herself from the group.

Eli seemed to relax after his publicist's hasty exit. Lang acknowledged Penelope's farewell with barely a nod.

"Aria," Leigh piped up, "have you seen Michael's pool table?"

"You shoot pool too?" Lang fairly vibrated with childlike excitement.

"About as well as I speak French," Aria admitted with a demure smile.

"I've yet to be beaten on my own table." Lang offered a bony elbow to Aria. "Let's to billiards then, shall we?"

He led her toward a hallway, Eli and Leigh following. He walked too close and his intense, penetrating stare gave Aria the creeps. But she kept a lid on her revulsion. She didn't want to risk Eli's career by turning him down.

Lang opened a set of mullioned double doors and gestured Aria and the others inside. A sharp contrast to the brilliance and bustle of the ballroom, the billiard room was hushed and dim, with cherry wood paneling and plush deep-red leather seating.

Lang handed Aria a stick from the rack on the wall. "Let's make it interesting. What shall we play for?"He raised an eyebrow at Eli. "How about a lead role in my upcoming film?"

Aria's mouth fell open and Eli emitted a low, "Whoa."

"Okay. And if you win?" Aria asked.

Lang fastened his gaze on Aria, daring in his eyes. "*Vous dormez avec moi ce soir.*"

She burst into laughter. Surely he didn't actually expect her to sleep with him.

When he simply smiled back, his gaze unwavering, a dread settled over her. She must have misunderstood. "You're kidding, right?" Aria met Lang's bold stare.

"*Non.*" Lang handed his stick to Leigh and racked the balls.

"*Vous me dégoûtez.*" She hoped her disappointment in Lang wouldn't be held against Eli.

Eli and Leigh exchanged worried glances.

Bent over the pool table, Lang broke without looking up. Three balls found pockets, two solids and a stripe. Straightening, he studied the lay of the table and pronounced, "We'll take stripes."

"*Si j'étais un home . . . je vous assommerai.*" Aria smiled sweetly for the benefit of the others and handed her stick to Eli. "Why don't you two decide what to play for? I need to powder my nose." She spun on her heel and didn't look back.

With floor-to-ceiling white marble, gleaming chrome, and crystalline wall sconces that could've graced Windsor Palace, the extravagance of the ladies' room matched the rest of the house. Aria smiled at the young attendant, who stood poised to hand out towels, and entered one of the four stalls. She would've preferred a few minutes of alone time before the mirror, but instead she made do in the relative seclusion behind the closed door.

A few deep breaths later, Aria squared her shoulders, resolving to put on a brave face for Eli's sake. No one, not even the most powerful movie mogul, was going to make her feel small tonight.

When she returned to the billiard room, Eli was alone, bent over the table, poised for a shot that sent the cue ball to the opposite end, where it bounced gently off the bumper. The balls were racked, ready for a fresh game. Eli looked up. "Lang changed his mind, said he shouldn't neglect his guests so long." Eli's cheeks rose with his smile. "Personally, I think he was afraid of you."

Aria hid her relief. "Oh, sorry about that."

Eli challenged her to a game. Still shaken, Aria was grateful for the excuse to delay rejoining the party. But when she ran the table in a single turn, Eli laughed good-naturedly and asked her to dance.

She could think of nothing more pleasant than dancing with Eli in the fresh air of the moonlit veranda. She'd had more than enough of the Hollywood fakes and leches.

At the door, Aria paused beside two wingback chairs positioned on either side of an ebony-and-quartz chess set. "How about chess?"

Eli chuckled and tugged her from the room.

Waltzing on the moonlit veranda, Aria tried to relax, to savor Eli's solid arms around her waist, his warmth, and the intoxicatingly male scent of him—an expensive-smelling blend of leather and cedar. But she sensed the army of beautiful women around them, watching her, wishing they were her. Eli could have any of them.

But she was the one he wanted, and he made her feel wanted. A feeling she'd missed more than she cared to admit.

Eli spoke against her ear, his voice deep and husky. "What did Lang say in the pool room?"

"Nothing important. It was silly."

He pulled back, brows raised.

Aria didn't want to ruin a perfectly good evening. "I'll tell you on the way to the beach house."

"Fair enough."

Aria melted into his arms while the mild ocean breeze and soft music swept her away so that only she and Eli remained on the moonlit veranda. All thoughts of Lang's insinuations and the myriad shallow conversations she'd overheard skittered away.

He spun her out, looking as happy as she felt. "Having fun?"

"Yes. I am."

He gave her a side-eye like he wasn't buying it. "But?"

"I'm enjoying this, dancing with you. But the conversations. I'm not used to being so . . . " She searched for the right word. "Superficial."

He winced and his gaze fell away. "That's a perfect description of these parties." Two beats later, his mouth curved into a wide grin, like he'd discovered something he hadn't known before. "Let's get outta here." He took her hand and led her back inside.

"Wait, we're leaving?"

"Yeah." With her arm firmly tucked in his, he urged her forward.

They'd crossed the ballroom when Aria overheard Penelope's voice, like a fingernail on a chalkboard. "Oh, her? She's a nobody, his latest shiny pebble. Trust me."

Aria searched the sea of faces for the offending voice.

Scowling, Eli pulled her out into the hallway. "Ignore her. She doesn't know what she's talking about."

Aria stopped his forward motion. "Eli, we should stay. These parties are important to your career, so producers and directors think of you when new roles come up. It's part of being in the movie business, right?"

"Yeah, but I don't want to be here. I'd rather take you to the beach house and . . . " His voice trailed off as he stared at her, his gaze a tender caress, and with a fingertip beneath her chin he tipped her face up to meet his kiss.

She melted against him. Every time he kissed her like that she went boneless. Oh, how she longed to be alone with Eli rather than fake one more hollow smile.

She was about to agree when Latisha popped her head out of the ballroom. "Y'all aren't leaving, are you? There's someone I want you to meet." She marched over and took Aria by the hand. "Come on, now. You can't leave a party this early. It's embarrassing." Her laughter filled the hallway.

Reluctantly, Aria allowed Latisha to pull her back inside, Eli right on their heels. Latisha introduced Aria to several friends. It didn't take long before the talk turned from pleasantries to real, honest-to-goodness conversation—and about things that mattered, no less. Even though it was obvious Aria wasn't someone who could help them get ahead in their careers, they embraced her like a college intern on her first day.

As Aria and Eli talked and laughed with Latisha and her friends, a woman's voice screamed Eli's name. Seconds later he was nearly bowled over by a petite blonde throwing herself into his arms.

Eli peeled her off of him, retreated a step, and with a patient smile said, "Kirsten, I'd like you to meet Aria." He draped an arm around Aria's shoulders. "Aria, this is Kirsten Allay."

Aria held out her hand. "Nice to meet you."

Kirsten had clearly passed tipsy hours ago. Ignoring Aria, she flashed Eli a flirty smile. "When did you get back from Montreal?"

"A few weeks ago. Sorry I didn't call. I've had a lot going on."

"I can see that." Kirsten's gaze flickered to Aria. "Are you an actress?" The woman blatantly sized Aria up.

Aria shook her head. "I'm not in the business at all. I don't even live here."

"Really?" Kirsten's voice held an inkling of hope.

"For now." Eli squeezed Aria's shoulders.

Kirsten's fake cheeriness vanished. Moisture glazed her eyes. She kissed Eli's cheek, wheeled around, and disappeared into the crowd.

"Well, that was awkward," Aria said with a chuckle.

"You could say that again." Eli puffed out his cheeks and exhaled. "Sorry about that."

So, she'd met Kirsten and seen Makayla. *Two down. One to go.*

As if reading her thoughts, Eli said, "Taylor's a music artist. She doesn't usually attend parties like this."

Aria suppressed a gasp. Oh, please, not *that* Taylor!

Eli led Aria to the veranda for some fresh air, then left to fetch refreshments. When he returned, Michael Lang stood beside her at the wrought-iron balustrade.

"You know," he heard Lang say, "you didn't have to make such a big deal about that earlier."

Eli paused inside the doorway to listen, grateful they were speaking English this time.

Lang placed a hand on her shoulder. Aria stepped away. Undaunted, Lang edged closer so they stood shoulder to shoulder.

She stepped back and faced him squarely. "That was extremely disrespectful back there, and I won't abide it."

"Pardon me?"

"You may treat all your Hollywood fluffs that way, but I'm not one of them."

Eli wanted to laugh at Aria's forcefulness—it reminded him of her righteous fury when she'd chased him down in O'Hare. He was about to step forward when Lang continued.

"I'll let you in on a little secret, my dear. The deal I'm working on that Eli and his people are so interested in . . . it's a remake of *Casanova*. " His eyes widened in mock surprise. "The most famous womanizer of all time. How's it feel to be dating a guy like that?"

Aria remained impassive. "If you think that's the kind of man Eli really is, then he's an even better actor than I thought. And all the more reason you should cast him."

Lang studied her for several long moments then laughed. "By Jove, you're right. Eli is a nice guy. He deserves better. My proposition earlier was out of line. Please, do forgive me."

Was Lang ridiculing her, or was that a sincere apology? With guys like him, it was hard to tell.

Aria's face softened. "Apology accepted."

"I'd still like to challenge you to a game of pool. I have a feeling you'd be a worthy opponent."

"I am. Another time perhaps."

"Until then." Lang lowered his head in a respectful bow. "Good night, Ms. Whitmore."

Eli quickly retreated to avoid being caught eavesdropping. As Lang continued down the veranda to greet another group of guests, Eli waited a few seconds, then rejoined Aria.

"I think we can get outta here now."

This time, they managed to get outside without being detected.

Eli punched in a text. Seconds later his phone vibrated. "Anders is a few minutes away." He placed her arm in his and they continued down the flagstone path toward the circle. Reaching the driveway, he stopped and turned to her. "Now can you tell me what Lang said to you in the billiard room?"

Aria's gaze wandered to the canopy of lighted palms. With a hand on his shoulder, she bent to slip off her strappy heels. "These are pretty, but my feet vehemently protest prettiness this tall." She straightened, shoes dangling from her fingertips. Barefoot, she strolled to a bench a few yards away, and plopped down.

Eli followed. "Well?"

"Can we just let it go?"

He crouched in front of her. "Please tell me."

She licked her lips, as though considering. "It's not worth repeating."

He sat beside her and pulled her into him. "You'd better tell me or else." He playfully poked her side. She jumped and squealed. He poked again, fully intending to tickle it out of her if he had to.

"Stop! Please." Aria laughed as she tried to slap his hands aside.

"I'll stop if you tell me." He continued to tickle her. She collapsed against him one minute, then wriggled to be free the next.

"Okay, okay." Breathless, she held his wrists away. Regaining her composure, she stared into the distance. "If he won the game, he wanted me to sleep with him tonight."

Eli bounded to his feet. "He said that?"

"Yes!"

A muscle in Eli's jaw twitched. "What did you say?"

"I told him he disgusts me, and if I were a man I would knock him out." She grinned, as though hoping he'd find the whole thing as amusing as she did.

Eli rubbed his chin, imagining his kickboxer girlfriend doing exactly what she'd threatened. "Oh, Ari, what am I going to do with you?" He pulled her up and against his chest.

"Why would he think he could say such a thing to me?"

"Some guys in this business are like that. They'll try to get away with whatever they can, especially with Hollywood fluffs, who typically abide it."

Aria yanked away. "You were eavesdropping!"

He laughed. "I was. And I'm glad I did, because you handled the situation really well."

The SUV pulled to a stop in the courtyard. Anders skirted the hood to open the rear door. Eli retrieved Aria's shoes and tucked her arm in his as they strolled to the car.

In the quiet of the backseat, Eli took Aria's hand. "Thank you for coming to the party tonight. I know my colleagues can be idiots sometimes, but one of them might get me a million-dollar role someday."

Aria shook her head. "You'd work for a guy like Lang?"

"I don't have a choice." He shrugged. "Don't get me wrong. I'm glad you shut him down like you did. But if I only worked for the good guys, I'd still be tending bar."

Aria shook her head. "In what universe is that kind of behavior even remotely tolerable?"

"Like my grandpa always said, sometimes you need to look a little harder to see the good in some people."

"I guess."

Eli relaxed into the soft leather seat. "Haven't you ever been propositioned where you work?"

"I have," she admitted. "Way too many times."

"How did you handle it?" She couldn't possibly have threatened to knock them out like she had Lang. Or actually knock them out like she did Matt.

"I dealt with it professionally." She grinned. "And most of the time, I still made the sale."

"Hollywood's like anywhere else. You can't always be selective about the people you work with."

Aria grimaced. "I hope I didn't ruin things for you."

He laughed. "If Lang was as impressed with you as I am, you probably helped my chances."

She brightened. "You're impressed with me?"

"You betcha."

She rested her head against his shoulder with a contented sigh.

Eli's thoughts wandered back to the overheard conversation. Of course Penelope was hot for him to get the lead in *Casanova*. What better story to punctuate the public persona she'd so carefully crafted for him?

Despite the inevitable stigma, he wanted the role. Lang's work was legendary. In all likelihood it would be a blockbuster, and wasn't that what he'd longed for? One more stellar success, an Oscar-worthy performance to get him to the top.

The thought of Italy with Aria made him giddy with excitement. He squeezed her hand and she squeezed his back.

At least she saw the real Eli Van Drie.

32

Aria awoke to orchestra music and an ocean scent carried in on a mild breeze. She could've sworn she'd closed the doors to the balcony before climbing into bed last night.

Disoriented, she sat up and looked around. Sheer white drapes puffed full with salty air and morning sunshine fluttered at the doors' edges. Like waking in a hotel room and not recalling what city she was in, let alone why, it took Aria a moment to remember she was in Bret and Olivia's Malibu beach house.

She tapped her phone for the time. Who played classical music this early in the morning? She threw off the coverlet, wiped sleep from her eyes, and slipped on her robe before stepping to the balcony to part the sheers.

Eli stood on the beach below. A trio of musicians—flute, violin, and bass—played off to the side. Not far beyond them a small yacht bobbed in the water, a scarlet mainsail flapping loosely in the wind, beckoning like someone with a kerchief lost in a crowd.

A breath fell out of her. Unbelievable!

Eli raised his arms, a silent *Ta-da!* Then he bowed low and came up grinning.

Aria laughed and shook her head. Surely, she must be dreaming.

"C'mon, chickadee, sail away with me!" he called.

She flew across the bedroom, scrambled down the stairs, burst through the rear door, ran across the beach as fast as her bare feet would allow, and barreled into his outstretched arms.

He scooped her up and swung her around with a hearty laugh.

"You read it!" He'd not only remembered her favorite book, Scarlet Sails, but he'd actually read it and brought it to life. For her. This was all for her.

"I did." He set her on her feet and leaned back to look at her. *I love you* lingered unspoken in the tenderness of his gaze.

She couldn't stop smiling. "My sea captain . . ."

The musicians played on. The morning sun shined like gossamer on the dark-blue water. The bright-red sail burned like a flame atop the white yacht. Her fairy tale stretched out before her eyes, and Eli had made it happen. Even his clothes were in-story: bare feet beneath tan breeches, a white puffy shirt with its laces open to the waist, his dark hair slicked back on the sides and bound into a ponytail at the back.

"Well? What do you think?"

"I can't believe you did all this for me."

He placed a palm over his heart. "Heroes in love do crazy things."

She spun around, taking in the whole scene, and seeing the beach house for the first time in the light of day. It was impressive, all white and glass and gleaming in the California sunshine.

"Don't look back." With his hands on her shoulders, he spun her to face him. "Only forward."

The setting was like a fantasy. But the unbridled joy in his eyes was real. "I'm dreaming, aren't I?"

A hearty chuckle rose from deep in his chest. "No. But I'm glad you think so."

His words from their first date unraveled in her heart. *Isn't that what we all want? To be someone's dream come true? Or better yet, the answer to their prayers.*

In that moment, held firmly in Eli's strong hands, her bare feet in the cool sand, his smiling eyes warming her in places she couldn't name, Eli was both her dream and her prayer.

Dressed and packed up minutes later, they hopped into the waiting dinghy, left the musicians and the beach house behind, and joined the yacht's three-man crew for a sail to the Channel Islands.

Eli had thought of every detail, from the scrumptious breakfast aboard ship while dolphins jumped playfully alongside, to the personal guide they met on Santa Cruz Island to lead their expeditions. They spent the morning hiking, kayaking the sea caves, and snorkeling the reefs.

The island was unlike anything Aria had ever experienced, a virtually uninhabited wilderness with scenery and wildlife so diverse it would make Tennyson weep. Seals and sea lions basked in the cool shade of the caves. Birds flew everywhere, especially the endemic island scrub-jay, which, the guide informed them, was found nowhere in the world except on Santa Cruz Island.

In the afternoon, they found a secluded beach, where they strolled hand-in-hand in the surf, then picnicked beneath an umbrella. Physically spent by the morning's excursions and lulled by the surf and a full stomach, Aria fell asleep in Eli's arms, blissfully happy.

She awoke to find Eli standing at the water's edge, gazing out to sea. Aria jumped to her feet, threw off the gauzy shirt she'd worn over her bikini, and ran past Eli into the water. Several yards in, she stopped knee-deep and turned around, playfully splashing him. "You coming?"

"You betcha." He whipped off his T-shirt, tossed it onto the beach, then ran to catch up to her. He swept her into his arms and carried her out into deeper water, laughing and breathless from the chilly Pacific.

Standing chest deep, he pulled her close. She wound her legs around his waist, seeking his warmth. He cupped her face and studied her. A kiss was coming; she could see it in his eyes. Her heart raced in anticipation.

He kissed her, soft and gentle, teasing her, making her want more. Her whole body tingled with desire.

He pulled back, his gaze caressing her face. "God, you're beautiful."

Startled by the raw hunger in his eyes, she broke free, swam away, and glanced back. He stood unmoving and solemn, staring after her.

A wave washed over him. Regaining his balance, he shook off the water and held out a hand. "Come here." The hungry gaze intensified.

Treading water beyond his reach, she felt like a cornered animal, despite the vast Pacific behind her. She shook her head playfully, held out a taunting hand, then pulled it back. With a mischievous smile she swam farther away.

He caught her easily and pulled her toward shore, where they laughed and kissed.

"Oh, look!" Aria pointed to their picnic area, where three island foxes pawed at the basket. Nearby, a fourth fox had Eli's shirt in its mouth. When its companions tipped over the basket, spilling the contents all over the sand, it dropped the shirt and bolted to join them.

Aria and Eli dashed from the water, shouting at the scoundrels. The foxes scurried up the rocks that hemmed in the crescent-shaped beach, each one carrying a remnant from their lunch basket. Aria and Eli collapsed on the blanket in a fit of laughter.

As they cleaned up the mess, Aria's cheeks ached. She couldn't remember the last time she'd laughed so much.

Back on the yacht and under sail, the ship gliding smoothly and silently through the waves, Eli convinced her to join him on the bow. Taking her hand, he led her beyond the furled jib to the very tip of the boat, then helped her into a sitting position at the rail, legs dangling over the prow. While she held on to the warm metal railing, Eli eased down behind her and wrapped his arms around her waist.

He pressed his cheek against her ear. "You know, you can learn a lot about a person from discovering their favorite things."

"Is that right?" She wanted to say something witty, but all she could think of was the wind in her face as the yacht flew across the water like a heron, effortless, silent, and graceful.

He planted his lips on her neck and across her shoulder, warm, wet kisses that cooled instantly on her skin in the cool ocean air. "You're a lot like the girl in your story, you know. Able to believe even when others don't. Never giving up." The tenderness of his voice, his words, his kisses, lulled her with a sense of utter tranquility.

"Do you really think so?" The young girl in the story was hurt, broken but resilient and determined. Oh, how nice it was to know Eli saw her that way, realized how hard she'd tried to just hold on— to the home she'd grown to love, to the future she and Adam had envisioned for their children, to the beauty and grace of life.

"You know what you want, and you do what it takes to make it happen."

She relaxed against Eli's chest, and his arms tightened around her. The wind whipped long strands of her hair free from her ponytail. Through her sunglasses, she squinted at the sunlight sparkling on the water as the yacht slid soundlessly through the waves.

"I don't want this day to end," she said with blissful contentment.

"This—" Eli kissed her neck—"Us. Doesn't ever have to end."

A poem whispered in her mind. *Time flies, tossed on the wind like dandelion fluff, and right now is sweeter than we know.* This, here and now, was Aria's next shining moment. And if she'd learned anything about Eli in their few short weeks together, there would be many more to come.

But this moment, this blissful moment, was too perfect to last forever.

TWO HOURS LATER, Aria and Eli were in the backseat of the SUV on the way to the GSI Conference in San Diego. During the drive, Aria reacquainted herself with the presentation she'd put together for Glen, which she was now slated to give the next morning. She would have to practice it in her hotel room after dinner. She had no idea if it fit the timeslot, but with plenty of material, she could always cut content on the fly if needed.

They arrived early evening, checked in at the Marriott Marquis hotel, and cleaned up. Then Eli treated her to that quiet dinner he'd promised—a relaxing bayside table at Top of the Market, not far from the hotel and convention center. Away from the glamour of Hollywood, there were no cameras, no paparazzi, no bothersome fans . . . although the waitress and a few patrons smiled with surprise as they recognized Eli. All in all, it was a languid end to a perfect day.

The stress of presenting at a large conference was draining no matter how prepared she felt, and despite staying up late practicing her speech, Aria had a hard time falling asleep. She stared at the door to the adjoining room for hours, imagining Eli on the other side, the comfort of his arms, the warmth of his body alongside hers, the soft spot where his shoulder met his chest and where her head rested so perfectly. But she resisted the urge to go to him.

The next morning, more nervous than she wanted to admit, she had an odd sensation as she stepped up on stage to give the keynote, knowing it would probably be the last time she'd speak in front of such a large group. The audience numbered well over a thousand if she had to guess—and, of course, Eli sat in the front row, smiling with anticipation, his presence in her business world tilting her on her professional axis.

After an initial pause, she looked out over the crowded hall, forced herself to forget Eli, and launched into her presentation to the healthcare industry on the importance of global standards. With the right amount of self-deprecating humor to keep the audience's attention despite the dry subject matter, it went flawlessly—and earned her a rousing applause.

With a bow of appreciation and a wave, Aria exited the stage with a sigh of relief, glad to be done with both public speaking and her tenure at Hewitt.

Backstage, as the conference coordinators thanked her for her presentation, Eli appeared, his face beaming with pride.

"Wow!" His brows knit together as he stared at her forehead. "What else have you got there in that incredible brain of yours?"

Aria felt a flush start in her neck and redden her cheeks. "You weren't bored to death?"

"Are you kidding?"

Aria stood a bit taller, Eli's admiration a welcome boost to her occasionally flagging self-esteem. If she could rock an audience this size, what could she accomplish with a law degree and the ideals formed from her impoverished youth? She added two things to her virtual to-do list: one, consider law school, and two, call Latisha.

33

The house was dark when Aria returned home. Travel-weary, she drooped against her daughter's doorframe for several minutes and watched her child sleep. A part of her wished she'd wake up. The opportunities to kiss her little girl good night were fading fast. With a heavy heart, she turned toward her own bedroom.

From her suitcase, Aria extracted the toiletries she'd need for the morning, and left the rest of the unpacking for tomorrow. Bone tired, she collapsed onto her bed, phone in front of her, and stared up at the ceiling as she waited for Eli to pick up.

"You're never going to guess who called tonight," he answered without preamble.

The enthusiasm in his voice was infectious, and her spirits lifted. "Lang."

"Seriously?" Eli frowned. She'd ruined his surprise.

"He liked you," she said, scrambling to sit up against the headboard. "Why wouldn't he call?"

"He liked *you*."

"And?" Aria prompted, even though she felt certain she knew what was coming.

"I got the part!"

So he'd be heading off to Italy to film *Casanova*. "That's awesome. Congratulations."

"You don't seem excited."

"I am. I'm just tired." Aria gazed longingly at her pillow. So tired, so far away. And soon to be much farther. She searched for a positive. "He knows how good you are."

"Do you, Ari? Do you know how good I am?" He sounded insecure, unlike himself, and it hurt knowing she'd made him feel that way.

"Of course I do."

"Filming starts in September. Monroe will be at college by then, right?"

"Yeah." And she'd be here, alone. Unless . . .

Silence hung in the air, as vast as the geography that separated them.

"So would you like to go to Italy with me."

"Oh, Eli." Was she crazy to even consider chasing this man halfway across the world? After the past few glorious days they'd spent together, how could she not?

"Will you at least think about it?"

"Sure." She imagined a quaint little villa nestled at the end of a long cypress-lined lane, on a vineyard, with an olive grove nearby. While Eli worked, she'd pass her days reading, maybe researching the idea Latisha and she had discussed. If Eli had weekends free they could explore the countryside, sightsee, and experience the culture together.

"Hey, I'll let you go. I know you're tired."

"Thanks again for the past few days. It really was amazing."

He exhaled, loud and long, as if he could sense her reluctance to cross over some invisible boundary. "Hey, I want you to know, I'm not some clown who performs grand gestures for every woman I meet. I'm crazy about you, Ari. And baby, yesterday was just a start."

"I don't need grand gestures."

"What do you need?"

Time. Sleep. She forced a smile. "You."

They said good night and she nestled beneath the covers, her mind racing. Reluctantly, she pushed Eli, the scarlet sails of the yacht, the sea caves, and Italy to the back of her mind and forced herself to think about work instead.

Tomorrow, in her weekly meeting that she'd rescheduled due to the conference, she would officially announce her resignation to her team.

Despite her certainty about her decision, she had mixed feelings. While she looked forward to leaving behind the incessant demands of the eight-to-five and the endless travel that had kept her from her children, she would miss all the good people she worked with.

But her greatest fear was how she would fill her days once Monroe went off to college. The inevitable loneliness was too wretched to dwell on—it lurked like a monster under the bed. And she feared if she looked too close, it would become all too real.

Suddenly, Italy with Eli hovered like a caramel-colored sunrise.

EARLY THE NEXT MORNING, in her office, Aria completed the company's online job requisition form for her replacement, a mere formality since Cadence had already been offered the position and accepted it.

She met with her team in their usual conference room and closed the meeting with the news of her resignation and Cadence's promotion to replace her. Although surprise registered on nearly every face, they all seemed genuinely pleased. A few questions were raised about procedural changes that might be forthcoming, and Cadence deftly took over, addressing each of their concerns as if she'd been in the role for months.

As their coworkers filed out of the room, just about everyone made a point of congratulating them both, most with a firm and heartfelt handshake, Caleb, her most recent new-hire, and a few others with hugs for Aria.

At lunchtime, Aria and Cadence left the office for Romano's Deli, where Mr. Romano affectionately greeted them as Signora Whit-amore and Signora May. At an outdoor bistro-style table, they enjoyed antipasto salads while Aria recounted her weekend in LA. Her friend practically swooned when Aria described the yacht with scarlet sails and what it meant to her.

Returning to the office, they agreed to regroup at two o'clock to begin the long and arduous process of realigning accounts until Cadence's replacement could be hired.

Back at her desk, Aria responded to several emails, copying in Cadence, then submitted her expense report for the San Diego conference.

Cadence arrived at her office at two, and they spent the rest of the afternoon reassigning accounts. Over the next few days, they would call most of Aria's new and larger customers to personally introduce Cadence. For the others, an email would suffice.

At a few minutes before five, Aria's cell phone vibrated. She bit her lip to hide the grin when she saw Eli's name.

Cadence stood. "Go ahead. We'll pick this back up in the morning."

Aria answered the call as her office door closed behind Cadence. "Hey there!"

"You obviously haven't seen today's *Hollywood Scoop*, or you wouldn't have picked up."

Her excitement evaporated like ice on a griddle. "What now?"

"Pics of me with just about every woman I spoke to at Lang's party, all looking angry or like they're about to cry."

She crumpled back in her chair. "Pictures of me too?"

"Right in the middle. Except you're walking away, and I'm standing there looking stupid and confused. It must have been taken when you left the game room."

Aria cringed. "What about the nice one Penelope took of us together?"

Eli chuckled bitterly. "Didn't fit the headline."

"Which was?"

A moment of silence hovered between them. "'Heartbreaker.'"

Aria sprang from her seat. *That woman and her forty-five miles of nerve!* Aria ached to all-out speedbag her. "Why do you let Penelope do this to you?"

Eli groaned. "She's my publicist. It's her job to build an image for me. I wouldn't be where I am today if—"

"You're giving her way too much credit."

"Image is important in this business."

"Maybe Your fans might love you even more if they knew what a good guy you are."

"I wouldn't even know where to start."

"Write your own story. Show them the man who shoots hoops with inner-city kids."

"Penelope would hate that."

Aria bit her tongue. It was Eli's career, and his publicist had obviously done a fine job for him so far. But now his reputation involved her. Surely she had the right to say something.

"She works for *you*, right?"

"Yeah."

"You don't have to give her carte blanche over your whole life."

Eli was silent.

"I'm overstepping, aren't I?" Aria sat on the edge of her desk.

"No, I appreciate your input. And you're right. Penelope turned down a fundraiser for a Detroit boys club I wanted to do in May and a golf outing for Special Olympics a few months before that."

"Well, *Heartbreaker* certainly isn't winning you any days in the sun."

She could hear him relax back in his seat. "You have a point. I'll give her a call. Let you know how it goes."

After they hung up, Aria plopped back into her chair. A part of her felt sorely tempted to rush out and buy the paper, to see just how bad it was. Another part refused to let it matter.

By the time Aria had shut down her laptop and packed her satchel, she received a text from Eli.

Eli: P agreed! But she's reserving final say on copy and pics.

Aria: No way. You should have final on both.

Eli: You're tough.

Aria: Bring it!

Eli responded with a Rolling on the Floor Laughing emoji.

Aria wanted to laugh too, but something rang false about the whole conversation. Who was she to tell Eli to reveal his true persona? She was doing the same thing, hiding the grieving widow wallowing in despair and loneliness behind what she allows others to see: the confident business woman, inventor, and defender of social justice.

Everyone has a weakness they hide from others.

Besides, she couldn't help the niggling feeling that this was much more than a battle won. More likely, it was the beginning of what would become an endless war. At least as long as Penelope Fenwick was in command.

34

———————

Aria stood on the back deck of her home, watching the flurry of activity below as the cadre of help, looking like worker ants, made final preparations for her daughter's open house. On one side of the lawn, Monroe helped the band— her friends from church—set up on a small stage. On the other side, caterers bustled about beneath a huge white tent while slushy and ice cream machines whirred with readiness beneath the deck. Strands of lights hung from the trees, deck, and tent, thousands of tiny white bulbs waiting to spring to life with nightfall.

All of Adam's family was coming. He would've been pleased.

Aria's phone rang. Eli. Turning her back on the frenzy below, she perched on the edge of the chaise and answered.

"Hey. On your way?"

"Still in LA. Looks like I can't make Monroe's open house after all. Lang invited me for a round of golf tomorrow morning, and I have to go. I hope you understand."

"Oh, sure." She didn't like it, but she understood. A round of golf was a golden opportunity to cement business relationships. Despite her own mediocre ability, she had made some of her best deals on the greens.

"You're not too disappointed?"

"I'll miss you." Of course she was disappointed, but not as much as she probably should be. Today, of all days, she wanted to focus on her daughter, not worry about whether someone would recognize Eli or whether he was enjoying himself. And what was one more day?

"How're the party arrangements coming?"

"Oh, good. Still setting up." Aria tried to imagine the scene from a drone shot, not from someone who'd spent hours and hours planning each minute detail. "Funny thing is, a couple of months ago, it was only going to be hotdogs and s'mores over the fire."

"And now?"

Aria went to the deck railing and turned the camera to pan the yard below.

"So why the big to-do?"

It took a moment for the reason to surface, but when it did, it made perfect sense. "It's the party Adam would have wanted for her." He had been the one who insisted on the big house on the lake, the high-end boat, the best schools. Monroe wouldn't have cared either way. And now, he wasn't here to appreciate it.

Aria swallowed the heartbreak and returned to the chaise. "How's your speech for the fundraiser coming?"

He groaned. "I'm so bad at this kind of thing. And I'm running out of time."

"Want some help?"

"Seriously?"

"You said you liked the presentation I gave in San Diego."

"It was brilliant!"

"All right, then. Will I see you tomorrow evening?"

"Any chance I can talk you into coming to LA next week?

She relaxed back in the chaise, her whole body smiling. "I shouldn't."

"Monroe?"

"No, she leaves in the morning for a senior trip, a week in the Rockies.

"Oh, fun for her. So . . . what are you going to do there? Rattle around that big empty house all by yourself?"

He had a point. "We won't have to go to a bunch of parties, will we?"

"Just the fundraiser for the boys club on Friday."

"I'd love to."

"Yes!" He threw his head back like a little kid. "Come tomorrow then."

A clash of cymbals made Aria jump.

"Sounds like you gotta go."

Aria hurried to the railing. Below in the yard, boys shouted as Monroe rushed to the backside of the stage. "Yeah. Sorry. See you tomorrow?"

"You betcha. Send me your flight details."

"You betcha," she echoed with a grin. Aria ended the call.

Monroe reappeared in the center of the lawn, caught her mother's gaze and gave her a wide grin and a thumbs-up. "All good."

Aria rested her head against the deck post, decided every task on her mental to-do list was crossed off, and virtually wadded it up and tossed it out—*whoosh*, like closing an app—everything was under control.

35

Never had Eli known a woman to be so agreeable. In a matter of days, Aria had settled into his leisurely at-home routine, astounding him with her carefree and easygoing manner. In the mornings, while he memorized his script, Aria worked on his speech and read another Ben Franklin biography.

They spent most days poolside, lounging beneath an umbrella, Aria reading lines with him. In the evenings they watched Italian movies, first with subtitles and then without. Eli was determined this time to learn at least a little of the local dialect, and given Aria's affinity for languages, she seemed eager to help him.

On Friday afternoon, after cooling off in the pool, Aria returned to her lounge chair and towel-dried her hair while Eli sat beside her, picked up his script, and wondered if he should save the scene they were about to read for later.

"What are we reading today?" She finger-combed her hair and braided it to one side.

"It's a love scene." He eyed her, sitting there all elegance and grace in her little white bikini, her body still glowing with tiny droplets glistening in the sunshine.

"I can handle it," she said with a confident grin. She snatched the script from his hands. "Can you?"

He cleared his throat and stifled a laugh. "Of course. I'm a professional." Was he up to it, though? She looked as hot as ever, and the memory of waking up beside her that morning still lingered like an all-night-long slow kiss.

Dismissing his reservations, he stood. "We're supposed to be walking." He gave her a hand up, then pointed to the page. "Start here. You're Henrietta today." He headed toward the garden path, and she followed at his side. "Whatever you may think of me, my dear Henrietta, know this. I do not seek to conquer."

"What then, Senior Casanova, do you seek?"

Beneath the magnolia, Eli stopped and turned to her, capturing her gaze, per the script. Nearby jasmine and honey-scented hibiscus danced with the trifecta of coconut, chlorine, and sunshine hugging her skin. "The ways of love and how it makes us one with the angels." He took her hand, raised it to his lips, and lowered his voice. "The taste of paradise before the fall." He kissed her hand. "A single moment to last a lifetime."

The script In her hand apparently forgotten, she eyed his lips on her hand with an emptiness he'd never seen before. While time stood still, her face tipped upward and her lips sought his in a moment of sheer perfection, setting him afire with their tenderness. His breath caught. Who was seducing whom here?

"Oh, my love." The words tumbled out, unbidden, and definitely not per script. Captured and defenseless, mesmerized by the hunger in her eyes, his emotions spilled like a glass of wine. "I see the heavens, the very moon and stars and galaxies in your eyes, and I am grounded to this place, this garden, this bench. I'm set aglow in your presence."

He pulled her down to sit beside him on the double chaise beneath the magnolia, then eased her back and stretched out beside her, half covering her with his weight. She blinked and fumbled with the pages. "Your eyelashes flutter like a butterfly's wings"—he placed her free hand on his heart—"setting my heart to beating madly in my chest."

He rolled to his back, pulling her atop him and undid her braid, then threaded his hands through her damp hair, arranging it forward, surrounding them both. "Your hair, like silken strands, cascades around me, wild and wavy and filled with sunshine, and I'm like the oceans tossed."

With the backs of his fingertips he caressed her cheek. "Your velvet skin"—his fingers trailed down her neck and across her bare shoulder, and she shivered, which excited him even more—" quivers at my touch."

"Eli—" Her breath was shaky.

"Oh, the sound of my name on your lips, like a siren's song, and I'm forever lost."

His hands roamed down her sides, her waist, her hips. She gasped for breath and moved against him, and his whole body rejoiced to know she ached for him. "Your curves, your softness, your very womanhood aches for my strength, my hardness, my possession."

She closed her eyes and arched her head back with a barely audible "Oh," arousing him beyond limits.

Wracked with a longing so deep he could hardly breathe, he pulled her to him, buried his face against her ear, and pleaded, "Oh, Ari, have pity on this poor besotted soul, and be with me."

She raised her head, her eyes dark with passion and a smile that was all *yes*.

She wanted him, finally. He'd waited so long to fully know this beautiful woman, to claim her as his own, to make her crazy with desire, like he'd been for weeks now.

"Wait." She raised her hand, which still held the pages. "My lines—"

He snatched away the script, tossed it aside, and wrapped his hands in her hair. "Baby, I went off script ten minutes ago."

"Oh."

He brushed his lips against hers, teasing, lost in their softness. "When you kissed me," he murmured against her open mouth.

"Well," she said with a half-laugh, "that wasn't very professional."

Eli stared up at her, dumbfounded that she'd thought it all a game, the way she'd so easily and carelessly toyed with him. He didn't know whether to be furious or laugh it off. It wasn't funny. In fact, it was getting downright serious, heartbreak serious, for him anyway.

He extricated himself, stood, and gazed down at her, the classy white bikini now slightly askew, her cheeks flushed pink, her chest rising and falling in rapid rhythm to her heavy breathing. Her impish grin disappeared, and she worried her lip sheepishly as though finally realizing her effect on him. Her gaze lowered, then averted altogether, no doubt to avoid his obvious state of arousal.

He spun on his heel and returned to the swimming pool, diving into the cool, blessed relief. When he surfaced ten laps later, his lungs searing from exhaustion, she was sitting at the pool's edge, unsmiling, feet dangling in the water. He stood, rubbed his face, and ran his hands through his hair.

"You're killing me here," he gasped, still catching his breath. Something about her undid him, the fleeting snippets of passion she couldn't hide, her tiny moan that screamed with wild abandon, the raw emotion in her touch that promised so much more. Beneath that tough exterior was a fire that burned and yearned, and yet, she jumped at every spark.

"I'm sorry," she said, her voice filled with nervousness. "I didn't mean to . . . " Her gaze softened, and she shook her head as though realizing her words and her eyes spoke two different languages. "I'm trying here." Her body seemed to curl in on itself, and she looked down as though shamed by allowing him to see this precious glimpse of her weakness.

He moved closer, parting her knees to stand between them and squinted up at her. "No, I'm sorry." For the briefest of moments he imagined lifting her down into the water to join him, her legs circling his waist, kissing her like he had that day in the meadow, a deep-down, meant-to-be-remembered kiss that would lead to . . . *oh, stop already*! He loosened the braid she'd redone, and her hair tumbled free in a ripple of wanton waves. "Wear your hair like this tonight."

"Wet?"

"Wild and loose." He ran his fingers through the unruly honey-brown strands, the drying parts reflecting the sun like rolling waves of wheat.

"But it's black-tie—"

"I want them to see you." He twirled a length around his index finger. "The real you."

He stepped out of the water, wrapped a towel around his waist, and turned to find her watching him. He saw love in her eyes.

The words no longer mattered.

Aria's heart pounded as she sat in the backseat of the SUV on the way to the fundraiser for the LA Boys & Girls Club. Eli had spent hours over the past few days practicing the speech she'd helped him write, but did he have any idea how much of herself she'd poured into it? If so, he'd given no indication.

The car stopped and Eli hopped out. "I'll be right back." He bounded up the steps of his friend Simon McGill's house, where they were to pick up him and Makayla. Penelope had insisted they all arrive together.

Aria gazed at the manila folder tucked into the seatback, containing Eli's speech notes. Unable to resist the temptation, she grabbed it, pulled a pen from her evening bag, and changed the closing line.

Makayla's laughter drew her attention as she returned the folder. In a slate blue sequined dress the exact color of Eli's eyes and an up-do that may have cost as much as Aria's dress, Makayla held Eli's arm so close it brushed her breast. Simon, in a well-fitted tux and red bow tie, followed behind. Aria scooched to the far side of the bench seat as Anders opened the rear door. Eli stepped forward to slide in first but Makayla deftly inserted herself in front of him. "I don't mind sitting in the middle," she cooed, cozying up beside Aria.

Eli, apparently oblivious to the chit's machinations, slid in behind her while Simon rode shotgun. Despite Aria's black Chiara Boni off-the-shoulder evening gown, the most expensive dress she'd ever owned, she felt dull beside the vivacious little blue belle.

Makayla chattered endlessly the whole way while the only thing Aria could think about was facing the press that would inevitably be there. At one point, Simon shot Aria a sympathetic smile, and she wanted to lunge across the vehicle and hug him.

Finally, Anders pulled to the curb in front of the Millennium Biltmore. A red carpet awaited, as if it were the Oscars, the media jostling for position along the cordoned off walkway.

Anders hurried around to open the rear door and Eli stepped out amid shouts and camera flashes. He offered a hand to Makayla who turned to the cameras, poised at his side, as if it were the most natural thing in the world—which it probably was, for her—to be the center of attention.

Aria waited, then waited a moment longer.

With a huff, Simon got out and offered an arm to Makayla who turned away, toward the hotel, clinging to Eli. And just like that, Eli and Makayla were walking the red carpet together, arm in arm, and smiling for the cameras.

Simon appeared at the door and Aria stepped out, took his arm with a warm smile of appreciation, and they followed the famous couple up the red carpet virtually ignored.

In the foyer of the Crystal Ballroom, Aria spotted Eli with Makayla still glommed onto his arm like a leech, posing for photographers in front of a large logoed screen.

Before Aria and Simon could reach them, Penelope appeared and whisked them away, leaving Aria and Simon in her purple-sequined dust.

Simon pointed to two long linen-draped tables covered with small tented place cards. "Shall we find our table?"

Still reeling with abandonment, Aria had half a notion to follow Eli. She was his guest, after all. Then remembering Latisha telling her it was good press for the two costars to be seen together, Aria decided to let it go. Simon was friendly, funny, and excellent company. She could certainly make do.

"Here we are," Simon said, handing Aria a card with her name on it. "Table twenty-four."

Simon offered his arm and they entered the ballroom together. White linen-covered round tables covered most of the carpeted floor, with a wide walkway down the middle. A bevy of gowned and tuxedoed guests milled between, searching for their assigned seating, or for someone they knew or hoped to know.

While Simon studied the table numbers, Aria succumbed to the grandeur of the room. With exquisite draping and soft lighting, a plethora of mirrors and glass, and intricate gilt arches and columns, the whole room pulsed with elegance and screamed Tinseltown. Aria had never seen anything more glamorous.

"Here we are," Simon announced.

Aria glanced at their table and the others around them—twenty-one through twenty-four, at the very back, nearest the doors—then scanned the room for Eli.

At the far end, rose three massive arches, each one inset with luxurious red velvet curtains and a white panel display screen. In front of the arches, spanned a stage, set with a podium and microphone. Eli sat at a front table, Penelope on his left, Makayla on his right. Michael Lang and a woman Aria assumed was his wife joined the table and Eli stood to shake his hand. Before returning to his seat, Eli turned, his gaze searching the room, finding Aria.

From her table in the back, Aria smiled and gave him a little wave, and an even smaller smile, then slipped into the chair Simon had pulled out for her.

While Simon left to fetch them both a beverage from one of the two bars they'd seen in the foyer, Aria lost herself in her surroundings. An upper level of intimate box seats, each one draped with red damask side curtains and subtly backlit lent the ornate ballroom a quaint yet expansive feel. She didn't know which was more enchanting, the ballroom or the people filling it.

Aside from a camera perched on a tripod on the balcony above the entryway, the room was surprisingly devoid of media. Aria breathed a sigh of relief.

Simon returned, handed her a red wine, and within minutes salad plates consisting of a Romaine wedge topped with carrot shreds, microgreens, and a pair of prawns were delivered by a bevy of well-trained wait staff. Two other couples joined them, a forty-something screenwriter and her husband, and a very young looking Silicon Valley tech exec and his expecting wife.

While they ate, Simon happily regaled Aria and their table-mates with the history of the Millennium Biltmore and the umpteen major motion pictures that had been filmed in that very room. Plated dinners appeared next—filet mignon, braised pota-toes, and a broccoli floret for most, a vegan plate for the tech exec's wife—and the conversation turned to each person's reason for attending the fundraiser. Aria had a hard time focusing on the conversation, much less eating anything beyond the salad, her stomach too twisted in knots. She turned to glance at the doorway only a few feet behind her. She could always flee.

Shortly after dessert was served—an intricate assortment of petit fours Aria couldn't even look at—the lights dimmed and a rotund little man with round spectacles lumbered onto the stage. Guests adjusted their chairs for a better view and the room hushed.

Aria stretched in her seat but could still barely make out the man's features. She eyed the darkened balconies overlooking the stage with longing.

A squeaky voice filled the ballroom as the man on stage intro-duced himself as the director of the local Boys & Girls Club. In a slow, hesitant drawl, he described the organization's guiding mission—to open doors and transform lives—and expressed how grateful he was for the community's support, and most especially for the evening's guest of honor.

Aria's insides thrummed as the little man droned on. She'd seen the evening's agenda so she knew the director's preamble was scheduled for eight to ten minutes. Refusing to miss a minute of Eli's speech, Aria leaned over and whispered to Simon, "I'm going to go powder my nose."

As Aria eased out one side of the wide double doors, taking care to not let it slam behind her, the man's voice faded away, muffled by the silence of the near empty foyer.

She glanced left then right and spotted the sign sticking out from the wall beyond a wide sweeping staircase. She headed that direction. Despite a placard draped across the second step that read "Balcony Closed," Aria's gaze drifted up the carpeted stairway as she passed by. The hall above wasn't completely dark, but it certainly wasn't inviting either.

Washing her hands before the gilt-edged mirror, bathed in a glow of crystal sconces, Aria knew exactly what to do.

Squaring her shoulders and donning her best "I belong here" façade, Aria exited the restroom, ignored the wait staff near the bar at the opposite end, and, dashed silently up the stairway as calmly as she could manage.

She made it to the opera box closest to the stage as the director, in a long-winded flourish, pronounced, "Eli Van Drie!"

The audience erupted in polite applause.

Tucked in the shadows of the balcony, suddenly grateful for her demure black evening gown, Aria enjoyed the best view in the house. As the audience quieted, Aria peeked back the way she'd come, to the dimly lit empty aisle.

Aria's breath caught in her throat when Eli's husky voice filled the cavernous ballroom. "Thank you, Director Hill. And thank you for all you do for the kids and for this community." Eli concluded his praise of the little man by clapping for him and the audience joined in.

"Ladies and gentlemen, it's an honor to be invited to speak to you tonight about a cause that's near and dear to my heart. Every chance I get, I visit the Boys & Girls Club in Central LA to shoot hoops with a bunch of inner-city kids. Because they matter."

Eli straightened the pages on the lectern. He'd done such a good job memorizing his speech, would he use his printed notes, notice her handwritten additions at the end?

"The first time I set foot on a basketball court—outside of ninth-grade gym class—was when I landed the role of Rummy in *Brotherhood*."

Eli told his story about being a hockey player and did his well-practiced goalie-save, sliding across the polished wood stage dramatically, one hand up, the other holding an invisible hockey stick. The audience roared with laughter.

Nailed it! Aria suppressed her own laughter.

Eli straightened his tux and returned to the podium as the audience quieted. "So I had to learn a new sport. I spent a lot of time with kids just like the ones in the film. The experience instilled in me a love of basketball and, more important, a heart for kids in crisis. If you haven't seen *Brotherhood*, I highly recommend it, and not just because I'm in it."

Another light titter from the audience. Eli picked up the clicker and began pacing the stage as if he owned it.

"See, the lead character, Rummy, is this poverty-stricken kid from a broken family who happens to be a stellar basketball player. When he makes All-American, his future is set, or so he thinks. But he has a really hard time accepting a more promising way of life. Sustained poverty has a way of warping a young mind, a whole community, to the point where people accept the way things are because it's all they've ever known. How can we even hope to convince a child to leave making mud pies in the ghetto in exchange for building sand castles in the suburbs when the child has never seen a beach?"

Aria's hand went to her heart as a soft "Oh!" tumbled from her lips. Hearing her words so eloquently given life by Eli's strong baritone, moved her, emboldened her, changed her. Aria scanned the faces of the audience, all captivated.

"Something powerful happens when adults say by their presence in a child's life, 'I could be anywhere in the world right now, but I'm choosing to be here with you because there's something in you I find valuable.' That message, when backed up by consistency and authenticity, breaks through to young people in ways that teachers and principals can rarely do. Sometimes having just one person who believes in a child helps that child to believe in himself."

Aria remembered discussing that line with Eli. She'd written "himself or herself," to be gender inclusive, but he felt it would come across as stiff, and everyone would know he meant girls too.

Eli pressed the clicker and the first slide appeared on the center screen, silhouettes of a mother and a young boy at a dinner table. They'd discussed this too. Aria had hoped to temper the sterility of espousing statistics by injecting profound images to help show the story.

"Young men who grow up in fatherless homes are twice as likely to end up in jail as those who come from traditional two-parent families. Every year, thousands of fatherless young men get stuck in the poverty-to-prison pipeline, their futures determined by their zip code rather than their aptitude, intelligence, or anything else for that matter. Who teaches a fatherless boy what it means to be a man when there's no man at home?"

Aria glanced to where Simon sat at their table, beside her empty seat. Too far away to see his face, but his posture, relaxed, beer in hand, said clearly, *No worries, mate.*

Eli clicked again and the first image moved to the rightmost screen and an image of a pregnant teen filled the center screen. "I hang out with the boys, but let's not forget the young girls. Teen pregnancy is strongly linked to poverty. Every year, one in four teenage girls gets pregnant. Only about half of young mothers finish high school, and just thirty-seven percent support themselves by holding down a job. Children born to teen parents tend to do worse in school than children born to older parents. They're more likely to apply for child welfare and enter correctional systems, drop out of high school, and become teen parents themselves."

Eli's next click brought an image to the leftmost screen of a man raising a hand to a cowering young woman, and a gasp from the audience.

"Who teaches a fatherless girl what a healthy marriage looks like when there's no man at home?"

All three screens went blank as Eli returned to the podium. "I'd like to introduce you to some of the young folks behind these statistics."

An image of Ricky Gonzales appeared on the left screen.

"This is Ricky. At fifteen, Ricky mugged a young classmate and almost slit her throat, an initiation ritual for a gang. Ricky dropped out of school shortly after the attack and was killed in a gang fight six months later."

Aria stared at Ricky's yearbook photo as her hand went instinctively to the scar beneath her chin. She shivered.

Ricky's photo flipped to the center screen and a picture of a smiling young girl Eli knew filled the leftmost screen.

"Delilah is an outgoing third grader who loves Double Dutch. Her mentor, Paula, takes her to dance lessons once a week. On the drive, they practice her multiplication tables and spelling words. Delilah has her sights set on Julliard, and Paula's determined to get her there."

Aria held her breath, knowing the next slide would be difficult to see again. As Ricky and Delilah's images cascaded to the right, a wrinkled old photo of Aria's older brother filled the far screen. Eli rubbed his face, as if it was as hard for him to tell this particular story as it had been for Aria to write it, to have lived it.

Aria hadn't expected three screens but it made for an interesting presentation. Leave it to Hollywood to turn a simple Power-Point into a cinematic experience. Seeing her brother was too much. The longing was so sharp she had to look away.

"Gibson, nineteen, was a fix-it whiz. He dreamed of going to college, getting an engineering degree, but his single-parent mom couldn't find time to complete the financial aid forms, so he was home on a cool October evening when a car raced by and shot up his fifteen-year-old sister's birthday party. With a bullet to the chest,

Gibs died in his best friend's arms. The three young men responsible were angry they weren't invited and are now serving life sentences."

Eli paced the stage as he continued.

"Miguel, a talented young artist, was arrested at fifteen for spreading graffiti. The police didn't care that it was nice art. It was on an overpass. During Miguel's six months in juvie, he met a twenty-six year old financial analyst, who introduced him to other artistic mediums and directed him to healthier outlets for his talents. Next month, Miguel has his first show, called Painting with Ashes, in Palm Springs."

As Eli clicked through the slides of more kids he knew personally, his face beamed with love and compassion.

A photo of a silhouetted man walking through metal gates, presumably a prison, filled the left screen as the other images bounced to the right and Eli continued.

"This is DJ, a wrongly convicted nineteen-year-old who pled guilty to arson. He may have believed his girlfriend started the blaze and was trying to protect her, or he may have been coerced into copping a plea to avoid the life sentence that came with the manslaughter charge for the man who died in the fire, the man who'd raped DJ's girlfriend. DJ left behind a loving grandmother and a guilt-ridden young girl."

It wasn't Dante's image of course, but it hadn't been hard for Aria to find one online that fit his story. There were so many to choose from.

"This little cutie is Lily."

With a tap of the clicker, Aria's kindergarten picture filled the far screen. A ragged young thing in a yellow dress smiled, cheery-eyed and pale with the chubby cheeks of youth, her honey-brown hair cropped short. Her mother had called it a pixie cut—adorable. Aria had called it boy-hair—horrid.

Aria had provided Eli the pictures of herself and her brother. Each one was a crop of the same photo that she'd taken with her when she'd moved out at fifteen.

"When she was a little girl, Lily's father left without even saying goodbye. Her mother became an addict, trading food stamps for drug money."

Aria swallowed the emotions churning inside her. She'd written it, hard as it was, and she'd heard it multiple times as Eli had practiced his speech, but it was still painful to relive the memories she'd tried so long to bury.

"A white child at a predominantly ethnic school, Lily's classmates teased her mercilessly, calling her Lily Whitetrash, honky, and worse. As she grew older—and prettier—the boys called her other things, most of them lewd. None of them nice."

Aria closed her eyes, willing this part to be over with. *He doesn't know. He's read it so many times and he doesn't have a clue who Lily is.*

"At sixteen, Lily begged her older brother's best friend to have sex with her so her first time wouldn't be a violation. Caring a great deal for her, he did as she asked. A week later, Lily's new stepfather committed the very act she'd feared."

Aria shuddered. Cueball deserved to burn. He turned her mother into an addict—but the fire . . . Dante shouldn't have gone to prison for that. She hadn't included those details in the story she wrote for Eli's speech though. No one needed to know that she was responsible for the fire.

"For weeks, feeling ashamed, Lily kept her secret, speaking to no one about it. Eventually, she told a school guidance counselor and then the police. But no one believed her."

Several people in the audience shook their heads, in disgust, disbelief, or compassion. Or likely all three.

"That wasn't even the worst of it. Three months after the attack, Lily discovered she was pregnant. For the next six months she wondered whether her baby's father was the gentle young man she'd begged to love her or the abusive grown man who'd so ruthlessly used her."

Eli paused for effect, as Aria had suggested. As he scanned the audience, Eli swiped at his eyes. Were those actual tears? Or was he just being the consummate actor?

"Friends, this isn't what poverty looks like in some third-world country. These are real kids right here in our own cities in dire need of just one person who cares. One person they can count on. One person who will stand up and say, 'You matter!'" His voice cracked.

Aria knew Eli well enough to realize that the emotion here was real.

Eli pressed the button on the clicker, and the screens returned to the Boys & Girls Club logo. "It doesn't take much to be a mentor. An hour a week, that's it, to share who you are with a young person who needs to know that someone cares about what happens to them. Like every kid in America, these children deserve a chance at the American dream."

Eli returned to the lectern and gazed into the faces of the crowd, creating another pause for the upcoming change in tone, as Aria had instructed.

He described The Butterfly Effect without missing a beat, ending with the question, "So was it Moses, or Carver, or Wallace, or Borlaug who saved a billion people? How far back would we have to go to determine who really saved those billion people? And how far forward would we have to go in *your* life to show the difference you can make? *You* have the power to change a child's life, and in doing so, change the world."

A sniffle broke the pin-drop silence. Aria scanned the audience and saw tears on the cheeks of a woman. More than one, actually. Whether it was the gut-wrenching snippets of the kids' lives or Eli's heartfelt delivery, the speech had definitely hit its mark. Aria blinked back the tears pooling on her own lids.

"Many of the children I just told you about are kids I've met here at the club."

Eli glanced down at his notes. The quick furrow on his forehead told Aria that he'd noticed her last-minute additions.

"Remember Lily, the sixteen-year-old pregnant teen? A couple of empty nesters took her under their wing, mentored and encouraged her, and showed her how life is supposed to be lived. She kept her baby, finished high school, earned a college degree, married, and had a second child." Eli squinted to read the chicken scratches at the bottom of the page. "Until recently, she led the sales and marketing division of a multi-billion-dollar medical device company whose products save millions of lives." Eli stopped abruptly and stared at the paper on the podium for a long moment.

His head popped up and he searched the audience, his face awash with bewilderment, heartache, and compassion. The audience sat in rapt anticipation.

Aria took a step back from the edge of the balcony, sinking deeper into the shadows.

"Ladies and gentlemen . . . Lily herself helped me write this speech."

The crowd leapt to their feet in deafening applause.

Aria's hand flew to her chest, her heart pounding wildly.

Eli's face held a mixture of surprise and humility at the standing ovation, and he bowed low. When he straightened, a tear coursed down his cheek. As he left the stage, Eli scoured the audience again.

Feeling suddenly exposed, Aria backpedaled from the opera box, eager to find some dark, shadowy corner to hide in. Propped against the wall, her legs felt rubbery and weak. She swallowed hard, willing her emotions to settle as she slumped to the carpeted floor.

"Lily?" came a deep voice from down the hall. Not Eli's.

She looked up to see her son's familiar silver-gray eyes in the face of a man she hadn't seen in years.

Dante had always been tall, but the gangly boy she'd known had filled out, strong and solid beneath the well-fitted tux.

"Lily Fair." The little-girl nickname rolled from his lips like a bittersweet memory as he closed the distance between them. "It is you!"

All the heartbreak of her adolescence came crashing back, her entire body infused with adrenaline. She stood and glared at him. "What are you doing here?"

"I'm the director pro—"

"What are you really doing here?"

"I saw you in the supermarket papers. What are you doing with him?" He nodded in the direction of the stage.

"What business is it of yours who—"

"I promised Gibs." He winced at the mention of her brother, his best friend.

"I hate you."

"I had no choice, Lil, you gotta know that." He shoved his hands in his pockets but not before she saw the scars.

"You sent me away. Returned all my letters. You didn't even bother to read them!" She studied his face. His soft, rain-colored eyes hadn't changed. They still spoke volumes, words from the heart she'd never heard from his lips but she knew to be true, all the same. The memory cut too deep. She had to turn away.

With a fingertip, he traced the edge of her jawline and tipped her chin, exposing the long scar. A somber cloud crossed his chiseled features. Was he remembering that long-ago night and how he'd failed her? Or how he'd once loved her?

She stared at him, afraid that if she blinked he'd be gone and she'd realize she'd only imagined him, as she'd done so many times before. "If you'd written me just once, I would have waited for you forever."

"I know." His eyes bore into hers. She felt the warmth of his breath on her skin, his pure, earthy, leather-and-cedar scent, still the same after all this time. She'd dreamed of this moment a million times—seeing him again, loving him again, belonging to him again. Her chest ached, and was it any wonder, after all these years, that her heart would feel bruised?

"I tracked you down when I got out. When no one answered, I walked around back, saw you run across the lawn and down the dock. You hopped into a ski boat and zoomed away, two littles riding behind on tubes, screeching with delight. The smile on your face said everything I needed to know." His gaze caressed her, like a beggar who's waited twenty years for this one life-saving morsel. "You found your handsome sea captain."

"He died."

"I know."

Dante pulled something from his pocket and handed it to her. It was the Tinker Bell from her music box.

"Oh, Dante." She breathed his name as her fingertip caressed the jagged edge where the tiny fairy's slippers should be.

He eased closer and tipped her chin, capturing her gaze. The scars on his face and the crook in his nose bore testament to his damaged soul, the price he'd so willingly paid for loving her.

A blinding light flashed. When her vision cleared, Aria caught a glimpse of a little man dressed in black duck behind a column, then scurry down the stairs with an oversized camera like a rat with cheese. Aria pressed her fists to her temples and squeezed her eyes shut. Like she really needed one more thing to worry about.

Dante turned to give chase, but Aria grabbed his arm. "It's too late." The energy to fight eluded her. How could she have forgotten cameras are everywhere.

He placed his hand over hers. Its warmth sent a current of longing straight to her core. "I'm sorry."

She yanked her hand away, not ready to feel these things again. "I have to go."

Before he could say another word, she walked away from him, from the life she'd ruined, from a past she'd tried so hard to forget.

Halfway down the curved stairway, she paused, a shaky hand still clutching Tinker Bell to her chest. The other hand gripped the railing so hard her knuckles turned white. The expanse below, now filled with people talking in small groups, made her feel like a stick about to be tossed into a rushing river, invisible to the flow of guests before her, inadequate on more levels than she could count.

Eli stood among the throng in the center of the foyer, Makayla draped on his arm, effortlessly working the crowd with grace and affability. As if he sensed being watched, he raised his head and scanned the foyer. His eyes landed on her.

Aria pasted on her most self-assured smile, and fluffed her hair, which she'd worn long and wavy for him. *You wanted to see the real me? Here I am!*

Eli's hand went to his heart, and he gave her a tender smile.

He extricated himself from Makayla and the group, then headed in Aria's direction, but he only made it a few steps before the throng swallowed him up again. Makayla pushed through to stand at his side, smiling, laughing, and glomming onto his arm.

Was this how it would always be? Forever a Makayla lurking on the sidelines, ready to swoop in and take her place?

Eli needed a woman like that—someone captivating, adorable, perfect. They made a lovely couple. He couldn't possibly still love Aria now that he knew where she came from, all she'd endured, seen how truly broken she was.

Aria ached for home. She missed Monroe, the lake, The Willows—places where she knew what to say, how to dress, and how to behave.

She tucked Tinker Bell into her evening bag and glanced to the doors leading to the hotel lobby. Anders could easily take her home and return for the others. No one would even notice her absence. Not even Eli.

Dante appeared on the step beside her and offered his arm. "May I?" He was still rakishly handsome with smooth, dark skin and a strong, clean-shaven jaw. And those almost girlishly long lashes that had once made her heart pound.

Wondering how long Eli and Makayla would orbit the room together, Aria took Dante's arm, her stomach quivering, as they descended the last few steps.

"Nice job on that speech." Dante looked at her with pride.

"Thank you," she said, though she felt anything but worthy.

"There you are!" Simon approached with a look of concern.

Despite her roiling emotions, Aria shrugged on a mantle of false bravado, and introduced the two men.

"I'm a friend of Eli's." Simon shrugged. "And a currently unemployed set designer."

Dante shook Simon's hand. "Director pro tem of the Detroit Boys & Girls Club. It's a pleasure to meet you."

Acting director, probably because an ex-felon could never hold such a position. There were probably a lot of things he couldn't do because of his prison record, because of her. And yet, here he was, among Hollywood's elite, conducting himself like a man comfortable in his own skin. No one would guess that he'd served time.

Aria turned to Simon. "Would you do me a favor? Could you please tell Eli I've gone home?"

If he even notices I'm gone.

37

———

You'll never be enough. The thought, like a whisper in the dark, reverberated in Aria's head, rising in volume, shaking her wide awake.

She'd heard Eli come home hours ago, the front door opening and closing below, and a few minutes later, her bedroom door as he peeked in to check on her. He'd stood there for several long moments as she feigned sleep, too tired, too overwhelmed, too dejected to have to explain why she'd left the fundraiser early. Images flashed in her mind: Makayla in her sequined gown draped on Eli's arm, her look of pure adoration, Dante's silvery gaze filled with love and longing.

She wasn't enough—not for Dante, not for Adam, and certainly not for a man like Eli Van Drie.

Dante lost eight years of his life because the police didn't believe her about the events leading up to the fire. If only she'd been brave enough to tell them what Cueball had done to her. If she'd come forward sooner. If she hadn't been so afraid. Instead, she'd holed up in her little room above the pool hall for days, shutting out the world, huddled and ashamed, until the police came knocking.

And months later when she discovered she was pregnant, she told herself she'd done the right thing. But after seeing Dante again, she wasn't so sure. Gone was the gangly boy who'd teased and adored her when she was a girl.

Did she ever really love him? Or had she simply fallen in love with the fact that someone, anyone, could ever love her? Was she devastated by the loss of him or by the loss of her innocence? Or knowing what he'd given up for her?

His grandmother was right—she'd been nothing but bad news for Dante Jackson.

She'd been wrong for Adam too. Oh, she'd made a nice home with him, cooked his meals and washed his clothes, given him a daughter, and learned to enjoy most of the outdoor activities he loved. But she'd ignored his thirst for adventure. He'd lived for the next breakneck adrenaline rush. He bought that motorcycle because everything else wasn't enough. *She* wasn't enough.

Perched on the edge of the bed, Aria gazed longingly at the door to Eli's room—so close yet out of reach. He thrived on accolades. He said he'd give it all up for true love, for her, but would he resent her afterward? Could he really live without his adoring fans and their constant reminder of how handsome, how talented, how worthy he was?

He once said he liked how she saw him for who he really was. That if she fell in love with him, it would be because of the man he was, not because of what he did or had.

Where does a person's self-worth come from? Their parents? Accomplishments, praise, the perception of others? A person should be enough simply because she is born, because she *exists*.

Aria's childhood was defined by shame: the hand-me-down clothes, the father who'd abandoned her, twice, and the mother who flat-out didn't care.

She could still picture her mom, sitting on the couch with her chocolate stars and Pepsi, solitaire spread on the coffee table while she watched *Jeopardy*. All those things were way more important than anything her daughter might've needed. Her mother's lack of affection shouldn't bother her, though. How could she miss what she'd never known?

Not all women are cut out for motherhood. Mona Farrow had given it a nickle try, a paltry twentieth of what it took to be a good parent. She paid the rent and put food on the table. It had to have been hard raising two kids with no help. But Mona Farrow's most serious flaw was her addiction to men. Like a junkie, she couldn't go more than a few days without bringing home some strange guy, affording her children a revolving door of father figures. Until she hooked up with Quentin, or Q as he called himself, who'd moved in with them after Gibs died. A huge man, pale as glue, bald, and chiseled, Aria had called him Cueball, though never to his face. That was when the real addiction began. Cueball was a dealer, and he'd gotten her mother hooked—first on him and then on smack.

If Aria had been enough for her mother, she wouldn't have needed all those men. She wouldn't have fallen for a loser like Cueball. They could have lived a decent life.

But Aria had overcome all of that. She was a good mother, had raised two amazing children, enjoyed a successful career, even patented an invention that would help the environment.

Her self-assurance felt forced most of the time. She'd spent so long pretending to be what others expected, she'd begun to convince herself. People could believe almost anything if they repeated it often enough. *Tell, believe, repeat.* But the façade she'd fabricated over the years was a brittle illusion.

When she left Detroit after her mother's funeral, she promised herself she'd never again depend on anyone for her happiness. But then Adam had come along, and she'd allowed herself to do exactly that, with the same painful effects. She hadn't expected it to happen with Eli too. She wasn't prepared for it. And now she felt herself sinking in the quicksand of his affections.

Of course she loved him. He was impossible not to love: smart, funny, kind, compassionate. He'd be a devoted father, and they'd have beautiful children. Was it too late to have all of that with him?

Eli said he wanted a family someday, but he couldn't possibly understand the responsibility, the sheer drudgery that comes with parenthood. Anyone can fall in love in the sunshine, in a butterfly meadow, or beneath the stars on a moonlit night. Life around a campfire or on a ship of scarlet sails isn't real. When the passion of their romance paled to everyday living—late-night feedings, diapers, exhaustion, and temper tantrums—would he still be happy and satisfied? Or would he eventually succumb to the endless array of beautiful, carefree women throwing themselves at him? Would Aria's solitary, domesticated love ever be enough?

The last few nights she'd slept peacefully, wrapped in the blanket of Eli's arms. She'd gone almost a full week without waking to a tear-soaked pillow. But now, in bed alone again, the thrumming anxiety tortured her in the wee hours before dawn. She felt like she was inching further and further out on a limb about to snap.

She stared out the window, the silence unsettling. No sound came from outdoors, only the soft whisper of a gentle breeze stirring the sheers. She longed for the comfort of Eli's arms, the sound of his heart beneath her ear, beating for her.

She could go to him, stand at his bedside and watch him sleep until he woke and held out a hand, beckoning her to join him, like he had the last few nights. But she'd already taken so much from him . . . and given so little.

As she took a step toward his door, her phone vibrated on the nightstand.

"Mom," Monroe said when Aria answered, "I'm scared."

Aria turned her back to Eli's door. "What's wrong?"

"I heard a noise, out back I think." Her daughter's voice quavered with fear.

"Where are you?" Monroe was supposed to be in Chicago with Rachel and her mom, a quick shopping spree tacked onto the end of their class trip. She wasn't due home until late Sunday.

"I'm home. In your bedroom."

Aria quietly hurried downstairs. "Tell me about the noise."

"It was a loud crash."

Aria slipped outside, her mind racing. "Is it raining, windy?"

"Yeah, it's really windy."

"Do you hear anything now besides the wind?" Aria sat on the patio steps, her heart in her throat.

Monroe hesitated, as though listening. "No. Just the wind."

"Turn on the yard light."

Aria heard sheets pulled back, feet hitting the floor, the faint *click* of a light switch. She pictured Monroe parting the blinds to peer out the slider toward the lake.

Her daughter sighed with relief. "The high-top's on its side."

Aria released a breath. "Well, that was it." The wrought-iron table hitting the brick patio would've made a loud crashing sound. "How's the boat?"

"Looks okay."

"Good." Aria waited while Monroe switched off the light and climbed back into bed. "You all right?"

"Yeah. When are you coming home?"

She's in my bed because she misses me. Guilt flooded in. She should be there, to rub her daughter's forehead, scratch her back, snuggle up beside her like she did after Adam passed. "I'll be home tomorrow night."

And I won't leave you again.

She may not have been enough for her mom, Dante, Adam, or Eli Van Drie. But she could be—needed to be—enough for her daughter. She would be there for Monroe as long as she could, in whatever ways possible. She would not repeat her mother's mistake of letting *anything* become a higher priority than her precious daughter.

38

____

Despite the heat and the sky hazy with smog, Aria sought the early morning solitude of breakfast on Eli's patio overlooking the gardens. Having rescheduled her flight, she closed her laptop and thought about how to tell him she'd be heading home a day sooner than planned. And why she'd left the fundraiser early last night.

Her croissant and strawberries remained untouched as her mind replayed the events of the evening. She still couldn't believe she'd run into Dante Jackson. He was the last person in the world she'd expected to see at a Hollywood gala.

The slam of the patio door shattered her moment of serenity. Eli stomped toward her, his face as dark as thunder. He tossed a tabloid onto the table beside her—*The Hollywood Scoop*. "Something you want to tell me?"

Two photos dominated the front page: one of Eli, glaring, arms crossed; the other a shot of Dante and Aria looking like they were about to kiss.

She'd never pegged Eli as the jealous type, but she suspected his anger went deeper than that. "I . . . he . . . we grew up together."

Eli's eyes narrowed. "I feel like I don't even know you right now."

I've told you nearly everything. You're just not listening.

He whirled away, as though reining in an explosive temper, then spun back to face her. "Do you have any idea what this does to my image?"

"That's what this is about? What your fandom might think?"

He slammed a palm on the table, making her recoil. "Aria, I need to know who you are. The real woman, scars and all."

How dare he use her words against her!

She picked up the paper and skimmed the article—an exposé on her childhood, including the violent deaths of each of her family members, Dante's confession and sentencing, her mother's drug addiction. Thank God, they didn't mention Jacks or Monroe. But they'd come up with a new name for her: *Ghetto Girl!*

He slid into the chair beside her. "Is all this true?" His voice softened. "I really need to know the person I'm falling in love with here." His gaze implored her, as though his whole future depended on what she might tell him.

Maybe it did.

Perhaps she should tell him everything. Find out if he really loved her.

She rose and wandered to the half wall that separated the patio from the gardens. Before she could speak, he stood beside her. The look on his face almost shattered her resolve. Hurt, distrust, and hope all rolled into one accusing, impatient stare.

She dropped her gaze. Everything went pin-drop silent. Even the birds stopped singing.

He lifted her chin. "Please talk to me. How well do you know that man?"

Aria shrugged out of his grasp, and his arms fell empty at his sides. Backed against the garden wall, she squared her shoulders.

"My story is what I wrote in your speech." She swallowed hard, gathering resolve. "My dad left when I was five. My mom was an addict. Gibson, my brother, was shot and killed right in front of me on my fifteenth birthday. I was sixteen when my boyfriend went to prison for killing the man who raped me. My mom died of an over- dose shortly after. Forgive me if I don't enjoy reliving my *happy* childhood."

His gaze wandered off, as if his mind were searching for an elusive truth, something—anything—to fit the pieces into place in the silence that burned between them. "DJ . . . was Dante the—"

"Boyfriend." Aria wished they could leave it at that. It had been enough for Adam. "I'll tell you more if you want, but I'd really rather not."

He held her shoulders. "I just want to know you."

Aria searched for peace in the bougainvillea-draped land- scape while the warmth of his touch lingered, a feeling she was going to miss. *If you knew what I did, you'd never look at me this way again.*

Eli wrapped his arms around her, pulling her against his chest. "Nothing in your past could ever change how I feel about you." He pushed her hair aside and kissed her neck. His warm breath curled about her cheek like a zephyr. "Talk to me, baby."

She shook her head. She'd been broken and put back together so many times, one more nudge and she'd crumble.

He pulled back, and his eyes bore into hers. "What else are you hiding?"

"Sometimes the past needs to stay in the past." She couldn't raise her eyes to meet his, afraid of what she'd see there.

"Ari, please. I only want to help."

"I don't need your help!" She wrenched free. "I was doing fine before you came along."

Eli flinched. "Oh, really?"

Aria glanced at the tabloid on the table. Eli was worried about more than his career, and rightfully so. Seeing that photo had to hurt. The look in Dante's eyes. The look in *her* eyes. The only thing worse than kissing the wrong man was *wanting to*.

"Dante Jackson was my first . . . everything."

Eli's brow furrowed as his mind put the pieces together: Dante

Jackson. Her son's name and caramel-colored skin. Her having a baby at sixteen.

With a fingertip, he lifted her chin to study the scar. "Did he do that to you?"

"No. Ricky did. But it happened the night Dante and I were . . . together." On her sixteenth birthday, she'd shared her pathetic one-candle wish: *for someone to love me.* Dante's earthy male scent of leather and wood had felt like a safe haven. Snuggled against his warmth on that cold October night, she'd blissfully lingered in her first taste of womanhood.

And she'd felt loved. Truly and indelibly loved.

"Ari?" Eli stared at her, brows raised, obviously waiting.

"What?"

"I asked if you loved him."

Tears pooled. "Very much."

His gaze held deep empathy. Or was it pity?

"No!" She backed away, hand flattened in the air between them, because she had to stop him. She knew it was going to hurt. "Don't. Don't you dare pity me. I can't bear it. This is why I didn't want to tell you. Now every time you look at me, you'll see a poor, wounded little girl. That's not me, not anymore." *That's Lily Farrow, not me.* Tears filled her eyes, shaming her even further. "Don't let that be who you see when you look at me."

She'd fought so hard for so long to forget Lily and become Aria. Lily was a weak, fragile flower that attended funerals. Aria, the name her father had wanted for her, meant "solo" in Italian, "lioness of God" in Hebrew.

Eli held out his hand, as though begging her to allow him to breach the chasm between them. "It's not pity. It's . . . pain. And anger. I feel sad for all the scars you carry, and I'm angry with the people who've hurt you. Everything you've endured hurts me too. Because I love you." His fingertip trailed the scar beneath her chin. "Your wounds are my scars too."

A tear ran down her cheek. She yearned for the compassion he was offering, but she didn't dare receive it. She couldn't risk one more heartbreak, one more loss, knowing the next one might very well kill her.

Cupping her face, Eli kissed away her tears.

How could she allow herself to love this man?

How could she not?

39

———————

Longing to start the day over again, Eli poked his head in the half-open door to Aria's room. She sat at the dressing table, her computer on her lap. She looked tired. All morning, she'd been quiet and withdrawn. A weight hung in the air, and he didn't know how to lift it. "*Buongiorno bellissima.*"

Aria closed her laptop and tucked it into her bag on the floor. "*Caio, mio amico.*"

"My friend?" She hadn't come to him last night and after their argument earlier, a distance seemed to have grown between them.

"*Cara mia?*"

"Much better." He sat on the bed opposite her, eager to share his news. "Max called. Two more producers want to meet with me before we leave for Italy."

"That's great. I knew it wouldn't be long before they realized how good you are."

The lack of conviction in her voice was unsettling, but he chose to ignore it. "And I've got a guy coming to look at the bike tonight. A collector. It's as good as sold."

Finally, a genuine smile.

"Mrs. Rodriguez made chicken enchiladas for lunch."

Her nose wrinkled almost imperceptibly. It was so cute he wanted to laugh.

"Not a fan of Mexican food?"

She shrugged. "I'm just not hungry. You go ahead." She went to the closet, then turned around as though she had something more important to say than she didn't like enchiladas.

"What's wrong?"

She raised her eyes to him, and he knew, before she even spoke a word, that he didn't want to hear what was coming. It was written in the misty green of her eyes, in the way her gaze held his, as though it may be the last time she'd ever see him this way, comfortable and easy, in a house they shared.

"I'm going home."

Those three little words shattered his world. For weeks, Eli had longed for a different three words to come from her lips.

She retrieved her suitcase from the closet, set it on the bed, opened it. "Monroe needs me."

"*I* need you."

She stiffened. "Don't make me choose."

He rubbed his face with both hands. She was right. He'd virtually monopolized her for the past six weeks, her last summer to be with Monroe before she went off to college. It was time for him to let her go.

But why did it feel so permanent?

"I could come with." He tried to capture her gaze, but she refused to look at him.

"I need some time, Eli." She glanced sideways at him. "Alone." She took clothes off hangers and tossed them onto the bed.

Eli sighed, crushed. He'd never seen goodbye from this side. Matt's words echoed in his head: *You've never had to fight for a girl in your life.* He was right. Eli had no idea what to do.

She'd been quiet and cool since her big reveal that morning. Or maybe he was the different one. Now that he'd seen the depth of her brokenness, it was hard to see her as whole again. He took her hands in his.

Her eyes were clouded, distant. She'd obviously struggled over her decision to leave.

"Talk to me." The smell of lunch wafted up the stairs, and his stomach growled.

"The image Penelope's fabricated for you is working. Doors are opening. And I'm happy for you." She swallowed. "But . . . I'm not the one you need at your side." She pulled her hands free and began folding. "You should be with Makayla."

The pain in her eyes as she'd watched him work the room last evening stung him afresh. "You know Makayla's just my costar. Penelope manipulated the seating at the fundraiser, and I'm sorry about that, but you didn't have to disappear."

She went into the bathroom, and he raised his voice over the sound of her collecting her toiletries. "You should have been the one walking through the crowd on my arm, accepting all the accolades." The only thing left hanging in the closet was his shirt that she'd worn the night she cried in his arms. It hurt that she didn't want to keep it. He yanked it from the hanger and stuffed it down into her suitcase.

She returned and dumped the contents of her arms into her suitcase. "Maybe."

"Definitely! That was your speech."

"I shouldn't have to fight for a place that's rightfully mine." Her voice sounded defeated, like she was giving up.

How could she stand up for other people with such ferocity and not stand up for herself? "What we have is worth fighting for, Ari."

At the dressing table, she stuffed her cosmetics into a small pink bag. "I can't be an empty-headed party fluff."

He almost choked. "You think that's what I want?"

She whirled to face him and scowled. "I don't know what you want."

"I want this." He spread his arms wide. "I want us. I want *you*. A real girlfriend. A lover. I want a wife!"

Her mouth dropped open, and she plopped down onto the bench. "A w-what?"

"Whoops. That just sorta popped out," he said with a nervous chuckle.

He rubbed his face in frustration. That was not at all how he'd intended to propose. Regardless, he dropped to a knee in front of her and took her hands in his. "I'm sorry. I know it's too soon. But I do want to marry you. I love you, Ari. I haven't told you lately because I get tired of not hearing it back, but it's still there, getting stronger every day."

She pulled free and stood. "You should be with someone who can help your career." She zipped her cosmetic bag, collected her hairbrush and straightener, and added them to her suitcase.

Eli sat on the bench she'd vacated. "You do help my career."

"Yeah, right." She picked up the emerald necklace from the nightstand and put it on.

"Lang liked you because you stood up to him, commanded his respect. I landed that role because of you."

She shook her head and closed her suitcase, zipped it up.

"You're why things are starting to happen for me. Being seen with a woman everyone admires, including me. You're the reason for my recent success."

She stared at her suitcase. "No, Matt was right. I'm just another one of your charity cases."

Eli jumped to his feet and gasped like he'd been gut-punched. "He said that?"

"'Street projects' I think was the term he used." She picked up her suitcase.

Eli took it from her and eased it to the floor, ruing the day he met Matt Desmond. "You're so much more to me than that, and you know it."

"I don't belong here, Eli." She dropped onto the edge of the bed, her lip trembling. "I'm not enough for you. I've never been enough and I never will be."

He sat facing her, took her hands. "You are enough! In fact, you're too good for the likes of me. You're more than I ever dreamed. Far more than I deserve."

Her silence said she wasn't buying it.

"How can I show you what you mean to me? Do I need to . . . paint you a picture and cut off my ear?"

His quip garnered a sympathetic smile, albeit a small one.

"Walk on water? I happen to know a top-notch set designer who could make it happen."

Her smile widened.

He stood and drew her into his arms. "Ari, you need to go be with your daughter, fine. I'll come see you in a few weeks. Or whenever you say."

Tears pooled on her lower lids, and she blinked them back, sniffed, and pulled away.

"Ari, look at me." He gently turned her face to him. "I need time too," he admitted. "As much as I've loved sharing my bed with you these past few days, I can't do it anymore. Sleeping with you and not having you is like death by a thousand cuts. Every night I bleed a little more."

Her eyes widened in surprise, as if she had no idea how much self-restraint it took for him to lie beside her, holding her, and nothing more. He'd wanted to go to her last night, but he didn't think he could bear it one more night.

"I'll miss you," she whispered softly.

Three little words. They would have to be enough for now.

40

———————

Packed and ready to go, Aria bent to sniff the fresh bouquet of Eli's pink roses, so beautiful but always fleeting, like life. She wandered through the connecting door to his room, which felt cool and inviting, like the man who slept there. She was going to miss waking up in that great big bed.

Eli appeared in the connecting doorway and leaned against the frame. "Anders is bringing the car around."

She nodded and eased past him, back to her room where she hefted her satchel onto her shoulder, then turned to find Eli gazing at the print of The Willows.

"Everything will remind me of you," he said wistfully.

With a daunting weight in her chest, Aria had to remind herself this wasn't the end. She was simply going home for a while. Monroe needed her. And she needed time.

"It would help if I knew you didn't want to go." His voice sounded like he'd lost something treasured.

"Help you or help me?" It came out sounding spiteful, and she regretted it instantly. This was hard on him too.

"Every time we say goodbye it hurts a little more."

"I know."

He picked up her suitcase with a sad smile. "I should hang onto this. Give you something to come back for."

She stared at the beautiful man with his hand on her suitcase and love in his eyes. "I already have plenty to come back for."

In the car on the way to the airport, Eli kept his eyes fixed on their intertwined hands like they were the last lines of a farewell letter. She didn't have to guess what he was thinking. The dread was written all over his face.

Anders pulled to the curb at LAX and jumped out to retrieve her suitcase from the back.

"Maybe you should see a therapist," Eli ventured.

"No one can help me get past what I need to go through." She squeezed his hand. "I just need time."

Eli kissed her gently, as though she might break—and maybe she would. He held her for a long time before pulling away. "I love you, Ari."

"I should go."

"You're still thinking about Italy, right? Monroe will be in school by then." The hope in his soft blue eyes was bittersweet.

A moment of silence unraveled between them. He stared at her as though peering over the edge of a cliff, deciding whether to jump. With a heavy sigh, he rubbed his face like he did whenever he was frustrated. "God, Ari. If you're going to break my heart, just do it already."

"No! I'm not. I don't . . . " Of course he would think that. She'd given him little to make him think otherwise. She tried to speak, but the words danced away like fireflies. She needed time, time to figure it all out.

"Oh, Ari." He slumped against the seatback, gazing upward as though giving up. "Why can't you let me in? Is it because you're afraid I'm going to leave you too?"

"The men I love always do."

He straightened, faced her, and grinned—no doubt at the mention of love, as though that was admission enough. But his smile quickly faded as he must have realized the truth of her declaration and what it meant to him. "Look, I can't promise to live forever. But baby, I'll give you the best I've got for whatever time we're given."

The compassion in his voice was her tipping point. *Go. Go now, while you still can.* Swallowing the emotions swirling inside her, she turned to the door and placed her fingertips on the handle.

"Ari, wait." He pulled her hand away. "Please don't leave like this."

She kissed him goodbye, and it was long and sweet as if it might be the last time she'd kiss him that way. Or any way. When she pulled back, her lip quivered. *Don't cry, not here, not now.* But oh, how bitter is the kiss that says goodbye?

"Aw, baby." He slid his thumb across her lower lip.

"I'm sorry." She sniffed.

He cupped her face, tipped his head, and studied her. "How long do you need?"

Aria could only shrug because she really had no idea.

His gaze softened, but he didn't release her or look away.

He deserved an answer. She couldn't leave him hanging on forever. "I need at least this summer."

His eyes spoke of things he probably wanted to say but couldn't. "You want me to wait?"

She melted at the familiar movie line. Did he even realize it was a line? His question was so heartfelt, his gaze imploring, searching, as if through her eyes he could see straight into her heart. But she couldn't bring herself to say the words he longed to hear. "You're making it really hard . . ."

A crease appeared between his brows.

". . . to not love you." Lame, but it was the best she could do.

He smiled his chivalrous, confident grin and released his hold on her face. "I'll wait."

She forced a smile. Before he could stop her again, she threw open the door and jumped out. Taking the handle of her suitcase, she mumbled thanks to Anders and walked away through a teary haze. She didn't look back—couldn't. If she did, she may never leave.

As Aria cleared security, her phone vibrated with a text.

Eli: Watch this when you get to your gate.

She hurried through the concourse, found a seat in the waiting area, connected her headphones, and hit Play on the video he'd sent.

"This is for you, Ari," Eli said, smiling for the camera, for her. Wearing jeans and a white dress shirt, he sat perched on a barstool on his patio, his gardens in the background, his guitar in his arms. He was clean shaven, and his eyes squinted in the sunlight. Her heart swelled. "Hold it close, 'cause it's got my heart all wrapped up in it. Watch it when you're missing me, and know that I'm thinking of you too." With two fingers, he blew a kiss.

He put his whole huge heart out there with his song, even included cutaways to videos and pictures he had taken of her—most she had no idea he'd captured—and a few close-ups of the two of them together. Throughout, his deep gravelly voice sang the words that now held so much more meaning than they had that first night when they'd sung them together.

I wanna draw you in
I wanna make you smile
Come on and take my hand
Let's dance for a while

I wanna steal your heart
I wanna be your dream
Come on and take my hand
You'll be my everything

Let me into your heart
Let me love you
Let me fill your life with love

Let me in, let me in

I wanna give you time
A while to heal your pain
I wanna love you so
You'll wanna let me in

I wanna make you mine
I wanna help you see
I wanna be with you
You'll wanna be with me

Let me into your heart
Into your life
Let me fill your days with love
Let me in. Let me in
Oh, let me in

THE VIDEO ENDED with a fade into the photo of the two of them lying together on the chaise, a peach-hued hint of sunrise reflected on the water, not in black and white like the tabloid had run but full high-res color, care of über-publicist Penelope, no doubt. He must have been working on the video for weeks.

Aria bent forward, elbows on her knees, head down, and a sob escaped. "I love you too." She should have told him! She tapped out a text—what was she doing? This was sheer madness. And yet . . . She counted down, 5-4-3-2-1. Before she could talk herself out of it, she pressed Send.

Aria: I don't want to go.

Within seconds her phone rang. Eli.

"Thank you for the video. It's beautiful." Her voice caught in her throat.

"You all right?"

"No."

"Oh, baby."

She pulled herself together and squeezed her eyes shut. "I'll be fine. I'm sorry."

"You're amazing."

Yeah, so amazing I'm choking on it. "I don't deserve you."

"Yes, you do, and it's only a matter of time before you let me in. I know it in my heart. We're meant to be together. Have faith in that, okay?"

She didn't know what to say, and the silence stretched between them.

"Okay?" he insisted.

"I'll try." He seemed certain she'd eventually come around, and he was willing to wait for her, but for how long? "Monroe moves into her dorm the last Friday in August." And there it was, the monster under the bed, exposed. It bought a fresh sharp twist to the knife in her heart.

"I won't call you until then."

"Okay."

"But I might text every once in a while. If you don't mind. I wouldn't want you to forget me." From the smile in his voice, she could picture the boyish half-grin.

"I'd like that."

"Call me when you get home."

"I will."

She stared at her phone as it went dark. *I am such a coward. Run, Lily Farrow, run. It's what you do best.*

Another text appeared.

Eli: Promise me you'll always remember: You're braver than you believe and stronger than you seem. A. A. Milne.

Oh, how she wished that were true.

41

Despite the overwhelming emptiness and uncertainty caused by Aria's early departure, Eli couldn't help but laugh out loud as he stood on his back patio step watching his new puppy scampering around his yard in the late afternoon sunshine. He'd planned to take Aria hiking in Malibu and pick up the dog as a surprise gift for her on their way home, but instead, after dropping Aria off at the airport, he and Anders had made the trip alone.

He clapped twice, and the pup came running. "Good boy." He rubbed Finn's tiny head then picked up the little ball of brown, black, and white fur. Barely the size of a cauliflower, he was pure cuteness wriggling in his hand. "She's going to love you." He nuzzled the dog's forehead, then took a selfie with him for Aria.

Before he could send it, his phone rang, the familiar train whistle.

"Eli, good." Penelope's voice was hesitant, not her usual clipped and harried pitch. "I'm glad I reached you, darling. You're not going to like this but . . ."

"What've you done now?"

"It wasn't me this time. I'm just doing damage control."

Eli didn't like the sound of that. He set his puppy down on the path.

"You should've told me what happened with Desmond."

Eli stood, paced, his puppy forgotten. "Why? What's he done?" Matt's parting words, something about regret, lurked in the periphery of his memory.

"You know he was the other actor Lang was interested in for the Casanova role, right?"

"No."

"Well, he was. And you broke his nose, Eli. When he didn't make an appearance at his party, Lang set up a meeting with him. Imagine his surprise when over a week later, Matt still looked like—"

"For crying out loud. Any cosmetic surgeon in Hollywood could fix it with their eyes closed. Cut to the chase, P."

"All right, all right. The film's delayed, a month, possibly longer. And Desmond has somehow talked himself into the lead role."

"What? He can't do that. We have a signed contract."

"Not according to Lang, or Max. You still have a part, but it's a supporting role, not the lead. I'm sure Max can explain. I'm sorry, Eli."

Eli slumped to the step, winded. "And your damage control is what exactly?"

"I'm running a piece about you and Makayla to divert attention. I understand you two met for lunch a few weeks ago. You'll love the pics. They're fabulous. And it's good press to—"

"Don't you dare."

"Eli, darling—" That condescending tone infuriated Eli.

"I said no, P. No more of that playboy crap."

"Too late." He could hear her straighten in her chair, light up a cigarette, then a breathy exhale.

Eli wasn't sure which enraged him more: that Matt had absconded with his lead role or that yet another article would hit the stands touting a relationship with a woman who wasn't Aria."

"Get it rescinded, P. Or else." Eli ended the call and his head fell into his hands. What happened with the contract? He'd signed it over a week ago.

Anders cleared his throat from the doorway. "Max Acres is here to see you, sir."

Eli scooped up Finn, urged him into his crate on the patio, then hurried through the house to the front door, swinging it wide as a white Lexus rolled to a stop in front of the garage. Eli's agent sat behind the wheel.

Eli propped against the doorjamb, arms crossed over his chest, and seethed, while Max extricated himself from the vehicle. "Just got off the phone with Penelope," he said as Max rounded the hood.

"You've heard then?" Red-faced, Max carried a manilla folder in one hand, while the other wiped sweat from his brow with a handkerchief. He wore a suit jacket over a crumpled white dress shirt stretched taut across his gut and puckering around the buttons. It made him look upholstered.

Eli nodded and glared at the little round man. "So I'm relegated to a supporting role, just like that?"

"Afraid so. I've got the new contract here." He raised the folder. "If you're still interested."

"I'm not." Eli's face felt like it was on fire.

Max backpedaled. "Pay's the same," he sputtered.

"Really?" Eli narrowed his gaze at Max.

"Hard telling what Desmond told Lang to cause the about face."

"Yeah, who knows what that lying, self-centered, piece of worthless—" Feeling caught in a maelstrom, Eli's head spun with fury, hurt, betrayal. "But I damn well intend to find out."

He stormed past Max and kicked the front tire of his SUV blocking the garage door, then eyed his motorcycle which stood ready and waiting for the potential buyer near the edge of the driveway. Eli grabbed his helmet off the handlebars, resisting the urge to hurl it at something, anything. Instead, he shoved it onto his head, threw a leg across the seat, and stomped on the kick-starter. Once, twice, a third time. Finally, the old Indian roared to life.

42

———

"Get out!" Eli yelled through his clenched jaw, chucking a water glass at his opening bedroom door.

Nick ducked as the tumbler crashed against the frame, sending shards of glass scattering across the floor and water puddling on the wood. "I'm only trying to help." He peered cautiously around the edge of the doorway.

Eli eased his head back onto the pillow and screwed his eyes tight, fighting the shooting pain exploding through his lower jaw like a star going supernova. *What was his brother doing here anyway?*

Suddenly it all came to him: the crash, waking up in a hospital bed, the antiseptic smell, the steady *beep, beep, beep* of a monitor, opening his eyes in a state of blurry half-consciousness to see his whole family at his bedside, their mournful expressions so distraught he thought surely he was dying.

"Go!" The intense pain slammed him again as he strained to eke out the word. *Broken jaw,* he remembered too late. He sighed heavily as tiny white lights sent him spinning again. He wasn't supposed to talk and definitely shouldn't be yelling.

A notepad lay on the table beside him, and he snatched it up and scribbled, "Sorry. Want 2B alone." He shoved it at his brother. "Please," he mumbled, careful to move only his lips.

Nick nodded with chagrin, set the pad on the nightstand, and left.

Eli had never felt so powerless. He could barely move, let alone get out of bed. His right side had taken most of the impact, leaving him with a fractured clavicle and femur in addition to the broken jaw and plethora of road rash. His whole body ached. But all of that was nothing compared to the razor-sharp pain in his chest for Aria.

He couldn't let her see him like this, not after everything she'd been through, not after he'd broken his promise to her. No, she could not find out about the motorcycle accident. How serendipitous that he'd told her he wouldn't call. He'd laugh if it didn't hurt so much.

Eli stared out the bedroom window, suddenly overwhelmed by a sinking feeling that he'd never see her again. He fumbled for his phone on the side table and brought up a picture of Aria driving her boat, smiling, carefree, the wind in her hair. He could almost smell the sweet scent of strawberries dripping off the pillow beneath his right shoulder, feel her warmth there beside him, taste her Napa Valley kisses. The fist around his heart tightened, the phone went dark, and his eyes closed, overcome.

Some time later, Mrs. Rodriguez appeared to clean up the mess. Shamed by his outburst, Eli feigned sleep while his mind roiled.

He'd been in the hospital, unconscious, for a week, or so he'd been told. He didn't remember the accident, the minivan that had T-boned him on Wilshire. The ordeal of coming home would stay with him for a lifetime, though. Even drugged up, he'd never in his life endured so much pain.

He'd made Penelope promise not to leak his accident to the press, and if there was one thing he could count on, it was Penelope controlling the media to suit her client. A story like that could put him out of work for months. All he could do now was focus on his recovery. Between Nick and his mother, and Leigh stopping by almost daily, Eli had all the help he needed. But Aria was the one he wanted.

He listened again to the brief voice mail she'd left that fateful evening letting him know she'd made it home, then he Googled Natalie's favorite poet. Thrilled to find the perfect excerpt, he fired it off in a text to Aria.

She responded within seconds, "loving" it.

Lying in the stillness of his bedroom, listening to the sound of the sprinklers pattering against the garden paths, he closed his eyes and she came to him, vivid as Technicolor, in his drug-induced delirium.

His bedroom door eased open. The drapes were drawn, the room dim. She stared at the bed as her eyes adjusted to the faint light. He was asleep, his right arm resting across his stomach in a sling, his right leg propped atop a mound of pillows. She stood quietly for a moment, taking in the extent of his injuries. His eyes fluttered open, and like a subhuman creature in a zombie flick, his head slowly rotated toward her.

A long white bandage covered his right cheek, from his temple to his jaw, the side previously turned away from her but now clearly visible. His right eye, puffy and purplish-red, was swollen shut. Her hand flew to her mouth to muffle a gasp.

He reached out to her, trembling. As tentative as winter sunlight, she neared and took his hand, her fingers soft and warm. Gently, he squeezed them and gave her a weak half smile because only one side of his face moved now.

"You gonna be okay?" Her voice broke, filled with the horror of reliving what had to be her worst nightmare.

He hesitated, then nodded.

She exhaled a shaky breath.

Panic filled her eyes, then she dropped his hand and backed away.

"Don't go," he pleaded, his jaw unmoving.

At the doorway, she shook her head, and her eyes went far away, as though she could no longer bear to look at him.

"Ari!"

Turning, she fled the room, her footsteps echoing with finality as she raced down the staircase. Then the slam of the front door— the sound that jolted him out of the wretched vision.

An errant tear escaped the corner of his eye, searing the patch of road rash on his cheek like lemon juice.

No, she couldn't know. Not ever.

43

The weeks passed quickly as Aria basked in the luxury of being home with her daughter, not stuck behind a desk or in a stuffy conference room on a glorious summer day. They played tennis, worked out together, and twice they kayaked the river north of Falls Creek. Jacks and Monroe had friends over often, and Aria enjoyed fun-filled days playing volleyball, surfing, and wakeboarding with them.

Determined to face her daughter's impending departure for college bravely and with at least a modicum of enthusiasm, Aria spent long afternoons shopping with Monroe for school supplies and dorm-room furnishings.

When Monroe was off with friends, Aria had time to read, so she checked out every Ben Franklin biography available in the whole countywide library system, even reread his autobiography. She studied his revolutionary ideals, his political *savoir faire*, searching for something that would give her own life purpose once her children no longer needed her.

Despite Aria's best attempts to fill her days, Eli was never far from her mind. In the wee hours when she couldn't sleep, she watched his movies, a couple of them more than once. She imagined him everywhere: beside her on the boat, at the volleyball net, reading by her side, brandishing his endearing *Ta-da!* from the side yard, reminding her how effortlessly he'd burst into her life, like sunlight at dawn, to brighten her world.

He sent a new text at least once a week, each one more touching than the last.

Eli: For always, night and day, I hear lake water lapping with low sounds down by the shore (Yeats) and I think of you.

Eli: Like a lover's prayer, I miss you, I need you. Come back to me. (C. Scyles)

Eli: My hope falls like rain before my eyes, a tranquil wonder. (A. Capelli)

Eli: Red rover, red rover, when can I come over?

Eli: Even heroes bleed sometimes. (E. Van Drie)

She didn't get that last one, but "loved" it anyway, like all the others.

They hadn't spoken since she left LA. When she'd unpacked her suitcase the next day and found his shirt, redolent with his scent, she'd started to text him, "Thank you. I miss you." But she'd backspaced each letter, one by one. Turns out, it was harder to try and fail to text something than to never text it at all.

A niggling of guilt insisted she should call him soon, but for reasons she couldn't explain—reasons she didn't even want to explore—she couldn't bring herself to do it. How would she know when she was ready?

Most nights, as she lay alone in her half-empty bed wearing his shirt, she watched Eli's music video. In the quiet moments before sleep, she found comfort in his seductive baritone and the intimate pieces of himself he had so openly and generously shared with her.

In mid-July, an *Us Weekly* magazine with Eli and Makayla gracing the cover appeared at the grocery store checkout. She had to buy it. Like a kid with a new comic book, in the privacy of her bedroom, she read the intimate interview, drinking in every word with an unquenchable thirst to know what he was up to, how he was doing.

When you read it, remember I was thinking of you, he'd told her. His words slaked her dehydrated soul. Until she remembered the article was written over a month before, and like air from a popped balloon, her joy vanished.

RELIEVED TO BE BACK in bed after an exhausting day of physical therapy, Eli closed his eyes. Even with the help of his therapist and a walker, simply shuffling along the length of the hallway had drained his last ounce of energy.

Leigh burst into the bedroom with an armful of magazines. "Have you seen it? Please tell me I'm the first."

Eli turned away, in no mood for Leigh's surprise, whatever it was, let alone her bubbly enthusiasm. It still hurt to smile, although he could no longer blame it on the road rash.

Leigh set a stack of magazines on his bedside table and held one up for him to see: *Us Weekly,* with a picture-perfect shot of him and Makayla looking happily in love. "You made the cover! Did you know?"

Eli stared. Maybe he knew. He couldn't remember. Penelope always took care of those details. Besides, it no longer mattered. His career was likely over. He was lucky to have a supporting role in Casanova now. If the road rash on his cheek didn't heal well, he'd be permanently scarred and forever relegated to secondary roles, or worse, cameos and background work. There was only so much makeup could cover.

"Want me to read it to you?" Leigh eased onto the end of his bed and leafed through the pages.

He didn't answer, knowing full well she'd read it to him anyway.

"'When you find that special someone, the stars shine brighter, you notice the birds singing, all of life gets sweeter, more beauti-ful.'" She looked up and shot him a sappy grin. "That's . . . wow."

A part of him wanted to smile at the memory, but it was all so bittersweet. Eli picked up his notepad and scribbled, "Aria."

Leigh's smile said she understood. "She knows how you feel, right?"

He nodded.

"Sure you don't want me to call her for you?"

Eli scowled.

"Right. She can't find out about the motorcycle." She studied him. "Are you feeling any better?"

He held up a finger and thumb, a small distance between.

"Anything I can do?"

He scribbled "Finn" on his notepad.

"Got it." Leigh tossed the magazine atop the stack, disappeared, and returned a few minutes later carrying the puppy in one arm, his small pet carrier in the other.

Leigh set Finn on Eli's lap and the carrier beside the bed, within arm's reach. He rubbed the dog's ears and shot Leigh a smile of appreciation. He'd had precious little time with his new pup.

"He's adorable."

Eli brought his fingertips to his lips and lowered them—the sign for thank you—and nodded toward the stack of magazines.

"You're welcome." Leigh resettled herself on the end of the bed. "You missed a great party last weekend."

The last thing Eli wanted to hear about was the life he was missing. With one hand on Finn to ensure he stayed put, Eli scribbled on his pad, "Tired."

"Oh, sure." She bounded to her feet and bent to kiss his cheek, then stared down at him. "You're going to get better. Hang in there, okay?"

Eli forced another half-smile.

"Text me if you need anything."

He flashed an okay sign and Leigh disappeared, closing the door behind her.

He didn't know which was worse: the dull, empty ache of the last few years or the all-consuming desperation for something he now couldn't live without.

I'll get Aria back. She loves me. I know she does. His insides squeezed in a fist of despair as a whisper of doubt gnawed at him. If she found out about his accident that could totally push her over the edge. She could decide to never love again.

No, she was stronger than that.

Please, baby, be strong. Be brave with me. Come back to me. He silently willed it, with all the courage, faith, and hope he could muster. *God, please bring her back to me.*

ARIA SPENT her mornings clearing out Adam's things: emptying his closet, his office, his workshop. She'd unintentionally made a shrine of his personal spaces, unable to face the task until now. Once she started, though, she found the undertaking therapeutic, as if with every taped box, every cleared shelf, every empty rod, she grew nearer to the closure she sought.

Occasionally she became emotional when she came across little mementos of their life together: a poem she'd written for him, love notes he'd saved, a robe she'd made for him, a cherished scent memory still clinging to it. Such meaningless little things, but they tore at her heart.

Early one morning, at the back of the closet in Adam's office, she found her brother's toolbox. She ran her hand across the cool blue metal. Gibson's hopes and dreams had once fit into that small box. And like a ghost from the past, it beckoned, its eerie call silent and insistent. *Open me. Remember me. Cry for me.* She swallowed her hesitation and opened the lid, expecting to find her brother's meager supply of hand tools, but to her surprise, the toolbox was filled with the letters she'd written to Dante. She leafed through them. Across each one was scrawled RETURN TO SENDER.

She thumbed through the envelopes, eight years' worth, all in order of the postmarks. Every single one had been opened with a clean slice through the top. She glanced to Adam's desk where his letter opener rested point down in the Mason jar he'd used as a pencil holder.

No wonder Adam never asked about her past. He'd known all along the worst things about her . . . and still he'd loved her. She choked back a sob.

Unable to help herself, she began with the first one.

November 4, 1995

Dear Dante,

It's been three days and I still don't understand. You didn't need to cop a plea for me. I didn't do it! And I know you didn't either.

Please, D, you've got to help me make them listen.
Please write me back, and tell me when I can come visit again.
We can find a way. Trust me.

"Have faith, son," as Mrs. Wyatt would say. Have faith in me, D.

Prayers and kisses. I love you.

Always,
Your Lily Fair

As she read them all, she relived the painful days following Dante's incarceration, her search for her father, her pregnancy. How Adam must have laughed at the way she'd described him to Dante: "worldly," "a good son," and "he treats me like a little girl." At sixteen, she *was* a little girl.

She'd written less often after marrying Adam. The annual letters simply chronicled her son's childhood and included a birthday snapshot and school picture. She stopped asking him to write and switched to signing the letters *Love and blessings, Lily*.

Regret formed a knot in her throat. She should have told Dante about his son at the fundraiser. She leafed forward through the letters, finding the one that contained the news. If only Dante had read them instead of returning them, he'd know.

If only. Her whole life played like an elegy of too many if-onlys, could'ves, and should'ves, always second-guessing herself.

July 6, 1996

Dear Dante,

This is a big day for me, for us. You're a father! We have a beautiful, healthy baby boy. He has my little ears and nose and the most beautiful caramel-colored skin, dark curly hair, and silver-blue eyes—the best of you and me, all in one perfect, tiny being. I named him Jackson, after you. Now you have two reasons to get out.

I know how you felt about not knowing your dad, how you vowed to do better if you were blessed with a child of your own one day.
I'm sorry I didn't tell you sooner, but since all of my earlier letters came back unread, you probably would have missed the news anyway. I hope you'll read this one and that you're as happy as I am.

In January I came home from work, tired as usual, and went to the loft for a nap. Lying on the bed was a home pregnancy test and a pamphlet for this place called Cradles of Grace. I looked at them for a long time before it finally sank in. Mrs. W. suspected I was pregnant.

I hadn't been feeling good in the mornings, and I'd gained weight to the point where my clothes no longer fit, but I thought it was because of Mrs. W.'s good cooking. At first, when I saw the test result, I laughed out loud, so excited to have your baby. Then I remembered what Cueball had done to me, and I cried. That's why I waited to tell you. Sometimes you don't know how strong you can be until strong is the only choice you've got.

I joined the Cradles of Grace support group. Their mission is to come alongside young women like me and help us make wise decisions about life and birth and family. They've been so helpful. They drive me to my doctor appointments and the weekly meet-ings. I've learned what it means to be a good mother and a godly woman. Which is great, because aside from Mrs. Wyatt, I didn't have the best example growing up. I have a mentor named Lucy. How cool is that? She's a kindergarten teacher, and she was my birth coach. She's super sweet.

I never knew there could be so many kind people in my life. I feel like I'm in heaven, surrounded by angels: Mr. and Mrs. Whit-more, Lucy, and the other ladies at Cradles of Grace. I think people who believe in God have a greater capacity to love each other, and this town is full of them. "It's a place where you can count on the kindness of strangers," as Tennessee Williams once said.

Mrs. W. loves country music, I think because it's full of love and God and an overall belief in the goodness of people. Like Falls Creek.

I know you'll like it here too, D. This is where I'll be when you get out. Please come find me. I'll be the young mother with the long chestnut braids and the beautiful little boy who looks like you. I can't believe I've been so blessed! I hope he loves me back.

Mrs. Whitmore insisted I move into the house and take her son's old room, but Jackson and I are going to stay in the loft. It's cozy here, and we won't wake them. I know she only wants to help— she's like the grandmother I never had. But if Adam didn't like me

horning in before, he'd be furious to come home and find his
parents had given me his room.

I hope you read this letter. That it doesn't come back to me like all
the others.

Love and blessings,
Always,
Your Lily Fair

Hours later, the late afternoon sun streaming in, she unfolded
the last letter—the only one that had been forwarded and stamped
NO LONGER AT THIS ADDRESS, like a eulogy in bold black ink.
He'd been released. And she didn't know where he'd gone.

It was the last time she wrote to him.

The letter read much like the ones that had preceded it, but this
one had a postscript.

Jackson saw me putting his picture into the envelope. "Will he
come visit me when he gets out of jail?" he asked.

I didn't have the heart to tell him you don't even know about him,
so I promised him someday you would. I think he's looking
forward to it, so please don't disappoint him.

Aria swallowed the lump in her throat and stared at the snapshot of her sweet silver-eyed, fawn-skinned boy of eight in a fishing
hat, brandishing a huge walleye and an ear-to-ear grin, taken on
one of their annual family trips to Canada. She brushed her thumb
across the photograph.

Jacks was almost four years old when she married Adam, so
he'd known all along Adam wasn't his real father. Standing beside
Adam at the altar in his miniature tuxedo, Jacks had tugged at
Adam's pant leg. *"Can I call you Daddy now?"*

Adam knelt and pointed to the rings on the pillow Jacks held.

"Just as soon as I put that ring on your mommy's finger." They'd always talked openly about Jacks's real father, but Jacks, in his childlike naiveté, said he only needed one daddy, so he seldom expressed interest in hearing about Dante Jackson—at least not until the third grade.

At a Donuts with Dad event at school, Jacks told his friends he had two dads, but the other one couldn't come. Of course, his classmates didn't believe him, which upset Jacks, and that evening Aria had explained that his birth father was in prison. It was the last time they'd talked about Dante Jackson.

"Hey, Mom," Jacks called from the back door, breaking her reverie. "I'm heading out."

Still sitting on the floor of Adam's near-empty office, Aria sniffed and straightened but couldn't find the strength to stand and face her son.

A few moments later, Jacks stood in the doorway. He never could leave without a *Love you* and a hug. "Mom?" His gaze scanned the letters piled around her.

"He doesn't even know about you." She almost choked on the words.

"Oh, Mom." Jacks lowered himself to the floor to sit beside her, shoulder to shoulder, back against the wall, his long legs bent at the knee. He picked up a letter from the nearest stack, studied it for a moment, then tossed it back. "You obviously tried."

Yes, she'd tried. The neat piles of her failed attempts evidenced eight years of waiting for a single return letter that never came.

"He's a good man," she said quietly.

"I had a great dad."

Aria nodded, too rattled for words. He was right. Adam couldn't have loved Jacks more if he'd been his own flesh and blood.

Jacks was about six, and Monroe a toddler, when she and Adam started talking about having more children. *"I'd never want Jacks to feel less of a son,"* Adam had said. They decided not to have more kids, and Adam got a vasectomy three weeks later.

Jacks rubbed his chin as he stared at her letters to Dante. "What did he do?"

Tried to protect me. "He went to prison for arson." *And manslaughter.* "But he didn't do it."

"Isn't that what they all say?"

"He didn't. I know he didn't." *Because I know who did.*

She'd been hiding in Gibs's room when Dante pounded on the door. Afraid and ashamed, she couldn't bear for him to see her, broken and used by Cueball.

After Dante gave up and left, she came out and found Cueball passed out on the couch, a lit cigarette in his hand and drool trickling from the corner of his mouth. His zippo sat on the coffee table beside the can of lighter fluid he'd been too stoned to open. She'd heard him cursing as he stomped to the kitchen, the *click-click-click* of the stove before the gas ignited to light his smoke. The idiot left it on. The place reeked of it.

A fire waiting to happen.

She'd wanted it to happen. Cueball deserved to die for what he'd done to her and her mom.

She could have turned off the gas, but she didn't. How could she have known the whole place would go up like the Hindenberg, that the police would blame Dante?

She tried to tell everyone she was the guilty party, not Dante. If they'd believed her, Dante wouldn't have gone to prison. She could've pleaded ignorance or self-defense and being a minor, they probably would've let her go. Then Jacks would've had his real father.

"Would you like to meet him?"

"Is he out of jail?"

She nodded. "He's the acting director of a boys club in Detroit."

Jacks stood, brows knit. "If you want me to meet him, I will." His voice conveyed a childlike compassion. "We could invite him to my graduation in the spring."

She smiled up at him through tear-filled eyes. "That'd be nice."

Jacks gave her a hand up, and they hugged. "Love you," he said, lingering a few seconds longer than usual. When they parted, his beautiful rain-colored eyes searched her face, his love pure and unfiltered. They said, *Don't be sad. I didn't miss a thing. You've given me everything a son could ever want.*

Or maybe that was only what she needed to hear.

ELI LAY IN BED, nearly suffocated by the weight in his chest, as though every day since Aria left, a stone had been placed on top of his heart. The load grew heavier and heavier as she slipped further from his grasp, and now only a cairn remained.

He settled into the pillow and closed his eyes, longing for sleep so he could wake up to find the last few weeks had been nothing more than a bad dream. But his mind refused to shut down. He couldn't stop thinking about her. She was the golden needle in his crazy haystack life. He'd never find another woman like her. His grandpa had told him he'd know when the right one came along. He was right.

Eli had already prayed, more times than he could count. The only thing to do now was focus on his recovery. When he got better, he'd fly out to see her. Hopefully, she'd be ready by then.

He breathed deeply, exhaled slowly, panic rising like a dark cloud in his belly.

"When life gets hard, don't forget what you know," his grandpa's gravelly burnt toast voice echoed in his head.

He mulled that over for all of two seconds. *I know she loves me.* He pushed the lingering doubts away and forced himself to focus on that one vital tidbit. She hadn't been able to say it, not yet, but it was there, in the way she looked at him, in the way her body responded to his touch, in the way she kissed him like the world might end. Yes, she loved him, and for now, believing would have to be enough.

44

Aria stood in the doorway of Adam's lower-level office, empty except for the desk, a file cabinet, and the blue metal toolbox shut away on the closet shelf. Boxes of files and office supplies lined the wall outside, each one neatly labeled Donate or Discard.

She breathed a sigh of discontent. *Now what?* The calendar read late July—she had a lot of summer left to fill.

"Hey there." She whirled at the sound of Justus's gentle voice. Jacks stood behind him.

"Oh, hi, guys." Aria gave them each a hug.

"Jacks thought you might need a hand," her father-in-law said, perusing her work.

While Jacks and Justus carried the furniture upstairs and loaded it into Adam's pickup, Aria carried the boxes, each one reverberating with finality, like nails in a coffin, as she slid them into the bed of the truck.

Back downstairs she stood in the office doorway. A lake view and sunshine filled the empty space. Dents in the carpet, like shadow-phantoms, were all that remained of the successful construction business that had once run from within the now-bare walls.

Justus appeared behind her and placed a comforting hand on her shoulder.

"Monroe and I signed up to teach English as a second language," she said, yearning for a positive thought and hoping to ease her father-in-law's obvious concern. "We start Thursday." Somehow it seemed insignificant now. "I've also been thinking about becoming a foster parent, taking in a pregnant teen, like you and Bea did with me." She gave him an affectionate smile.

How different her life would have been if she'd never met Justus and Bea. She wouldn't have been able to keep Jacks and balance work, school, and college. And she'd never have met Adam.

He raised a bushy white eyebrow. "You could do more than that."

"What are you thinking?" She knew he was leading her, and she was happy to follow. He always led her to good things. She'd always depended on his intuition and his advice.

"Your guy, Eli, has a heart for kids same as you. And he has quite a platform.

I watched that speech online and I read about the results of that fundraiser. Seven million dollars from a few hundred people. Over three million hits on YouTube. Mentoring programs across the country seeing more volunteers than they can handle."

She couldn't argue the impact of Eli's speech. "It's easy to open your wallet when you know good people are behind the request. And that audience certainly had fat wallets."

"Seems to me you're right where God wants you to be."

She moved to dusting the windowsill, anything to keep busy.

"I have to admit, I wasn't too keen on that boy at first, his reputation and all, but he's got passion, and that's a wondrous thing. Maybe you've come to where you are *for such a time as this*."

Of course her father-in-law would quote Scripture, the story of Esther the young Jewish orphan, beloved of a pagan king, who used her influence to save her family—her entire race.

Aria paused in her dusting and faced her father-in-law. Justus crossed his arms over his chest, a familiar look in his rheumy blue eyes. If he'd heard the speech, he knew that she'd had a big hand in writing it. He was also aware that she was at a crossroad. A glimmer of hope seeped into her heart.

"There're a million kids out there just like you were. Kids who need somebody like you and Eli to speak up for them, to lift them up."

Her hand with the duster fell to her side. "Oh, Justus." She wilted like a seedling in a bed of weeds. "I'm just trying to survive." She slumped against the wall.

"Don't let your grief drag you into the shadows. You were meant to become the light, Aria Whitmore."

As she studied his wise old eyes, self-doubt crept in like a cancer, attacking the good parts, sapping her will to live. "I'm not enough," Aria said, nearly choking on the admission. She'd said it to herself plenty of times, even tried to convince Eli how *not enough* she was. But voicing it aloud to Justus, who'd always believed in her, made it sound devastating.

Justus shook his head, his face soft, his arms open. She fell into them. "Oh, my beautiful child." He rubbed her back. "You are most definitely enough."

He held her in his powerful arms. The lingering scent of earth and sunshine, Brut and horses, washed over her grieving soul like a soothing balm.

"Come sit with me." He led her to the sofa in the rec room. Facing her, he took her hands into his gnarled ones. "Trust me on this, Aria-girl. Great things are in store for you on the other side of that fear and doubt. Sometimes you can't hear God in the midst of the storm that rages around you. It's in the hush that follows, with senses heightened, that you can truly feel His presence." He squeezed her hands, his gentle touch reassuring. "You're like the violin in 'The Touch of the Master's Hand.' Do you remember that poem?"

She remembered, and something inside of her warmed. She,

the battered and scarred old instrument . . . Eli the master, playing her, bringing forth her beauty, her worth, helping everyone, including her, to see her true value. How reassuring that Justus, like the auctioneer in the story, saw her that way.

"I don't deserve him."

"Life isn't about deserving or earning. It's about believing and receiving. Be still and rest in your faith, girl. The past can be transformed into hope, even if it takes a lifetime."

That evening, Aria sat on the lakeside patio alone, staring into the flames of the fire pit as Justus's words sang in her heart. *You were meant to become the light.*

She replayed Eli's music video, and when the song ended, she stared at the screen until it went dark. She should call him. More than anything she wanted to call him, to hear his beautiful voice.

After a brief mustering of courage, she pressed Call. It rang twice, then the call ended. Seconds later, she received a text.

Eli: Can't talk right now, but the full moon reminds me of you, so beautiful, so bright, so far away.

The soft spot in Aria's heart softened a little more.

Aria: Call me later?

After a few minutes he responded

Eli: Shoor.

She smiled and replied with a laughing emoji.

Aria stayed awake as long as she could, not wanting to miss him. But the phone never rang.

The next morning, she saw another text.

Eli: Sorry I didn't get back to you. It got late. I'll call soon.

Maybe she'd waited too long.

45

———

As Aria eased open her daughter's bedroom door to say goodnight, Monroe scrambled to tuck something beneath her pillow. Monroe hadn't hidden anything from her since she was six years old and had lost her first tooth, as if her mother wouldn't notice the gap in her smile. Aria wondered but chose not to ask about it. Her daughter was almost an adult now and deserved her privacy.

"Sure you don't want me to turn the air on?" The humid August heat melted everything from ice cream to sunny dispositions.

"No, thanks. I like to hear the night sounds. You could turn on my fan, though, please."

Aria's heart lifted. Adam had preferred air-conditioning on hot summer nights, but Aria loved to sleep with the windows open no matter the outdoor temperature. She flipped on the ceiling fan and moved to the bed, where Monroe lay propped against the headrest, half-covered with a sheet, her knees pulled up in front of her.

"You're not going to Italy, are you?" Monroe's question took Aria off guard, and the unreturned call from Eli sliced like a knife through her fragile heart. By now he had probably found someone else, Makayla no doubt, to join him on the trip.

"I don't think so, honey." Aria sat on the edge of the bed and picked up her daughter's cell phone, resisting the urge to scroll through the texts. When her children got their first cell phones in middle school, monitoring had been part of the deal. Parental rights, Adam called it. Parental responsibility, Aria called it. But she'd stopped checking her daughter's texts and social media when she turned seventeen. Now being unaware of her daily activity felt like a sad harbinger of the distance that would inevitably grow between them when Monroe left for college.

Monroe plugged the phone into the charger and set it on the nightstand. "Are you going to see him again?"

"I don't know." She had no idea why Eli had gone silent on her. Hopefully it was simply his way of giving her time, and he'd call any day now to invite her again.

"Well, he's a jerk anyway." Monroe nestled back onto her pillow and yanked the sheet up.

Aria startled at her daughter's comment. She had encouraged her relationship with him from day one. What could have changed her perspective so drastically?

Something colorful peeked from beneath the edge of Monroe's pillow, and Aria pulled out the *Us Weekly* magazine with Eli and Makayla's picture on the cover. "Oh, sweetie." She should have known Sutton's mom would show it to her. She'd probably gloated too. *See the kind of man your mother was carrying on with?*

Monroe scowled at the magazine. "He's a liar."

"Baby, that interview was in June, and he told me he was talking about me the whole time." It sounded lame now. Was she naïve to have believed him?

"Well, either he lied to you or he's lying to the whole world."

"He's an actor. It's his public—"

"Is that why you broke up?"

"We didn't break up." Aria said it like she believed it. She wanted to believe it, wanted her daughter to believe it.

"Oh, really?" Monroe's brows shot up in disbelief. "I know

you've called him and texted him, and he hasn't called back. He's ghosting you, Mom."

Aria gasped. "Have you been checking my phone?"

"You check mine."

"Monroe!"

Her daughter's eyes softened and she took Aria's hand. "I'm sorry, Mom. I just want you to be happy."

"Oh, my sweet baby girl. Don't worry about me." She turned away, knowing full well her daughter would see right through her false bravado. "I'm fine."

Monroe shot up to a sitting position. "You have dark circles under your eyes 'cause you're not sleeping. You barely eat. You're not fine."

The concern in Monroe's voice brought a lump to Aria's throat. "I will be," she insisted, needing it to be true. "It's just going to take time." She hugged her daughter, eased her back down, and stood as she pulled up the sheet.

Monroe took her mother's hand, held onto it, her silent, *please stay and talk to me.* Aria sat back down.

"I could stay here and go to CC."

"Don't even think about it. You earned that scholarship at Hope, and you're not throwing it away." Aria had gone to community college, but she wanted more for her daughter, the whole college experience: dorm life, roommates, sorority sisters who'd become lifelong friends, formals and football games, all the things Aria had missed out on.

Monroe brushed a stray lock of hair from Aria's cheek. "You once told me that a boy would break my heart someday because sometimes the one you choose doesn't choose you. You said it would hurt, but I shouldn't cry because he probably wasn't the one God picked for me."

"Oh, baby." Aria's eyes burned with unshed tears. It was good advice—easy to give, hard to accept.

Aria wanted to tell her she had it all wrong. *Eli chose me, he loves me, or at least he did. I'm the one who wasn't ready to be chosen.* But nothing came out.

Monroe wrapped her in a hug. "It's going to get better, Mom."

"I know, sweetie. I know." Aria kissed Monroe's forehead, and Monroe smiled up at her, her father's wide grin and shining blue eyes. At least she'd always have those cherished little pieces of Adam in her daughter. "Go to sleep now."

"I love you."

"Love you too."

Aria eased the door closed behind her and collapsed against the wall, finally able to exhale. In the kitchen, she tried to get ahold of herself, focusing on the simple act of pouring herself a second glass of wine. Somehow she made it back to her bedroom.

Stacks of books related to her social reform idea littered the floor near the foot of the bed, while a plethora of research articles and notes about everything from persistent poverty to US welfare programs lay scattered across the quilt on Adam's side.

She'd convinced her company to condense their North American sales and marketing teams, a major reorg that saved the company millions in overhead. She'd turned a paper craft idea into a recycling solution that garnered worldwide attention, a lucrative patent, and in all likelihood would save billions of trees in years to come. She'd raised two incredible children. Who better to show the impoverished the path to a better life than one who'd traveled it?

She plucked the acceptance letter from Cooley Law School from the jumble. She'd wanted that law degree to help Dante, but it was too late for that. He didn't need her anymore. Seized by weariness, she let the letter float back to the pile.

No, Eli was her path now. If he still wanted her. Aria set the wine glass on the nightstand and picked up her cell.

Eli's phone buzzed with a text from Aria.

Aria: Hey, I said I needed time, but you don't have to ghost me.

He stared at it until his phone went dark. More than anything, he wanted to call her, hear her voice, tell her how much he loved her, how much he needed her. What he wouldn't give to see her smile, to smell her hair, to hear her laughter. But he wasn't ready for her to see him. Or hear his voice through teeth set into a clenched position.

He only needed a few more days. On Wednesday he'd see the oral surgeon again and hopefully be rid of the wire in his jaw. Who knew six weeks could feel like a lifetime?

He'd wanted so badly to text her. But if he texted, he'd have to explain why he couldn't see her. Better to let her believe he was just giving her time with her daughter.

His phone buzzed with another text.

Aria: Unless that's what you need, a clean break.

A half dozen times he typed out a reply only to delete each one.

He stared at the print of The Willows he'd had moved into his room and imagined the life they might have had if he'd taken things slower, if he'd sought her out at the fundraiser, if he hadn't raced off on his motorcycle.

He sighed, closed his eyes, and forced his aching body to relax as he welcomed his dream world, where she still lived and laughed and loved him.

She's wearing the green dress with the leather belt. Her strappy heels dangle from one hand as she strolls up the bank of the pond in the fading light of dusk. At the water's edge, she looks like a wood fairy. Her hair is wet and wavy and pulled to the side in a long, loose braid—a little messy, almost ethereal, very sexy. He waits for her on a blanket beneath the willow. The branches are tied back, open, welcoming. He's on fire for her, anticipating, aching, his strength for her softness, yearning to become hopelessly entwined, knotted together as one for time eternal.

Eli's eyes flew open, and he was overcome with a desire so

intense it physically hurt, a need so deep, so elemental, like a breath, he thought he might die without it. And maybe he would.

His phone buzzed with another text.

Aria: I guess that's what you need.

Oh, Ari! It felt like all the air in the room had been sucked out. He fired back,

Eli: That's NOT what I need! I need YOU. Come to my premiere with me, as my date.

He deleted the last word and replaced it with *girlfriend.*

After a pause that seemed to last forever, he saw the row of dots indicating she'd begun to reply.

Eli: Please

Aria: I'll think about it.

Eli: Good enough. I'll call you in a few days, I promise.

He hoped this time it was a promise he could keep.

THREE DAYS LATER, at almost midnight, Eli finally called. Aria sat up in bed, closed her Bible, and answered. "Hey."

"Sorry I didn't call sooner. Lots going on, you know."

His voice sounded off, his speech slow and slurred, like he'd been drinking.

"Sure."

For the first time, he didn't make fun of her accent.

"How've you been?"

"Good. You?"

How could a few months turn their free and easy conversation into awkward small talk, their sad goodbye now haunting the space between them?

"Busy. Having fun with Monroe?"

"Yeah."

"God, I miss you. Can you come to my premiere?"

Her gut twisted at the thought of a repeat of the fundraiser fiasco. "When is it?"

"September eighth. A Friday night. Prime time." A hint of pride colored his voice.

"I thought you were leaving for Italy soon."

"Not for a while yet. We'll probably start filming here, on set."

"Oh." She knew he needed an answer.

"Baby, we don't get to be here long, but . . . " He hesitated and she imagined him struggling with the words that would keep them apart. "But if you need more time, I understand."

"I do. I'm sorry."

"It's all right." He sighed heavily, and her heart broke for the disappointment in his voice. "Call me as soon as you decide, okay? I really hope you say yes."

He wasn't giving up on her after all. She nearly wept with happiness. But she bit back her tears. She hadn't cried in days and she wasn't going to start again now.

46

———

Like a blood-chilling rollercoaster Aria would never get to ride again, Monroe's college move-in day finally arrived. For years, Aria had been looking forward to this day with mixed emotions. And now, as the inevitable goodbye loomed, she wasn't ready to face the heartbreaking sense of finality, to relinquish this last tenuous grip on motherhood. It seemed impossible to be so excited about her daughter's future and yet so reluctant to walk away and allow her to embark upon it alone.

Outside the dorm, Jacks hugged his sister goodbye then turned to his mom. "I'll wait in the truck."

Aria sat with Monroe on a bench along the sidewalk. All around them, the campus bustled with life in the early autumn sunshine as excited freshmen appeared lost and upper classmen directed. Hulky young men carried mini fridges and futons while parents and children hugged their goodbyes.

Aria breathed deeply, steeling herself, before raising her eyes to her little girl. "I love you so much, baby, and I'm so proud of you."

"I know, Mom. I love you too." Monroe looked all around the courtyard, anywhere but at her mother.

Aria resolved not to cry, but like the autumn leaves, she was barely holding on. She took her daughter's hand and touched the moonstone ring she and Adam had given her for her fourteenth birthday. "I'm only forty minutes away. If you need me, I'm here for you."

"Thanks, Mom." Monroe frowned with thinly veiled impatience.

Aria sniffled. "I know I wasn't always the best mom, especially after Daddy's accident, but I want you to know that being your mother has been the best thing I've ever done, that I will ever do. And that doesn't stop just because you're away at school. Understand?" A tear escaped to trickle down her cheek, and she swiped it away.

Monroe nodded but didn't look at her.

Aria held her daughter so tight for so long she couldn't believe Monroe didn't pull away. She needed time, just a little more time.

Eventually Aria released her and attempted a smile. "I did okay, didn't I?"

Monroe's face softened, and her eyes went misty. "You've been the best mom ever."

Aria laughed and dabbed at her eyes. "Thanks. But I meant today, with not crying. Too much."

Monroe stood, tilted her head and smiled. "Aw, Mom. Yeah, you did great."

"I love you, baby, so much." She blew her daughter a final kiss then watched as she walked away. *It doesn't take much to let go of a child. Just everything.*

Aria wasn't sure how long she sat there, alone on the bench amid the flurry of activity, before Jacks eased down beside her. "Ready?"

She couldn't look at him. She'd fall apart completely if she did. "God, I'm going to miss her. I miss you all. So much."

Jacks draped an arm around her and squeezed. "Was it this hard the first time you and Dad dropped me off?"

Aria nodded, breathed. "But at least I had your dad."

Jacks patted her knee. "Well, you've got me. Come on."

⌒

AT HOME that evening Aria wandered through the house, past empty chairs at an empty table, half-empty bedrooms—too much emptiness. With the deaths of so many loved ones, she'd swallowed the misery life had dealt her. And now, here she was, alone in her beautiful house, her family all but ripped away one by one.

She escaped to the back deck, stood at the railing, seeking comfort in the serenity of the lake. The quiet yard below swept her mind back to snippets of her children's lives. Jacks holding out his arms to his newborn baby sister—he'd thought she was his present because she was born on his birthday. The way Adam had openly cried at his daughter's birth. How she'd worried because Monroe, comforted by her thumb and her *Goodnight, Moon* bunny, almost never cried.

Images flipped in her mind like pages in a scrapbook. Monroe playing with her Bitty Baby on the lawn with Sutton, swimming in the lake, doing little-girl cartwheels, then big-girl back tucks. Echoes of birthday parties down by the water shimmered like a desert mirage, all the pictures she'd taken before dances, home-comings, and prom. The happy, carefree days of her children's youth, now nothing but hauntingly sweet memories, slashed Aria's fragile heart to tatters.

How she longed for those simpler days when her only dream was a home that felt nothing like the one she grew up in. Almost twenty years married to Adam and two amazing children to love, nurture, and adore. What a gift life used to be. It had all gone by much too fast.

The ache of missing them nearly made her knees buckle.

Stop living in the past. There's hope in the future.

Hope—such a dangerous thing. Nebulous and fleeting, it didn't fit in the physical world of things you could count on. But what did she have left if not hope?

On that stormy afternoon in the pavilion, Eli had told her he wanted a family. *We'll figure it out when we get to it,* he'd said. She would turn thirty-seven in a few months. Was it too late for her to have another child . . . if Eli still wanted her?

"Hey, Aria," her neighbor called from his deck.

"Hey, Jim." He could probably see her loneliness glaring like a beacon.

"Join us for a cocktail?"

"Thanks, but not today." She paused to gather her resolve, but it morphed into a heavy sigh instead. She needed to get used to being alone with her grief, not to wallow in it but to face it head on, accept it, get comfortable with it. Her grief, like the scar beneath her chin, would be a part of her life forever.

"You okay?" he asked.

"I will be." She was going to keep telling herself that until it was true.

"Okie-doke. Well, if you change your mind . . ."

"Thanks, Jim." Oh, how she wished Adam would rescue her from this awkward conversation. Would she ever get used to the aching hole left by her husband's death?

Don't look back, only forward, Eli had said. Right. Next week she'd start law school. With her new volunteer job at the West Michigan Literacy Center, teaching English as a second language, and her social reform ideas, she had plenty to look forward to.

So why did it all feel so wrong?

Because they're nothing more than meager attempts to ease the ache of loneliness. Aria screwed her eyes shut and extended a hand as a prayer circled her heart. *Oh, please, God, please.*

Something tickled her hand, and her eyes shot open. A spicebush swallowtail fluttered from her fingertip to her palm and stilled. She'd never seen one at her house before, only at The Willows. Its wings fell open, relaxed, basking, trusting. A sun-bleached image of Eli looming over her in the meadow filtered into view like a watermark. With all the clarity of a summer morning, a silent voice spoke to her. *Go to him. Now. Become the light.*

For some reason, she thought of a book she'd read years ago, astounded that the words that had touched her heart then surfaced so readily now. "What is hell?" Dostoevsky asked in *The Brothers Karamazov*. "It is the suffering of being unable to love."

The doorbell yanked her from the quicksand of despair, and the butterfly flew away.

Aria peered through the house to the front porch. Anders! Her heart soared.

She raced through the house and threw open the door. "It's so good to see you," she gushed. Parked in the driveway stood a black sedan, empty. Disappointment returned with a thud.

"Ms. Whitmore," he said, so formal, as always. "Mr. Van Drie asked me to deliver this to you." He held out a pet carrier a little bigger than a shoebox, and a small whine came from within. Anders's solemn expression seemed to say, *I'm sorry, it's all I have for you.*

Aria took the carrier and peeked inside, meeting a tiny set of brown eyes in a mass of chestnut, black, and white fur. The puppy gave an excited yip. "Aw." She backed into the foyer, set the bag on the floor, and knelt to unzip it. The puppy ventured out, sniffed her knees, and climbed onto her lap. When she stroked the dog's tiny head, its eyes closed, and her heart melted like chocolate in sunshine.

"His name is Finn," Anders said, clearing his throat. He set a canvas bag on the floor beside the open door. "His food, leash, a few toys."

Aria pulled the bag closer and peered into it, searching for a note or card from Eli. Nothing.

"How is he?" she asked.

"Mr. Van Drie?" Anders straightened his tie. "As good as can be expected, ma'am."

"Leaving for Italy soon, I guess." She could be going with him, if only she wasn't so damaged, so weak. If only.

"Anything you'd like me to tell him?"

Aria thought of all the things she wanted to say but couldn't: *I miss you. I need you. I love you.* Tears stung her eyes as she snuggled her new puppy. "Tell him I said thank you."

47

———

Aria's phone vibrated for the fourth time in the past hour. Shuffling through the papers strewn across the kitchen island, she found the phone under her class schedule. She rubbed her neck. Cadence again. She didn't feel like talking to anyone, but she hadn't spoken to Cadie in weeks, and she missed her. And based on the number of times she had called, it must be important.

Aria picked up. "Hey, girl."

"I've been trying to reach you all day."

"I know. I'm sorry. I was—"

"I'm coming over."

"What? No, I'm—"

"It's about your dad."

"Cadie—" The last person Aria wanted to think about was her father.

"Be there in twenty." Silence. She'd ended the call.

Aria glanced around the kitchen. Empty take-out bags, dirty dishes, and wine bottles covered every inch of counter space. The island where she sat lay buried beneath piles of books, research articles, and notes related to her welfare reform project.

As she poured another glass of wine, she tried to push her father from her mind. She needed to focus on her research into the current welfare laws. Aria stared at the laptop screen and tried to read, but her mind wouldn't hold the words.

A memory found her, one of the few she had of her father when she was little. Perched on his lap on the front stoop, she'd listened in rapt attention as his voice rang with encouragement.

You can be anything you want to be when you grow up, Lily-bear.

Even a princess?

Even a knight.

What's a knight?

Someone who fights battles for people who can't defend themselves.

A sob escaped. She cradled her head in her hands and squeezed her eyes shut.

Some time later, Aria jolted awake in the darkened kitchen to Finn barking, the doorbell ringing, and Cadence's muffled voice calling out, "I know you're home!"

Reluctantly, Aria slipped off the barstool, wiped sleep from her eyes, and shuffled to the door.

"Oh, my God!" Cadence pushed her way in, flipped on the lights, and gawked, first at Aria and then at the house. "Look at this place."

Aria shielded her eyes from the sudden onslaught of light. She staggered to Finn's cage and fumbled to attach his leash. "I'll be right back," she mumbled, leaving Cadence, hands on hips, assessing her messy kitchen.

Outside, night had fallen, and Aria let the blessedly cool, quiet darkness envelop her.

When she returned to the house, Cadence stood propped against the kitchen sink, arms folded across her chest, staring at a half dozen empty wine bottles lined up like toy soldiers on the counter. The overflowing recycle bin, which included a few more, stood beside her along with the mounded trashcan.

Carrying Finn, Aria returned to her barstool at the kitchen island.

"At least you're taking care of the dog," Cadence said with a huff.

"Of course I am." Finn settled happily on Aria's lap while she rubbed his ears. She reached for her unfinished glass of wine, but her friend snatched it away and dumped it into the sink.

Cadence approached the island, concern etched on her face. "You look like you haven't slept in days."

"I've been working on something." Aria closed her laptop and straightened the papers within reach. "Something important."

Cadence picked up several of the books and read the first few titles aloud. "*The Truly Disadvantaged, Good Kids from Bad Neighborhoods, Understanding Persistent Poverty, Ben Franklin: An American Life*." She stared at Aria, eyes wide.

Aria motioned to her laptop. "I'm preparing a proposal for social reform." It was the first time she'd said it aloud, and it sounded big. It was big. Probably too big for her.

Cadence turned over the Cooley orientation guide. "Law school?"

"Words are the weapons that are going to win this battle. I need to know how to wield them."

"You could sell light bulbs to the Amish. You don't need a law degree."

Aria wanted to chuckle but couldn't find the energy. She set Finn on the floor, and he toddled off to his bed beneath the hall table.

"I'm worried about you. Are you all right?" Cadence's tone softened with genuine concern.

"I'm fine." It didn't sound convincing, and Aria knew Cadence wouldn't let it go. "At least I will be."

"Talk to me. I haven't seen you in forever. You're not working. You're always home but never available for lunch."

"You said it was about my father."

Cadence opened the fridge, stared inside for a moment, then closed it and turned back to Aria. "When's the last time you ate?"

"Cadie!"

"He died."

A fist tightened around Aria's heart. "How—"

"He was on his way home from a gig," Cadence said, her voice breaking. "A drunk driver going the wrong way . . . It was on the news." She slipped onto the stool at Aria's side and placed a hand on her shoulder. "I'm sorry."

Aria's eyes burned with unshed tears, but she sniffed and willed them away. That man did not deserve her sorrow.

The first time Aria had seen Adam lying in the casket in the funeral home parlor, she'd stepped back, hand to her mouth in shock. *Is this really my husband?* Lifeless and still, face colored by makeup, he looked like a painted wax figure, not the vibrant man she'd loved. Steadied by Justus's hand at the small of her back, she'd stood transfixed while Monroe leaned her head against her shoulder and wept quietly.

She'd provided the funeral home director with pictures, thinking they were to display during the visitation so their friends and family could remember Adam the way he used to be. She didn't realize they would also use them to guide the restoration, to set his facial features. They don't tell you that.

It wasn't the way she wanted to see her father.

Aria turned to her friend, and Cadence's face crumpled like a paper bag.

Aria retrieved a box of tissues from the powder room and held it out. Cadence took one, wiped her eyes, and gazed out to the lake, quiet and still in the dark of night. Silent moments passed like sand in an hourglass, trickling grain by grain.

"I wish I could be as strong as you." Cadence sniffed.

Aria pinched the bridge of her nose. If only she could be the person others thought she was. "I'm not strong."

"Are you kidding me?"

Aria shook her head. "I cry all the time."

"Strong people cry."

"Aw, Cadie."

"I love it when you call me that. No one else calls me that. I admire you, Aria, more than anyone in the world. You're like the big sister I never had."

Aria almost choked on the lump that filled her throat.

Cadence plucked at Aria's sleeve. "Nice shirt."

Aria glanced down and tried to remember when she'd slipped into Eli's shirt. She was so tired her head felt like it was going to roll right off her shoulders.

Cadence huffed then returned to the fridge and started pulling things out. "I'm going to make you something to eat. Then I'm putting you to bed and cleaning up this kitchen."

"You don't have to do that."

"I know, but I'm going to because I know you'd do it for me." She gave Aria a sappy grin that reminded her of Gibson. The knife in her heart twisted at the thought of her brother. "Besides, I need you to snap out of this—whatever it is—so you can attend the visitation tomorrow. And the funeral on Monday."

Aria shook her head. Her father didn't want her. She'd accepted that long ago.

"He has two daughters."

"I don't even know if . . ." She couldn't even say it. What if he really wasn't her father? Was finding two half-sisters worth the risk? She could just as easily end up having no idea who her father was.

"You need closure. At least go to the funeral. You'll regret it if you don't."

Aria glanced at the calendar on the wall.

"Today's Saturday." Cadence raised an eyebrow.

"I know."

"Want me to go with you?"

"No, but thanks for the offer."

"You sure you're okay?" Cadence asked with a wry smile.

"I will be," Aria repeated, hoping it was true.

48

Attending her father's funeral was almost more than Aria could bear, but she donned resilience like a cloak, tucked into its sturdy fabric, for the sake of closure.

After the burial, the pastor invited everyone back to the Farrow family home for a small reception. In the quaint, well-kept little ranch house on a quiet tree-lined street on the south side of Grand Rapids, Aria felt like an impostor. The two twenty-something daughters, lost in their grief, distant and distracted as though medicated, moved slowly among the other mourners in the cramped space.

As Aria meandered down a narrow hallway, its walls covered with photos of the happy little family, a gaping hole threatened to swallow her from the inside. She had no such pictures. Even before the fire, she couldn't remember any photos adorning the walls of their rental on Bowser Street. Her school pictures, if her mother even bought them, never made it to the refrigerator, let alone a frame.

Toward the end of the hall hung a print of a single white lily rising from a bed of ashes, a burning cityscape in the background. Aria stepped back, bumping into the opposite wall as though kicked in the chest by the macabre tribute. *That's all I get, Daddy? A dollar-store print on the Farrow family wall?*

Disgusted by feelings of self-pity, Aria's fists clenched as she found anger instead. Anger she could hold onto. Anger never left her in a puddle of tears. Anger turned to strength.

The older sister appeared and stood beside Aria, shoulder to shoulder. "My dad loved that picture," she said, eyeing the print. "No matter how many times my mom tried to move it, it always ended up back on this wall."

"Was he a good dad?" Aria sputtered.

"The best," the young woman said, her voice colored blue with grief.

"I'm sorry for your loss." Aria nearly choked on the words, swallowing the loss she couldn't share.

Numb, Aria left the house, slipped into her car. *Breathe. Just breathe.* Thoughts of her father roiling in her mind, she started toward home but minutes later found herself at The Willows, staring at the chain and the two-track beyond, wishing she'd had the forethought to stop by the house to change clothes and grab the gate key and her gun.

She didn't understand why being at The Willows now made her feel unsafe, why she always brought the pistol whenever she came alone. Perhaps it was the depth of aloneness she felt being there without Adam.

Despite her unreasonable fears, she was drawn to this place. She imagined it might be like someone who cuts herself, how feeling the physical pain of sliced skin dulled another, much deeper, intangible pain . . . like the death of a father who didn't want you.

After slipping into a pair of boots and grabbing a wool blanket, two winter necessities she kept in her trunk year-round, she headed to the pond on foot.

The glorious early-autumn day seemed an assault. The trees, full of sunshine, whirled in a kaleidoscope of magenta, rust, and gold. Aria seethed with renewed anger. It should be raining, cold, and dreary. A thunderstorm would have been perfect.

She strolled across the meadow, the wild grasses up to her chest, and brushed her hands across their feathery tops. She felt like she was sleepwalking and didn't know how to wake up.

At the willow, she stamped down the grasses and spread the blanket, then opened the branches, braiding each one to the side. Settled on her blanket, she allowed herself a small smile.

Sometime later she awoke to her phone vibrating on the blanket beside her with a text from Eli: *Two together are so much more than one and one. A. Whitmore*

How did he always know when she needed him? Wiping sleep from her eyes, she sat up and pressed Call.

"Ari," he said, relief and a smile in his smooth, husky voice.

"Hey." She closed her eyes, imagining him there beside her.

"I hear birds. Are you on your deck?"

"At The Willows."

"You okay?"

She sighed heavily. "It's been a tough week."

"Tell me."

Silence filled the phone line while she considered the last few days. It was all so convoluted, and more than anything, she wanted to put it behind her. "It's complicated."

"You don't always have to be brave, you know. Let me be the strong one for once, for both of us."

That sounded so nice. If only she could give it all over to someone else. "I don't know how." She managed to keep the tears out of her voice but barely.

"Let me show you. Come to my premiere on Friday, spend a few days."

"Oh." She'd forgotten. "It's this Friday, isn't it?" Time, the spin of the earth, the orbit of the sun—such an existential and insolent nuisance—of course it didn't falter because another man died.

"Can I book you a flight?"

"I can do it myself."

"So you'll come?"

The hope and excitement in his voice made her heart hurt.

She lay back down on the blanket and stared up into the tree. The leaves gleamed like gold bangles in the early-autumn sunshine, taunting her with their vibrant color.

Classes started tomorrow. Despite the years since dropping out of law school, she'd been accepted again, and she couldn't miss the first day. She needed that law degree. Besides, she was supposed to teach Thursday night. And if her children needed her, she'd be thousands of miles away. And who would take care of Finn? A hundred little reasons to say no.

"I miss you, baby."

And one simple reason to say yes. "I can be there Friday morning."

"That's kinda last minute. You'll need a gown. We could go shopping if you come earlier."

"I'm teaching Thursday evening."

"Teaching?"

"ESL, English as a Second Language, to Spanish families."

"Oh, wow! That's great. Well, Friday then. Text me the details and we'll pick you up at the airport."

"I will."

"Do you mind bringing Finn?"

"Not at all."

"And don't worry about a dress. I'll take care of it."

"I can find something."

"It's okay, baby. I've got this."

Aria rubbed her forehead against the memory of how she'd described a good marriage. She should've known better than to venture too close to this crater of misery called love, with its edges that crumbled so easily. Was it any wonder she was on the way down?

～

THE SKY IS HYDRANGEA BLUE, vibrant and cloudless, the air warm and pungent and filled with birdsong. A swarm of spicebush swallowtails flutter past with a whoosh like pheasants bursting to the sky in a flush, startled by some unseen danger. A young girl in a yellow sundress strolls through the waist-high meadow grasses, arms outstretched, setting the long blades dancing.

A heavy cloud appears overhead and darkness descends. The girl whirls, lost, unseeing, and in a blink the music of nature is replaced by sounds of screeching metal, like prison doors slamming, men's voices raised in anger, words indistinguishable, fists connecting with flesh.

A man emerges from the blackness: tall and thin, his silver-gray eyes hauntingly bright against ebony skin and the darkness from which he'd sprung. He reaches for her and—

Aria bolted upright in her bed, heart racing, hands trembling, her hair wet with perspiration and plastered to her face and neck. Finn whined from his cage at the foot of the bed.

She'd dreamed about Dante again. He had sacrificed everything for her while she selfishly went on with her life—while she fell in love, raised a family, and tried to forget.

She stared into the darkness, willing her heart to find its rhythm. She eased from the covers and knelt beside Finn's cage, lifted him out, and pressed her nose to his soft, tiny head. "It's okay, buddy. We're going to be fine."

Cradling her trembling puppy, Aria rested her head against the side of the bed and closed her eyes, the dream fading to a distant memory. *Yes, we're going to be just fine.*

Funny how easy it is to forget your own troubles when someone —or something—needs you.

49

———————

"**P**lease!" Eli smacked the wardrobe assistant's hand as she attempted to tuck the puffy white shirt into the too-tight breeches he wore. He finished the task himself, and when he looked up, she stood staring at his crotch like a wolf eying a rabbit. He could guess what she was thinking: If the rumors were true, he'd be up for anything, anytime, with anyone . . . even an easy wardrobe assistant.

The text from Aria that he'd awakened to rankled in his mind.

Aria: Sorry, but I can't come tonight. There's something I have to do.

What could be more important than his premiere?

When he cleared his throat, the wardrobe assistant finally raised her eyes, caught his angry glare, and blushed.

Stepping back, she gestured to the trifold mirror. "Well, what do you think?"

Eli didn't recognize his own reflection. Dark circles ringed his eyes. His cheeks were pale and gaunt, accentuating the pink stain where the road rash had been. The stranger in the glass looked angry, haunted, and wretched.

He ran his hands through his too-long hair and smoothed it

behind his ears, but that did little to improve the apparition before him.

He put on his well-practiced Hollywood smile, like a doctor donning a white coat and stethoscope—the tools of his trade. "Not bad," he lied.

His phone, sitting atop his backpack across the dressing room, vibrated.

The girl caught his glance. "Need to get that?"

"If you don't mind."

"No problem." She disappeared into the back of the wardrobe area.

He limped across the room, hoping Aria had changed her mind about coming. He didn't want to go alone—or worse, with Makayla.

Eli snatched up the phone. Nothing from Aria, but Anders had texted the number for her in-laws' therapeutic riding facility.

He stared at the phone, pacing the floor of the small dressing room, careful to avoid the mirror, while he considered what to say to the Whitmores.

His fingertip poised over the number, he froze when the door burst open with a crash and Penelope breezed in. "OMG! You look fabulous!" Her ample bosom nearly overflowed a skintight purple blouse as she circled Eli, appraising him as though he were a rotisserie chicken. "Fab-u-lous!"

Eli seethed with renewed fury. Penelope had insisted on picking out Aria's dress for the premiere and had dropped it off at the house. A white silk Sherri Hill original with a daring plunge front and back—something Aria could have easily pulled off but wouldn't have been caught dead in.

"Aria's dress . . . I explicitly said something conservative." His voice sounded foreign to him, so filled with rage. He glared down at her, using every bit of his six foot four inches to make the gravity of his displeasure crystal clear.

Penelope backed away, stammered something unintelligible, then bit her lip. Bright red lipstick glommed onto her overbleached teeth.

"What were you thinking?"

Penelope picked an invisible thread from his shirtsleeve. "What, too daring for your little ghetto girl?"

Eli brushed her hand aside. "You're the reason she's gone! The seating at the fundraiser. The way you've treated her from day one. And that exposé in *The Scoop* . . . that was you, wasn't it?"

"Darling," she drawled with a tilt of her head, as though speaking to a child throwing a tantrum. "I check out all of your playmates. It's my job."

"Not anymore."

"What?"

"You're fired."

She clutched at his arm. "Eli, darling—"

Eli wrenched free, stormed across the room, and snatched up his backpack. "And if you so much as leak anything more about Aria—anything, P. I mean it. I'll make sure you never work in this town again." It wasn't an idle threat. With three more films lined up after *Casanova*, he held all the power now. As long as his face healed, that is. He slung his pack onto his shoulder and headed for the door.

"I didn't even give 'em the dirt on her son," Penelope cooed. "Yet."

Eli whirled around to glare at her.

Penelope sauntered to the three-way mirror, whisked her bangs to the side, and smiled at her reflection. "What?" She eyed his reflection and wiped the color from her teeth. "You didn't know her son's father is the young man, DJ, who went to prison? She didn't share that little tidbit with you?"

Eli slammed through the doors and stormed out of the studio, aching for a smoke even though he'd quit months ago.

Alone on the back lot, Eli slumped against the brick wall and with trembling hands he Googled her in-law's riding facility, clicked on the phone number but had to leave a message. While he waited for the return call, he paced like a caged animal. Time trickled by like water torture. After several long minutes, his phone vibrated.

He quickly introduced himself then cut right to the point. "I'm sorry to bother you Mrs. Whitmore, but Aria was supposed to fly to LA this morning and I received a text from her saying that something had come up. And now I can't reach her. Do you happen to know where she is?"

"Well yes, she went to visit a friend in Detroit."

Eli sagged against the building.

"I'm sure she'll get back to you, dear."

Michael Lang came out the side door. Eli straightened. "Yes, of course. Thank you, Mrs. Whitmore. You've been very helpful."

As Eli ended the call, Lang lit up a cigarette. "May I?"

Lang eyed him warily as he handed him a smoke and his lighter. "No hard feelings, I hope."

"Nope," Eli mumbled around the cigarette between his lips. His hands shook as he lit it.

"Rough day, sport?"

Eli took a long drag and coughed, his lungs rudely reminding him it'd been months since they'd endured the assault of cigarette smoke. He forced a smile. "Look, I don't know what Matt Desmond told you, but I wasn't the one who did that to his nose."

Lang's eyes widened in surprise then his thin lips curved into a knowing smile. "Your girl?"

"He deserved a lot worse, if you ask me."

Lang nodded and studied Eli's cheek, then his gaze slowly raked the length of him. "How's the leg?"

"Better."

"Can you run?"

Eli's brows knit together. He knew why the producer was asking —the lead role might still be his if he could own it. At the moment, he could barely walk, let alone run, and while he hated to admit it, he couldn't lie either. "Today, no. But in another two or three weeks, I'm your man."

Lang rubbed his chin. Somewhere in the distance the *beep, beep,*

beep of a construction vehicle backing up filled the silence that hung in the space between them. "Premiere tonight, huh?"

And just like that Eli's spark of hope was snuffed. He swallowed the disappointment. "You betcha. You coming?"

"Wouldn't miss it. Bringing your girl wonder?"

"Naw. She's in Michigan." Eli watched a studio cart race across the empty lot.

Lang eyed him as though he knew Eli had messed things up, that he'd known all along Eli wasn't man enough to hang on to a woman like Aria Whitmore.

Propped against the building, Eli tried his best to present a cool façade. "She'll be back."

Lang raised a brow.

Eli ran a hand across his eyes. "Hell, I don't know. I might've lost her." It was hard to think about, harder to say. Impossible to accept.

Lang took a long pull from his cigarette and exhaled slowly. "Look, I'm on my third marriage, so I'm the last one who should be giving advice. But if I were you, I'd go after her."

"Really?"

"Inside every strong, independent woman I've ever met lies a shattered little girl who's had to learn the hard way not to depend on anyone. The ones who won't tell you they need you are usually the ones who need you the most."

Uncanny how accurately Lang had pegged Aria after one brief meeting. "I think she went to Detroit to see her high school sweetheart."

"All the more reason to go."

"But I have this fitting." Eli nodded toward the door. "And the—"

Lang raised a hand, cutting him off. "It fits. And hey, that kind of woman doesn't come along every day."

"What kind is that?"

"The kind who makes you want to be better." Lang shot Eli a knowing smile.

Eli glanced at his watch. If he left now, he might be able to catch a flight east.

"Take my jet." Lang pulled out his wallet and thumbed through it.

"Seriously?"

It was one thing to borrow a friend's beach house or sailboat, but no one had ever offered him their private jet.

"Absolutely." Lang handed Eli a business card. "My pilot can be ready to take off in an hour. And a car can be waiting for you when you land."

Eli entered the number from the card into his phone. "Why are you doing this?"

"I like to keep my *lead* actors happy." Lang's smile was warm and genuine.

"Lead?" Eli perked up as a lingering ember of hope reignited.

Lang gave him a curt nod. "Does she make you happy?"

"You betcha."

"Then go get her."

As JITTERY AS a seventh-grader at his first school dance, Eli settled into a plush leather seat on Lang's Gulfstream and wiped his sweaty palms on his jeans. While it felt great to be back on top—he still couldn't believe Lang's change of heart—he needed to focus on Aria now. He needed a plan, a good one. Movie endings flashed through his mind, the happily-ever-after ones: *Pretty Woman, Jerry McGuire, Princess Bride*, and Aria's fave, *Meet Joe Black*. He imagined himself pounding down Jackson's door and finding—what? Aria in his arms? Or worse, in his bed?

Eli rubbed his face, trying hard to erase that image.

He looked at Anders, who sat across the aisle, thumbing away on his phone. "Anything?"

Anders glanced up. "Got it."

Suddenly thankful for Anders's past connections, Eli felt a small rush of relief. At least now they knew where they were going.

The plane eased out of the hangar, and Eli peered out the small window at the sun-drenched tarmac. But in his mind all he could see was the face of Dante Jackson, Aria's son's father, the ex-con. *My first everything,* her voice echoed.

The plane thundered down the runway, lifted off, and banked right. At the sound of the wheels tucking into the plane's belly, Eli sat back in his seat and tried to relax, think, and plan.

50

———

ria had vowed long ago never to return to Detroit. The last time had been for her mother's funeral, a wet and dreary November day. She could still see her sixteen-year-old self, numbed by the cold and the all-too-familiar grave site ritual, expected to grieve for a junkie who'd overdosed within hours of leaving rehab, a woman who'd died of shame and weakness, a mother who'd never wanted her. Mrs. Wyatt, her only remaining friend, stood at her side. Aria had never felt so utterly alone.

Thankful for the bright summer day, she exited the interstate and merged onto West Fisher. It had been over twenty years since she'd been back, but it could have been yesterday for all this part of the city had changed.

She drove past miles of the same dead factories, apocalyptic monoliths of graffiti-covered concrete, crumbling brick, and broken windows. Once a proud testament to the industrial revolution that had lured the tired, poor, huddled masses with promises of good-paying work and a chance at the American dream, they now stood as harbingers of joblessness and hopelessness, the indubitable backdrop of violence and poverty in America.

Her old neighborhood resembled a ghost town, with block after block of burned-out bungalows, boarded-up storefronts, and vacant lots sprinkled with broken glass that glistened like dewdrops among the weeds. She remembered the frequent house fires, amusement enough for penniless hoodlums because a can of gasoline was cheaper than a movie ticket.

A few things had changed. The grocery store was now a tattoo parlor, the dry cleaners a pawn shop. Liquor stores anchored every other corner.

She turned onto Waterman Street. Dilapidated houses lined the pot-holed street, like endless rows of beggars—some damaged, most empty, all grayed and drooping, worn down by life in the hood. Every few blocks, a large tenement building rose. Despite the heat and humidity, groups of faceless indigents—some young, some old, all scruffy—huddled together on street corners, their heads turning to watch as she rolled past in Adam's pickup.

She parked curbside in front of a small electronics shop with bars across the plate-glass window front. According to the receptionist at the Boys & Girls Club, this was where Dante worked. Outside, two teens lingered beside the building, smoking cigarettes. One nudged the other and nodded in her direction. Dread settled deep in her bones.

She peered across the front passenger seat through the shop's dirty glass. Inside, a multi-hued group of children sat cross-legged on the floor, gazing at a man sitting on a cube with an open book on his lap. How ironic that the boy who'd once scoffed at her love of reading was now passing along that gift to others.

She could feel the loitering teens staring at her, but that didn't matter as she considered the prospect of walking into the shop and facing Dante again. She couldn't do it. *"I hate you,"* she'd railed at him at the fundraiser. He probably hated her too. He had every right to. Directly or indirectly, she'd been responsible for his prison sentence.

She'd almost bolstered the courage to go in when the children stood and began moving about. Dante appeared at the door, propping it open with his tall frame. As the littles filed out, they consumed his attention with high fives, fist bumps, and giggles.

When the last one skipped off down the block, he looked up and his eyes met hers.

He strolled to the truck and leaned in the passenger-side window, his elbows resting on the door. "I was hoping you'd come."

"You were?" What was she doing here, really? Looking for happiness where she'd lost it?

He answered with a smile that said he was happy to see her. "My house is close by. We can talk there. Give me two secs to lock up."

Dante disappeared inside the shop, and Aria climbed out of the truck and rested against the tailgate as a trickle of sweat ran down her spine. When he returned with a jangle of keys, she said, "I thought you were with the local Boys & Girls Club. Director—"

"Pro tem. Temporary and part-time. This is my day job."

"Your boss doesn't mind you reading to kids while you're working?"

"I'm the boss," he said with an enigmatic grin. "You know, a little girl once told me books held all the knowledge of the world."

She turned from his watchful gaze to glance inside. "It's nice."

"It's a living, barely." He pulled down a sheet of corrugated metal over the front windows, padlocked it, then turned a key in the door. "I live just down the street. You can leave your truck here."

"Okay." She retrieved her satchel from the passenger seat, locked up the truck, and fell into stride beside him, half expecting him to take her hand like they'd done as kids. A small pang of disappointment stung when he didn't.

"Ain't easy to get a job when you get out. Pretty much had to start my own business. Gotta start somewhere—ain't that what Gibs used to say?" He shot her a side-eye.

Dante moved with a slow hobble she hadn't noticed at the fundraiser. "You're limping."

He bent to rub his knee. "Must'a pulled something shooting hoops this morning. I'll be fine in a day or two."

An image of Eli shooting hoops with the kids at the boys club popped into her mind. Eli had no place in her mission here. Might have no place in her life at all anymore.

Dante glanced up. "This is it." He stopped in front of a small Cape Cod with a wide front porch. Unlike the other homes on the street, this one appeared fairly well maintained. At least the windows were intact. Several young men sitting on the porch turned to gawk as Aria and Dante started up the cracked sidewalk.

A tall young man, maybe pushing twenty, with beefy arms, sporting a crew cut and a sleeveless T, stood. His eyes boldly raked over her, then fixated on the satchel.

"These are my roomies." Dante motioned to the hulk staring her down. "This is Hookie." He nodded to the other two slightly younger guys, one lanky with a high-top fade and a smaller looka-like with cornrows. "That's Andre and Aki. Guys, this is Lily."

Aria squared her shoulders, locked eyes with Hookie, and rested her hand on the satchel, bolstered by the weight of the Glock within. "Pleased to meet you all." Aria kept her tone level—friendly, not scared. Never scared.

The two smaller teens mumbled a polite hello while the big one straightened, making himself even bigger. "You look lost," he growled derisively.

"Hey!" Dante stepped forward, crowding Hookie's personal space. "She's my guest. Show some respect."

With a glare directed at Hookie, Dante ushered Aria into the sweltering house. "Sorry about that. Sometimes they forget their manners." He raised his voice at the end, obviously intending to be overheard.

She followed him down a dimly lit hallway to a much cooler kitchen at the back of the house.

"I do what I can to keep them in line, but I gotta pick my battles, you know? They're good kids, though."

He pulled out a chair for her at a small, cracked-enamel table. "I'm glad you're here."

"I needed to see you." She set the satchel on the floor at her feet, the weight of the metal box inside reminding her why she'd come.

"You should'a called." He opened the fridge and stared at the contents, just the way Jacks always did. "Want something to drink? Soda? Water?"

"No, thank you." She didn't dare lift a glass. Her trembling hands would betray her.

He slid into the seat opposite her and sat back in his chair, balancing it on two legs while he appraised her. He smiled, obviously pleased by what he saw. "You still take my breath away."

She broke eye contact, embarrassed by the emotions his compliment stirred in her. Her gaze landed on a small tattoo in the hollow between his neck and shoulder. She hadn't noticed it at the fundraiser, hidden beneath the collar of his tux shirt, but now, with only a T-shirt stretched taut across Dante's muscular chest, it was hard to miss. A tiny, sinister-looking fairy—Tinker Bell, no less—held a double-edged dagger without a handle, blood dripping from her palms. Like love, eventually it cuts you, no matter how you hold it.

She glanced around the kitchen. While unlikely to win any *Better Homes and Gardens* contest, it was tidy and boasted some homey touches. Clean, crisp white blinds on the windows slivered the sunlight while a red-checked towel hung neatly on a hook beside the sink. A wooden napkin holder, the kind a high schooler might make in shop class, graced the table where they sat. "I like your place."

"I don't need much, so it's plenty for me," he said, not taking his eyes off her.

"How's your grandmother?"

A deep sadness settled on his features. "She passed while I was . . . away."

"I'm sorry."

"Thanks." He stared at a stain on the tabletop. "She was an amazing lady."

Aria tried not to think harshly of the wiry old woman who'd

called her *white trash* and *nothing but trouble*. "What you're doing here is great. I always knew you were one of the good ones."

"Just doing the best I can, with what I got, where I am."

A Teddy Roosevelt quote. Apparently, he read more than children's stories. Part of her felt proud to have given him a love for reading, especially considering all she'd cost him. "I'm glad you're not bitter about prison and . . . everything."

He narrowed his gaze thoughtfully. "When I walked out that gate, feeling my first taste of freedom after eight long years, I knew if I didn't leave my anger behind, I'd still be in prison." He sat forward, the chair's front legs crashing to the floor. "Life is too short to dwell on a past you can't change."

He was talking about his own choices, but he could have easily been referring to hers.

She pulled Gibson's toolbox from her satchel, set it on the table, and pushed it his way. "I came to give you this."

The sad tilt of his head said he recognized it.

She opened it and turned it so he could see her letters inside. Their eyes met, and the years melted away like snowflakes in sunshine. He was still the handsome silver-eyed boy she'd loved since childhood.

"Lily."

She swallowed the lump at the back of her throat. "The words I wrote to you were things I needed to say. You still need to hear them."

He stood, turned his back to her, and rubbed a hand across his face. His shoulders heaved with several deep breaths.

She had to tell him. There may never be another chance. She stood and took a step toward him. "I didn't mean it, you know."

He whirled to face her and gripped her shoulders, holding her at arm's length.

"I don't hate you. I just don't understand why you sent me away when I came to visit you. Why you wouldn't even talk to me. Did you think I started that fire? Is that why you copped a plea?"

"I didn't do it to protect you. I ain't no saint."

"Then why?"

"I was facing a death sentence, Lil, for manslaughter. Ten to twenty was a way out."

Her hand flew to her mouth. *No!* He was a good kid; no priors. He shouldn't have needed a way out. "I might've been able to save you." She wanted to believe it, needed to believe it.

Dante shook his head slowly. "Naw, you couldn't."

"I never stopped loving you," she whispered. The sweet gangly boy she'd loved since kindergarten had transformed into the benevolent strong man before her. She moved closer and touched his face. "We were beautiful together, weren't we?"

He gazed down at her and his eyes softened. She pulled him to her and kissed him. He tasted of pure male warmth and white-hot passion. Just the way she remembered.

He returned her kiss like he couldn't get enough, taking everything she offered, consuming every breath of life she gave. He moved to her neck, and his hands wandered lower. She melted against him with a sigh.

"I thought I'd never see you again," she murmured against the warmth of his neck.

Dante held her against his chest, so close she could barely breathe.

"If you knew what I went through, how much I loved you, how much I still love you."

He pressed a feverish kiss against her lips. "Stay with me," he breathed.

Oh, how easy it would be to say yes. But even as she sank into Dante's passionate embrace, she knew this was not where she was meant to be.

She pulled free. "I have to go."

He groaned and stumbled back against the sink. His hands rubbed his face as if he could wipe away the love she'd placed there. "You're still such a little girl," he growled. "You can't kiss a man like that and walk away."

She smiled, his obvious desire warming her in places she shouldn't be thinking about.

"You can't look at a man that way, neither."

She eyed the open toolbox on the table. All those letters she'd written so many years ago, bursting with expressions of love, returned, unopened, unread.

Silence hummed in the empty kitchen. "You love him?" Dante asked softly.

She nodded. "Eli's a good man."

"Yeah, he's not as bad as I thought, but then again, none of us are as good as you hope."

"You've always been a . . . a good friend."

He cringed as though she'd physically wounded him. In truth, he was far more. Surely he knew that.

"You could have a beautiful life with him, an easy life."

She stepped away. "Promise me you'll read the letters."

His gaze caressed her face. "I will."

Though it took every ounce of her willpower, she turned and left the house. Dante followed.

At the truck, she touched his cheek. She could feel the boys on the porch watching, certain he could too, and yet his gaze never left her, unmistakable desire shining from his rain-colored eyes.

"I know you loved me once," she said. "We were kids, but it was real, wasn't it?"

He rubbed his neck and glanced back to the house. "You should take the toolbox."

"Bring it to me after you've read my letters." She turned and slipped behind the wheel of Adam's truck.

As she pulled away, the figure of Dante receded in the rearview mirror, his hand raised in a frozen goodbye. Would she ever see him again? For Jacks's sake, she hoped so. With an unexpected peace, she pulled her gaze to the road ahead. *Don't look back, only forward now.*

DETROIT WAS HOT, the air so steamy it felt to Eli like breathing water. Dante's neighborhood was scary, especially in the fading daylight: endless streets of boarded-up homes, crumbling concrete, and empty lots.

Anders pulled to the curb in front of a little bungalow that resembled an old man sitting in a shopping mall: well-kept but haggard and lonely.

Eli approached the wide porch, where three young men stared at him. "I'm looking for Dante." His voice didn't come across near as confident as he'd hoped.

The tallest one stood. "Ain't you—"

"Yeah." Eli hoped being recognized might work to his advantage.

With a distrustful side-eye to the other two, the kid let him in. He stopped at a door off the main hallway and knocked loudly. "D! Someone's here for ya."

The door eased open a crack, and Dante's weary face appeared. "Lily?"

Hearing Aria's childhood name almost undid him and it took every ounce of restraint for Eli to not barge through the door. "Hey, Dante, right? I'm just looking for Aria."

51

Aria had never been to The Willows alone at night before. A harvest moon ducked in and out of the cloud's inky darkness, illuminating the meadow in dancing patches of silvery light. Despite the heat and humidity, she shivered.

After the long drive home from Detroit, she'd picked up Finn from her in-laws and settled him at home, but the house felt too big, too bare, filled with too many ghosts. She couldn't stand the deep and overwhelming emptiness, the barren landscape that had become her life—a life that had once been vibrant and beautiful, full of love and family.

At least the solitude out here seemed natural. She could lose herself in the moonlit pond and the smell of moist earth. A gust of wind stirred a tornado of leaves on the path before her.

Going to see Dante had been a step in the right direction. Like clearing out Adam's things, moving on, once and for all. She was trying.

Dante deserved to know about Jacks. But oh, what a coward she'd been, shoving the box of letters across the table at him like an unwanted responsibility instead of telling him outright, facing his reaction, discussing next steps.

What if he didn't want to be a father? She couldn't bear for her sweet, tenderhearted son to suffer the kind of rejection she'd endured at the hands of her own father. Better to discourage Jacks from ever reaching out. There's nothing sadder than an unwanted child.

The rumble of distant thunder shook the ground. Rain was coming—hopefully, enough to ease the late-summer humidity but not so much as to soak her grassy little patch beneath the willow.

Pushing aside her tangled thoughts, Aria braved the woods for an armful of twigs and logs for a fire. She dug a shallow bowl in the dirt beyond the edge of the tree's canopy, and within minutes, the fire sparked and took off. She added some larger sticks, then sat back on her haunches, stared into the flames, and sighed.

What are you doing here, Aria? The voice came in a gentle whisper.

She was searching. For healing, for strength, for the next right thing.

She needed to choose her own next steps. Eli had opened her eyes to the yawning chasm between what she'd always dreamed of and her current existence. She felt good about the headway she'd made on her social reform proposal, and with Eli's influence, together they could make a real difference in the lives of impoverished teens.

But what are you doing here?

Aria looked inward but came up empty, too ashamed to admit, even to herself, that she was hiding.

I sent him just for you, came the still small voice.

Her whole body gripped with fear, but she couldn't deny her overwhelming feelings for Eli. Of course she loved him. His charm, charisma, and boyish enthusiasm, his silent Ta-das, were adorable. With a generous heart, he'd tried to make her happy: the print of The Willows on his guest room wall, the yacht with scarlet sails, the way he held her when she needed to be held. And he was patient and kind, with strong roots—*like Adam. No!*

Aria collapsed onto her bottom. *God, no!*

I know what you need. Trust me.

Oh, how her heart wanted him, longed for him, for love, dangerous, unpredictable, and scary as it was. But. . . did she dare to love again?

She would not give up her own dream of becoming a warrior for social justice. Not this time. Not for Eli, not for children. Not for anything. *This time, I will have it all.*

She thought about calling Eli, but what could she say? She'd probably blown it with him completely, having ignored his calls and texts all day. Besides, he would be sitting in the theater watching his film about now, having walked the red carpet without her. Not alone, though. A man like Eli Van Drie was never alone.

Unlike her. Aria's life had been one long series of losing the people she loved. What if she was the common denominator, the reason everyone around her died? The thought sucked her down like quicksand. She couldn't lose Eli too. Better to end it with him now and let him live than—

The soft crack of a snapped twig pierced the stillness of the woods. Aria's whole body tensed.

She peeked around the tree. Clouds had swallowed the moon, but she could barely make out the shape of a figure, tall and thin, limping along the tree line like a vagrant skulking in the dark.

Crouched low, she reached for her pistol, then remembered she'd left it in her satchel, in the truck, at the barn. She ducked back behind the tree. *Breathe. Think. Think!* As silent as a held thought, she skirted the pond, and crept into the woods from the far bank. After making a wide arc, she stepped from the shadows into a ready stance, arms raised.

"You're here," Aria said with a languid smile.

"Ari." Eli's legs felt as wobbly as two willow limbs, but he.lumbered forward, closing the distance between them. Her eyes softened but he could see her brokenness in the way she stood, the way her gaze flickered away.

"How did you find me?" As he neared, she backpedaled, apparently not wanting him to come closer.

He stopped. "You're predictable."

"No, I'm not," they said in unison.

Eli grinned, and she turned away, unsmiling. Her sorrow must be deep.

"Ari—" He took a step forward and stumbled. His thigh felt like it was on fire.

With her back to him, she didn't notice. She knelt before the fire and placed a log on it. "What are you doing here?"

A woman who knew how to start a fire, in the rain even—now, that was impressive. At one point, he'd questioned her independence. He'd never met a woman who didn't need a man for something. It seemed unnatural. Now he knew better. Aria needed him on a deeper, more intimate, emotional level.

And being needed in that way was by far the most powerful thing he'd ever felt.

"I had to see you." He limped forward.

She straightened and tipped her head in that cute way she always did. "Aren't you missing your movie premiere?"

He shrugged. "Heroes in love do crazy things."

She smiled at that, a real smile this time. "But that was important to you. To your career."

"Nothing's more important to me than you."

She turned back to the fire. "Penelope's probably furious."

"I fired her." If she'd checked her phone, she would've known that. "I don't want to be the man she's made me out to be. I like the way you see me, the person I am when I'm with you. I'm the best version of myself when we're together. That's love according to Aria Whitmore, right?" He inched forward, hoping she wouldn't notice that he could barely walk.

She eyed him with a hint of compassion. "What's wrong with your leg?"

"Long story." He couldn't tell her about the motorcycle accident, but then again, he owed her the truth. Swallowing a rising panic, he described Matt's attempt to steal his Casanova role, and then racing off on his bike and the accident. "That's why I didn't call you back. I literally couldn't talk for six weeks."

In a heartbeat, her face went from empathy to hurt, anger, and distrust all in one accusing glare. "You promised." Her voice broke as she seemed to wither before his eyes.

His heart in his throat, he forced a grin. "I admitted I was never a scout."

"Really? That's the best you've got?" She turned back toward the fire, dismissing him.

Eli clasped her hand. "Please don't shut me out."

She whirled, and her eyes darted to the toolbox under his arm. Open-mouthed and wide-eyed, she gaped at it. "How'd you get that?"

"Dante asked me to give it to you." He extended it to her and she snatched it from him.

"You went to—"

"Looking for you."

As though fearing something deadly might jump out of it, she eased open the lid and peered inside. She took out the single envelope and stared at it like someone facing death. She slid down the tree trunk to sit cross-legged in the grass, the toolbox on her lap. The flames danced, rain dripped from leaves, and frogs croaked as time ticked by and still, she stared at the envelope. She was so inside her head, she may as well have been on the moon.

Eli eased down beside her, ignoring the white-hot pain pulsing through his thigh.

She closed her eyes. Her chest rose and fell with a heavy breath. "You have no idea how long I've waited for a single letter from that man."

Silence shivered with misery between them.

"Ari—"

She thrust the envelope at him. "Read it to me." It was both a command and a plea.

Reluctantly, he opened the envelope, unfolded the single sheet, angled it toward the firelight, and read aloud.

My Forever Lily Fair,

He glanced up. Aria stared into the flames.
He cleared the apprehension from his throat and continued.

You asked me to read your letters, said I'd understand. Well, I read them, and I've done a lot of thinking, and it all adds up to one thing. You belong with Van Drie.

Eli collapsed back against the tree. Aria's hollowed out expression remained unchanged.

Together, the two of you can make a real difference in the world. And if you throw that away for me, you'll regret it. Maybe not today, or tomorrow, but eventually. And forever.

I have a good life here, but you know what you'd have if you shared it with me. The poverty, the violence, the hopelessness. I wouldn't be able to protect you, although God knows I'd die trying.

All this time, you've felt responsible for me going to prison. But it wasn't your fault. None of it was.

Sounds like you raised a fine young man, Lily. I always wanted a son. I look forward to meeting him someday.

I will love you forever.
Dante

The contents of the letter were somehow reflected in her expression, like someone losing her last thread of hope. A sob escaped from somewhere deep inside, like her whole soul was turning inside out.

With shaking hands, Aria took the page from Eli, folded it carefully, and replaced it in the envelope. She returned it to the box and closed the lid. "He's a good man."

Eli couldn't argue with that. When he found Dante at his ramshackle bungalow in Detroit, after the initial surprise had settled, Dante paced the room with feverish eyes as he opened up to Eli like a dying man reliving the best moments of his life.

With Aria's letters scattered around him, Dante had shared stories of his Lily Fair and their growing-up years: how she'd loved to read and fix things, her brother's sudden death, the mugging on her sixteenth birthday that left the scar beneath her chin. He'd been unable to protect her, but he had comforted her when she asked . . . because it was all he had left to give.

Eli had never seen a man so in love and so bereft. He'd never forget Dante's desolate gaze as he'd perused the room as though his next words would cost him everything.

"I got nothing to offer her," he'd moaned. Then he looked up at Eli and said, "You treat her right, you hear?"

Yes, Dante was a good man. "One of the best," Eli said.

Aria's whole body sagged, like a marionette cut from its strings. "I've cost him so much."

"You've given him the one thing he's always wanted."

She nodded. "A son."

After several heartbeats, she set the toolbox aside, cradled her knees, and stared into the fire. She sniffled, then wept, the kind of strangled, silent crying that she sometimes gave herself over to when she thought he was asleep. Great lonely tears streamed down her cheeks and dripped from her chin. She didn't move, as if by refusing to wipe the tears away she could defy the weakness behind them.

He'd never seen someone so strong so overcome. He didn't trust his voice, but he had to say something. "I wish I could tell you everything will be okay."

She sucked in a breath.

"I can't take the pain away." He placed a hand on her shoulder. "But I'm here for you. Tell me what you need."

Aria wiped her eyes on her crossed arms, then raised her head. "Hold me."

He swallowed her in his embrace, and she sobbed against his chest.

After several long moments, she drew back and gave him a sad smile.

He wiped the tears from her cheeks with the pad of his thumb. Her eyes held a tenderness that made his heart ache with longing. He leaned in for a kiss, his lips brushing softly against hers, savoring the warmth of her life-giving breath, the salt of her tears, tasting her pain and making it his own.

"Be with me," he murmured against her wet cheek.

She swallowed hard and pulled away, gazed at him as though seeing him for the first time, taking his measure. A glimmer of hope—or was it something more?—shined in her eyes, and it was soft and vulnerable, like he'd never seen her before. A smile spread from her eyes to her lips and then disappeared. "I'm not what you need," she said with devastating finality. "I wish—"

"You're everything I need."

"Your career—"

"Is taking off like never before. That speech you wrote—Max says I'm on fire. My fans adore the new me. They adore you."

"That's all you need? Someone to improve your image?" Her words stung, and now he was the one feeling like he wasn't enough, could never be enough for a woman like her.

"It's a good start." He shot her one of his grins that usually made her smile.

Oblivious to his well-practiced charm, her warmth vanished like a spark in the wind, his words falling way short of what she needed to hear.

She blinked. "There's something I have to do."

"Whatever it is, I'm in."

"How can you say that?"

"Because everything you do is good and pure and worthwhile. And I want to be a part of it all. We're so much more together than we are apart."

"Oh, Eli." She gave him a withering look.

He struggled to one knee and held her hand. "Marry me, baby. Right here, right now." He dug into his pocket for his grandmother's ring and held it out to her. It seemed small and unimpressive in his big, clumsy hands.

Aria sprang to her feet and looked down at him, speechless. The fire crackled and popped behind her, outlining her thin silhouette, her body aglow in a halo of light. He could no longer see her face.

Eli had imagined proposing on the red carpet that very night, and a dozen other ways, each of them a grand gesture, but he couldn't be certain of her answer. Scarcely able to breathe for the pounding of his heart, he waited. The firelight twinkled in the diamond like magic. "I hope you don't mind a little hand-me-down. It belonged to my grandmother."

"Do I seem like a girl who'd wear a Gibraltar?" She gave up a half-smile.

He breathed a sigh of relief. It wasn't exactly a yes, but . . . "I didn't plan to propose this way." Eli chuckled nervously, trying to dispel the silence unraveling between them like a fraying lifeline.

Aria turned away and fell to her knees. Her shoulders shook as she sobbed.

Eli collapsed against the tree and stretched out his injured leg. Physically exhausted, he didn't have the strength to go to her. Wasn't even sure she wanted him to.

He stared at the ring, imagining the moment when his grandfather had offered it to his beloved. Had he been as tied up in knots as Eli was now, with so many hopes and dreams hanging in the balance?

Maybe he'd only imagined Aria's feelings for him because he'd wanted so desperately to believe the kind of love his grandparents had was finally within his grasp. "Baby, if I make you this unhappy, I'll leave you alone." He suppressed a rising panic. "But Ari, if there's any chance—"

She whirled to face him. "That's not even my real name!"

"I know. And it doesn't matter. I love who you are and who you were. I hate everything you've been through, but I appreciate it because it made you who you are. That scar you try so hard to hide is the most beautiful thing I've ever seen because it shows how you got knocked down, rose up, and persevered."

She sniffed, firelight dancing in shadows across her face. The soft pitter-patter of rain filled the darkness beyond the fire's glow.

For a moment he wondered if she really was too broken to accept the happiness he offered, if she'd ever be ready to accept it. He gazed at the ring, feeling his grandpa's faith in its circle of perfection. He held it out to her again.

Gentle raindrops chased the tears rolling down her cheeks. "I'm —afraid," she said so quietly he wasn't sure he'd heard it.

Eli understood the courage it took for her to admit her fear. She'd been strong for way too long. "You're the bravest person I've ever met," he said, not taking his eyes off her.

She looked away, beyond the darkness where rain dripped like tears from the willow's long arching branches. Now he knew how the willows wept.

He twisted the ring in his fingertips. It was too soon. She'd wanted to take it slow, and he'd promised. And now, he'd been reckless and impulsive. He should have waited. And yet . . . He leaned into her line of sight, extended the ring again, recapturing her attention.

She crept closer and stared long and hard at the ring, as though considering all it represented: The happiness, sure, but the risk, the inevitable probability of another soul-crushing loss, for in her eyes, right now, that was bound to be her overriding perspective. The loss. He was just one more person to lose, one more gaping, aching, hole in her heart.

Slowly she offered her hand as if allowing him to place the ring on it. Her hand trembled as she raised her eyes to him.

He pulled back the ring and arched his brows. He needed to hear the words.

She yanked her hand back to her chest, palm to heart, as if protecting the one thing she was most afraid to lose.

"Trust me."

She inched closer and kissed him, soft and sweet and so tender it hurt, as if it was all she had left to give.

When she pulled away she cupped his face. It must have been the solitary tear—his own—that trickled down his cheek.

"I love you." She kissed the tear away. .

"So, marry me?"

"Shoor."

EPILOGUE

I search the house as a niggling panic begins deep in my belly. It's late morning and the bed is made, the kitchen tidied, but my wife is nowhere to be found. After a week in New York, I'm exhausted, worn ragged by a relentless flurry of talk shows and interviews to promote not only the release of *Casanova*– already being touted as the greatest epic romance since *Titanic*—but also Aria's social reform proposal. Boarding the predawn flight home this morning seems like a distant memory as I race from room to room, quietly calling her name.

Finally, on the back deck, I breathe a sigh of relief as I peer across the expanse of lawn to the lakefront patio where she's nestled on the double chaise beneath the cottonwood, Finn at her side. A warm summer breeze stirs the creamy white puffs floating down like oversized snowflakes. The air is redolent with the scent of freshly cut grass, evergreens, and lake water. Almost two years since we met and it still astounds me, this life we share. My heart swells with pure joy. Not many people actually get to live in their happy place.

I rub the weariness from my neck and creep down the steps, careful not to wake them. A wide grin stretches across my face as I take in the two little bundles tucked into the pram beside her, and I recall how she'd sprung the news on our flight back to Italy after spending Christmas in Michigan.

"I have one more present for you," she'd said, reaching into her satchel under the seat and pulling out a small gold wrapped gift. She held it a moment before handing it to me.

From the box, I lifted out an antique picture frame. Engraved across the top were the words, 'Hopes and Dreams'. The frame held a black-and-white print of two milky gray shapes on a black background. I studied it closely but couldn't figure out what it was supposed to be. "What are you trying to tell me here, babe?"

The smile she'd been trying to suppress beamed wide. "It's our family."

"What?" I peered at her and she nodded. "This is . . .? You're . . .?" I laughed out loud. "That's our baby?"

She laughed with me. "Actually, it's two babies." She pointed to the shapes facing each other in the picture.

"Twins?" I touched the framed image, processing the news. "Oh, Ari!" My heart nearly launched right out of my chest. "This is the best Christmas gift ever." I kissed her, hugged her, and took a deep breath. "We're having a baby!" I shouted for the whole plane to hear, thrusting a fist into the air.

Passengers around us cheered and shouted congratulations.

"Two babies," she reminded me.

"Twins!" I shot both fists into the air.

Again our fellow passengers erupted with applause and well wishes, even a few Uh-oh's.

I tried to talk her into going back home but of course, she adamantly refused, and like any attorney worth her salt, she had a whole arsenal of prepared arguments: She'd seen a doctor while we were in Grand Rapids, she was fine, the babies were fine; she had ten days of Christmas break left; I only had four more weeks of filming, five tops; we weren't far from Florence, a big city with a modern hospital.

I didn't stand a chance and truth be told, I was glad for it.

The extended honeymoon we spent in Italy, despite her working through law school while I filmed, was sheer bliss. We rented a small villa on a vineyard not far from the set, and though I often had to work weekends and my days were long, I eagerly looked forward to her visits, the nights filled with easy, passionate lovemaking and a slowness I'd never known. I often found myself distracted long afterward by the remembering.

While I worked, Aria balanced her studies with reading, researching, and blogging about Ben Franklin's ideas for social reform. I am still in awe of her avid determination to get her law degree and change a broken world with her words.

Last November, she launched a website where she explained the basic premise of her proposal, including the creation of Franklin's four committees. She and Latisha talked often, and the early feedback Aria received from her online following was remarkably encouraging.

The afternoon Aria posted the final proposal, her in-box filled up from her website's contact page, including emails from a congressman and a senator who both gushed with praise and requested a meeting.

She'd prepared a media packet to send to news magazines and cable news channels to get the word out, but the overwhelming response—from The Hill of all places—was far more than she'd anticipated.

The legislators we met with in Washington paved the way for the formation of the committees and staffed them with qualified bipartisan leaders. The media response was hyperbolic. For months, Aria's cell phone rang nonstop with political pundits and talk show hosts offering live interviews. Back in LA, we met with movie stars and musicians who, like Latisha, wanted to help in any way they could to ensure widespread acceptance.

"You're home!" Aria whispers sleepily, tugging me from my reverie. She smiles and holds out her hand, beckoning me while birdsong and cottonwood fluff swirls in the air.

Finn yips softly, already well trained to not wake the babies.

I rub the dog's ears and he settles down, then I stretch out beside Aria on the chaise and snuggle against her, reveling in her warmth and love and the unique smell of babies.

Aria is so much more than I imagined that morning in the airport. A woman of resilient strength and indomitable courage, my wife has not only renewed my faith in God, she's taught me to live, love, learn, and grow in ways I never would've believed possible. She's given me hope for a better future for impoverished kids across the country and shown me firsthand what it means to be brave.

The busy week finally catches up with me and I drift lazily toward sleep with a final thought. *Yeah, I'd swap a plane ticket any day for a chance to be with you.*

IF YOU ENJOYED *The Bravest Among Us,* I would love it if you let your friends know so they can also experience Aria's journey! As with all of my books, I have enabled lending on all platforms where it is allowed. If you leave a review on the site from which you purchased *The Bravest Among Us*, Goodreads, or your own blog, I would love to read it! Email me the link at **kathryn@kathrynsuemoore.com**

Stay up-to-date on upcoming releases by joining my newsletter via my website KathrynSueMoore.com or the QR Code below.

RESOURCES

What's Next?

America's children need your help. Become a warrior for social justice by checking out one of the following resources to help a child in crisis.

Affinity Mentoring - AffinityMentoring.org

> Affinity Mentoring is an organization in Grand Rapids, Michigan that partners with local businesses, organizations, and schools to match students in K-8th grade with a caring adult role model to journey alongside them one hour a week.

> Affinity's mission is to facilitate equitable growth in academics, social emotional skills, and self-esteem through mutually beneficial mentoring relationships, cultivating a brave space that amplifies the voices of young agents of change in a diverse and inclusive community.

BeUndividded - BeUndivided.com

Can you imagine...
300,000 churches serving 100,000 schools
Because churches serving schools can change everything.

Big Brothers Big Sisters - BBBS.org

Since 1904, Big Brothers Big Sisters has operated under the belief that inherent in every child is incredible potential. As the nation's largest donor- and volunteer-supported mentoring network, Big Brothers Big Sisters makes meaningful, monitored matches between adult volunteers ("Bigs") and children ("Littles"), ages 5 through young adulthood in communities across the country. We develop positive relationships that have a direct and lasting effect on the lives of young people.

Mission: Create and support one-to-one mentoring relationships that ignite the power and promise of youth.

Vision: All youth achieve their full potential.

Boys and Girls Clubs of America - BGCA.org

Mission: To enable all young people, especially those who need us most, to reach their full potential as productive, caring, responsible citizens.

Vision: Provide a world-class Club Experience that assures success is within reach of every young person who enters our doors, with all members on track to graduate from high school with a plan for the future, demonstrating good character and citizenship, and living a healthy lifestyle.

Christian Community Development Association - CCDA.org

The CCDA's mission is to strengthen and inspire Christian Community Development practitioners for community transformation through equipping and connecting.

Mirror Me Inc. - MirrorMeInc.org

Mirror Me Inc. is an organization in Grand Rapids, Michigan focused on developing characteristics of virtue, integrity, and leadership in girls ages 11-18. We help reveal identity by exemplifying the characteristics and nature of God.

Mission: To affirm identity and inspire destiny through empowerment, education, and mentoring.

National Church Adopt a School Initiative - ChurchAdoptaSchool.org

Change a life through reading with kids one hour a week.

Youth who develop a meaningful mentor relationship with an adult are:

- Five times more likely to graduate high school
- 46% less likely to start using drugs
- 27% less likely to start drinking
- 52% less likely to skip school

Young Life - YoungLife.org

Active in every major city and works through school and community-based partnerships to introduce adolescents to Jesus Christ ad to help them grow in their faith.

- Going where kids are and building personal relationships with them
- Providing fun, adventurous, life-changing experiences
- Working in community alongside like-minded adults (volunteer leaders, committee members, donors and staff)

Together, each of us with our own little candle, we can set fire to a movement to eliminate persistent poverty in America.

ACKNOWLEDGEMENTS

There is only one author listed on this book, but I could never have written this story without the following people:

My father. You always told me I could be anything I wanted to be. And you still do.

My mother. Thank you for instilling in me a love for the written word, and the legacy we've passed along. You never said no when I asked for more books, even when money was tight.

Mrs. Wyatt. The only babysitter I remember having as a child, I thank you for helping me learn to read by myself through the bible verses you introduced me to in your after-school program. And thank you for leading me to Jesus, my forever friend, my hope, my savior.

My beta-readers. To those who read early drafts of this story and offered honest and constructive critiques—Nancy Mosier, David Strickland, Debbie Wagner, Claire Fawcett, and Jennifer O'Hara—I offer my heartfelt gratitude for your help in making each new version better than the last. Your feedback, support, and unfailing friendship are more than I deserve.

My editors, Kathy Ide and Erin Bartels. Your invaluable expertise has made this manuscript not only presentable but a joy to read.

My children, Jake and Rachel. You're my greatest accomplishments in life. Motherhood has been a roller coaster of a great time and, yes, I will always miss the story time cuddles.

My husband, Alan, who has shared my story for thirty-plus years. Thank you for remembering my phone number when you'd forgotten my name the night we met. Thank you for calling back when I told you there was no Debra here. Thank you for the endless phone calls when we lived three hours apart for the early months of our relationship. Most of all, thank you for making the promise of an "ever after" a reality.

ABOUT THE AUTHOR

K. S. Moore is the award-winning author of Angel Beneath My Wheels. She grew up in a neighborhood not unlike the one depicted in this story, and with God's grace and Pell Grants, she attained a college degree. She now lives in Michigan with her husband, Alan, where she mentors inner-city kids.

Find her online at KathrynSueMoore.com.

facebook.com/KathrynSueMoore

x.com/KathrynSueMoore

instagram.com/kathrynsuemoore